Silver Lies

Silver Lies

Ann Parker

Poisoned Pen Press

Copyright © 2003, 2006 by Ann Parker

First Trade Paperback Edition 2006

10 9 8 7 6 5 4 3 2

Library of Congress Catalog Card Number: 2003104912

ISBN: 978-1-59058-278-7 Trade Paperback

Poisoned Pen Press
6962 E. First Ave., Ste. 103
Scottsdale, AZ 85251
www.poisonedpenpress.com
info@poisonedpenpress.com

Printed in the United States of America

Acknowledgments

If I were to thank properly all who offered encouragement and shared their expertise, suggestions, and ideas, this acknowledgment would begin to approach the length of the book. Instead, I'll try to be brief. For any who don't appear here, please know I'm grateful.

First of all, my family. Bill for his love, support, and critical reader's eye. Ian and Devyn for understanding (or at least tolerating) my mind-fades into the 19th century at the dinner table. My father, Don, and mother, Corinne, and sibs and their partners for abiding interest. Special thanks to my Colorado relatives including Walt, Bette, Dorothy (bless you for stockpiling the family history!), and Dave for his reference books, network of experts, and great homebrew.

I owe much to those who shared their time and expertise including Roger Neuscheler for historical assaying techniques; Ed Raines for mining history, maps, and assays; Roy Marcot for arming Inez appropriately; and Larry Hamby for information on guns and knife-fighting techniques. Any inaccuracies, slipups, or wild flights of fancy are mine alone.

This book would never have been if not for Leadville and its people, past and present. I'm grateful to Bob Elder for answering my many questions and for sharing his grandfather's letters, to Hillery McCalister and the Apple Blossom innkeepers for tours of their historical abodes, and to the

Honorable Neil Reynolds for sharing his expertise on historic Leadville. Thanks also to the staff at the Lake County Public Library, the National Mining Hall of Fame & Museum, and Leadville's Historical Society, who keep the spirit of the past alive for those who seek it.

Along the Front Range, the Colorado Historical Society and Denver Public Library deserve special mention. Their historical collections provided invaluable fodder for my fiction, and their staff were always helpful and patient.

On the writerly end of things, I am indebted to Camille Minichino and Penny Warner—friends, authors, teachers—and to the every-other-Thursday-night critique group including Claire Johnson, Kay Barnhart, Carole Price, Janet Finsliver, Mike Cooper, Rena Leith, Gordon Yano, Mignon Richards, and Colleen Casey. Thanks to Jane Staehle for her quick and eagle eye, as well as to the folks down on the cubicle farm for music, musings on Milton, and moral support. Members of the Northern California chapter of Mystery Writers of America and Women Writing the West provided advice and encouragement. I also wish to acknowledge the e-communities of DorothyL, CrimeThruTime, HistRes, and Prock-research (now carmelsloop), where I've mostly lurked and learned.

I'm indebted to all the folks at Poisoned Pen Press who have helped bring *Silver Lies* to light.

And finally, to the original Inez Stannert, thank you for lending me your name.

For Walter Underwood Parker,
who set me on the road to Leadville.
And for Bill, Ian, and Devyn,
who walked every step beside me.

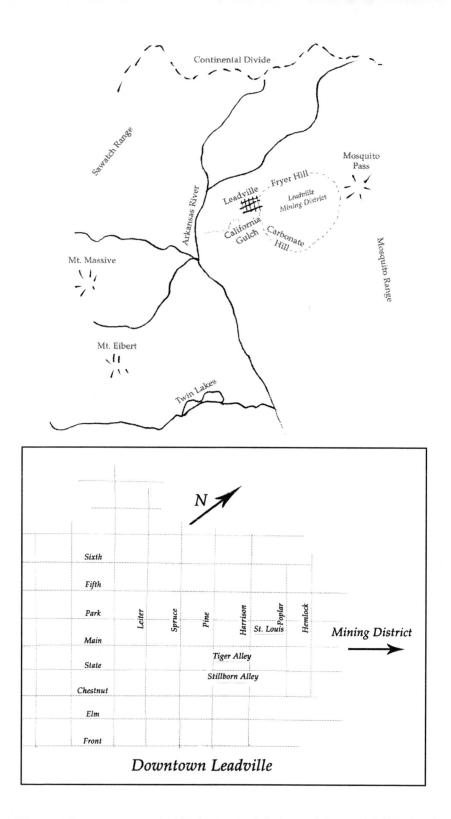

Continental Divide

Sawatch Range

Arkansas River

Leadville — Fryer Hill

Leadville Mining District

California Gulch

Carbonate Hill

Mosquito Pass

Mosquito Range

Mt. Massive

Mt. Elbert

Twin Lakes

N

Sixth

Fifth

Park

Main

State

Chestnut

Elm

Front

Leiter

Spruce

Pine

Harrison

St. Louis

Poplar

Hemlock

Tiger Alley

Stillborn Alley

Mining District

Downtown Leadville

Prologue

If there was an arctic version of hell, Joe Rose was living it in Leadville, Colorado.

Hugging the ten-thousand foot mark in the Rocky Mountains, Leadville in December 1879 had winter air cold enough to freeze a man's lungs, if he wasn't used to it.

A light, white snow, soft as angel wings, descended to the black mud of Tiger Alley in Leadville's red-light district. The icy paste—mixed with a season's worth of animal excrement and human garbage—had been churned up by beasts of burden, carts, and lost souls. In some spots, it lay knee deep.

At 2:30 in the morning, Tiger Alley was no place to fall down. Joe knew that as he flailed about, trying to regain his footing and his dignity. Raucous voices and honky-tonk music blasted through the saloon's half-open back door, the door through which he'd been unceremoniously ejected moments before.

On his feet at last, Joe reached for his pocket handkerchief to wipe the filth from his face. His fingers touched the slime coating his favorite waistcoat. "Damn!" He tried to scrub the mud off the silver and gold threads. "Ruined!" The word reverberated in his head, and Joe pictured it all again. The dealer raking in his last gold eagle across the waxed cloth of the faro table, the bouncer closing in on him to haul him away.

"I'm ruined," Joe whispered. Money, gone. Reputation gone as well, thanks to Harry. He owes me, Joe thought. We had a deal, we shook on it. I risked my neck meeting my side of the bargain, and he backs out.

As if through a haze, Joe remembered the curses he'd screamed at Harry just hours before, the cold, dismissive look on Harry's face, and, most frightening of all, Harry's silence. Panic welled up, bitter and black, in Joe's throat.

There was no future for him in Leadville. For him, his wife Emma, or their son. Joe closed his eyes in anguish. An image of Emma, her face pale and serious, rose before him. He spoke as if to a ghost: "I did it for you." Even as he said the words, he realized they weren't entirely true. He'd tried to protect her, true, but his troubles had really started when he tried to be someone he wasn't. Someone who'd gamble a fortune on a hunch at the poker table or a promising claim. Now, with the last of his five thousand dollars gone, any hope of making that elusive fortune in silver had disappeared. Worse, he could see no way of extracting himself from the mess he'd created.

The only money he had left was a fifty-dollar bill he dared not gamble. It all whirled around in his brain: his debts, the fifty, Emma, the deal gone bad between him and Harry, Denver.... The bleakness of his situation penetrated his whiskey-induced fog. "How will I ever explain to Emma?" he said to the night. His hand automatically strayed to the waistcoat pocket where he kept the pocketwatch she'd given him six years ago on their wedding day.

It was gone.

Heart sinking, he searched his trouser pockets frantically and tried to strike a deal with God: Just let me find the watch. I'll go straight home, tell Emma everything. I'll use that damn banknote to buy three stagecoach tickets and we'll start over with a clean slate. I swear I'll never touch cards or another glass of whiskey.

The lack of moonlight made it difficult to see in the alley. Crouching, Joe scrabbled through the frigid muck. His fingers felt, then closed on a familiar metallic disk. He clutched the watch to his chest in relief and thought, now I can go home. Everything will work out.

A slight vibration in the ground. A soft "whuff," barely heard.

Something was behind him.

Joe sprang to his feet and turned to see a monstrous dark shape. Too tall for a man. Joe heard a jangle of bit and bridle, an equine snort. The shape moved, became a horse and rider. The rider urged the mount forward. Straight toward Joe.

"Hey!" Joe shouted, trying to get out of the way. The horse jerked its head up with a snort and pranced backward. It unexpectedly lunged forward as the rider applied the whip. Joe stumbled to one side. Mud sucked at his boots, slowing his escape. The horse's bulk slammed into him, knocking the breath out of his body and nearly toppling him backward. The rider pulled up short with a vicious rein. Breathing hard and cursing, Joe grabbed a stirrup leather, staying well to the side to avoid being stepped on. He peered up, trying to discern the rider.

The voice that floated down to him was filled with menace.

"Well, well, if it isn't Joe Rose."

Fear crawled over Joe, freezing the sweat on his back, choking the curses in his throat. Oh Jesus, he thought. Not here. Not now. He couldn't force his thoughts any further, couldn't frame a reply.

Words poured over him with increased fury. "Looks like Lady Luck's deserted you for good this time. Are you short on silver again? Greenbacks? Or are you cheating at cards now?"

The rider leaned over, seized the dangling fob, and yanked. The pocketwatch flew from Joe's grip, a comet streaking beyond his reach.

Joe let go of the stirrup leather and made a futile grab, desperate to recapture the watch. The rider shifted athwart the saddle, away from Joe. The next instant, a booted foot smashed into Joe's face, sending bright daggers of pain streaking through his vision.

Joe cried out and fell backward, breaking through a thin icy crust into the scum below. Blood, warm and wet, poured from his battered nose and bathed his lips and chin. The pain loosened his tongue at last. He struggled to raise himself, searching purchase in the slime. "Wait! I was coming to see you." He tried to sound assured, sincere. But all he heard in his trembling voice was desperation and fear. "I...I've got what you want. All of it. The shipment arrived today. About the other business, the chemistry was wrong, but it's straight now."

"You liar. You double-crossing son of a bitch. Your next drink is with the Devil!" The whip hissed through the air.

Joe flinched, raised a hand, anticipating the cut of the lash across his palm. Instead, he heard—but didn't feel—the smack of lash on flesh.

The horse brayed and reared. For a moment, Joe saw mount and rider looming over him, an enormous shadow against night-dark clouds. The whip fell again. The horse pawed the air, then leaped forward with a grunt. Joe recoiled in terror. He heard, then felt a bone-crunching snap. And screamed.

His leg.

Intolerable pain engulfed him like a black avalanche. He tried to grab something, roll away. His fingers closed on ooze and shattered ice.

The horse reared again, fighting rein and whip. Hooves plunged down, flashing past Joe's face, crushing his ribs with a sound like dry wood splintering.

Joe's last scream was muffled by mud and honky-tonk music.

And the piano played on.

Chapter One

"Sweet Jesus," Inez Stannert muttered, surveying the ruins of her drinking establishment. "Looks like the North and South settled their differences right here on the floor."

Inez stood at the rear of the Silver Queen Saloon, hands on her hips. She eyed the splintered remains of what had once been a twenty-foot mirror gracing the mahogany backbar. Shards of glass lay about the sawdust like so many stars fallen to earth. She sighed. Her stays pinched beneath her green cashmere dress, a reminder not to inhale too deeply. A new mirror would run a thousand dollars. Freighting fees, another five hundred. At least.

Inez shook her head and turned her attention to the rest of the room. Busted chairs mixed it up with overturned tables. Her husband's favorite lithograph, a depiction of boxing champions Heenan and Sayers, bare-knuckled fists raised and ready, lay ripped and crumpled in one corner. The gilt frame looked as if it had been used to batter someone's head. Cold December air swept through the saloon's wide-open front door, doing little to alleviate the stale smell of tobacco and the heavy scent of whiskey, brandy, and beer leaking from broken bottles. She thought of the imported Scotch whisky, soaking the floorboards, worth its weight in gold. And groaned.

Abe Jackson, dark and silent as a shadow, emerged from the kitchen with two porcelain mugs of steaming coffee and stood beside Inez. They began walking the length of the room, wordlessly examining the damage. When they reached the front door, Abe handed Inez a mug and closed the door on the early morning light, extinguishing the stars on the floor.

"Looks worse than five hours ago," he ventured, scratching one end of his coarse black mustache.

Inez twisted the two rings on her finger—one gold, one silver—while she did a quick mental calculation. "We've lost several hundred in liquor alone, never mind the furniture. As for the mirror, it'll be spring before we can afford to order another from Chicago. Unless the house gets lucky at the poker table."

Turning away from the door, the two walked toward the staircase, passing a dusty upright piano. Inez lifted her long skirts to climb the steps. "Let's go to the office and you can tell me what happened."

On the second floor, Inez unlocked a door and the two entered a sitting room flooded with light from a large, west-facing window. A fire in the pot-bellied stove battled the cold, while a rag rug captured what warmth the winter sun offered.

Inez waved one hand at a calico cat dozing on a russet-colored horsehair couch. "Shoo. Go chase those rats I heard in the storeroom last night. Earn your keep, you lazy thing." The cat scooted under the couch, tail flicking.

Inez sipped her coffee before balancing the steaming mug on a stack of payables. She sat, banged up the rolltop to her desk, and pulled out a ledger. The window beside the desk over-looked the false-fronted saloons, dancing halls, and brothels of State Street to the distant snow-covered peaks of Massive and Elbert.

Abe sank onto the couch, knees cracking as he stretched his long legs. The calico, sensing a friendly and familiar lap, leaped to the sofa. Abe picked her up, his fingers disappearing in the thick winter coat.

Inez hooked half-glasses over her ears and opened the ledger. "Let's hear the story. Was it the liquor? The cards? Or some combination?"

Abe scratched the cat between her half-closed eyes while she worked her claws on his pant leg. "I think folks were spoilin' for a fight last night. Take Joe Rose, bustin' up your Saturday night game and callin' Harry Gallagher a liar to his face. Seems cussin' out his best client wouldn't be in Joe's best interests. Especially Harry, bein' that he and the other silver barons run the town. But Joe'd calmed down by the time he set up Harrison."

Inez peered over the top of her glasses. "Could he walk?"

"He made a mighty attempt to stagger in a straight line."

Inez nodded once, a quill pen balanced between her long fingers. "Joe knows the house rules. No married men gambling. No drunks served a drink. He failed on both counts. I hope he was sober enough to appreciate the favor you did him, walking him away from Harry."

Abe's deep brown eyes creased briefly.

The cat wiggled, turning over to present a belly for rubbing. Abe obliged. "We probably should've closed for the night after you shut down the game. Anyhow, about an hour after you went home, the second fight broke out. I was in the storeroom and didn't see it. Useless was tendin' bar. He says Chet Donnelly was arguin' over a claim with the twins Zed and Zeke. Chet heaved one of them into the mirror and the place exploded. By the time we hauled everyone out into the street, the damage was done. I told Chet he'd be payin' for a new mirror. Probably won't remember, though."

Inez slammed down the rolltop. The cat bolted under the couch. "Damn Chet Donnelly! There's too many men like him in this town. Someone looks at them cross-eyed and they start swinging!"

Abe coaxed the cat out and settled her on his lap again. "Yep. Just like some women I know. Act first, think later."

Inez faced him, opening hands in mock defeat. "Point taken. Your game, Abe. You always know when to play the winning card." She glanced at the grandfather clock by the door. "I'll be late for church! Not a good impression to make on the new reverend." She hurried to the door, pulling her winter cloak off a nearby hook.

"Well, now, he's only there 'til June, isn't that what you told me? What do you care what he thinks?"

She adjusted her hat in the mirror by the door. "He's the interim minister, true, but I'd like to start off on the right foot. Who knows? Maybe he plays cards or takes a nip now and again." She winked at Abe's reflection in the mirror.

"If he's gettin' paid what most preachers do, he's not playin' any high-stakes games. Unless he's got stock in some high-flyin' mine like the Denver City or Silver Mountain." He sauntered out after her. "Besides, you walk in late, everyone can admire your Sunday-go-to-meetin' outfit."

"Oh, they gawk anyway," Inez grumbled. "They believe all the business women on State Street work on their backs."

She stopped and glanced apologetically at Abe. "Perhaps the new reverend will say a few words on the virtues of holding one's temper. See you after supper, Abe. And thank you for handling the trouble last night."

"What are partners for? Gotta back each other up, if San Francisco's ever gonna be more'n a dream."

For a moment, Inez could almost hear her husband, Mark: "Inez, meet Abe Jackson. Ablest Negro soldier in the Union Army. I should know, I ended up at the business end of his rifle back in '65. Only man I ever met who can best me in a straight game of poker. Abe—" Mark's hands had been warm on her shoulders. "Meet Mrs. Mark Stannert. Inez and I outran her family and got hitched a week ago while you were lollygagging up north. Pretty sudden, I know, but that's how love is. Besides, she'll be an asset to our partnership. Inez plays piano like no one you've ever heard. Mozart from the heart. If we can teach her to play poker like she does music, we'll retire to San Francisco before the decade's out!" Mark's laugh echoed in her memory.

It's been nearly ten years since that promise. And nearly eight months since Mark disappeared.

"We're not in California yet," she said. "And the decade's almost gone. As is Mark." Her bitter words hovered in the air.

"There are many things that can happen to a man in these mountains. Things that'd keep him from coming back." Abe's voice was gentle. "Mark loved you and the young'un, Inez. It wasn't his nature to pick up and leave."

"Well, he's long gone in any case." She started down the stairs again.

"Inez." Abe held up two wrapped candies. "Joey Rose'll be expecting these. Don't break the boy's heart."

The candies sailed through the air, landed in her outstretched hand, and disappeared into her pocket. "I won't disappoint him. And I'll inquire from Emma about Joe. He most likely won't be at church, given his inebriated condition last night. I do wonder what's going on between him and Harry."

Abe turned to lock the office door. "Didn't Harry say anything?"

She continued down to the ruined room below. "Harry said, 'He's drunk.' Nothing we didn't already know. But I'll tell you this. If looks could kill, Joe Rose'd be a dead man."

Chapter Two

Once downstairs, Inez passed by the wrecked card room, its oil lamps silent and dark, and entered the clattering furor of the kitchen. Bending over a cooking stove of enormous proportions, a sturdy figure in a long gray dress busied herself among the sounds and smells of breakfast.

"Good morning, Bridgette. Thank you for offering to help out today."

Bridgette stopped stirring a massive iron pot of beans to beam at her employer. "No trouble at all, ma'am. Gives me a jump on the week's cooking, it does."

"And how was Mass this morning?"

"Father Briggs was in rare form, truly."

"Hmmm." Inez lifted an eyebrow. "Sober, for a change."

Bridgette wiped the sweat from her round face with the hem of her white apron. "Now, that sounds like blasphemy, indeed! It's a miracle that he stays on at all. A wickeder place than Leadville I haven't seen in my forty years, and I've been laundering and cooking since Sutter's Mill. Now, didn't I hear that Leadville's evils were just too much for your minister... Reverend Johnson, wasn't it?"

"Johnstone. And it wasn't the evils of Leadville. It was the winters."

"Well." She turned her attention back to the stove. "I hear your new reverend cuts a fine figure. The school-ma'ams are all a-twitter over him. He's unattached, they say."

"How do you know all this? He only arrived Tuesday."

Bridgette clunked the cover back on the iron pot and attacked a skillet of sausages. "I read the papers. And I hear things, I do."

Inez shook her head. "I'm in awe, Bridgette. And not just of your culinary skills. I hope your information travels one way. In, not out."

"Oh, ma'am. No need to worry about me blathering about who comes, who goes, and who says what. I couldn't keep my five boys in shoes and shirts if it weren't for you. Why, with the prices in this town, I couldn't take in enough laundry to pay for a tent! Not with the mister gone down the shaft of the New Discovery and on to a better place."

Her eyes misted for a moment, then cleared. She pointed her long-handled fork at Inez. "Along with you. And I want a report back as to whether the good Reverend J. B. Sands is as fine a gentleman as all are saying." She smiled, her anticipation not at all marred by a missing left incisor.

After locking the front door behind her, Inez walked to the corner and turned up Harrison Avenue. She pushed against a surging, restless tide of humanity, ninety-nine percent of it men. Even at this early hour, most were turning down State Street, searching for entertainment and liquor to numb the ever-present cold, lingering homesickness, and the pangs of silver fever. Long accustomed to the peculiar glitter of hope mixed with despair that branded nearly every face in the silver boom town, Inez lost herself in private ruminations even as her feet automatically adjusted their pace to the uneven elevations of Harrison's boardwalks.

Sunday. A day of rest, when the saloon was closed. She and Abe had stood together on that, united against Mark's initial enthusiasm to keep the establishment open around the clock, seven days a week.

She remembered when Mark had won the saloon from a Denver fellow with piggish eyes. During a break, and before the poker game in which he'd staked all their savings—hers, Mark's, and Abe's—against the business, Mark had pulled her aside.

"Now darlin'," he'd murmured into her ear. "I know when he's bluffing and when he's holding a good hand. I'm just waitin' for the right play. You remember that assayer, Joe Rose? He says this place is the next silver bonanza, the biggest yet. I figure we'll settle into business with this saloon and mine the miners. We'll celebrate tonight, sweet lady!" He'd kissed her hard, winked, and returned to the table, leaving her mouth tingling.

Mark had parted that fellow from his property, smooth and neat. Later that night, he'd twirled her in a wild polka across the empty saloon floor. Afterward...ah yes. Celebrate they did.

Oh Mark. Why did you leave? Without a word?

The steeple of the small white church beckoned. Shaking off the memories like she shook the mud and ice from the hem of her dress, Inez mounted the church stairs. She slipped into place next to Joey and Emma Rose and smiled at Joey. The five-year-old was already losing the battle against the urge to wiggle and kick at the pew in front of him.

"Joey." She opened her hand, revealing the candies. Joey's twitching stilled. "One when the sermon starts. The second when it's done. Deal?"

With his dark blue eyes and slicked-down black hair, Joey looked like a miniature version of his father. "Deal, Auntie Inez." He snuggled between the two women, muffled by their wool cloaks.

Inez took advantage of the general buzz to lean over Joey. "Emma?"

Emma Rose turned to Inez. The freckles across her nose stood out against her pale skin. Her red hair, wound up under a black velvet hat, still managed to wisp about her face, framing eyes close to tears.

"Emma?" Inez leaned over a fraction further, keeping her voice low. "What's wrong? Are you feeling ill?"

Emma turned to gaze straight ahead, her gloved hands clasping the small prayerbook in her lap.

Inez persisted. "Is Joe all right?"

Emma's hands twisted around the book, burrowing into the folds of her Sunday dress. "He didn't come home last night." She faltered. "He's never done this before."

Inez frowned.

As Reverend Sands strode to the pulpit amid anticipatory murmurs from the congregation, Inez heard a rustle of petticoats and felt a faint pressure to her right. Susan Carothers sank next to her, panting.

"Hello, Inez," she whispered, tucking a strand of shiny black hair behind her ear. "Sunday morning sittings are always a mistake. It takes forever to pose the clients and expose the plates."

Susan pulled her prayerbook out of her reticule and straightened her crooked hat, eyes darting around the church before settling on the man at the front. "Have you met Reverend Sands yet? He has the nicest smile. I was part of the welcoming committee that took him to tea at the Clairmont on Wednesday." She leaned sideways, gaze still fixed forward, and softened her voice another notch. "He's handsome, don't you think? I'm glad he doesn't have one of those ugly soup-strainer mustaches that all the men wear."

"Shhh! Susan, later, please. After the service." Inez scrutinized the reverend, standing at ease and waiting for the arpeggio of murmurs to die.

Her first impression was not of a man focused on the ethereal or spiritual side of life. Far from being an attenuated, pale cleric, Reverend Sands appeared physically fit and well acquainted with long days in the sun. He rather reminded her of the circuit riders who would snowshoe in sixty miles to preach to the lost in Leadville.

Other than that, Reverend Sands struck her as fairly ordinary looking: medium height, mid-thirties, light brown hair, clean-shaven face, a faint but pleasant smile. A mien designed to blend into the crowds. Nothing about him would have caused Inez to glance at him twice if he'd strolled through the Silver Queen's doors. Nothing, that is, until he spoke.

"Let's all stand." Reverend Sands' voice rolled over her. Warm, almost sensual in its invitation. "And turn to hymn sixty-three."

Something about his timbre reminded Inez of butter spread on one of Bridgette's just-baked biscuits. She stood, shaking off the spell of his voice. *I should have had something besides coffee for breakfast.*

Emma opened the hymn book but didn't sing. Joey shuffled, but not too much, obviously mindful of the promised treat. Inez's attention shifted from the music to the Roses.

Where's Joe?

"...a pleasure to join your community, even if only for six months." The reverend's intimate tone surrounded her, brought her back to the church. "At the earliest opportunity, I hope to become acquainted with each and every one of you."

"Ha!" Susan nodded toward a woman with hennaed hair coiled beneath an extravagant hat. "I bet Catherine DuBois would love to have him drop in for a 'cup of tea.' When did she take up religion anyway?"

"Shhh."

Sure enough, the owner of the Crystal Belle Saloon and Leadville's leading parlor house sat with two of her "soiled doves" in the front pew, as bold as you please.

Inez twisted a little to her right. *Ah yes.* And there was Harry Gallagher with his diamond stick pin and impeccably tailored frock coat, looking rich as a banker and friendly as the Devil himself. His glacial blue eyes froze on Inez, then slid back to the pulpit.

"...As our Lord says in chapter eighteen of the book of Matthew, 'If a man have a hundred sheep, and one of them be gone astray, doth he not leave the ninety and nine, and goeth into the mountains, and seeketh that which is gone astray?'"

Joey wiggled a bit. Inez fished out one candy and surreptitiously handed it to him, saving the second for later. A small crinkling sound of paper, and Joey sat still, one cheek bulging like a squirrel with a nut.

The service ended not a moment too soon for Joey. "Greet your neighbors!" concluded Reverend Sands, gathering his notes. Joey grabbed Inez's skirts in a hug, then wiggled past her to join a gaggle of children heading outside.

Emma, following Joey with her eyes, frowned. "Is that the marshal?"

Lounging by the door, Marshal Bart Hollis scanned the crowd, his jaws working rhythmically on a plug of tobacco. A thin man with the look of a hungry rattlesnake, he hunched his shoulders as if expecting a bird of prey to grab him by his collar and haul him away. His gaze snagged on Inez, and he began elbowing his way through the congregation, a tin star winking on his sheepskin vest.

Inez watched his approach with growing unease. "What's he doing here? Hollis probably hasn't been in a place of worship since he was a babe in arms."

"Miz Rose?" He looked the three women over, stroking his drooping tobacco-stained mustache.

Emma took a half step forward, dread on her face.

"Ma'am, I've got bad news."

Emma clutched Inez's arm. "Does this have to do with my husband?"

Marshal Hollis sent a stream of tobacco juice angling under the pew, just missing Inez's skirts.

"Well, mebbe." He paused. "At least, we're thinkin' it's him."

Inez put a steadying hand over Emma's. Emma whispered, "Something's happened. Has he been arrested? Is he hurt?"

Marshal Hollis cleared his throat. "Ma'am. I don't rightly know how to say this, but, about an hour ago, we got word about this body."

Emma closed her eyes.

"Findin' a deceased fella or two ain't anything rare after Saturday nights." He floundered. "But this one, we think he's, uh, your husband, ma'am. It's a little hard to tell."

"Joe." Emma's knees buckled.

Inez helped her sit in the pew.

Marshal Hollis belatedly removed his battered Stetson. "Right sorry, Miz Rose. If you'd come along with me, he's in Tiger Alley." He shifted his narrow eyes, pinning Inez. "Mebbe Miz Stannert here can tell us what he's doin' propped up behind her saloon, the Silver Queen."

Chapter Three

Disbelief flooded through Inez. "That's impossible! How dare you insinuate—"

"Deputy." The reverend escaped from a knot of school-teachers. "I'm Reverend Sands, the new minister of this church. Until June, that is. I don't believe we've met. Is something amiss?"

"Marshal!" snapped Hollis. "Marshal Bart Hollis. And I got a heap a trouble, but it's none of your funeral." He stopped, his face squeezing in several degrees further.

Inez turned to Susan. "Take Joey. I'll go with Emma."

Susan swiped at her eyes with her wadded-up gloves. "Marshal, I hope you're wrong." She moved quickly out the door, calling, "Joey! Your mother says you can visit my studio. Come, I'll show you how the camera works."

"What's this about?" Reverend Sands' voice took on an edge.

"Reverend. A moment, please." Inez moved to one side, motioning him over. She spoke softly, with emphasis. "I'm Mrs. Stannert, a friend of the Roses. This entire business is probably a ghastly misunderstanding and doesn't bear repeating. Given that you're new to town, it might be best if I deal with this…problem. If we need your assistance, I will send word to you within the hour. Where are you staying?"

Reverend Sands seemed to weigh the question before answering. "I've a room at the Clairmont."

Harry's hotel. Inez suppressed an involuntary shudder. "Within the hour then, Reverend Sands."

"Very well, Mrs. Stannert." His voice was level, the warm quality that had infused the service, gone.

Inez guided Emma outside. The sky, so brilliant blue two hours earlier, now pressed down a soft, doleful gray. The temperature had plummeted, bringing biting cold.

"Now, Emma, it's most likely a mistake." Inez pulled up Emma's fur-lined hood, as if the red-haired woman were a child. "With the marshal so new in town, I doubt he's ever met Joe."

Hollis bristled as he gingerly stepped up and down Harrison's multi-level boardwalks. "Been here almost three weeks, feels like three years. Your cook, what's 'er name, says it looks like Joe Rose."

"Marshal." Inez's voice was venomous. "Bridgette is a wonderful cook, a dedicated mother, and an honest woman. But I don't think she could pick out her own parents from ten feet away. Her eyes are worse than a mole's above ground."

The trio maneuvered down the crowded thoroughfare past tobacco shops, saloons, a book store, and a jumble of mercantile shops. Except for the recently completed brick opera house across the broad street, most of the buildings had the raw look of wood structures, hastily constructed to beat Leadville's early winter. Up north on Harrison, sounds of construction mingled with the clatter of horse- and mule-drawn wagons and the thunder of a thousand boots on wooden walkways. A hollow boom signaled that someone had set off a charge to break through the frozen ground. Another foundation would be set that day. It might have been Sunday, but that didn't stop the building or real estate speculation. Frames continued to rise on prime real estate at a frantic pace, snow or no.

The marshal and the two women paused at the corner of Harrison and State streets. Snow fell weeping on their shoulders and at their feet.

Emma gazed down State. The red-light district was an undulating sea of hatted humanity spilling from crowded boardwalks and into the street. Two brass bands faced each other from opposing dance halls and blatted out tunes to lure passersby inside. Inez was grateful that none of State's frail sisters were in sight and that the weather was too cold for the tightrope walkers who occasionally balanced on ropes strung high over the street.

"Just around the corner." Inez gently prodded Emma. Emma took one step.

"Inez, I've never set foot on State much less been inside your…establishment."

"There's no one there now besides our cook Bridgette and maybe Abe."

Hollis brushed past them to the door of the saloon. "This way, ma'am."

Emma squared her shoulders and entered, eyes straight ahead.

Hollis paused, examining the broken chairs and overturned tables. "Jest a regular Saturday night, eh Miz Stannert?"

Inez shot him a look of disgust. Emma quickened her pace and clutched her prayerbook before her as if it were a small shield.

The group passed through the devastation to the kitchen. Steam from a pot of wash water on the stove imbued the room with a heavy, wet warmth. Inez recognized the deputy slouched by the back door as Curly Dan, a mild-mannered sort who frequented her saloon—*sans* badge—on his days off. He nodded at Inez and lifted his hat briefly to Emma, his bald pate appearing and disappearing fast as a wink. Bridgette, her face red-splotched, sat at the plank table surrounded by dirty crockery. Abe slumped nearby, gabardine trousers muddy to the knees. He looked at Emma, then Inez, and shook his head.

Inez's heart sank.

"Oh ma'am, it's just awful," babbled Bridgette. "Mr. Jackson sent for the marshal—"

"And now we got to find out who that is back there," interrupted Hollis. He crossed to Curly Dan and asked, "Any trouble?"

The deputy moved aside to let Hollis pass. "Nope. Not a speck."

Hollis leaned out, peering left. "What in tarnation?"

Bridgette blew her nose on her apron. "Mr. Jackson took the wash water and threw it at the—"

"Cleaned him up right nice," observed Hollis.

Emma's face paled. With a moan she covered her mouth, looking around.

Maternal instincts aroused, Bridgette leapt to her feet and, grabbing an empty pot, steered Emma out of the kitchen. Sounds of retching followed.

Abe looked at Inez. "I don't think she oughta see what's out there."

"Marshal." Inez tried for a reasonable tone. "Abe and I, we know Joe well. Perhaps our identification of the body might suffice."

Hollis set his jaw stubbornly.

She tried again. "If you were to also remove some personal effects for Mrs. Rose. A ring. A pocketwatch. Wouldn't that be enough? If it is Joe, I would hate for her to carry that image of her husband as her last."

Curly Dan spoke up. "Might not be a bad idea, Bart. He's pretty bad smashed up for viewing."

Hollis glared at him. "You takin' their side, Curly?"

He shrugged. "Just thinking of the widow. That's all."

Hollis turned to Inez, his mouth twisted beneath the scraggly mustache. "Okay, Miz Stannert. He's right out back. Curly here'll show you where." He faced Abe. "Boy. You and Curly get whatever'll help Miz Rose identify those remains."

Abe tipped his chair back and leveled a stare at the marshal. "I'm not your 'boy,' Hollis. Do it yourself."

Hollis glared at Abe and then turned to his deputy, who gazed across the alley as if he wished himself a million miles away. Curly Dan finally spoke in a conciliatory tone. "Seems like you'd best handle this one, Bart. If I remember correct, Joe Rose is Gallagher's assayer for Silver Mountain. Works for him almost exclusive." He shifted, causing the boards to creak beneath his boots. "Don't want Gallagher blaming me if something's not done right."

"Then it's you an' me, Miz Stannert." Hollis grabbed Inez's arm and jerked her through the back door. She yanked her arm away. Once on the narrow walkway, Hollis faced her, blocking her view of the alley. "Seems to me, you an' that nigger ain't exactly co-operatin' with the law. And I *am* the law, like it or not."

Inez folded her arms and glared back. "You talk like that in Abe's presence, he'll carve you up quicker than a Christmas turkey, star or no. Everyone knows you're just a two-bit gunslinger from Texas. The only thing placing you on *this* side of the law in Leadville is Gallagher and the other silver barons who hired you to keep the peace after last month's lynching. If that isn't an irony."

"I been in town long enough to know you're good at makin' enemies, Miz Stannert. Mebbe one of these days, you'll holler for help and it'll be too slow in coming." Hollis turned up the collar of his jacket. They took a few steps along the walkway. After a moment's hesitation, Hollis gingerly stepped off the narrow planks and into the icy slime.

As he stepped down, Inez saw the body sprawled in the mud and snow, lying half under the raised walkway. The dishwater had lent a frozen sheen to the skin while removing most of the filth. The face was smashed, obliterated, along with the torso. But Inez recognized the waistcoat. Joe had been so proud of that extravagant vest, bought on one of his many trips to Denver for assaying supplies. "Makes me look like a real high roller, don't you think, Inez?" He had smoothed the ornate gold and silver trim.

Best you don't see, Emma. Inez looked away, overwhelmed by the grief that crashed upon her.

Hollis squatted over the body, cursing as the freezing mud poured over the tops of his boots. "Dang this shit! The only thing that could make this worse is if it were warm and stinkin'. Okay, Miz Stannert. Who is he?"

She wanted to sink down right there on the walkway. "It's Joe Rose."

"Well, well, Mr. Respectable hisself, Honest Joe Rose. And what was he doin' out here last night behind the Silver Queen? Okay. Let's see. Here's his ring. I'll take that for Miz Rose. What else?"

Inez closed her eyes to the sight. "He should have a wallet, unless some footpad got to him first. How did he end up so... mutilated?"

"That's for the coroner to say. Mebbe a horse stomped him while he was passed out drunk. Mebbe someone dropped a piano on him. Here's the wallet. What else does he carry?"

"A gold pocketwatch." Inez opened the soaked leather wallet as she spoke. "JR engraved on the cover, a photograph of his wife and son inside."

She pulled out a sodden fifty-dollar bill. *He couldn't have been lying here since midnight. This would have been long gone.*

Her gloved fingers squeezed an invisible stiffness beneath the leather. Frowning, she opened the wallet wide, displaying the spotted silk lining.

Empty.

She could, however, see the impression of something, about the size and shape of a coin, trapped between the leather and the silk. Inez tried to coax the object out from a rip in the bottom of the lining.

Hollis rooted through Joe's waistcoat pockets, sucking through his teeth.

The round object, which at first glance looked like a brass coin with the center punched out, fell into her palm.

Hollis spat. "No watch."

Inez looked up. "Are you sure? Check his trouser pockets. He never went anywhere without it."

She refocused on the object in her hand. It looked like no token she'd ever seen. The center was punched out in the shape of a heart. Small letters stamped around the outside proclaimed: "527 Holladay Street, Denver, Colo." Frowning, she turned it over to read: "Good for one free screw. Mattie Silks, Prop."

Chapter Four

Inez slipped the brass check into her pocket as Marshal Hollis looked up. "I ain't diggin' through his guts any further."

He waded to the walkway and pulled himself up with a grunt. Extracting a soiled neckerchief from a pocket, he attempted to wipe off his boots. "You give those things to Miz Rose. We'll see what she says. After that, I got a few questions for you and anyone else who closed up last night." What could have been a neutral statement came out as a not-so-subtle threat.

Time to lay our cards on the table. At least, some of them.

"Let's not put Mrs. Rose through any more pain than necessary," Inez began. "I'll tell you what I know. Abe and our hired man Useless will back me up. Joe *was* here last night, but only briefly. He and Harry Gallagher had a…" she searched for a neutral word, "disagreement. Joe left about midnight. Abe saw him heading up Harrison. That was the last we saw of Joe. I have no idea how he ended up here. Like this."

Hollis snorted derisively, examined his neckerchief, and threw it into the mud with the rest of the garbage. "Curly!" he hollered. "Get out here. You stand guard 'til the undertaker's wagon gets here. Don't let any alley scum come sniffin' around too close."

Back in the kitchen, Inez laid the ring and the wallet in front of Emma. The stricken expression on Emma's face said it all. She began to rock in the chair, knuckles pressed to her mouth. Inez sat down and put an arm around her. In a muffled voice Emma asked, "His pocketwatch?"

Inez squeezed her shoulder. "We didn't find it."

Covering her face, Emma whispered, "He promised, he gave his word that nothing more would happen. I was a fool to believe him."

Inez bent closer, not certain she'd heard Emma correctly.

"What's that?" Hollis leaned forward. "So these're your husband's?"

Emma nodded.

Inez turned to the marshal. "You've got what you need. We're taking Mrs. Rose home now. If you have further questions, talk to me or Abe."

The brass check weighed heavily in Inez's thoughts as she wrestled with the Silver Queen's massive doors.

Joe, visiting a Denver whorehouse? He fancied cards and an occasional drink, but this....I had no idea. Either Emma knows and is keeping silent or she's in the dark. In any case, I'd best keep my suspicions to myself.

The wind pounded her with waves of snow as she jammed the heavy key in the lock. Bridgette gave Emma a last comforting pat and hurried away, pulling her shawl close about her head. Marshal Hollis clutched his Stetson to keep it from taking wing. Abe offered his muffler to Emma.

"'Scuse me, ma'am." Inez jumped at the unexpected voice behind her. She turned to find Useless, hands stuffed into the pockets of his damp brown corduroy pants.

Useless glanced at Emma, then at Abe and the marshal, before addressing his remarks to his boots.

"I thought maybe you could use some help cleaning up today." He wiped his nose with the back of his hand.

Inez pulled her cloak tight as the wind tore at her skirts. "Goodness, Useless, after last night, I'd thought you'd be home recovering." Seeing his eyes fix on Emma, whose red hair was coming unpinned and whipping over the top of the muffler, she added, "Mr. Ulysses Assenmacher, Mrs. Joe Rose."

Useless yanked off his hat and held it to his chest. His mousy hair collected clumps of snow. "I've met your husband when he's come around. Nice fella. Hope he's feeling better. After, uh, last night."

Inez winced at his ill-timed remark and its delivery. Useless was hopeless around women. She had introduced him to Susan once when he'd happened upon them in the Eureka Restaurant. Inez had mentally rolled her eyes at his bowing and stuttering, but Susan's response after he'd left had been far more visceral.

"Ugh! He works for you, Inez? How can you stand it?"

"Stand what?"

"The way he stares." Susan shuddered. "Makes me want to scrub up with soap."

Yes, Useless needs to be taught some basic manners. And soon.

Inez watched Emma turn away from him, clutching her hood closer about her face. His smile faded.

Marshal Hollis stepped forward. "Joe Rose's dead. Behind the saloon."

"Oh jeez." His face slid into dismay and froze.

Hollis pressed on. "You here last night?"

Useless replaced his hat, sneaking a guilty glance at Emma. "Until two. Locked up with Mr. Jackson."

The marshal's eyes seemed to grow smaller, shinier. "Miz Stannert, me'n your help here are gonna discuss last night's events. Inside."

Inez unlocked the door reluctantly, thinking of the marshal's penchant for hard liquor. "Useless, Abe will be back soon to lock up. We'll deal with the mess tomorrow. The marshal may have two shots of Red Dog on the house." She paused for emphasis. "Two."

Useless nodded. Drops of snow flew from his hat and nose.

Snow scuttled over the floorboards with the two men before the door slammed behind them. "Lord, it's cold! Let's take State to Pine. It's quicker."

"No!" Emma spoke vehemently under the muffler. "I will not walk another step down this evil street!"

Abe sighed. "We're gonna freeze if we keep standin' here. Let's go up Harrison. When we reach Park Street, you take her on home. I'll get Joey, close up, and come see you before I head home myself."

The trio turned onto Harrison, where tall store fronts cut the wind, and promptly came face to face with Cat DuBois and her companions from church.

"More travelers adrift in the storm," purred Cat from deep inside her fur coat. "Mrs. Stannert, you didn't stay to welcome Reverend Sands. Such a charming gentleman. We plan to extend every courtesy to him during his brief stay and show just how friendly Leadville can be. Right, girls?" Her gaze shifted to her companions. They responded with tentative nods. Cat turned back to Inez. "We saw you rush off with the marshal in tow. So, something dire afoot? Trouble at the Silver Queen?"

"Save the chit-chat for church, Mrs. DuBois," snapped Inez.

"Scant civility in the streets of Hell today." Cat shoved past Inez, crowding her toward the edge of the boardwalk.

One of Cat's women, a petite, well-endowed blonde, hurried by with downcast eyes. The second paused before Emma Rose, blocking her path.

Her thick black hair curled over her fur coat nearly to her waist. Damp and flecked with snow, it seemed nearly alive, springing about her face and shoulders with an energy that filled the space around her. In contrast, her heart-shaped face was still. No heavy powders or face paints marred skin the color of cinnamon. Eyes dark, deep as midnight, seemed to swallow light, giving nothing back. She stared at Emma and tentatively raised a hand.

"Angel!" Cat's voice cracked like a whip. Angel lowered her gaze and darted around Emma.

"Angel, dear, your manners. These *respectable* people prefer we remain invisible." Cat's melodious voice floated back as she turned the corner.

Inez, Emma, and Abe continued up Harrison in silence.

"How old is she?" asked Emma suddenly.

Inez and Abe exchanged a glance over Emma's head.

"Angel? Seventeen, eighteen," said Abe.

"Seventeen. Just a child," murmured Emma. "Why is she here?"

Inez picked up the pace. Park Street was in sight. "Life's choices. Or lack of them. Sometimes, that young, they're runaways with nowhere else to go. Only Angel could say."

"She can't speak," said Abe. He cleared his throat as the two women stopped and looked at him. "At least, that's the talk over whiskey and cards. The gentlemen say Angel keeps her secrets and others' too."

"That's horrible." Tears trickled down Emma's face and froze on her cheeks. "What kind of God could let it happen? And now Joe's dead. We should have left Leadville long ago. I begged. I pleaded. I did everything I could. And now it's too late."

Chapter Five

"Leave Leadville?" Inez, who had started moving, stopped again. A gaunt man, hard on her heels, bumped into her, muttered an apology and kept going. Inez ignored him. "You never breathed a word about this before."

Emma compressed her lips, as if regretting her words. Finally she spoke. "We've been moving from one mining town to another since before young Joey was born. Georgetown. Central City. Silverton. Leadville. I told Joe, I wanted to settle someplace civilized. And things…things weren't going well here for Joe's business. Or for me. Oh, Inez. I can't talk about it now. I need to think on what I'm going to tell Joey."

Hearing the pain in Emma's voice, Inez swallowed her questions.

At Emma's house, Inez found a tartan wool throw for Emma's shoulders and settled her in the rocker by the kitchen stove. As she moved hesitantly about Emma's kitchen searching for teapot, strainer, cups, canned milk, Inez remembered how miserable she'd been as a housewife.

She and Mark had moved with high hopes to their small home on Park Street, just two down from the Roses'. Inez, exhausted in the last stages of pregnancy, had been relieved to vacate their quarters above the saloon. State Street never slept, day or night, making it hard for her to rest. Furthermore, it was no place to raise a baby.

The Stannerts' visions of domestic bliss soon withered. In a silent concession to Inez's non-existent cooking skills, Mark began bringing home leftovers from the saloon for their supper. After William was born with his weak lungs, Inez abandoned all pretense of keeping house to care for him.

Doc Cramer was a constant visitor that winter as they struggled to ease William's breathing. Once spring arrived and William's condition improved, Doc advised them to leave the mountains. "Your boy won't make it through another winter. His constitution's not built for it."

Expression grim, Mark had relayed Doc's words to Inez. She knew what he was thinking: Sell the saloon now? Go where? Do what? It was May 1879. Strike after silver strike rolled through the district and business was booming.

"Maybe we don't have to sell," Inez said. "Abe could manage the place. We could move to Denver. The winters are milder there."

Mark rubbed his face with both hands, shoulders sagging under his black velvet waistcoat. "That's up to Abe." He hesitated. "With all the good ol' boys and Eastern high society hitting town, Leadville isn't as…open…as it was a year ago. I don't know how folks would respond to a man of color being in charge. He may not want to put up with the trouble."

Mark walked to the parlor window and gazed at the sapling he'd planted the day of William's birth. His fingers drummed on the varnished top of Inez's piano. "Harry Gallagher's interested in buying the Queen. Cat DuBois is mighty eager too. I swear that woman'd buy all of State Street if it were for sale." His tone was noncommittal. "Maybe I'll play them off each other. See who raises and how high."

He turned and kissed her on the nose. Inez was too disheartened to demand when and where he'd conversed with Madam DuBois.

Mark continued, "Doc says William can't make another winter, so we'll be on the train out of Denver by July. August at the latest." He settled his hat on his head, preparing to go to the saloon. "I hear autumn's mighty fine in California."

The next day, he disappeared from Leadville and her life.

<>‹›<>

After promising to return the following day, Inez left Emma and walked home in the dwindling winter light. Emotionally exhausted from reliving her memories and keeping Emma company, Inez settled into her own, silent parlor, wrapped in one of Mark's old sweaters. She flexed her toes in their soggy green-striped stockings and stared at the small fir tree struggling to stay erect in the front yard.

Her feet ached, as did her heart. And something dark waited along the edges of her grief. Questions, but no answers.

With a sigh, she lifted the keyboard cover of her parlor grand piano. Her fingers ran up and down the scales, letting a waterfall of measured notes pour into the silence. Exploring tones by touch in the darkening room, she picked music to fit her mood. The melody line surfaced from the liquid language of the piano's strings and wrapped about her.

Closing her eyes, she let her sorrows, old and new, rise and fall with the music. The precision and beauty of Mozart anchored her, pulled her back from emotions that threatened to swallow her whole.

Inez surfaced at the end of the sonata to a persistent knocking on the door. *Abe.* He'd promised to stop by. She decided against forcing her damp stockinged feet into shoes. Stockings were not going to shock Abe. In their years together, he'd seen worse.

She abandoned Mark's sweater to the keyboard and moved toward the sound. "Coming."

Inez opened the door.

Reverend Sands stood on the small porch, ankle deep in drifting snow, looking none too happy.

"Pardon, Mrs. Stannert, but when I didn't hear from you…"

He stopped, as if her expression had finally registered past his displeasure. "May I come in?" He curled a hand around the edge of the door as if to prevent her from slamming it in his face.

She contemplated that hand for a moment. Long fingers, square clean nails. Strong, capable. The hand of a physical man, but not of a prospector or laborer. Fighting a vague uneasiness, Inez looked back at his face. Concern settled across his features, although the blue-gray eyes were far too piercing to be sympathetic.

"My apologies. I did say I would send for you, didn't I. Please, come in." She stood aside and gestured toward the parlor.

He used his black hat to knock the snow off his shoulders before entering. His boots echoed on the varnished hardwood floor of the entryway.

Boots.

She looked down. The tips of her green-striped stockings were barely visible beneath her long skirts.

Reverend Sands glanced around the parlor, his gaze lingering on the piano. She followed and indicated the maroon loveseat.

He sat and idly began flapping his hat up and down on the back of the small sofa, watching her. Inez felt disinclined to take his hat. Her reluctance grew as his gaze shifted slowly downward, pausing at her stockinged feet. This visit, she decided, would be brief.

Mustering dignity learned in the deportment lessons of her youth, Inez moved toward the sideboard. "Tea, Reverend Sands? Or something stronger?"

'No. Thank you."

"Well, I'm having both." Inez opened a door on the sideboard and pulled out a decanter. She measured a generous amount of brandy into her tea before returning to the piano seat. As she sipped, the warm liquid slid down, untying the last cold knot of sorrow. For the present.

"Reverend, you have your work cut out for you. Mrs. Rose's husband was killed last night in a terrible accident."

Accident. The word mocked her. An image of Marshal Hollis' skeptical face floated through her mind.

Reverend Sands stopped tapping and leaned forward, sympathetic. "I heard as much this afternoon. Normally, I would have gone directly to the family and offered my assistance. But in this case, I'm at a disadvantage, having just arrived in town." He leaned back, looking relaxed, except for those eyes. "Since you're a friend of the Roses and a member of the congregation, I thought you could advise me on the best course of action. Perhaps Mrs. Rose prefers the company of those close to her right now." He shrugged, acknowledging his status as an outsider.

Inez studied him. On closer examination, she had to admit that Susan and Madam DuBois were right: He was rather attractive. Although, she felt that, even as she watched, he shifted, wasn't quite in focus. It was, Inez decided, like looking at someone through a pair of bad spectacles. Behind the relaxed demeanor, he seemed to be watching, waiting for her to reveal through some throwaway gesture who she was, what kind of hand she held.

"I'd have pegged you as a gambler rather than a man of the cloth."

The reverend's eyebrows shot up. "Excuse me?"

Inez hoped the twilight hid the flush crawling up her face. "Pardon. How inexcusable of me."

She placed cup and saucer on top of the piano. "I own a drinking establishment downtown. It's in my best interest to divine those who walk through my doors before the liquor flows and the cards are dealt. When people arrive in Leadville, they shed their pasts like old coats. Not all are what they seem."

Inez rose to light a small lamp. "It's getting late. Let's speak of the Roses."

The warm lamplight chased away the shadows, revealing the concern etched in the reverend's face. He nodded, looking, for the moment, like a proper clergyman.

Inez drained the lukewarm tea and forced herself not to look at the bottle on the sideboard. "As with everyone in Leadville, they're from somewhere else. Joe's from Nebraska, or maybe it's Kansas. I think Emma's the same. They met in Colorado, in one of the mining camps. I believe Emma was a schoolteacher. Joe is—was—an assayer. He came to the district in seventy-seven, seventy-eight. As anyone will tell you, Joe's well respected. A man of integrity. Devoted to his family." She said the last almost as if she expected him to challenge her.

Sands merely asked, "Any relatives nearby? Family that Mrs. Rose can turn to? "

"None that I know of." Inez rubbed her forehead, feeling the fine strands of hair that had pulled loose from her chignon. "Joe's business, the church, their friends. Everything's here. Leadville is their home. I'd just assumed that they planned to stay until the silver boom goes bust. If it ever does. But this afternoon, Emma indicated they'd talked of leaving. I don't know why." Inez glanced away, considering Emma's dilemma. "Emma Rose is going to have a difficult time. Oh, not financially, Joe's no doubt left her well provided for. However she, ah, she…"

Inez debated a moment. *Well. He's her minister now after all. If he's going to help, I've got to tell him.* "Mrs. Rose is in a family way. She told me a few days ago." Inez remembered the devastated look on Emma's face when she'd delivered the news. "I don't think," Inez finished lamely, "it was a particularly welcome development."

Sands leaned forward. "I'll hold what you've told me in confidence, of course. Am I right in thinking tomorrow afternoon is soon enough to pay a call and offer my support?"

"I believe so. When I left her a while ago, she was very clear that she wanted time alone to talk with her son, Joey." Inez stood.

Reverend Sands followed her lead. "Mrs. Rose is lucky to have friends such as yourself to help her through these times.

Perhaps I might come around your place of business. We could talk further."

Inez walked toward the door. "It's the Silver Queen, corner of Harrison and State. We serve only the best and never water it down."

He shook his head, a tad regretfully, she thought. "I'm not a drinking man myself."

"Well, I also employ the best cook in town. So if the liquor doesn't tempt you, Bridgette's biscuits and stew might."

Sands grinned. "Now that kind of temptation I find hard to resist. And I'd enjoy speaking with you more. Under different circumstances." His smile finally reached his eyes, matching the warmth of his voice.

Inez smiled back, feeling lightheaded. *Must be the brandy.* She pulled the door open. "Until later, then."

Standing outside, hand raised to knock, Abe looked as startled as the reverend.

Inez recovered first. "Why, Abe. How fortunate you're here. Reverend Sands and I were just discussing the Roses. The reverend is interim minister for the church until June. Reverend, this is my business partner, Abe Jackson."

Sands held out his hand. "You're a friend of the Roses?"

Abe's hand engulfed the reverend's. He looked the cleric over and smiled. The same smile he gave to strangers as he dealt the cards. A smile to keep the suckers easy in their chairs. "Mighty fine to meet you, Reverend." His drawl became more pronounced. "Lord's taken Joe to a better place. Now we got to help Miz Rose through these troubled times, raise our voices to the Lord and say His name in praise and prayer."

Inez stared. The only times she'd ever heard Abe raise his voice to say the Lord's name, it wasn't in praise. Or in prayer. Abe rolled on. "Yes, God Almighty's gathered Joe to His bosom. Called him home. Right, Reverend?"

"Yes. Exactly." Sands extracted his hand and glanced up at the black sky. Whirling snowflakes appeared and wheeled lazily down to vanish in the drifts at his feet. "The wind has dropped. Pleased to meet you, Mr. Jackson. I look forward to seeing you again sometime." With a last smile at Inez, he walked out of the small pool of light on the porch and into the darkness.

Inez and Abe stood at the door, watching Sands disappear down the street.

"He's no reverend," Abe said flatly.

Chaper Six

Deep in dreams, Inez heard a woman's long wail curl about the scream of a child.

She shot from sleep to wakefulness. Under the pillow, her right hand clutched the cold comfort of Mark's War-issue Navy Colt: an automatic response to danger.

Moonlight crept through lace curtains over drawn roller shades. Outside, two cats yowled and spat.

Her nightmare still burned in her mind. Joe Rose, dead. Covered with mud and blood.

She fumbled on the nightstand, searching for the small porcelain bowl of lucifers. Her hand shook so that she could hardly hold the match steady enough to light the kerosene lamp. The flame finally leapt in the glass chimney and settled into a warm glow. An ominous shadow by the wardrobe melted into clothes draped on the high-backed corner chair.

Inez threw back her comforter, dislodging a book that thumped onto a small braided carpet. She rounded the foot of the bed and picked up the leather-bound volume of *Paradise Lost*. Flipping open Milton's classic, she read: "Accuse not Nature, she hath done her part;/Do thou but thine, and be not diffident/Of Wisdom…"

I need something stronger to banish Joe's ghost.

Inez padded across the hall to the parlor and poured two fingers of brandy into a tumbler. The clock on the mantel ticked: 2:30. Dance halls and saloons would be jumping. After hours of gambling, drinking, and pinching the waiter girls, the patrons would be surly and murderous.

Murder.

Was Joe murdered?

The question would no longer be pushed aside but twined round with the lingering scent of wood smoke from the potbelly stove. Inez wrapped Mark's old sweater around her shoulders and sat on her piano stool, extending rough-knit wool socks to the faint warmth.

She glanced out into the hall. The hall-tree stood thin sentry beside a spindle-legged table. She pictured M. Silks' brass token lying deep inside the drawer. Her initial impulse had been to throw the incriminating bit of brass away. Finally, reluctantly, she'd tossed it in the back of the drawer. She couldn't believe Joe would visit a brothel, even a high-class one far from home, much less carry such a thing around on his person.

Now if I'd found it in Mark's wallet—

She shut her mind against the voiceless whisper as firmly as she'd slammed the drawer shut on the token, and turned her thoughts to Joe Rose.

To hear Joe tell it, he had been one of the first to hear the sweet whispers of silver in the heavy black sands of Leadville's California Gulch. He'd set up shop early, built a reputation for honesty and accuracy among his clients: penniless prospectors, mining company magnates, buyers, and sellers. Inez couldn't imagine any of them having a bone to pick with Joe. Joe was genial, easy going. Like Mark.

Back when the assayer and saloon-owner were thick as thieves, she and Emma had mused on what lay behind the peculiar friendship.

"I think, when they look at each other, it's like looking in a mirror," Inez had offered. "They're both charmers, through and through."

Inez was certain Joe's fascination with poker, whiskey, and flashy waistcoats had its genesis with Mark. Whereas Mark's sudden enthusiasm to settle down, buy a business, start a family echoed of Joe's good example. And how those men loved their children.

Children.

Memories of her son, never far away, surfaced and would not be ignored. Sighing, Inez rose, lit a small peg lamp, and carried it past the bedroom where she slept alone. She opened a door at the end of the hall and entered the cold, dusty room holding the discards of her married life.

In one corner, William's cradle lay empty.

Inez stooped and ran her hands over the smooth pine frame. "I should just give it away and be done with it," she said aloud.

She pulled the satin-edged blanket from the bottom and held it to her cheek, remembering its twin wrapped around her nine-month-old son. The blanket had rippled through her hands as she'd shifted William to her sister's lap in the Denver train station, four months ago.

"Inez, we'll take good care of William until you're ready for him. He'll have the best of everything. We'll not add to your sorrows." Harmony's hazel eyes, mirrors of Inez's own, looked as if she would gladly take all Inez's sorrows, real and imagined.

Inez held out a finger for William to grasp. The train was preparing for boarding; she dreaded the final good-byes. The nursemaid that Harmony had hired shifted on her well-padded rump and eyed William as if he were a sweetmeat.

Inez gathered up William for a last kiss. "It's only for a while," she whispered as he grabbed her nose. "By summer, we'll be together. I promise."

She handed him to the nursemaid, who pounced, cooing. He responded with a drooling grin. Inez took a deep breath to block a sudden stab of jealousy.

Harmony bent toward Inez. "My husband gives me a generous household account and a free rein. I could send you something every month. No one would know."

"I don't need money, Harmony. I need time. Time to decide what to do next, where to go." She forced the trembling from her voice. "Besides, if you send money to me and Papa finds out, he'll disown you too."

"Oh Inez. That was ten years ago."

"Are you saying he's ready to forgive and forget? That doesn't sound like Papa."

Inez could see him: face purple with rage as he roared, "You *eloped?* With a nobody. A Johnny Reb and a damn fortune-hunter to boot! You'll never get a dime from me and neither will he. When he leaves you high and dry, don't bother coming back."

The boarding whistle blew. The porter grabbed the last of Harmony's hat boxes. William smiled at Inez and held out his arms.

Inez spoke through the lump in her throat, "When he cries, give him this." She handed Harmony a small calico stuffed dog. Its black button eyes gleamed forlornly.

"Inez, if you decide to come home—"

Inez shook her head.

"Let me finish. Just tell Papa that he was right. That you made a mistake marrying Mark. One look at William, and Papa'd forgive you anything. But you have to take the first step." Harmony added softly, "Mama misses you. She never says a word, but I know."

Inez turned to pay the porter. "I'll write every week. You do the same."

The small group boarded the first-class car. William peeked over the nursemaid's shoulder, the creases on his face deepening in puzzlement. As the conductor closed the door, Inez fancied she heard a protesting wail.

She walked away, head high, holding back a flood of tears.

‹›‹›‹›

A long ride from past to present. Inez felt chilled to the bone in the silent room. She refolded the blanket and left, closing the door behind her.

Rubbing her arms through the flannel wrapper, she puzzled over the sudden surge of memories. Focus on the present with an eye to the future, that was her way. Run the saloon, balance the books, put money in the bank, watch the balance grow. Wait for word of Mark, although hope on that account was melting faster than snow in July. But all this wallowing in the past, over things that couldn't be changed…

She stopped in the hall, debating between the bedroom and the parlor. She turned right and headed for the sideboard and the bottle.

Last one, she promised herself, as she poured another inch of brandy.

She blew out the peg lamp, returned it to its holder, and carried the glass back to bed. Surrounded by her down comforter and bolstered by the fortifying properties of the Silver Queen's finest, she started to drowse. Until her nightmare image of Joe loomed again, demanding answers.

Who would leave the money and take the watch? No cutpurse would pass up fifty dollars. Was Joe's death a random event in a town riddled with violence, or did it involve the "business trouble" Emma mentioned?

She sat up, struck by a sudden thought: Did Joe's business trouble involve Harry Gallagher? Harry was close about his business and tight with his money, hoarding every silver piece and letting it go only when it stood a good chance of returning with more of its kind. He played only when the odds were in his favor. And always sat next to her at the poker table, even after their falling-out in October. *The bastard.*

Thoroughly awake, Inez threw back the comforter, went to the parlor, and returned to bed with the bottle.

Inez filled her tumbler. A regular wolf, Harry was, with an appetite for mutton. Did he renege on some deal with Joe? It might explain Joe's drunken tirade the night of his death. She didn't think Harry would bloody his own hands, but there were plenty of roughs that would do his bidding for a price. Including Marshal Hollis.

Inez didn't want to walk that street in the dark.

The glass was now empty, the bottle nearly so. "No use leaving a bit in the bottom," she said to the wardrobe before draining the bottle. The tightness eased, warmth spread like molasses throughout her body and mind. Her last vision, as she slid into dreamless sleep, was of Marshal Hollis standing over the bloody remains of Joe Rose.

Chapter Seven

Inez rocked on the heels of Mark's hobnail boots, squinting at the exterior of Cat DuBois' parlor house on the corner of State and Pine streets. The too-bright morning light knifed through her pounding headache, a headache due, she knew, to the contents of the empty bottle under her bed.

Dressing in Mark's abandoned clothes with her long hair hidden under his jacket and hat guaranteed her anonymity. Carrying Mark's Navy Colt in hand and her Smoot Number Two Remington in pocket guaranteed her safety. She preferred the pocket Remington for serious problems, but to walk the streets as a man without a visible display of firepower was asking for trouble.

Inez had taken the long route that morning, wandering up State Street and surveying the competition as she went. She was particularly curious about Cat DuBois' parlor house and the adjoining saloon. The original buildings had been destroyed by fire the previous spring. Cat, then newly arrived in Leadville, had snatched up both lots, rebuilding the saloon quickly. She'd spend much more time—and money—erecting her three-story "boarding house." Inez thought the brick edifice looked more like a bank than a whorehouse. Indeed, town wags said more money passed through Cat's house than through Leadville's five banks combined.

Inez surveyed the street-level bay windows. Closed damask curtains rebuffed sunlight and prying eyes. She wondered if the stories about polished walls, silk-covered Turkish couches, and five-hundred-dollar rocking chairs were true. *It must cost her plenty to keep the champagne flowing and the patrons happy.*

"Come back after noon and you'll find us more hospitable."

Startled, Inez turned to see Cat's blonde companion from church descend a carriage and land, with an undignified hop, on the boardwalk. Holding her fur coat and satin skirts away from the muddy planks, she waved farewell to the driver before turning to Inez and shielding a yawn with her hand. "'Scuse me. Late night."

Her bloodshot gaze swept Inez's face. "You weren't at last night's party. I'd remember those green…" She hesitated, then leaned closer. The scent of stale smoke battled tired violet perfume. "Brown? Gray? Well, I'd remember your eyes, honey. Gentleman's eyes. Come back later, we'll get to know each other better." Her gaze lowered to Mark's corduroys, nearly done in at the knees. "And be sure to wear your Sunday best. We deal in quality here at Mrs. DuBois'. New to town? You'll need this to get in."

She reached into a small beaded purse and extracted a small business card. She seized Inez's wrist, forcing the card into her gloved palm. "Florence Sweet's the name. Everyone calls me Frisco Flo. Here in Leadville by way of Denver, Georgetown, San Francisco." Her fingers, nails painted red, stroked Inez's wrist and began to walk up her arm. Inez stepped back, nearly falling off the boardwalk.

Flo lifted her eyebrows and smiled, not unkindly. "Cat got your tongue? That's a joke, honey. Cat DuBois owns the house and the bar next door. No matter. You come by tonight and ask for Flo. We'll have our own private party, and I promise you'll be howling at the moon before I'm done."

Flo sashayed up the steps and fluttered her fingers at Inez, pursing her red-painted mouth in a kiss before disappearing behind the mahogany door.

I suppose this means I can still "pass" when I must.

Thinking how Mark would have hooted with laughter over the encounter, Inez glanced down at the card. The spidery embossed printing read: "Florence Sweet, Gent's Furnishings." Shaking her head, she slipped it into her pocket. As she maneuvered around a tipsy tower of crates and through the milling crowd, Inez wondered if, perhaps, something similar had happened to Joe in Denver. *Maybe he was just walking by and some woman who furnishes gentlemen took a shine to him.*

Even as she composed the thought, Inez knew it didn't sing. Giving away a business card to a stranger, that made sense. But offering up tokens for a free ride....And if that was so, why would he keep it? Not just keep it, but hide it in the lining of his wallet?

Inez turned down the narrow passageway squeezed between the Silver Queen and a neighboring dance hall to reach Tiger Alley and the rear of the saloon. She made the short journey with the heavy Colt in hand and visible. Alleys, although convenient shortcuts, were notoriously unsafe. Inez rapped on the door three times before unlocking it. The tantalizing scent of biscuits nudged out the sour smells of the alley.

Inez stepped into olfactory heaven. "Good morning, Bridgette."

The cook was busy peeling apples, while a line of pie tins, crusts at the ready, waited to accept their due. She looked up, squinting. "Mornin', ma'am. My goodness, it's good you said something. I'd not have recognized you otherwise."

Inez glanced at the shotgun on the table, close to hand. "I'd rather not muck out broken glass and beer kegs in skirts and corsets. And I plan to stop in at the livery afterward."

"Antelope steak on the table. Eggs, gravy in the warmer. Biscuits out in a moment. You're the first one here, asides myself, that is." Bridgette returned her attention to the paring knife. The peels seemed to unroll on their own accord forming long red ribbons before dropping into the bucket at her feet.

Inez opened the warmer and loaded a tin plate with fluffy yellow eggs, smothering them with gravy. She sat with a contented sigh. "This is what it must be like to breakfast in Heaven."

Bridgette frowned at the apple, now using the paring knife to whittle bite-sized chunks off and into the large earthen bowl before her. The mountain of apple pieces grew larger. Her downturned mouth disappeared into the folds around her neck as she attacked the next apple, undressing it with nearly vicious speed. Inez scooped up a forkful of dripping eggs and watched Bridgette as she chewed.

Inez finally broke the uncharacteristic silence. "Is something wrong?"

"Wrong, ma'am?" The apple chunks flew into the bowl.

"That's what I said."

Bridgette puffed out her cheeks and exhaled. "Biscuits are done. Now, you just stay put, I'll bring them over." She rose and opened the maw of the iron stove, which belched a cloud of heat and the smell of baked buttermilk biscuits. The wool underclothes prickled Inez's skin.

"You know, ma'am. Maybe I ought to get some spectacles. Like yours. Only to help me see better at distance. Why, the good father greeted me on the street yesterday, and if it hadn't been for his voice, I wouldn't have even known it was him." Biscuit tins clattered on the rangetop. "Sometimes..." Her voice trailed off. She shoveled a dozen hot biscuits into a serving bowl and set them at Inez's elbow.

"Yeeees?" Inez prompted.

Bridgette plopped into her chair, staring at the bowl of apple pie innards.

"Yesterday was the first time I'd met Mr. Rose's wife. God rest his soul." Bridgette crossed herself perfunctorily. "Now, ma'am, you know I don't hold with gossip, carrying tales and such." Bridgette squinted, searching her employer's face for any hint of displeasure.

Inez nodded encouragingly and reached for a biscuit.

"When I met Mrs. Rose yesterday, I thought to myself, I thought, 'She looks just like that woman I saw coming out of the back of the Clairmont with Mr. Gallagher.'"

Chapter Eight

Inez sat back, attempting to digest this news along with the eggs and gravy.

"Emma—Mrs. Rose, that is—and Harry, ah, Mr. Gallagher? A most unlikely couple, I agree. Leaving the hotel together?"

"Oh yes, ma'am," Bridgette rushed on. "I was chatting up my neighbor Maggie, she works the Clairmont kitchen, and I saw Mr. Gallagher and a red-haired woman by the back door. She was crying, and they seemed, ah, familiar with each other. Now, Mr. Gallagher, it was he for certain. Well, it's his hotel, so that's not so strange. The woman was probably a local fancy woman. After all, why would Mrs. Rose be there? And with him?"

"Why indeed," murmured Inez. "When was this?"

"Oh, early November, I'd say. I'm sure it was just Mrs. Rose's hair that made me think of it."

The back door creaked open.

"Mr. Jackson!" Bridgette pounced on him. "You're just in time for breakfast. By the time you're finished cleaning up, there'll be pie as well!"

"Promise of your apple pie'll make the mornin' tasks bearable." Abe set his knife and a folded newspaper on the table before heading for the coffee.

The wet edge of the eight-inch blade bled onto the crumpled front page of last week's *Dodge City Times*. Inez eyed the stain. "Run into trouble?"

"Nothin' I couldn't handle." Abe sat down with a full cup, tore the back page from the newspaper, and began cleaning the knife. "Just a tenderfoot, new to town. Lost his bankroll on a shell game couple days ago. Tried to jump me in the alley. I didn't take his fingers, just his weapon. 'Bout the size of..." He gestured at Bridgette's paring knife.

Inez's fork clattered to her plate. "I hope you had him arrested!"

"Now, Inez. You really think the law's gonna bother over a white man taking on a colored man in an alley? Especially when the white man's the one who's cut? Nope, I didn't."

"Well, what did you do?"

"Gave him four bits. Told him to get a shave, some grub, and a job."

"Stray cats and lost souls," muttered Inez. "Abe, you're hopeless."

"And I expect you'd of shot him then spat in his eye." Abe speared a steak off the platter. "The boy didn't hurt me none." He cut the steak and offered a hunk to the calico, who sniffed at it, tail twitching.

"Don't feed her, Abe. She's already lazy. The rats will just take over."

The cat snatched the meat as if sensing that there was not a moment to spare and streaked into the storeroom.

"Changin' the subject." Abe pointed his knife at the paper. "Looks like a friend of yours lost the Ford County sheriff election. Got accused of gamblin' with county funds durin' his last term."

Inez's full stomach flip-flopped beneath her ribs. She rose from the table and approached the rag box by the storeroom. "I didn't follow the Kansas elections," she lied. "But if it's Ford County, you must mean Masterson. Bat, gambling with public money? What nonsense."

Bridgette's voice soared half an octave. "Bat Masterson? The Kansas sheriff that was in the railroad wars last spring? You *know* him, ma'am?"

"Knew him. Only incidentally and long ago." She locked eyes with Abe, silently warning him to say no more. Abe cradled the coffee mug, face unreadable. Inez added, "Abe, Mark, and I met him when we passed through Dodge on our way to Colorado. He owned a bar there at the time."

She glanced down at the cat who'd emerged from the storeroom, looking furtive. "I'll bet she sleeps all night and never catches a thing."

"Oh, she does all right." Abe dug into a mountain of gravy-soaked biscuits. "Bridgette, you cook 'em like back home."

Bridgette smiled, and the apple peels flew. "Well, now. There's nothing to biscuits and gravy. I could do them in my sleep."

Inez carried her armful of rags and a broom across the kitchen.

Abe crossed fork and cutlery knife on the gravy-smeared tin plate and stood. "Guess I'll see what I can save with a hammer and nails."

As she passed him by the door, he said, low-voiced, "Sorry about bringin' up Masterson. I know you don't like thinkin' about Dodge."

She mustered a wan smile. "And I'm sorry I jumped on you about that greenhorn. I suppose we're both on edge, what with Joe."

Abe followed her into the barroom. "I keep wonderin' how he ended up back of our place." Abe sorted through the wreckage, lining up repairable chairs against the wall and tossing unsalvageable pieces into a pile.

Inez used the broom to sweep broken glass off the bar. "And I keep thinking about the scene at the card table." She rubbed her thumb over two new gouges in the dark wood. "Joe roared into the room, put his face up close to Harry and shouted, 'You owe me, you son of a bitch! We had a deal!' Then he grabbed the table and gave it a heave-ho. Everyone hit the deck. Except Harry. He just sat, cool as a cucumber, as if he was taking in a show at the opera house. But his face."

Inez shuddered. "Harry's not a man to cross. Particularly in public. Joe knew that. 'You owe me.'" Inez mulled over the phrase. "Maybe Harry wasn't paying his bills."

"Maybe." Abe didn't sound convinced.

Inez gathered the largest pieces of glass and tossed them into an empty crate. "Abe, do you remember that time in New Orleans when I dressed up in Mark's clothes and we all went out on the town?"

"Sure. We made decent money playin' vingt-et-un and lansquenet. Drank some damn fine cognac. Charmed the ladies. As I recall, you made a passable fine gentleman." Abe set a table leg to one side.

"I went by Cat DuBois' place this morning and ran into Florence Sweet."

"Frisco Flo?" Abe leaned on his broom and took a good look at Inez. "Don't tell me you fooled Flo with that getup."

Inez grinned. She tugged her waist-length braid out from under her shirt collar and knotted it at the nape of her neck. "Flo invited me to a private party. Even gave me her card."

"She's gonna be disappointed when her mystery stranger don't show."

"Well, it wasn't intentional. I count on these clothes to help me blend into the crowd. I wasn't expecting a State Street hooker to get friendly."

"Flo's no hooker, Inez. The women in that house don't come cheap."

"Oh? You've priced them?"

He started sorting again. "Fact is, no one gets in without a card and a pocketful of cash. You could probably sell that card for a hefty sum."

"Think I'll hang onto it. I've always wondered what Cat's house looks like inside. Maybe someday, I'll pull Mark's evening clothes from the wardrobe upstairs and find out."

"You go lookin' without buyin', Mrs. DuBois won't like it."

Inez sniffed. "If I buy enough champagne she probably won't care one way or the other. Speaking of buying," she hefted the crate onto one hip, "you heard she's trying to buy Slim McKay's place?"

"Yep. Offered him plenty, to hear him talk."

"He's next to her saloon. Maybe she's thinking of expanding." Inez frowned, an unwelcome memory intruding. "Remember that time she showed up here. After Mark left."

"Not likely to forget," Abe said shortly. "Thought you two'd kill each other. She damn near scratched my eyes out when I showed her the door."

Inez looked down into the crate of broken bottles. Their jagged edges reminded her of Cat DuBois' cutting words, delivered five days after Mark's disappearance. Cat had marched into the Silver Queen early in the afternoon, heading straight for Inez. All chatter had ceased. State Street's leading madam had slammed her closed parasol on the bar, sweeping glasses and bottles to the floor. "Where's that smooth-talking man of yours?" she'd hissed. "He took my deposit *and* the contract. I bought this damn business. You honor the fucking deal or give me back my eight hundred dollars. Else there'll be the devil to pay and you, Mrs. Stannert, will pay in spades!"

For a reply, Inez dashed a glass of whiskey in her face.

Abe interrupted her thoughts. "You, Mark, me, we own the Silver Queen, thirds all around. He wouldn't of sold without talkin' to us first."

"Well, she hasn't mentioned it since, so I suppose you're right. She was probably just trying to hoodwink us." Still, whenever she thought of it, Cat's claim raised painful questions. *Would Mark light out and leave us—me, William, Abe—for eight hundred dollars?*

Carrying her secret doubts and the glass-filled crate, Inez hurried through the kitchen and dumped the trash in the alley. She returned to find Abe, hands folded over the broom handle, staring reflectively at the backbar.

"How 'bout a painting, Inez?"

Inez followed his gaze to the empty planks framed by the backbar's mahogany pillars. "A painting of what?"

"Battle scene. Mountains. Don't suppose you'd cotton to nymphs."

Inez set the crate on the floor by Abe. "I'm not interested in having a painting of scantily clad women behind me as I'm working the bar." She tapped her lower lip as she examined the blank wall. Then smiled.

"What?" said Abe. "I've seen that look before. I'm not sure I like it."

"*Paradise Lost!* I was rereading it last night."

"Most of my readin' is from the papers or the Bible."

"Well, you'll feel right at home, then. John Milton's epic speaks to the ultimate battle between Heaven and Hell, good and evil."

"Inez," Abe moved in front of her. "I think we're safer with scenery. Or dancin' girls. Sinners don't want to be reminded that they're gamblin' their souls as they toss their money on the bar. Religion and liquor don't mix."

"No, listen." Inez grabbed his arm. "You yourself suggested a battle scene. So, make it a battle between God's heavenly host and Satan's legions. If the painter's a fair portraitist, he could include some of Leadville's citizenry in the fray! Come to think on it, we could sell spots on the wall!"

"I don't know. When you start talkin' about real faces up there—"

"I'm certain there's more than a few that might enjoy seeing themselves portrayed, silver swords held high, on one side or the other."

Abe pondered. "Might keep folks entertained through the winter months. All right. But come May, when the snow melts and we can afford it, we get another mirror hauled in from Chicago."

She squeezed his arm. "Deal!"

Abe smiled at her. "Inez, sometimes you're like one of those mountain storms. A force of nature that a man's just gotta go along with."

"Er-hem." A cough and shuffle from the direction of the kitchen shattered the moment. Inez and Abe shifted away from each other hastily.

Useless emerged from the shadows. "Didn't mean to interrupt."

"You're not interrupting." Inez moved behind the counter and began sweeping the debris to one end. "Mr. Jackson and I were talking about what to do with the back wall. A painting, we thought. Classical, on a grand scale."

"A painting?" Useless sounded mystified.

"The fellow who did our signage last summer. Isn't he also a portraitist?"

Useless looked around as if she might be addressing someone else.

"Come on, Useless. You were working for Cat but you used to drop in with him for a drink. A Cousin Jack, a Cornishman. Short. Dresses like a swell."

Abe tipped a round table on edge and rolled it toward the wall. "Llewellyn Tremayne. Hear he painted Mrs. DuBois real lifelike. Supposed to be hangin' in her private rooms."

"Uh. I don't know about that." Useless shifted on his feet, gazing uneasily at the blank wall behind Inez.

"But you remember Tremayne," she persisted.

"Yeah. Sure."

"Well, he's the one I want. Useless, after we finish here, find him and tell him I've got a business proposition. Now, let's restock." Inez finished wiping the backbar. Useless disappeared into the back. Thumping ensued from the storeroom, interrupted by the sounds of crates being dragged about. The thudding was echoed by a pounding on the front door.

"Closed!" shouted Inez. "Come back tomorrow!"

The pounding ceased.

"Abe," Inez dropped the rag into the crate. "I promised Emma that I'd go over Joe's accounts and his assay office."

Lopsided footsteps approached unevenly from the kitchen. Inez reached below the bar to the shotgun. "We're closed!"

"Now my dear, if I'd said that every time your husband appeared in the middle of the night about your boy...." Dr. Cramer, leaning on his cane, limped into view.

"She means closed to all but friends, Doc." Abe pulled an unbroken chair close to the bar. Doc waved it away.

"No thank you, Mr. Jackson. I just dropped by for a quick libation before heading on to another case of consumption."

He hooked the silver-headed cane on the lip of the bar and propped his elbows on the surface. He rubbed his long, droopy face with both hands, before looking up with bloodshot eyes. "How about some of your soul-bracing brandy." He stretched his gimpy leg, then bent it tentatively. "The old war wound is acting up again. More precipitation before day's end."

At one time, Doc's physique had been impressive, giving him the look of a lumbering grizzly as he limped down the boardwalks of Leadville on his rounds. But the past year had sheared the meat from his frame, leaving skin that, around his face in particular, looked pouchy and deflated, as if it could use a good bit of steam or some of Bridgette's meals to fill it out.

Useless staggered by with a crate of bottles and set it on the backbar. Inez found Doc's favorite brand and hunted up a clean snifter. "Bad night?"

Doc removed his top hat and smoothed back iron gray hair. "Lost Mrs. French and her baby." He sighed, and his face sagged further. "The miners and their endless consumption is bad enough. But losing a woman in travail...." He shook his head, mutton chops quivering. Inez hesitated, then filled the snifter further, before pushing both the bottle and glass toward him.

"I'm sure you did everything you could."

He rested his huge hands around the bulbous glass. "Thank you, my dear."

Inez watched sympathetically as he drained the drink with hardly a pause. He sighed and wiped his mouth with a damp pocket handkerchief.

"Ah, the medicinal properties of alcohol. Some call it the devil's drink. Yet, I maintain it brings solace and strength to thousands." Doc moved to take up his hat. Inez held it to the counter.

"Speaking of tragedy," she leaned forward, "you heard about Joe Rose?"

"Ah yes. Yet another casualty of the violence that periodically boils out of this city. The coroner called me in for my opinion."

Inez hesitated, then pushed on. "What happened to Joe? I was asked to identify him when they found the body."

Doc eased his hat from her grip. "Not a pretty sight. But the trauma from a trampling never is. I saw it often in the War."

"So he was run over by a cart? A sleigh?"

"No evidence of that." Doc patted his chapped nose with the crumpled handkerchief. "Most likely a horse. Certainly equine. Straight and simple."

She drummed her fingers on the wood, frowning. "Most horses would throw a rider before stepping on someone."

Doc nodded and carefully refolded the limp white square of linen. "Yet, Mr. Rose did not suffer from an isolated misstep. He was thoroughly trampled and probably dragged as well."

Inez clutched the collar of her faded flannel shirt. Behind her, she heard the musical tinkle of glass against glass as Useless lined up the bottles.

"My God," she said softly. "Someone murdered Joe, dragged him behind our saloon, and left him there."

Chapter Nine

Her gaze switched to Doc. "I'd swear that Marshal Hollis thought we had something to do with Joe's death. What you're saying proves otherwise. Did you tell this to Hollis?"

Doc settled his hat on his head. "I voiced my opinions to the coroner and the marshal, of course. The law will follow whatever course it deems appropriate. I suspect, in the end, Rose's luckless demise in Tiger Alley will be just one more item in the 'Breakfast Bullets' column of the *Chronicle*." Doc patted her hand. "There, there. We'll all do what we can to help Mrs. Rose. Take a care to the living, and so on. Will you be back in business by Saturday night? The evening's the high point of my week, you know."

Inez, focused on his previous words, flashed him an absent smile as she withdrew her hand to pick up his glass. "On the house, Doc. Of course we'll be open Saturday. In fact, we're hoping tomorrow, right Abe?"

"Just need a handful of chairs and a couple more tables." Abe walked the limping physician to the kitchen door. "See you Saturday, Doc. Sooner, if you get thirsty."

"Thank you, Mr. Jackson. Thank you." The doctor scrunched his shoulders at the doorframe, his hat nearly brushing the lintel.

Abe walked back, looking grim. "I sure hope you're not thinkin' what I think you're thinkin'."

Inez said to Useless, "Go get the forty-rod that was delivered last week."

Useless glanced from Inez to Abe, then headed toward the kitchen.

Inez waited until he was out of earshot, then faced Abe. "You and Doc are always saying, 'Take a care to the living, the dead take care of themselves.' Well, I'm taking care of Emma and Joey by tidying up Joe's business affairs."

Abe crossed his arms. "I heard what you said to Doc. That Joe was murdered. Maybe so, maybe no. As long as the marshal leaves us alone, I say let sleepin' dogs lie."

"But what was Joe doing in Tiger Alley in the dead of night? Look down the block. There's our place, a restaurant, a hotel, a dancehall, five saloons with the requisite gamblers and girls, and Cat's place. The next block, the cribs get smaller and the drinks get weaker." The brass check flashed through her mind. "Abe, did Joe ever frequent the brothels on State?"

"What in blazes makes you ask that? Think I'd know the man's private business? Joe was a family man, plain and simple."

She gripped the rounded edge of the bar. "Family men stray. It happens all the time. As you and I know well."

The clanking of bottles heralded Useless' approach. He bent, knee joints popping, and set the crate of whiskey on the floor. "Here y'are. Want me to put 'em on the shelves?"

She turned a furious eye on him. "Go search out a hammer and nails. You can help Abe salvage some of the furniture."

Useless disappeared to the back again.

"Inez." Abe gripped the broom handle so tight the knuckles of his dark skin paled. "I know you don't cotton to advice. But I'm serious here. I don't see any advantage in pursuin' this accident."

"Trampling, dragging, hardly seems like an accident. And it's very peculiar that he argued with Harry Gallagher just before he died."

"Now why don't you let that man be?" Abe sounded impatient. "Harry's a payin' customer, a regular on Saturday nights. Been a model of courtesy since that business last fall. Let bygones be bygones, Inez."

That business. The unspoken veered into the open. Inez abandoned cleaning the bar and glared at Abe. "How can you say that. Harry nearly swindled us out of the Silver Queen. I admit I was stupid, blind, to fall for him like I did. I let my guard down, what with Mark gone and sending William east. When he started coming around I thought... well, you know what I thought. But how could that even begin to explain *his* behavior?"

Abe's face closed as if somewhere inside a door had slammed shut. "That ain't the way it happened, Inez, and you know it. All I'm sayin' is, you're followin' a road best left untraveled."

A metallic symphony drew their attention. "Oh jeez." Useless knelt to gather the nails that had rained from the box when he'd tripped.

Abe hunkered down to help Useless. Inez, fuming, turned her back. In the past, flare-ups between herself and Abe had always been mediated by Mark, who knew how to smooth the ruffled feathers and lead them to middle ground. Since Mark's disappearance, it often seemed that she and Abe were tiptoeing around each other, careful not to start something that neither would know quite how to stop.

Until now, they'd scrupulously avoided any mention of "the business" with Harry since its denouement. Their first and last discussion on the topic had occurred on an Indian-summer morning in September, the day after Harry had left on a month-long business trip. She'd been working on the books on the second floor, the air sweltering, even with the window open. Abe had folded his long frame down onto the horsehair couch before delivering a short, gruff speech: "Harry Gallagher stopped by on his way out of town. He wants to buy my share of the Queen. Said you and he had an arrangement. Now, he didn't say what kind of arrangement, but I've got eyes. He offered a price more'n fair, wanted me to sign right then." Abe had shifted on the couch, uncomfortable. "Wish you'd talked to me about this, Inez. It put me in a real awkward position with a man who doesn't like 'no' or 'maybe later' for an answer. I'm willin' to sell and move on, if that's what you want. But I gotta hear it from you. Not Gallagher."

Inez's cheeks stung at the memory. What a fool she'd been. And it had taken Abe to rip open her eyes so she could see. *The flowers. The gifts. The words. All lies. That day at Twin Lakes most of all.* It still hurt, how she'd opened her heart to him. Her heart and more.

All he wanted was the property. And if that meant taking me in the bargain....

"Useless." Abe picked up a chair leg that Useless had split while attempting a repair. "Why don't you help Mrs. Stannert with that crate."

"Sorry." Useless looked miserable. "I never was much of a carpenter."

"Well, it just ain't your talent, son, that's all." Abe picked over the sticks of furniture, found another leg, and pounded it into the chair seat as if he could hammer down the silent walls that lurked in the room.

〈〉〈〉〈〉

The day's work done, Inez trudged down State Street, ignoring the jostling throngs of humanity. Miners coming off shifts on Fryer Hill and Stray Horse Gulch mingled with workers from the smelters. A few women moved through the crowds, lugging parcels home from bakeries and butcher shops, small children clinging to their coats. Occasionally the sea of bodies would part, allowing a brightly dressed denizen of the street to glide past. The men admired. The women averted faces. The children stared.

Inez glanced up as she turned onto the alley that ran behind her home. The afternoon sky shaded from pearl gray overhead to beige at the horizon. *Doc's right: More snow's coming.*

Nearing the Roses' property, she heard the whack of wood on wood. Joey stood behind an outbuilding, whipping at a spindly fir with a stick and a vengeance.

Inez called, "Joey."

He looked up warily.

"It's Auntie Inez. Want to visit the livery?"

He nodded.

"Go ask your mother."

A few minutes later, he joined her, slipping his mittened hand into her gloved one. "Mama says I have to be home in half an hour."

Inez loved the smell of the livery, the dusty smell of hay mixed with the sweet scent of horses. They entered the cavernous barn, moving slowly toward the back stalls.

A small, dark shape darted in front of them.

"Ugh!" She jumped backward. "A rat!"

Joey clutched her hand tighter.

The rat zigzagged across the hardpacked dirt before scooting between nearby hay bales.

"It's all right, Joey. It's gone now."

Joey peered up through the gloom. "Are you scared of rats, Auntie?"

"Scared?" She stamped her feet, trying to rid herself of the feeling that traveled up her spine. Almost as if little rodent feet were skittering up her back. "No. I just don't like them. I suppose I've spent too many nights lying awake, listening to them scratch around."

They went deeper into the livery, Inez aware of the whisper of horses: a snort here, a swish of tail there. She finally stopped, whistled softly. A black horse, ears pricked, approached from the back of a stall. Joey retreated. Inez noted the wariness on his face. *I wonder if he knows how his father died.*

She lit an oil lamp hanging from an iron hook on the wall and retrieved a curry brush from a peg. "Why don't you stay by the gate while I brush her, Joey."

He climbed the gate's wooden slats and hung his arms over the top. Inez advanced with the curry brush. Lucy whickered.

"Uncle Mark…" Joey stopped, then forged on. "Uncle Mark told me Lucy's the very devil. She's not. Is she?"

Inez chuckled, then frowned. "Oh, Joey. It's a joke. Her real name is Lucifer."

"Why'd you call her that?"

"I didn't. Her previous owners did. They didn't treat her right, and she, well, she gave them the devil for it. Lucy's one of God's creatures. Handle her with respect, she responds in kind."

Joey swung on the gate, mind obviously elsewhere. "Auntie?"

"Yes?"

"Papa's not dead." His face in the half-light was serious.

Inez paused, the brush on Lucy's neck. "Whatever do you mean?"

"Mama said," he hesitated. "She said Papa and Uncle Mark are in Heaven. But they're not. They're gonna be here for Christmas."

Inez was at loss for words.

Joey crossed his arms on top of the railing, looking so much like his father that Inez felt she'd entered some strange twilight world. He continued, "Uncle Mark and Papa promised me a pony for Christmas. A real one." His eyebrows drew together. "But then, Papa brought me that rocking horse and said it was my pony. He said it would bring us luck, and we'd ride it to a new home."

He looked up, pleading for understanding. "Uncle Mark and Papa are coming back, Auntie. And they're gonna bring a real pony. They promised."

Inez came over and hugged Joey, staring over his head at the dancing oil flame.

His voice was muffled against her jacket. "Papa said not to tell Mama. But he didn't say I couldn't tell you."

"I'm glad you told me." Inez untangled herself from his small arms and hung the brush back on its peg. "We should go. Your mama needs you." Subdued, she gave Lucy one last pat before leading Joey toward the waning light outside the livery. *I should tell him the truth. That his father is gone forever. That there will be no horse at Christmas. But who am I to say this, when I myself listen night after night for Mark's footsteps at the door.*

Chaper Ten

Inez stood outside the door, jangling the ring of keys Emma had given her. JOSEPH ROSE, ASSAYING OFFICE was inscribed in gilt-edged black letters on the narrow-paned window.

Susan Carothers nudged her. "Inez, open the door."

Inez lingered, taking in the mid-morning aspect of upper Chestnut Avenue. *Prime real estate. The sale of this building should provide well for Emma and Joey.*

Susan jiggled Inez's elbow. "I need to be back at my studio in an hour."

Inez inserted a key. There was a click, and the door swung inward. The two women entered, long skirts swishing. Subdued light filtered into a small reception area. Down the passageway, a dimmer light glimmered from the rear of the building.

Susan breezed past Inez, making a beeline for an unlit kerosene lamp. "Now what are we looking for again?"

Inez peered about, struggling against her unease. "Joe's books, his ledgers, accounts receivables, client lists, assay notes, whatever sheds light on the condition of his business. If he's got assaying half done in the laboratory, maybe you can determine what he was up to."

"I'm not sure how much help I'll be. The chemistry for assaying is not at all like that for photography. What about his assistant? The Swede? He would know."

"Nils Hansen. Useless tried to track him down. Turns out, no one's seen him for days."

Feeling like an intruder, Inez walked around the counter and approached Joe's desk. It seemed a likely place to start. A dozen pigeon holes gaped on either side of a writing surface. A bottle of ink stood in the inkwell, capped. An unmarked blotter, empty. No papers, no clutter.

Inez remembered how particular Joe was about keeping everything in its place. By closing time, he'd have surfaces cleared, glassware washed and arranged on the laboratory's shelves, the delicate scales used to weigh the final precious metal extracts pristine in their glass cases, and chemicals locked away inside tall glass-doored cabinets.

While Susan lit the lamp and adjusted the wick, Inez sat at the desk. The swivel chair squeaked as she explored the pigeon holes and drawers. Extra bottles of ink. Pens. Pencils, sharpened and ready. A stack of printed assay certificates. She examined one, its empty lines waiting for the number of ounces of gold and silver per ton to be filled in, and wondered how many inquiries she'd have to make in a town where fortunes rose and fell depending on those numbers. She folded it and slid it into her pocket.

"He must have had a ledger," Inez muttered. The bottom drawer appeared empty as well. Exhaling in frustration, she slammed it shut only to hear a muffled thump. Opening the drawer again she saw, leaning at an angle, the familiar rectangle of a bookkeeping ledger.

It must have been pushed up against the back wall of the drawer. Inez opened it on the blotter. Pressed between the cover and the first page was a bill of lading from the Denver Mine and Smelter Supply Company. She squinted at the date and winced. *Joe's last trip to Denver.* Inez turned her attention to the first page: columns of dates, names, initials, and numbers, inked in Joe's small, controlled handwriting.

Her reading light faded as Susan carried the lamp toward the laboratory. "Susan, I found his ledger. Could you bring the lamp over?"

Susan's footsteps halted. "Inez! Come quick!"

Holding the large record-keeping book, Inez moved as swiftly as her skirts would allow through the narrow passageway to the rear of the building.

The alternate source of illumination became obvious as she stepped into the assaying laboratory. The rear door hung ajar, held half open by a drift of snow on the plank floor. Wavering lamplight sparkled off the windblown snow and smashed glass. The scales were a tangled mess of metal, their casings broken. The air smelled acidic, and the tall cabinets gaped open, glass doors destroyed. Notes and paper littered the floor. Drawers yanked from under countertops and emptied lay every which way. Only a medium-sized black safe, tucked in one corner, appeared undisturbed.

Inez closed her eyes, unable to keep the Silver Queen's recent disarray from crossing her mind. "Oh no!"

Susan grabbed her arm. "Who would have done this? We'd better get the marshal."

"And what do you think he will do?" Inez retorted. "Nothing! We'd better look around now, while we have a chance."

The lamplight danced over the walls. "What do you think happened?"

"My guess is someone was looking for something. Whether they found it is hard to say. The office is untouched, and the safe looks secure."

Inez spied a trash barrel under the sink, still half full. She pulled it out and tipped it over, spilling debris and adding to the chaos underfoot. Digging through bits of rubbish— rubber tubing, paper, rags—she touched something more solid than the rest. Inez pulled out a loosely wrapped bundle. The paper gave way and a stiff black form thudded at her feet.

Susan's shriek was loud enough to break any remaining glassware.

"What *is* that?"

Inez clutched reflexively at the revolver in her pocket, her palm damp in the leather glove. She forced calm she didn't feel into her tone, as if she were trying to soothe a panicked horse. "A rat. A dead rat."

"Ugh!"

Inez gingerly nudged the rat with the toe of her shoe.

"Inez, what are you *doing?*"

This rat hadn't keeled over from cold or starvation. A gash pierced its plump body, stomach to back. The brown fur was stiff with dried gore. The eyes were sunken, nearly gone. Small yellow teeth shone dully.

Far behind them, the front door banged shut. Both women jumped.

"Who's there?" a gruff voice demanded.

Inez slid into the shadow of the rear door, revolver trained on the hall. Susan gripped the lamp tighter as a shape materialized from the corridor.

"Abe, you old fool, I almost shot you!" Inez slumped against the wall, feeling weak at the knees.

"Looks like Miss Susan was 'bout ready to throw the lamp at me as well." Abe looked around the laboratory. "Loooord have mercy."

"Mr. Jackson. It didn't sound like you." Susan leaned against the countertop.

Abe eyed the two women. "I suppose you didn't think of doin' something sensible-like, like, say, sendin' for the marshal."

"He'll have his turn soon enough." Inez slumped further, feeling drained.

"Who'll have their turn?" Another voice echoed from the corridor.

Susan's shriek faded to a squeak as Nils Hansen stepped forward. The tall Swede, wrapped in a worn waterproof and carrying a scuffed saddlebag, scratched his jaw as if the stubble along his jaw itched. The blonde beard mixed with a mustache so light it was nearly invisible. He took in the destruction. "What happened?"

Inez stepped forward. "Where've you been? My hired help scoured the town for you yesterday."

"I was on my claim. I don't waste my time or money in honky-tonks." Nils' voice trailed off at the gun in her hand and the knife in Abe's. "What's going on?"

"Joe's dead." Inez watched for his reaction.

It wasn't what she'd expected.

Nils nodded once. And turned to leave, muttering.

Inez grabbed a corner of his saddlebag. "What did you say?"

He didn't look at her. "God is not mocked: for whatsoever a man soweth, that shall he also reap."

"We don't need platitudes," snapped Inez. "We need help! You're Joe's assistant. You can tell us what he was up to before he died."

Nils eased the bag from her grip. "He was probably up to no good. But I'm not the one to say. I quit after Joe got back from Denver. I work at Kelley's assay house now."

Inez stared at his retreating back. All she could muster was "Well!"

Abe's knife vanished under his coat. "Sounds like Nils and Joe didn't part on the best of terms."

Inez heard the front door slam shut. "Up to no good. What did he mean by that?"

"Boy's probably just blowin' off steam. Sounds like he wasn't around last week, in any case. Let's see, front wasn't tampered with, so they must've come in the back." Abe examined the door. "Yep. Lock's jimmied. Now what's this?"

Abe ran a finger over a deep gash about shoulder level in the door's exterior. A rust-colored blotch surrounded the wound and tailed off into a streak that meandered down the weathered wood.

Inez examined the door, her stomach suddenly squeamish. "Maybe a knife."

Abe turned, eyebrows raised.

Inez returned to the trash barrel. "Susan, bring the lamp over."

Inez didn't have far to dig before her fingers closed on a smooth wood handle. She sat back on her heels and held up a knife, its blade dull with dried blood.

Chapter Eleven

"So. You refuse to do anything." Inez crossed her arms to contain her frustration.

Marshal Hollis rocked in his swivel chair, the heels of his mud-splattered boots planted on the desk.

"Waalll, Miz Stannert, you're the one that said finding Joe's body behind your saloon was some strange accident." He punctuated his patronizing tone with a squirt of tobacco juice aimed at the nearby spittoon.

"I never said his death was an accident. Doc himself said Joe was trampled and dragged up the alley."

"And you and Jackson, who seems to be the last to have seen Rose alive, don't know a thing about it."

"No! We don't!"

"So I'm supposed to ignore Rose's death and look for someone who broke into his business and skewered a rat to his door, right?"

"Right. I mean, no." She heaved a frustrated sigh. *This is hopeless.*

Hollis removed his hat, scratched a greasy thatch of hair, and brought his boots down with a thump. "I'll bet some drunks found the door unlocked and went in to get outta the cold. You said yourself, nothing's missing. Case closed. Just like this here conversation. Now I've got important things to do."

"Like wait for Harry Gallagher or one of his cronies to crook their finger?"

Curly Dan stifled a snort from his position by the door.

Hollis lunged to his feet. The chair careened into the wall with a bang. He walked around the desk, his thin lips disappearing under his mustache in a tight scowl. The stench that assaulted her senses was a vivid reminder of how few baths Leadville's citizens indulged in during the winter months.

"Day in, day out, men get cut up, shot up, for walking in the wrong place at the wrong time. I'm not gonna cry over one more body in State Street's alleys. I done my duty, got Rose identified, and notified the next of kin. Now, get outta here, before I change my mind."

Inez felt like pounding him with her umbrella. Instead, she pulled up the hood of her cloak and headed for the door.

"If you're so all-fired up over Rose, take some of that money from that crooked poker game you run and hire a Pinkerton!" Hollis snarled.

Curly Dan opened the door for her. Inez marched out of the city marshal's office, holding the umbrella in a strangle-hold. "My game's a hell of a lot straighter than you are!"

As the door closed she heard Curly Dan say, "Steady, Bart. She's leaving."

Another mess to clean up. I wonder if Emma has the combination to the safe.

There was nothing for it but to return to Emma's house and ask. She had to get a better handle on Joe's finances. And soon.

That morning, Emma had dropped the office keys into Inez's hand before announcing, "Joey and I are leaving Leadville the first of the year. I can't stay after what's happened. Don't try to talk me out of this."

Stunned, Inez had sunk onto a nearby parlor chair covered with Emma's meticulous needlepoint. "Where will you go?"

Emma sat by the bay window, hands clasped so tightly that the knuckles showed white, blotting out the freckles. "Someplace where no one knows us."

"I'll try to settle Joe's accounts by then. But even assuming the best, at some point, you may need to earn a living. Have you thought of that?"

"I worked before I met Joe." She bit her lip, looked away. "If worse comes to worst, I'll sew. Or take in laundry. With God's help, we'll get by."

Emma smoothed her hands over the lap of her black crepe dress. Small twists of copper hair escaped from the pins, framing her face. All in all, she was a striking woman. Inez doubted that Emma would remain a widow for long.

"I wish you'd reconsider, Emma, but I won't argue. And I'll help you any way I can."

"I know you will." Emma sat back. "I want to leave this place free and clear. No outstanding business. No blot on Joe's name. No loose ends."

<〉〈〉〈〉

No loose ends.

Inez stopped in front of Emma's home. The snow on the path to the front door was well trodden, a sure sign that the neighbors and churchfolk were helping the family through the crisis. A black crepe ribbon draped the door handle. Only days ago, the door had sported an evergreen wreath in anticipation of the coming Christmas.

Inez sighed.

She decided not to mention the break-in at Joe's assay office but just to ask about the safe. She raised the door knocker and tapped it once. The knocker ripped from her grasp as the door flew open. Inez and Reverend Sands eyed each other in mutual surprise.

Sands raised a hand to his head, before smiling crookedly in acknowledgment that he was already hatless. "Mrs. Stannert. We seem to meet on thresholds. I was expecting a couple of ladies from the church."

He stepped aside for her to enter. The warmth of the interior matched the warmth of his smile. Once again, the sentiment didn't reach his eyes. "May I help you with your cloak?"

"That's not necessary." Inez faced away and undid the clasp. She felt the weight of the cloak lift from her shoulders.

"Allow me, *Mrs. Stannert*." His voice at her ear sounded disconcertingly intimate.

The emphasis on her married title set her on guard. Inez stepped a safe distance away and turned. "I said it wasn't necessary. *Reverend* Sands."

With a glint of amusement in his eyes, he hung her wrap on the hall tree. "I'll let Mrs. Rose know you're here."

"Let's dispense with the formalities, Reverend. I'm not a church acquaintance come to offer my condolences." She sidestepped him and, holding her pearl gray overskirts close, proceeded to the parlor.

Emma was at the window seat with a cup of tea in her hands and a flush in her cheeks. "Inez!" She patted the cushion, inviting Inez to sit beside her. "I was talking to Reverend Sands about where to go after Leadville. He suggested Sacramento. California is a good place to raise children, he says. And he knows many people there."

"He does, does he?" Inez sat back, looking coldly at the reverend, who had materialized beside them.

He smiled blandly at Inez and held out a steaming cup of tea. "Sacramento's a warm, friendly place. Not too big and not too small. I know the community well."

"And what were you doing in California?" Her tone suggested that it must have been something unsavory.

His expression altered not a whit. He merely moved the cup closer to her, forcing her to take it lest he set it—or pour it—in her lap. "Ministering. Of course."

Emma plucked at Inez's sleeve to get her attention. "Reverend Sands says he'll telegraph the minister in Sacramento and ask him to find a place for Joey and me. And he even knows a woman who runs a respectable hotel in Denver if we need to stop over."

Inez clutched her cup furiously, nearly burning her fingers. "Reverend Sands knows a lot of people. How convenient."

He leaned forward, capturing Inez's eyes with his. "Just part of the job, Mrs. Stannert. If I can call on people and connections from the past to help someone, well, that's all to the best. The past can be useful. Don't you agree?"

He sat back. "In fact, I'm all for Mrs. Rose and her son proceeding to Denver as soon as the funeral's over. With friends like you to handle matters here, why wait?" The reverend's gaze slid over her body in a manner she found thoroughly annoying. "Wrapping up Mr. Rose's business affairs should be straightforward. After all, he led such an...exemplary life."

He's baiting me. Why? Inez carefully set the tea cup on a side table, taking a moment to compose herself. "Emma, I hate to ask, but I need to act quickly. Particularly if you're leaving town soon. Do you have the combination to Joe's safe?"

"Why, no." Emma looked alarmed. "Is there a problem?"

Inez smiled in a way she hoped was reassuring and stood. "No matter. There's more than one way to open a safe."

Reverend Sands had come to his feet as well. "Allow me." He walked her toward the entry.

"I can see myself out."

"No, no, I insist. Besides," his voice lowered, "I'd like a word with you." Sands pulled her cloak from the hall tree and set it on her shoulders. "Pity about Joe Rose. 'The righteous live for evermore; their reward also is with the Lord.' The question is, just how righteous was he?"

She decided to play innocent, see what he knew. "What do you mean?"

The butter-smooth tone melted away in favor of steel. "Come on, Mrs. Stannert. No more games. Joe's death was no accident. He was up to his neck in trouble and it finally drowned him. He wasn't the fine, upstanding fellow everyone paints him out to be. You know that and more. I can see it in your eyes."

The break with Nils, the fight with Harry, the brass check. None of it added up to the Joe she knew. Her shoulders tensed before she realized that the reverend's hands still rested there, heavy.

"And then there's Joe's best friend: your husband, the elusive Mark Stannert. I've heard about him and your sad and sorry circumstances. My sympathies." His voice in her ear sounded anything but sympathetic. "Yet here you are, still in Leadville. Why? Who are you, Mrs. Stannert? The grieving friend of Joe Rose's widow, a faithful wife waiting for word of her long-lost husband. Are you the real McCoy or as counterfeit as Joe Rose?" The sword was now out and pointed at her throat.

She grabbed the lapels of her cloak and faced him. He had backed away and was leaning against the door, awaiting her response.

She fastened her cloak. Slowly, deliberately. *This. Is a dangerous man.*

Instead of denying his words, slapping his face, or doing the thousand other things that rose to mind, she said, "I could ask the same of you. Who or what are you? Besides unbearably rude? And why are you so interested in Joe Rose?"

He opened the door. A blast of cold air heaved into the entry, prowling about for loose items to engage. "I'm just one of God's foot soldiers, a temporary shepherd: 'Be thou diligent to know the state of thy flocks, and look well to thy herds.' Proverbs twenty-seven, verse twenty-three. I'm looking for wolves in sheep's clothing, counterfeit souls. Like Joe Rose."

She dug into her pocket for her gloves. "Smoke and mirrors. You haven't answered my questions."

"Neither have you." He watched as she worked the gloves on, finger by finger. "You're an intelligent woman. I like that. We could work together to lessen Mrs. Rose's grief and lay her husband to rest. Think on it, Mrs. Stannert. Think on what you know about Joe Rose, his life and his death, and how they intersect with your absent husband. We'll talk again."

Chapter Twelve

Early afternoon. The customers at the Silver Queen were saving their energies for the evening. Inez stepped inside and surveyed the long room as she removed her doeskin gloves. A few desultory card games were in action, but most of those hunkered at the tables and along the bar were focused on eating and drinking. Abe worked the bar while Useless carried bowls of stew from the kitchen. Inez inhaled. Venison and onions mixed with tobacco and the unwashed.

Useless stopped, balancing four bowls. "Found the painter. He'll be by."

Abe looked up from mixing a Mule Skinner—whiskey and blackberry liquor. "Get the combination?"

She shook her head. "Looks like we'll need your special talents." She mimed rotating a dial in the air and headed for the upstairs office.

Once at her desk, she pulled out the small package she'd retrieved at the post office. The brown paper carried her sister's careful script. She wondered if the small package had crossed paths with the one she'd sent to Harmony. The parcels, each deep in the belly of a train, passing on some snowy plain in Kansas. Travelling in opposite directions.

The paper rustled as she unwrapped it, layer after layer, before revealing an intricately tooled leather case.

A folded page of ivory stationery fell out as she opened the case. William's baby face peered out from the photograph mounted behind the glass window. She traced his image behind the glass, feeling the pain of separation all over again.

Some of the pudginess had left his cheeks. He sat in a garden on a small, wooden stool, clutching his stuffed toy dog. One of the dog's button eyes was crooked, as if it had fallen off and had hastily been re-sewed. Inez closed the case and opened her sister's letter.

Dearest Inez,
William's cough has passed with none of the complications
you feared. This news and the enclosed photograph will, I
trust, bring you peace this Christmas season—

The door squeaked open. Abe said, "The painter's downstairs."

She handed him the photo case. Abe turned it over twice, examining the embossed cover, and opened it. He tugged at one corner of his mustache, gently closed the case, and handed it back. "A right fine likeness. He's got your eyes. Let's hope he doesn't inherit your temper."

"And that he grows into a whole lot more common sense as well." She opened the case and balanced it on the desktop. William's hazel eyes, so like her own, stared back. "You'll have to open Joe's safe. Soon. Tomorrow, if possible."

Abe wiped his hands on the bar towel tucked into his apron. "Haven't done that sort of thing in a long time, Inez. Might've lost my touch."

She snorted. "Abe, anyone who handles a knife and mixes drinks the way you do hasn't lost his touch, I guarantee."

"What's the hurry?"

"Reverend Sands was at Emma's." She tapped the desk blotter with a finger, frowning. "He's talked her into moving to Sacramento. Before I left, he pulled me aside, quoted the Bible, asked questions about Joe, and threw out innuendoes about Joe and Mark. He was quite intimidating."

"And you, what? Quoted the Good Book right back at him?"

She waved a hand. "I just threw his innuendoes back in his face." She rocked the chair gently. "He doesn't believe Joe's death is an accident either." She stood and moved toward the door, casting one more look at the lone image on the desk. "I pray every night that I made the right decision. Sending William east and staying here."

"Well, if I remember rightly, goin' back to your family wasn't in the cards." Abe locked the door behind them.

"If I'd arrived on the patriarchal doorstep Papa'd thrown me right back out on the streets. And how would Mama explain to her society friends that her eldest daughter is not widowed, not, God forbid, divorced, but abandoned by her worthless husband." Inez gripped the raw wooden banister, scanning the crowd below. "I did what I had to do. Now, I must ensure that, when I next hold my son, I'll never have to leave him again."

From her vantage point on the landing, Inez spotted Llewellyn Tremayne conversing with Useless at the bar. The sign-painting business must be lucrative, she thought, or perhaps his portrait work funded his wardrobe. A coat with a dramatic overcape complemented a ruffled-front shirt and doeskin breeches. His dark hair was tied back. That and his neat pointed beard and flowing mustaches gave him the air of an English poet from the previous century. The only concession to the climate and the condition of the streets was his boots, nicely blacked, but laced high for practicality and deep mud.

How he escapes being assaulted in the streets for a swell is beyond me.

Useless looked up and met Inez's eyes. He blushed, said something short to Llewellyn, and began to clear away dirty glassware. Llewellyn turned, watching Inez as she descended the stairs.

"Mr. Tremayne. You painted our sign last spring. You've gained a reputation for portraiture as well."

He bowed deeply over her proffered hand. "Bankers, mining magnates. Not to mention the cherubs on the ceiling of Tabor's new opera house."

"Rumor has it, you've also painted Mrs. DuBois."

"Twice." His smile widened, revealing the whitest, most perfect teeth Inez had ever seen. "The more public of the two hangs in her drawing room. The second, my masterpiece, is in her private chambers. Catherine DuBois as Venus, rising from the sea in her natural state, surrounded by nymphs."

Inez raised her eyebrows. Abe broke the awkward silence. "Mrs. Stannert here has some notions she'd like to see up on the wall where the mirror used to be."

She nodded. "Actually, I'm pleased to hear you're acquainted with the classics, because I had my heart set on something classical on a grand scale."

Llewellyn smoothed his mustache as he pondered the twenty-foot length between the backbar's mahogany pillars. "Greek Gods? Helen and a thousand ships?"

"Rather the ultimate battle between good and evil, as in John Milton's *Paradise Lost*. I'll show you the appropriate passages later. Now, here's my vision. To the right," she pointed, "Heaven. But not a city of gold, not for Leadville. Let's make Heaven a silver city. And over here," her arm swept to the left, "Hell. But not fire and brimstone. Something dark and cold enough to freeze your soul. Ice. And put a little spot of Eden in the corner."

She brushed her hands together briskly, pleased. "When you paint Heaven and Hell's legions, leave the faces blank. We'll sell spots on the wall. You'll get to do portraits of Leadville's highest and lowest."

Llewellyn rocked on his heels. "I'm intrigued. For the right price, Mrs. Stannert, I'm yours, body and soul, for the winter."

He smiles like a fox. And all those white teeth.

Inez smiled back. "Keep your soul. Let's draw up a contract tomorrow." She addressed Abe. "Now, don't you think some citizen will pay handsomely to be portrayed as Saint Michael holding a silver sword?"

"You're askin' the wrong man. I was votin' for scenery, remember?"

"And you shall have it. A spiritual landscape peopled with all the souls trapped here, as well as those who are just passing through." She turned to Llewellyn. "May I offer you a drink to seal the deal?"

"Clouds the mind and dulls the imagination. Not to mention what it does to the hand that holds the brush. That stew smells good, though."

He placed a one-dollar note on the bar. Inez made as if to hand it back. "No, no, Mrs. Stannert. I'll pay for my meals, like the rest."

She fingered the worn greenback before placing it in the cash box. "I swear I see more paper notes every day. I'll never get used to them. They just don't seem real."

Llewellyn laughed, a short hard bark. "Backed by the government, they're as good as gold. Or silver. I'd rather carry a roll of these than tote a bag of coins. Mark my words, paper money is the future for the world of commerce."

After Llewellyn left Inez asked Useless, "What were you two talking about? You looked like the cat that swallowed the canary."

"Uh." His Adam's apple bobbled. "Just old times. I worked for Mrs. DuBois when he was painting her picture. I'll go help Bridgette." He scurried away.

"That's right. We didn't steal him away from Cat DuBois until mid-October." Inez directed her comments to Abe and a smile at the miners coming off-shift.

"I'm still wonderin' why you did that. It's not as if we couldn't've found help elsewhere."

"I enjoy annoying her. Besides, if she'd really wanted to keep him, she could've offered him more to stay." She winked at Abe, then turned her attention to the clatter of tin lunch buckets as the miners staked a place at the bar. "Name your poison, gentlemen."

Chapter Thirteen

With afternoon deepening into twilight, Bridgette layered on coats, shawl, hat, gloves, and galoshes, as she talked to Inez. "Stewpot's half full. Extra biscuits in—" she nodded toward the tin-door pie safe. "And I put something aside for Mrs. Rose. Tell her my heart goes out to her."

"I'll deliver your words with the stew, Bridgette."

"When's the service for the mister?"

"Soon, according to Reverend Sands." Inez stacked clean bowls on the table.

Bridgette peered nearsightedly at Inez. "And how is that new reverend of yours? As handsome as they all say?"

Inez frowned, then raised her eyebrows to smooth away the creases. "Handsome depends on who's doing the looking. He has a certain charm, I suppose. When he chooses to exercise it."

A triple knock tapped out on the kitchen door. "There's my Michael now, come to walk his mother home."

"Good night, Bridgette."

No sooner did Bridgette leave than Useless crashed through the passdoor. "Chet Donnelly's here and he said—"

A shove from behind sent Useless sprawling into the table, rattling the bowls. A bass voice boomed, "He said he's hauled his no-account ass back in here to 'pol…apologize and to, whaddya call it, make reso-loo…resta-too…Aw shit. Make good on another fancy mirror to hang behind your bar."

Inez calculated the distance between Chet and herself. She doubted her pocket revolver would even slow him down, if he was really drunk and dangerous. And she wasn't up to heaving a kettle of stew at him.

"Ma'am." Chet swept off his battered broad-brimmed hat, revealing a rat's nest of tangled graying locks. "I hereby 'pologize for tearin' the place up Saturday last. Weren't 'zactly my fault. Them twins, they don't see we're sittin' on a bonanza on Fryer Hill. And the longer we sit, the better it gets. But, hey, I'm willin' to pay for a new mirror, you let bygones be bygones."

"That mirror came from Chicago. Cost us plenty." Inez looked at his patched canvas overalls and worn boots. "So, to what do you attribute your sudden fortune? Did you sell a claim, rob a bank, or buck the tiger and win?"

He lumbered forward and thumped huge pawlike hands on the table. The bowls clinked. His breath was so heavy with alcohol, she could ignite it with a match. "I got lucky. But I know to keep my mouth shut. Sometimes, just talkin' drives Lady Luck away. Or worse. She's got her own ways of gettin' even. Now. How much for the mirror?"

"That mirror cost us a thousand," snapped Inez. "And since you're so flush, there's the broken chairs and tables too. That's another hundred at least."

One paw disappeared into his jacket pocket. Inez's stomach knotted. She slid her hand into her pocket, fingers curling around the grip of the pocket revolver. Chet's hand emerged, holding a roll of bills.

"Huh. Chicken feed." He lined up fifties on the table like soldiers. The roll, hardly diminished, disappeared back into his pocket.

Inez eyed the money as if it might explode. "My Lord. You *did* rob a bank!"

Chet guffawed, then patted the scraggly beard that reached halfway down his sizeable belly. "Like I said. Lady Luck's bein' real agreeable." He swayed, a shallow-rooted giant in a wind storm. "Let's shake on it, and you tell Jackson to pour me a drink." The paw extended across the table. Inez examined the blackened nails, the hand cracked and tough from seasons of prospecting in the Rockies.

They shook. "Done. But next time you get snockered, I'll have Jackson toss you out in the alley."

"Thatta girl." His mouth split open—a grin populated by small rotten stumps of teeth. He lumbered back into the crowded saloon, hollering, "Drinks are on me, fellers! Pour 'em, Jackson!"

Abe reached under the counter, face tense, as Chet shouldered his way through the crowd. Inez slid behind the bar and stayed Abe from pulling out the shotgun. "It's all right. He's got the money."

"The man's a damn nuisance." Abe glowered. Chet belched.

Drinkers rushed the bar. Chet downed a shot and a chaser, slammed another fifty by the empty glasses and, weaving toward the exit, roared, "Keep the change!"

Shots of rye were grabbed up as fast as Abe could pour them. Opening another bottle, he asked Inez, "What in blazes was that all about?"

Inez pulled the wad of paper money from her pocket and directed Abe to where she held it, out of sight below the bar. "He bought a pardon."

Abe froze. "Where'd he get that? God amighty, he rob someone?"

Inez locked the money in the cash box. "He swears not." Shouts for refills and new orders escalated. The round of free drinks had awakened the crowd; naptime was over.

Toward midnight, Inez frowned toward one card game where the shouting was beginning to intensify. "Looks dangerous. Maybe we should shut them down."

"Here's more trouble."

Inez thought at first Abe was responding to her comment. Then she noticed he was staring toward the entrance. Just inside the door, snow still on the shoulders of his overcoat, Reverend Sands surveyed the scene.

Chapter Fourteen

Inez watched, bottle and glass in hand, as Reverend Sands strolled toward the escalating shouting match. If—or rather when—the men stood up and the chairs fell back, Inez knew it would be too late.

The reverend reached the table. The shouting ceased as the men looked up, no doubt startled to see a stranger standing over them. He leaned forward, placing one hand on the table. Judging from the sudden alterations in the players' expressions, his words must have been persuasive.

Reverend Sands straightened up. The men slumped in their chairs like schoolboys chastised for winging spitballs at each other.

"Did you see that?" Inez was stunned.

For the second time that evening, Abe shoved the shotgun back under the counter. "Wonder what chapter and verse he called up."

Reverend Sands lifted his hand and, at first, she thought he was hiding his smile. That impression was crowded out by the familiarity of the gesture: she'd seen it thousands of times, performed by Mark, Abe, countless other men. Absently smoothing his missing mustache, Reverend Sands scanned the room until their eyes met. As he moved toward the bar, she cleared off several used glasses and an empty bottle.

"What brings you to State Street this time of night, Reverend Sands? Looking for sinners? More counterfeit souls?"

Abe winced at her tone.

Sands smiled. Gently, reprovingly. "Appearances don't always tell the innocent from the guilty, the true from the false. You said something similar, as I recall."

Abe hastened, "Thanks for handlin' that bunch, Reverend. You got there quicker than I could have."

"Whatever did you say?" She still couldn't believe the transformation. The two men hunched over their cards, motionless.

Reverend Sands' set a well-worn pocket Bible on the burnished wood. "I suggested that if they hoped to reap any rewards in the hereafter, they should mend their behavior in the here and now."

A patron who'd been waiting more or less patiently took advantage of the pause. "Miz Stannert, I need that bellywash bad."

Inez started, poured a measure, and accepted his coin before returning to Reverend Sands. "At least we can offer you a drink. You saved us a whole lot of grief." She set a glass before him. He turned it over.

"No thanks."

Inez lowered the bottle. "Second time today someone's turned down a free drink. What next, I wonder. Hell freezing over? No, I forgot. It already has. It's winter in Leadville." She regarded him. "So, you're not here to drink, you're here to…?"

"To talk with you about that business earlier today. But—" men jostled on either side. "You look busy. Maybe later. Perhaps a cup of coffee? I'll hunt down familiar faces."

"You'll find more than a few from Sunday's services," she said, then shouted, "Useless!" beckoning him over. "Useless, this is Reverend Sands, new to town. Please get him a cup of coffee and some stew."

She addressed the clergyman. "The coffee's strong. The stew's the best in town. I believe in quality." She bent over to reshelve the clean glass.

"I too appreciate quality. In all its forms."

Inez straightened and caught his eyes on her décolletage. She smiled frostily. "Yes. Well. Make yourself comfortable." She turned pointedly to the next customer. Being stared at was part of the job. She'd built up armor early, traveling with Mark and Abe. The world considered any woman traveling with professional gamblers and playing the tables to be fair game, married or not.

The stares and speculations about her moral life had become more pronounced once Mark disappeared. She stared down the whisperers or ignored them, depending on the circumstances. Still, the way Reverend Sands looked at her was...disquieting.

A while later, Doc limped in.

She pulled his favorite brandy from the backbar. "How was your day?"

He peeled off winter gloves before he answered. "Not bad. Not bad. No one died, no one appreciably worse."

Doc swirled the liquid in the glass before draining it. Sighing once, he motioned for more. "Warms this old man's bones." He pushed a quarter eagle toward her. "I offered my condolences to Mrs. Rose. She'll be leaving town soon, I understand. Sorry state of affairs."

He rubbed his face, rearranging the folds and wrinkles, as he looked about the crowded room. "Why, isn't that the new minister? I met him at the Roses. Sands, isn't it?"

"That's right." Inez followed his gaze. Reverend Sands must have felt their scrutiny, for he looked up, winked at Inez, nodded at the doctor.

Doc waved back before turning to Inez. "Pleasant fellow. We had a most interesting conversation. War stories and so on."

Curiosity piqued, Inez asked, "Sands was in the War? Not ministering, I suppose."

"No no, my dear. I gather that's a recent development. Nasty business, the War. I still dream of the amputations. Brrrr. Think I'll join him." Doc moved toward the reverend.

"Inez." Abe's voice caused her to jump. "Jed Elliston wants a word." Abe nodded at the far end of the bar. The newspaperman held up his glass to draw Inez's attention.

Abe continued, "He's curious about Joe. Knows he turned up in the alley, that there was some ruckus Saturday last. Told him I wasn't discussin' it. We don't need that kind of stuff in the papers about the business. Now, he wants to talk to you."

Inez wiped her hands on her apron and reluctantly headed toward Elliston, who was making circles with his wet glass on the polished dark wood. He had the voracious look that plagued the young men who thronged into Leadville and the other Colorado boom towns. Only, Elliston wasn't after silver. Everyone knew he was comfortably supported in his publishing efforts by a wealthy and indulgent father whose stock rose with each mile of track laid down by the Atchison, Topeka and Santa Fe Railroad. No, Elliston had that kind of fortune aplenty, and the ease with which it vanished at the gaming tables indicated how little he valued it. He dug, not through soil and rock for precious metals, but through casual conversation and rumor for stories to splash across the pages of his newspaper, *The Independent*.

"Evening, Mrs. Stannert. Quite a crowd tonight."

"Actually, Mr. Elliston, it's morning now. And I can't spare you much time."

"It's about Joe Rose." He held up a hand, as if anticipating her protests. "I understand he came in last Saturday, tore up the place, then turned up dead on your back porch."

Inez rubbed her eyes, which stung from the smoke. Beneath the flowery prose of Joe's obituary in the paper, she'd sensed Elliston's unspoken questions. Now, here he was, true to form, nosing around. She didn't want him dwelling on the corpse at her door. Abe was right. That kind of story would do them no good.

On the other hand, if she could get Elliston to take an interest in Joe's death and find out who was responsible.... Suddenly, she saw a way to direct Elliston's curiosity away from the Silver Queen and still focus him on Joe's untimely demise.

"I found Joe's death peculiar myself. Did you know," she leaned forward in what she hoped was a conspiratorial manner, "someone broke into his assay office?"

Elliston's patrician face mirrored her intensity. "No. When?"

"Don't know. But the marshal's not taking much of an interest." Inez ignored Abe's increasingly pointed stare from the other end of the bar. "Look, I'm settling Rose's accounts. I'll be in his office about nine tomorrow. Why don't you stop in and we'll talk."

"I'll be there." Elliston ran a finger along the brim of his bowler.

Closing time arrived. The patrons, as always, thought differently. Abe and Useless were merciless, herding out the diehards, more or less forcefully as required.

At the door, Inez bid Doc and others good-night. When Abe and Useless went to roust the last customer, snoring nose-down on a table, Reverend Sands turned to Inez. "May I walk you home?"

Inez let the question hang as she tried to read his expression. He waited, hat in hand, looking for all the world like a hopeful suitor.

She took the easy way out, raising her left hand before her and twisting the double bands on the ring finger meaningfully. "No, Reverend. That's not possible."

He waited, as if expecting more explanation. When none followed, he said, "Another time, perhaps."

He stepped away just as Abe propelled the last drunk out the door. Inez and Abe watched Sands, nearly invisible in his black garb, melt into the State Street crowds.

Back inside, they took the cash box up to the parlor office. In silence, Abe put the day's take in the safe while Inez exchanged her thin leather shoes for a pair of sturdy walking boots.

"For a moment, I thought you'd take him up on his offer." Abe closed the safe door and spun the dial.

She finished tying the laces. "Offer?"

"His offer to walk you home."

"Abe. He's a con. All smooth talk and smiles. Why would I?"

Abe straightened and stared out the window at the darkness. "The man's hidin' somethin', and I bet you're gonna keep circlin' until you find out what. I've seen you fall for that kind before."

"Leave it, Abe. I don't need the lecture." She yawned. "Tomorrow, I've got to talk to the bank about Joe's accounts. And, oh yes, Joe's safe. Think you can give it a shot?"

He wound a muffler around his starched collar and shrugged into his overcoat. "Just don't go advertisin' my old talents around town. I'd rather be known for slingin' gin than pickin' locks. Folks think we're an odd pair as is."

"Bah. I don't pay attention to that talk and neither should you. As long they keep drinking and playing cards, it doesn't matter."

In the kitchen, Useless stacked dirty crockery and glasses. The brass spittoons were lined up, ready to be emptied into the alley.

The cat came out of hiding and wrapped herself around Abe's legs. He lifted her and carried her into the dark saloon. His voice drifted into the kitchen: "Go get them rats."

"Ha," muttered Inez. "That'll be the day."

"I'll lock up." Useless filled the wash tub.

Inez and Abe eased out the back door and set out through a drifting snowfall. She took a deep breath of the cold air and held it for as long as she could. It was a game she'd played as a girl: Take a breath of winter air. *Hold it…hold it…* It was like swimming, gliding through a green, underwater world. Only this world was clear and sharp like crystal. She let out her breath, watching it curl away like steam. They walked companionably up Harrison.

"So what'd you tell Jed?" Abe broke the silence.

"He's going to meet me at Joe's office tomorrow. You know, it's strange. Marshal Hollis seemed so suspicious of us and the circumstances around Joe's death. Now, he's dropped the whole thing. It might not be all bad if Elliston should take an interest. A carefully directed interest, of course. If we don't pursue this, no one will. And what if it's not over? What if Emma and Joey are in danger? Sands implied that could be the case."

"You believe him?" Abe interrupted incredulously.

Inez looked away at the silent store fronts, interiors masked by darkness. "Bridgette thought she saw Harry with Emma at the Clairmont. Coming out the back."

Abe stopped walking. "Inez, don't be lookin' for what isn't there. Emma's a decent woman. And Harry calls the shots with Tabor and the rest in this town."

"He doesn't call the shots for you or me. Anyway, I'm just thinking aloud. Consider. Right before Joe dies, who comes to town? A new marshal, a new reverend—"

"And probably a thousand others."

"The marshal is backed by the silver barons," Inez pressed on, "while the reverend takes room and board in Harry's hotel. And I'll bet he doesn't pay a dime."

Abe groaned and walked away. "Lord, I'm too old for this. I don't like it, Inez. Don't like it at all. I swear, for a woman who's supposedly so all-fired smart and educated, you sure like makin' things difficult."

Inez hurried toward him. "Now Abe." She tucked her gloved hand about his arm. "It's just that Joe's death is like a musical score with a missing page. It bothers me. It's not right. I won't do anything rash. Or anything that would ruin our good standing with the townfolk." She didn't bother to hide her sarcasm. "The way I see it, Jed Elliston has questions about Joe's death. You know how persistent he is when it comes to digging up a story. He wants to nose around? Fine. I'll sound the horn, slip the leash, and let him run. Don't you see? We'll let Jed flush out the fox for us."

Chapter Fifteen

At eight-thirty in the morning, the fresh snow on Chestnut Street was already churned into gray slush beneath wheels and hooves. Outside Joe's office, Inez hugged the ledger under her arm and fumbled for the key. The letter in her pocket crinkled, a reminder that she needed to stop at the bank later. The note, in Emma's hand, authorized Carbonate City Bank to release information about Joe's accounts.

Inez unlocked the door and entered the abandoned office. The very air seemed cold and forlorn. Shaking off the gloom, Inez lit the kerosene lamp on the counter and opened the accounting book. Some of the entries had recognizable names attached, others were cryptic letters and numbers.

Harry Gallagher's Silver Mountain Consolidated appeared frequently until…she flipped through the pages. Mid-October.

"Odd," she said aloud. Hinges creaked behind her.

"What is?" Susan stood at the threshold, knocking icy mud from her shoes.

"I wish I knew more about Joe's business." Inez turned more pages, then stopped. "No more entries." She ran her finger down the last page. "Peculiar. Almost no entries for November."

"Wasn't he in Denver until Thanksgiving?" Susan drifted around the counter as she adjusted her small maroon hat. "The office was probably closed while he was gone."

"But Nils was here then." Inez tapped her finger on the counter, staring at the page.

"I have a ten-thirty sitting. What are we going to do about that safe?" She lingered at a small mirror by the desk, fluffing the frizz of bangs above her dark brows.

Inez sighed, closed the ledger, and looked at her young friend. Susan always struck her as the epitome of a modern young woman. Heeding the siren call to "head West," women like Susan left their families in the farms and small towns and boarded the westbound trains alone, chins held high and plans aplenty. Schoolteachers, laundresses, newspaperwomen, they flourished in the boom towns and new cities. Other women, half-heartedly following husbands struck by gold or silver fever, faltered and pined, always looking over their shoulders toward "home."

In the mirror, Susan's reflection directed inquiring eyes on Inez.

"Abe knows someone who can handle the safe," said Inez. "I'll go to the bank about Joe's accounts and arrange for the sale of the building. I'm surprised real estate promoters aren't lined up to make an offer. After all, this is Chestnut Avenue and Joe owned the building, free and clear. Now, Jed Elliston is coming over any minute. When he does, let me do the talking."

"Elliston of *The Independent*?" Susan frowned. "Why is he coming here?"

"He's taken an interest in the events surrounding Joe's death. I thought perhaps, with a nudge in the right direction, he might prove useful."

"His father's a robber baron, rubbing elbows with the Santa Fe Railroad! And he turned me down flat when I tried to take out advertising in his paper!" She paced in indignation as Inez tried to decide what bothered Susan more: the casual wealth of the father or the dismissive nature of the son.

"The man is positively medieval about women. 'Now, Miss Carothers,'" Susan mimicked his cultured drawl, "'Women *rahlly* belong in the domestic sphere, *not* meddling in masculine pursuits.'"

"Yes, yes. He can be annoying. But he may be able to help us resolve Joe's death."

"Inez, we don't need him! We can do it ourselves!"

"Susan, we both have businesses to run. And neither you nor I can go from banks to bars asking questions about Joe and his business connections. Who would tell us? Jed, on the other hand, has access to the whole of Leadville. People *expect* him to ask questions, for heaven's sake."

"What makes you think he'll tell us anything? He'll just take what we give him, and the next thing you know, we'll read about it in his paper!"

"That's fine with me. The point is to bring Joe's killer to justice. If Jed can do that, I'll give him free whiskey for a year."

The front door squeaked open. "Mrs. Stannert, I accept your challenge. But only if we're talking proper Kentucky bourbon, not tonsil varnish."

Both women started guiltily. Inez hoped all he'd caught was the concluding sentence and not the preceding argument.

He removed his hat. Inez caught a whiff of bay rum as he appraised Susan.

Susan thrust out a hand over the counter. "Miss Carothers. I approached you once about advertising."

"Oh, of course." He took her hand, shook it limply. "Charmed to meet you again."

She sniffed, unmollified.

Elliston faced Inez. "So, what's the story? You said someone broke in?" He glanced about the office, doubt plain in his expression.

She pointed toward the rear of the building.

Elliston tipped back his bowler, walked through the swinging gate, and disappeared down the passageway. A long, low whistle drifted to the women, who joined Elliston.

"We cleaned up some." Susan brushed past him to crack open the rear door. Light speared the gloom, illuminating piles of trash glittering with broken glassware.

"Too bad." His condescension hung in the air. "Sometimes, you can deduce a fair amount about the perpetrators by the crime scene. When the scene is undisturbed, that is."

Susan rolled her eyes.

"Oh, I agree," Inez interjected smoothly. "Susan and I drew conclusions of our own. And we found this." She set the ledger on a cleared countertop.

Elliston's dark eyes snapped into focus, as if he'd been only half awake before. "And that is?"

"Joe's business records." She fanned the pages. "There's something odd about the last month of entries."

The hunger in his face was palpable. Inez placed both elbows on the closed ledger, gazing at him almost tenderly. *Jed's such a sucker. His face gives him away, every time.*

He cleared his throat. "As I said. I would be happy to offer my assistance."

"Of course you would." Her elbows remained on the book.

He looked around as if seeking allies. Susan glowered at him, arms crossed.

Inez continued, "We could help each other. Joe's widow asked me to settle his business affairs."

Shock warred with caution in Elliston's face. He looked as if he was trying to think of something suitable to say. "That's...commendable."

"Peculiar is probably what you mean. Well, peculiar has never stopped me before. In any case, I can ask the bank questions that you can't. And Susan and I have—" she tapped the book. "So, here's how it stands. It seems to me that your newspaper could greatly benefit from a part-time assistant."

She smiled at Susan, who, in a heartbeat, saw where she was heading. It took Elliston longer. But from his morose expression, Inez could tell he'd caught her drift at last. "Well, Jed. Do we have an agreement? The offer of free drinks still stands."

Elliston rubbed his jaw and looked sideways at Susan. Inez added, "And I'm certain you'll find some space in your paper to advertise Carother's Photographic Studio."

He finally bristled. "Mrs. Stannert, *The Independent* is my paper. You have no right to direct placement of adverts or articles."

"Of course, Jed. You know your business better than I," she soothed, watching his ruffled feathers settle. "You and Miss Carothers are quite capable of working it all out. And I promise to read *The Independent*, first page to last, with great interest from now on. Might even take out advertising myself." She opened the ledger and moved aside.

Elliston wavered, but the temptation was too great. He bent over the pages. "We need more light."

When Inez returned from the front counter with the lamp, Elliston and Susan were poring over entries. "'SilvM' must be Silver Mountain, Mr. Gallagher's company." Susan glanced at Inez for confirmation. "Wasn't he Joe's main customer?"

"Was is right. Until Old Harry decided to hire a company man," said Elliston.

"He did?" Inez's mind raced over bar talk and rumors, turning up nothing. "I don't recall hearing that."

A satisfied smile tweaked his lips. "It's not common knowledge."

"Well, I'm intrigued. Tell us more."

Elliston turned and leaned against the counter, hands thrust into trouser pockets.

"Harry's bringing in some chap from back East, come spring. He's been using Kelley's assay house for over a month now."

Inez stared at the lamp's flame. *I wonder if Emma knew.*

"Inez." Susan's face flickered with excitement. "Look at this."

Inez and Elliston crowded close as Susan pressed down on the open pages. Barely visible, a small knife-ridge of paper split the seam. "Someone's removed a page."

Chapter Sixteen

Elliston peered over Susan's head at the pages. "The last date on this page is the fifteenth of October. From there, it jumps to…Miss Carothers, you're standing in the light."

"The next date is November twenty-ninth," Susan said with some asperity. "And there are only a handful listed after that."

The front door opened with a crash that shook the floorboards.

"Joe, old coot. Ya in?" bellowed a familiar voice.

The three exchanged startled glances. Inez arrived in the office area first, followed closely by Elliston and Susan.

Chet Donnelly prowled by the counter, looking almost sober. His last resting place must have been quite firm, judging from the way his hat and hair were squashed flat on one side. He stared at the trio, puzzled.

"Rose in?" Chet snatched off his lopsided hat, clutching it before him in a vague remembrance of manners.

Elliston spoke first. "Don't you read the papers? Rose's dead."

Chet's furry eyebrows pulled together. "Wadd'ya mean, dead?"

"Died in Tiger Alley, Saturday night."

Chet sucked in his lips under the tangled beard. He seemed to be chewing something. Maybe his mustache. Suddenly, it was as if a cloud hanging in his mind blew away, revealing something he didn't want to see.

"Damn." He passed one shaky hand over his eyes. "Sorry, ladies. I'm tryin' to remember."

Inez spoke up. "You don't remember? That was only four days ago."

He hawked and spat. "I recollect wakin' up this morning on the floor of the Red Garter with my head half out the door. Felt like I'd been stepped on a few times."

"That's all?"

He looked slantways at her, still chewing.

"Well, allow me to refresh your memory. Saturday night, you and the twins, Zed and Zeke, started a fight at my saloon. Last night, you rolled in, paid for a new mirror, and bought a round for the house. Paid for everything with fifty dollar notes."

He looked as if she'd slapped him with a rotten fish. "I did?" His hands plunged into his pockets, searching for leftover change. "Ya sure that was me?"

"Of course it was you." Inez was exasperated.

A small notebook and pencil magically appeared in Elliston's hands. "Were you a client of Rose's?"

Chet stopped chewing, and his features rearranged themselves along crafty lines. "You a newspaper man?"

"Owner, editor, and chief reporter of *The Independent*. Say, Chet, what's your last name? And when did you last talk to Rose?"

Chet glowered, looking like a demented Saint Nicholas. "Never you mind." He lowered his head and barreled through the counter gate. "Rose has somethin' of mine out back. I'll get it and be on my way. S'cuse me." He lumbered toward the laboratory.

Inez followed. "Perhaps you'd best tell me what you're looking for," she said as he stared about the chaos.

Chet jammed his greasy hat back on his head. "Assay samples. Left 'em last week."

"You mean rocks in bags?" Susan managed to push past Elliston, who blocked the hall. "We've found nothing like that."

"Damnation." He hooked his thumbs in the rope that served as a belt and attempted to hitch up his pants over his sizeable gut. Gravity won, and the pants sagged back down below his belly. "He said he'd take care of them. Lady Luck was comin' through at last."

Something clicked for Inez, and a couple of small, musical notes fell into place. "Last night, you mentioned Lady Luck."

Chet peered around as if he expected his sample bags magically to appear. "Hell, she's the saint we pray to, every time we stick a shovel in the ground."

He eased out the back door. Then glared back through slitted eyes. "If you find bags with my name or initials, it's my property."

He lurched off.

"C.D.," said Inez softly. "Did C.D. appear in the last entries?"

Susan frowned. "No. Why?"

"Chet's initials. If he left something here last week, why isn't it in the ledger?"

‹›‹›‹›

"We've a deal, then. You supply the paint, I'll supply the faces." Inez handed Llewellyn a signed copy of their agreement.

"Done." Llewellyn touched the inked signatures with a finger. Satisfied they were dry, he rolled up and pocketed the agreement. As they left the second-floor saloon office, he added, "Now that that's settled, I'd like to prepare the surface. When's the best time for me to work?"

"Mornings, before we open. Someone's always here by eight."

"I'll time my arrivals for eight, then." He rubbed his hands together, smiling in a self-satisfied manner.

Inez couldn't help but smile back. At least this part of the morning's efforts had concluded satisfactorily. Llewellyn had promised to have the mural completed by February. And he hadn't even haggled over the price. *That's an artist for you. No sense for the bottom line.* The mural would cost far less than a new mirror, and there'd be nothing else like it in town.

Joe's ledger still troubled her, however. The missing page had whetted Elliston's appetite. He'd promised to look at the records and ask around. Still, Inez felt uneasy about letting the ledger leave her control. *After all, one page is gone. What if more turn up missing?* She wished she'd asked Susan to count the written pages. Just as insurance.

<>‹›‹›

"And what can I do for one of Carbonate City Bank's best customers?" The round tones in Nigel Hollingsworth's voice betrayed him as a native of England's shores. He steepled his fingers and beamed at Inez.

"Two things, Mr. Hollingsworth." Inez turned slightly in her chair by the assistant bank manager's desk and crooked a finger at Useless. "First, a deposit. A large one."

Nigel shifted aside a stack of papers restrained by a large, faceted crystal paperweight to make room on his desk. Useless plunked a satchel square on the blotter. Nigel laid a narrow hand on the rough leather, patting it like a father soothing a squalling babe. "So glad to hear you're open again, Mrs. Stannert. A day's lost profits is no mean figure. Leadville is booming, even now, in the dead of winter. Why, last night I met a Prussian count who's itching to invest in the right hole in the ground."

"I prefer making my fortune aboveground." Inez watched as Nigel opened the satchel and extracted bundled bills and rolls of gold and silver coins.

"Mark my words." He tweaked his cuffs before opening the bank ledger. "Leadville has only begun her ascent in the silver firmament. Just between us, confidentially and all that, if you ever consider expanding your enterprise, you can count on us for financial backing. Astute businesses stand poised to profit enormously in Leadville."

"As do astute institutions such as yours." She accepted the note of deposit. "Now, the second matter." Inez laid Emma's letter on his desk. "I'm here on behalf of Mrs. Rose, concerning her husband's business. He was also one of your best customers, I believe."

Nigel took on a properly somber air. "Ah yes. A tragedy." He glanced down at the letter, absorbing the impact of her words. "Oh, I say, you're here on behalf of the widow?"

"I'm settling Joe Rose's affairs. I need to know the status of his business and personal accounts so Mrs. Rose can plan accordingly."

She stopped. Nigel was not reacting as anticipated. Instead of nodding solicitously and saying soothing things, such as "We'll have those records straightaway," he was silent. He touched the note on his desk as if it might erupt in flames. Or poison him.

Inez heard the murmurs of bank clerks and customers out front and the squeak of nearby floorboards as Useless shifted from one foot to the other.

Nigel cleared his throat. "I say, perhaps we should discuss this privately."

Inez frowned, puzzled, then turned to Useless. "Why don't you wait in the lobby."

Once the door clicked shut, Nigel refolded Emma's note in careful quarters and pushed it gingerly across the desk to Inez.

"I can pull the records for you, Mrs. Stannert. But Mr. Rose closed his accounts with us about a month ago. I conducted the transaction personally."

Inez sat utterly still, not touching the folded note before her. Her starched lace collar scratched her neck as she swallowed. "Joe left your bank? Do you know where he moved his accounts?"

Nigel's pencil-thin mustache twitched above his compressed lips. "He cashed out. The whole bloody lot. And there's more."

He stopped. Then pulled a pipe from his frock coat and twirled it aimlessly between his fingers. "He took out a substantial loan with his business as collateral. Our manager,

Morris Cooke, handled that. I don't know the details." Nigel looked supremely unhappy. "I hardly need say that, unless there are funds elsewhere, we will have to foreclose."

Nigel repocketed his unlit pipe. The lace scratched mercilessly at her throat, like fingernails searching for a hold. Finally, she asked, "Anything else, Mr. Hollingsworth?"

"I think that's probably quite enough. Don't you?"

Inez shut her eyes. *I hope Emma has more than pin money tucked away for a rainy day. Because the skies just opened up.*

<>‹>‹>

"I hardly knew how to tell Emma." Half an hour before opening time, Inez held up the clean shot glass, inspecting it for spots. *Not that the customers ever notice.*

A warped image of Abe behind the bar wavered through the double thickness. "Did you tell her we'd tide her over, help her get settled?"

"I did. But she refused to listen. I think she's too distraught to think straight."

Emma had stared right through her when Inez tried to explain about the closed accounts, the loan. She'd whispered, "The wages of sin."

"What?" Inez had leaned forward in the window seat of Emma's parlor, not certain she'd heard correctly.

"Harry Gallagher. He ruined us."

"What do you mean, Emma?"

She'd turned away, pulled a black-bordered handkerchief from her sleeve, and dabbed her eyes. "Joe told me. Mr. Gallagher said terrible things about Joe, then took his assaying business elsewhere. He killed Joe just as certainly as if he'd shot him."

At Emma's mention of Harry, Bridgette's words drifted through Inez's mind like wisps of smoke. On impulse, Inez asked, "Emma, did you meet with Harry Gallagher? About a month ago in his hotel?"

Emma looked at her as if she'd gone mad. "I won't even honor that with an answer."

Beneath her chagrin, Inez grew nettled. "Emma, I wasn't suggesting you had an assignation with Harry Gallagher."

"Well, I hope not. You know, Inez, I always defend you when people talk." Her mouth trembled. "I know you're a Christian woman, a devoted wife and mother. If you hear rumors about me or Joe, vicious, untrue lies, I hope you defend us as well." She turned away. "There's no value in pursuing Joe's death. Just straighten out his business affairs. Work with the bank on the loan. I'm sorry I reacted as I did. But Joe, Mr. Gallagher…it's over. And I'm leaving Leadville forever."

In the saloon, Inez's mind wandered tentatively over Emma's words and tone, like hands picking out a piece of familiar music on an unfamiliar keyboard.

I don't believe I'd ever heard Emma lie before, but I'm certain she was lying then. She did meet Harry. But I'll learn nothing more about it from her.

Inez sighed and slid the glass under the counter.

She decided against relating the rest of that painful conversation to Abe. Instead, she remarked, "Normally, I would send an anonymous donation to the church's Widows and Orphans' Fund and earmark it for Emma. But I don't trust Sands."

Abe grunted, methodically drying glassware. Useless bent over a nearby crate, adding bottles to the backbar.

"Nigel said he'd ask Morris Cooke about Joe's loan. I still can't believe Joe emptied his accounts and took out a loan without telling Emma. And there's no sign of the money. What did he do with it all?"

"You talking about Joe's widow, the pretty lady with the red hair?" Useless hugged his empty crate. "She in trouble?"

Inez winced. *I should be careful about what I say and where.* "Please don't repeat any of this, Useless. I must count on your discretion, since mine has fled."

"Rose have gambling debts or something?"

Inez paused, glass in hand. "You saw Joe gambling?"

"I'd seen him around," Useless hedged. "Shoot, everyone in Leadville gambles." He squeezed around Abe and tried to pass Inez. She barred his progress with her arm.

"Where, exactly, did you see him?"

Useless bumped her arm once with the box, then resigned himself to an interrogation. "Uh, the Board of Trade. Red Garter."

"The Red Garter?" Inez was incredulous. "That dive?"

Gold and silver clinked as Abe counted coins into the cash box. "Inez, the boy's right. It don't mean much that Joe picked up a hand of cards here and there. I saw Joe myself at the Crystal Belle a few times."

"Cat DuBois' place?" Inez felt a stab of betrayal. Abe looked neutral. Useless looked guilty. "Useless, you too?"

"Well, sure," Useless said defensively. "I go there sometimes for a drink and to talk with the girls."

The notion of tongue-tied Useless chatting it up with Cat's women was hard for Inez to picture.

"Now, Inez." Abe added two more glasses to the growing line in front of her. "Checkin' out the competition's a good idea. I do it m'self. Leastwise, at those places that'll let me in the door. Speakin' of doors..."

Abe walked to the entrance and unbarred the door, opening it to the harsh white light of winter and the first drinkers of the day.

Chapter Seventeen

Mornings, Inez reflected, were her favorite time of day. When she wasn't hung over or hadn't been working until dawn.

She clucked and shook the reins. "Come on, girl."

Lucy swiveled her ears in response and quickened her pace, her winter shoes flinging bits of crusty snow into the cutter.

They headed west. The smelters, the town, Fryer Hill, and Mosquito Range receded, while Elbert and Massive loomed ahead. Inez took a deep breath of cold air, reveling in the silence and wide open spaces.

The previous night had been exceedingly profitable. Patrons of Leadville's new opera house had swelled the after-midnight crowds until the saloon was bursting at the seams. She and Abe had discussed fixing up the second story to house games of chance. Hiring a dealer or three. With the profits they were seeing, it could happen by summer.

Inez touched the pocket holding her copy of *Paradise Lost* and recalled the directions to Llewellyn Tremayne's workshop she'd wrung from Useless an hour before.

Llewellyn's certainly on the outskirts of town. Of course, given the price of real estate, maybe it's all he can afford.

Finally she spotted the place Useless had described: two log outbuildings with a more finished, slab-sided structure facing the road. The sign above the front door proclaimed "Portraits, Engraving, Signs."

After hitching Lucy to a post, Inez brushed her cloak free of icy clumps and entered. A tarp curtain divided the space into a small reception area and a larger workshop in the rear. The curtain hung askew, revealing a stove and a long table. Moving closer, she spotted a covered easel positioned by a north-facing window, paint jars and tins of various sizes. The diminutive painter was nowhere in sight.

"Mr. Tremayne?"

No answer.

Inez skirted the half-counter and ducked under the tarp. The worktable held scattered papers, copper plates, and various sharp implements used, she assumed, in the engraving trade. A small printer's press squatted to one side. Turpentine tinged the air, strong enough to make her scrunch her nose. Some of the scraps sported intricate designs that reminded her of the borders on her Silver Mountain stock certificates.

The rear door opened, and Llewellyn entered, wiping his hands on a rag. The fancy duds were absent, replaced by an ink-smirched leather apron, a worn woolen shirt, and canvas pants.

Llewellyn halted, his expression anything but welcoming.

"Mrs. Stannert. What are you doing here?" He hurried to the table, dropping the rag over the copper plates.

She held up *Paradise Lost*. Seeing his blank expression, she added, "For the painting."

He looked at the volume, then down at his inkstained hands. "I'll wash up. We can talk out front."

Inez glanced again at the table. A small engraving of a woman, dressed in classical garb, holding shield and sword. A pencil sketch of a pair of double-Xs—one with flourishes, one plain—lay side-by-side with a small-scale line engraving of the same. The images seemed familiar. Llewellyn moved forward, blocking her view and gathering the sheets together. "Please, Mrs. Stannert." He nodded pointedly at the curtain.

Once he'd joined her at the counter, she pulled a sheet of writing paper from the book. "I noted pages you might peruse for a sense of Milton's Heaven and Hell."

Her eyes strayed over his head to the hidden workroom. "I didn't realize you do engraving."

He reached out to take the book. Ink still stained his cuticles. "A sideline. My bread-and-butter is signs for the new businesses in town." He gestured at a stack of boards leaning against the wall. The one on top read P.T. WARNER BOOKS & STATIONERY. The scent of varnish melded with that of paint and new wood.

"I'm hoping my recent notoriety in portraiture will make the sign-painting unnecessary. Although I'd sooner paint signs or whitewash fences than go underground with the other Cousin Jacks."

Tremayne, Trelawney, Treleaven, Trevelyan. Inez recognized Llewellyn's last name as one more note in a litany of Cornish surnames that flooded Leadville's city directory. The Cousin Jacks came to work the mines, leaving behind Nevada's silver, the Midwest's lead and coal, and Cornwall's tin. "Mining's not for you, hmmm?"

Llewellyn's eyes were black pools, iris to pupil. "A blast in a Pennsylvania coal mine killed most of my family. I vowed I'd never join them. Now, let's see your book."

<> <> <>

Back in Joe's office, again. Inez pinched her nose, still numb from the ride back to town. *All I do these days is trudge in circles. With little or no result, it seems.*

The office door opened and Abe walked in. "Mornin' Inez. How was your ride?"

"Cold. Took me half an hour to get there." She picked up the lamp and followed Abe to the laboratory.

Abe dropped a scuffed saddlebag with a clank.

Inez eyed the bag. "You haven't explosives in there, have you?"

"Nope." Abe hunkered down in front of Joe's safe. In one fluid motion, he pulled out his knife, flipped it, and caught the blade. He tapped the safe's front panel with the hilt. The metal rang.

"Bring that light over, Inez." He examined the safe. "Ordinary plate iron. I can do this fast, if you don't plan on sellin' it. Or see if I can work out the numbers."

"I don't care about the safe, only the contents."

Abe opened the saddlebag and removed a pick and a jimmy. "Take me 'bout twenty minutes."

It took him fifteen.

She looked at the ripped-out iron panel, pried-back bolt, and broken lock. "That was fast."

He stood, brushed off his trousers. "Guess I still have the touch. Not that I plan on revisitin' that line of work."

Holding the lamp high, Inez stooped and peered into the maw of the safe. A stack of mottled notebooks lay beneath two dusty canvas bags tied with frayed ropes. "Joe didn't hide his fortune here."

"Too bad." Abe loaded the tools back into the saddlebag.

Inez pulled out the notebooks and the sacks. She held the lamp as close to the safe's interior as she could. Floor, wall, ceiling: empty.

Well, what did I expect? Greenbacks and double eagles stacked to the top? Much as she hated to admit it, that was exactly what she'd hoped for. Or at least some clear indication of where the money from his accounts and the loan had gone.

A peek inside a sack revealed a jumble of fist-sized rocks. She took out one. Sharp-edged, black and brown, with pinpricks of silver catching lamplight. Its secrets, she knew, would only be revealed by the application of chemicals and intense heat of the assay process. She put it back with its brethren and retied the bag. The rope looked familiar. *Like Chet's belt.*

She hauled experimentally on one bag.

"Here, Inez. I'll take those." Abe reached for the two sacks.

"They're probably Chet Donnelly's samples. Put them in our office safe for now." She glanced at the broken iron box before them. "Not that it would keep out anyone who's really determined."

Abe hefted the bags. "You comin'?"

"Soon."

"Suit yourself."

After he'd left, Inez opened the top notebook. The pencil marks on the pages might as well have been a secret code. Rows of numbers, interrupted by cryptic notes and what looked like chemical notations, ran from first page to last. She recognized abbreviations for commonly assayed metals: *Ag* for silver, *Au* for gold, *Pb* for lead, *Cu* for copper. Finally, she spotted a date: *9 April 1879*. "Where's November and December?" she said aloud in frustration.

"Hello!" A cultured voice sang out from the front. "Mrs. Stannert?"

Jed. "In the back."

Inez shoved the notebooks into a nearby drawer as the gate squeaked a warning.

Jed Elliston walked briskly into the laboratory, crossing the room in four long strides. "Any luck with the safe?" He threw an indifferent glance at the wreck in the corner. "Empty. Pity. Now, look at this!"

Elliston opened the ledger to a page marked with a gros-grain ribbon. He cracked his knuckles, radiating energy and impatience.

"What is it?" Inez brought over the circle of light.

Elliston stabbed a finger at the columns. "The initials C.D. show up June and August. Nothing in July or September. Mid-October, he's back again. What do you think? Could that be that fellow Chet Dunney?"

"Donnelly. When's the last C.D. entry?"

Elliston paged forward. "Mid-October, there's several more. And that's it. But we don't know what's on the missing page. I've checked out these last few entries before his death. Local mines. Standard stuff."

"Sounds like I should talk with Chet." Inez gazed down at the ledger.

"Or I could." Elliston sounded hopeful, with an undercurrent of obstinacy.

"I think not."

"But—"

"Jed, if you start hounding Chet with questions, he'll break your nose and make himself scarce. Or get so drunk we'll never get any sense out of him."

Elliston glowered. "You're going to cut me out."

"Not at all. I'll just approach him when he drops by for a drink. Idle bar chatter. He won't suspect a thing. Good God, Jed. You run a newspaper. He's not going to sit down for a friendly chat with you."

Jed's lower lip began to jut in a juvenile pout. She sighed. *I can just imagine Jed at five years old when someone took away a favorite toy. I'll have to give him something else to occupy him.*

She laid a placating hand on his arm. "While I'm waiting for Chet to get thirsty and make an appearance, why don't you check the Recorder's Office? You can track down the claims Chet's recorded since spring, his partners, whom he's sold to and for how much. See what he's been up to."

"In other words, run down the paper trail." His eyebrows drew in over his eyes.

Sensing a tantrum was imminent, Inez hurried on. "He's been throwing a lot of money around recently. Perhaps he's sold off some of his workings. That should be listed as a change in ownership, right? Might be interesting to see who the buyers are. See if they were Joe's clients as well." She breezed along, making up the melody as she went, but she could see that Elliston was responding to her invention.

The pout receded and his brow cleared. "Hmmm. Perhaps some of the major mining interests are involved. Tabor, Gallagher, Chaffee, and the rest are gobbling up property as fast as they can. Won't be long before they own it all, if they don't already."

He began to look cheerful. "I could pose a question here or there. Find out what new ventures are surfacing."

She pasted on an expression of encouragement. "Wonderful idea. And with your access to the rich and famous—"

"Well, family connections and the male prerogative." His superior air returned. "Yes, you'd best wait for that Chester fellow to show up. You can verify whatever I uncover. We'll compare notes in a few days."

"Ah, Jed. Remember Miss Carothers."

He blinked.

"She could be most helpful with this."

His face cleared. "Oh. Of course. I'll find some suitable task for her."

"Of course you will," Inez said softly, watching him go.

She retrieved the notebooks after he left, an idea beginning to form. *I think I have something suitable for Susan to investigate as well.*

Chapter Eighteen

Inez peered through the window around the stenciled words "Carother's Photographic Portraits: Best Prices and Quality Work." Through the half-pulled velvet drapes in the sitting area, she could see Susan posing a young couple. Susan removed the portrait camera's lens cap, and their faces bleached white in an instant of powder flash.

Inez entered, a tinkling bell announcing her arrival. She smiled at the couple, noting the silver band on the woman's left hand, the store-bought formal clothes. *Newlyweds.*

Susan said, "Your photographs will be ready Saturday, Mr. McGowan."

"Thankya," he muttered. The McGowans hastened to the door. After the bell subsided, Susan threw herself into an upholstered corner chair, motioning Inez to its mate. An occasional table between them held a tea set.

"Married two days ago." She absently pulled at the curtain of bangs on her forehead, then brightened. "Reverend Sands performed the ceremony and recommended they come here. Wasn't that nice of him?"

"Mmmm-hmmm." *What better way to gain Susan's trust than send her customers.* "I know the reverend's been out and about, meeting the parishioners. Has he been to see you yet?"

"He was here Tuesday." Susan's normally frank brown gaze skittered sideways. She jumped up. "Would you like some tea?"

"Not now." Inez leaned forward. "Did you mention the situation with the Roses? The condition of Joe's office?"

Susan looked trapped. "Well, yes. He's concerned about Emma and Joey, and he *is* the head of our church. Until June, anyway."

"I'm not angry," Inez said gently. "But what exactly did you say? I spoke with him at Emma's. He seems to have formed certain impressions about Joe and his situation. And he knew about Mark."

"Oh." She looked crestfallen. "He asked about you. I suppose I did mention Mark's disappearance. I also told him how hard you and Abe work to keep the saloon going." She raised her eyes, her usual spirit returning. "I believe he thought you were a, ah, woman of loose character." Her cheeks pinked. "Because of your business, I mean."

"He wouldn't be the first," Inez said dryly. "What did you say about Joe's office?"

"Well, I described the mess and how you found the rat. He asked about Joe's trips to Denver. I told him Nils knew more than I."

"At least it was before we discovered the missing ledger page," Inez said half to herself. "Although, he may have gotten wind of that by now."

Susan turned the teacup in her hands. "You don't trust him, do you. I think he wants to help. He listens."

"Susan, consider this. What do you know about Reverend Sands?"

"He's ministered in California."

"That was in the newspapers. What else?"

Susan rocked the teacup, watching the tea slosh.

"What about his family? His background? Heavens, his full name? 'J.B.' What kind of a name is that? Yet that's how he appears on the church sign, in the newspapers. We really know very little about him. He's so smooth at drawing out information. Yet he tells nothing in return."

Susan looked deflated.

Inez hastened to add, "Perhaps he's exactly what he says, but it pays to be circumspect." She picked up the notebooks stacked by her chair. "I have something for you. But let's keep it between us. Agreed?"

"Agreed." Susan peered over at the notebooks. "What are those?"

"They're from Joe's safe. I'm hazarding they're his assay notes. We can't ask Nils Hansen for help, so—" Inez plunked them into Susan's lap. The topmost slid to the floor. "Can you look these over? It's a lot of chemistry, which I know nothing about. Can you fit it in with your work and whatever you're doing for Jed?"

Susan paused while picking up the fallen notebook and glowered. "Do you know what he wants me to do?"

"Do tell."

"Set type." Susan's eyes snapped sparks. "I set type for my father's newspaper when I was thirteen, and I'm not about to do it again, thank you very much." She banged the notebooks down on the table, where they emitted a puff of gritty dust.

"Jed is just a taste of what's going to happen when the Eastern establishment moves in to 'civilize' Leadville," warned Inez. "Don't be fooled into thinking the town will stay wide open forever. For anyone different, opportunities will come harder and at a higher price as time goes on. Mark my words."

"When that happens, I'm off. Maybe to Wyoming. At least women can vote there."

The little bell clinked as a woman shepherded in three small children.

"Oops. Next appointment. Inez, I'll look through Joe's notes in the next couple of days. And I won't breathe a word to anyone."

"I know you won't." Inez smiled warmly. "Next to Abe and Emma, I'd trust you with my life."

‹›‹›‹›

Inez leaned on the bar and closed her eyes, blocking out the smoky haze and the crowded saloon. She could not, however, block out "Carry Me Back to Old Virginny," which was being rendered with great enthusiasm by the pianist she had hired on a whim that evening. The saloon's piano, Inez noted, needed tuning. Again.

"Miz Stannert, don't hug that bottle too tight." A man with rock dust etching the lines of his face tipped his empty glass.

Two bits changed hands for another dose of Taos Lightning. Inez checked her lapel watch: quarter past midnight.

Marshal Hollis ambled in. His reptilian eyes fastened on Useless at the far end.

Best give him a free drink so he doesn't pester Useless for it.

"Marshal!" On tiptoe, Inez waved the distinctive turquoise-green bottle over the heads of the crowd.

The marshal elbowed his way to the bar, hands gripping the gun belts crossed on his narrow hips. The star of justice pinned on the dingy sheepskin vest showed dimmer from the splatters of a recent meal.

"On the house." Inez had to yell to be heard above the piano and the general din. She set a clean glass before him. "Opera over yet?"

"Just gettin' out."

She poured. "How's the law and order business tonight?"

"Waall, one fella sliced up over a fancy woman at the Red Garter. 'Nother lost an ear over a misplaced ace. A lotta drunks freezin' upright and flat out on the walks. Jeeeee-sus, it's cold out there."

He let loose with a stream of tobacco juice, ignoring the spittoons placed every few yards. After knocking back the shot, he cleared his throat. "Ah-hem. Word has it you're still chasin' after Rose's ghost."

Inez's grip tightened on the bottle. "And?"

"'Taint 'zactly a healthy thing. Furthermore..." He waggled the empty glass at her. His mustache was thawing. She hated to think about the composition of the dripping liquid.

"All right. One more. But you better have something interesting to tell me. I'm not in business to give it away."

Hollis sniggered. "Just what Cat DuBois'd say."

Her polite intentions dissolved. "Keep your insinuations to yourself. You're a sorry excuse for a lawman."

Marshal Hollis downed his drink. "You're lucky you're a woman. If you were a man..." His eyes looked like pebbles at the bottom of a frozen stream. "You want somethin' interestin'? How about this? You keep ridin' down the road after Joe, you just might join him." He slammed the glass on the bar.

Inez jammed the cork back in the bottle. *Every time I talk with this man, I feel the need to take a bath.*

Abe pulled the bottle from her grasp. "You're lookin' a tad ferocious, Mrs. Stannert." He glanced from her to Marshal Hollis. Hollis glared back, mustache dripping.

Useless came hard on Abe's heels. "Bourbon's gone and the opera crowd's here."

"I say, Mrs. Stannert!" Nigel Hollingsworth, adrift in a sea of silk top hats and cutaway coats, tried to move closer to the bar but was stopped by a solid wall of bodies.

"Mrs. Stannert," he bellowed. "Regarding Rose's loan. I've discovered," he glanced around the milling crowd, "some interesting connections." Jostling elbows threw him off balance. "Meet me Sunday morning. Say, nine. At the bank."

Inez waved to show she'd heard. He turned and fought his way out.

Abe turned to Useless. "Get a case of Kentucky from the back."

Useless grabbed the storeroom keys and fairly flew the length of the bar.

Inez heard a someone say, "Crowd's too rich for my blood." The knot of miners shoved through the opera fans, creating a vacuum that was quickly filled. The pianist swung into "Oh Dem Golden Slippers."

Marshal Hollis looked at Inez with the hooded eyes of a viper. He shoved the empty glass at her and stalked out the front door into the night.

Chapter Nineteen

"We are gathered in the eyes of the Lord...."

The wind whipped through Evergreen Cemetery and snatched Reverend Sands' words away, snarling uphill toward the town, the mines, and Mosquito Range. The mourners huddled together, as much for warmth as for mutual comfort. The brass band that had trumpeted down Chestnut Avenue before the casket-bearing carriage stood in a frozen cluster. It seemed that much of Leadville had braved the weather to see Joe Rose on his last journey through town.

Inez, standing by Emma and Joey, focused on Joe Rose's grave blasted out of the snow and unforgiving ground. At the bottom, Joe's coffin waited for the first shovel of icy dirt. Inez gripped Joey's shoulder tighter. Joey peered up at her, blue eyes barely visible above his wool muffler and below his knit hat. A gust tugged at her cloak and wrapped it tighter around her black button boots.

Seemingly oblivious to the cold, Reverend Sands stood, head bowed, gloved hands clasped before him as he measured out Joe's eulogy. From time to time he scanned the crowd as if weighing the strength of his words against the growing storm. "We say good-by to a father, a husband, a citizen of unparalleled reputation in this worthy city."

The mourners stood motionless, bundled in copious winter outerwear.

"Ashes to ashes, dust to dust...."

Inez saw Nils Hansen, standing with two assayers from Jay G. Kelley's and looking miserable, whether from cold or emotion, it was impossible to tell. She also spotted Nigel from the bank, Doc, and the foreman from the Denver City Mine. Behind them, she detected what could only be Chet Donnelly's stove-in hat.

No Harry.

"Amen."

The wind moaned into the silence. Snow peppered the bowed heads of the crowd. Reverend Sands nodded to Abe, who shoveled the first clot of ice into the open pit and passed the shovel to the next pallbearer.

Inez's heart contracted with each thump of dirt. She remembered Joe. Building a snow fort with Joey, lecturing on assaying for silver in carbonate of lead, holding Emma's hand. And Joe with Mark. Arguing politics, discussing the finer points of poker, debating the merits of the latest silver strike. All those common memories now lay at the bottom of that dark hole. Joe was gone. Another link to Mark, broken.

The crowd shifted toward the welter of sleighs, cutters, and carriages. As Inez watched, a short, voluptuous figure wrapped in fur slipped away from the main crush of mourners. A gust lifted the veil of the fashionable black hat briefly, revealing brassy curls.

Frisco Flo?

The woman stepped nimbly into a red cutter trimmed in gold and flicked the reins.

Nils started toward Emma, met Inez's eyes, and beat a hasty retreat. Chet, hovering at a distance, finally spat into the snow and walked away. Inez felt an undefined anger growing, searching for a target.

Abe, Useless, and Reverend Sands approached from the gravesite. Sands stopped by Emma. "Mrs. Rose, it's time to go."

His eyes met Inez's briefly. Somber gray, with a genuine sorrow that surprised Inez. Emma squeezed Inez's hand, then let him guide her and Joey to a nearby sleigh.

Inez turned and caught Nils ducking away from her gaze. On impulse, she strode through the snow toward him.

"Nils Hansen." She blocked his path. "You've been avoiding me."

His two companions exchanged glances and kept walking.

Nils' reaction was exactly as she'd hoped. He flushed bright red and looked around to see who was watching. "What do you want, Mrs. Stannert?"

Inez grabbed his coat sleeve, ignoring the startled looks of passersby, and raised her voice. "Last week it was Inez. Why so formal now?"

She calculated what she knew of Nils: avoided honky-tonks, quoted the Bible, probably an obedient Lutheran son. She lowered her voice to a fierce whisper. "If you don't want the good folk of Leadville to think you've taken up with a lady saloon owner, you tell me what I want to know. Right now. What sort of 'no good' was Joe Rose up to?"

He tried to pull away. She knew he was too well-mannered to throw her off. In fact, she was counting on it.

"What happened last month?"

He said nothing, so she decided to up the ante and the volume. "Nils, remember that night? The things you said?"

One of the assayers, leaning on a wagon, shouted, "Give her what she wants, Nils, and let's go!"

Nils squirmed with embarrassment.

Inez twisted the cloth in her fists. "Joe hasn't a penny left to his name."

He looked stunned. "Then Mrs. Rose is—"

"Destitute. Now, Silver Mountain Consolidated. Why did Harry drop Joe?"

Nils jumped as if she'd rammed him with a hot poker, guilt plain on his face. "I reckon you'd better ask Mr. Gallagher about that."

"I reckon I will." She released his arm. As he plowed through the snow toward his companions, she shouted, "I'm not through with you, Nils Hansen!"

She walked with dignity to her buggy where Abe and Useless waited. Lucy rolled a dark eye toward Inez, indicating by a turn of ear how much she disliked standing around in the blowing snow. Inez patted her mare's neck absently, her thoughts on Frisco Flo. *Why did she come to Joe's funeral?*

"What was all that about?" Abe leaned down, reins gathered loosely in his hands. In back, Useless tucked his long neck deep into his canvas duster.

She waved dismissively and gathered up her petticoats, layered skirts, and cloak before climbing up to sit beside Abe. Pulling the hood of her cloak over her hat, she said, "I'll take her, Abe."

Abe handed over the reins.

Concentrating on the ruts fast disappearing under the pelting snow, Inez urged Lucy up State Street. Even in the storm, it was jammed with men, freight sledges, carriages, and delivery wagons. As Lucy trotted past Cat DuBois' parlor house, Inez risked glancing away from the slush-filled road to the elegant rigs lined up on the side street. The red cutter was there.

Inez stopped in front of the Silver Queen. As Abe and Useless climbed down, she threw the saloon keys to Abe. "I'll be in later."

Abe lifted his eyebrows.

"I have business to attend to."

"Somethin' we can send Useless for?"

"No. Not that kind of business."

Abe grabbed Lucy's harness. "What kind of business, Inez?"

As she stiffened, he added, "With a storm blowin' in, I'd like to know where you're headed, in case I gotta send a search party."

Inez relented. "Silver Mountain."

"The mine?" Abe didn't relinquish his hold.

"Oh, all right. The mining office. Harry's office."

"This have to do with Joe? Is that what's got you in a lather? Has Harry got outstandin' business on those books?"

"It has to do with something Nils said." Inez was suddenly aware of Useless, hanging back from Abe but within earshot. "It would take too long to explain. The sooner you let go, the sooner I'll be back."

Abe let go. "You watch your step, Inez. Harry ain't a man to trifle with."

"Trifling is the last thing on my mind. I have questions for Mr. Gallagher, and I intend to get some answers."

She snapped the reins and turned up Harrison, urging Lucy into the driving snow.

Chapter Twenty

Inez encountered a tangle of traffic on the way to Fryer Hill and the Silver Mountain Consolidated Mine. Alternately freezing and perspiring as she guided Lucy through the crush, Inez had plenty of time to consider Harry Gallagher and his possible role in the Roses' circumstances.

Harry won't tell me why he stopped doing business with Joe, but he might let something slip. Particularly if I mention Nils and imply that I know more than I do. Then, there's Emma. She said straight out that Harry ruined Joe. And she almost certainly met him at the Clairmont. But I won't play those cards unless I must.

"Whoa up!"

The cry behind caused her to yank the reins. A team of draft horses pulling a sledge heavy with timber thundered by, inches away.

Bastard!

By the time she and her mare had reached the offices of Silver Mountain, they were out of sorts and out of breath. Inez slid off the seat and dug through her pockets until she found two sugar lumps covered with wool fuzz. Lucy sniffed suspiciously at the meager offerings before deigning to lip them off Inez's gloved palm. Inez rubbed her hand on her cloak and examined the armed men lounging nearby, dressed in dark blue greatcoats and military-style hats. *Harry's private troops.*

The previous summer, Leadville's silver barons hadn't wasted any time in forming their own personal armies. Lip service had been given about creating the forces as insurance against lawlessness. *Hogwash. The barons raised these armed camps so they wouldn't kill each other in the rush to get rich.* Constant ownership disputes over land and mineral rights often erupted into physical violence.

Inez hitched Lucy to a nearby rail and turned her attention to the two-story frame building. One door, sheltered by a small portico, looked a likely office entrance.

The door flew open and a figure sailed out, landing hard on the slick ice. A militiaman appeared in the doorway. "You don't like the work, find another job. There's a dozen Cousin Jacks to take your place and Gallagher don't hold with organizers or agitators."

The miner staggered to his feet, spat on the frozen ground. "With the profits he makes, he can afford a living wage for his men."

Several workers coming on shift slowed to listen, tin dinner buckets glinting silver in a landscape of dirty snow and dark timbered structures.

Several tense seconds passed. He spat again, then turned away, walking toward Inez. Inez finally placed the face: One of the group who had abandoned the Silver Queen when the opera let out. He said in a voice meant to carry, "Here to make a deal with the Devil, Mrs. Stannert? Take care. He drives a hard bargain."

She smiled tightly as she passed him. "I've dealt with this particular devil before."

Inez mounted two stairs, slippery with frozen mud, and opened the door to a dark and muffled world. The reception area held a heating stove and a man seated behind a desk piled high with ledgers.

He squeaked, "What's your business, Mrs. Stannert?"

Renquist. Pince-nez clung to his nose, much as the few desperate strands of hair clung to his scalp. *At least he shaved off that hideously patchy beard. It made him look like he was molting.*

She said formally, "I'm here to see Mr. Gallagher."

He clutched a quill pen, glaring. She'd seen that expression before. An occasional customer at her saloon, Renquist would order a drink and nurse it at a vacant table. He would fix her with a look that—if it weren't for the thinly concealed lust behind it—she herself would've applied only to rats and other vermin. No one ever joined him at his table.

"He's a busy man, Mrs. Stannert. You can't drop in and demand an audience."

Inez spotted a paneled mahogany door. "Is that his office?"

Without waiting for a reply, she moved forward and grabbed the ornate bronze knob. Renquist jumped up, spilling ink on a ledger.

As she pushed the door open, Renquist shouted, "You haven't an appointment!"

Inez walked in.

Harry and another man were leaning over a large map, holding its curled edges down on a massive desk. They looked up, startled. Inez paused inside the threshold, as much to compose herself as to wait for Renquist to stop yammering.

"I told her you were busy, Mr. Gallagher. That she needed an appointment!"

So this is his office. Once that summer, Harry had driven her up to Silver Mountain and pointed out some of the mine's obvious features. As she recalled, it had been a quick detour on their way to dinner at Soda Springs. *It seems a million years ago.*

Renquist kept yapping. Harry, his silver-blue eyes on Inez, ignored him. Even though it was late afternoon, Harry's fine linen shirt was unwrinkled, the collar starched, and his dark gray vest entirely buttoned. Only the shirt sleeves, uncuffed, and a slightly loosened cravat indicated that Harry might have done something more that day than just dress for dinner.

His expression was unreadable. She looked away first, out the large mullioned window to the towering A-shaped timbers of the main headframe. She'd heard about Harry's window. Folks said he'd built it facing the mine so the men would know he was watching them and every ore bucket that rose up the main shaft.

"Enough," Harry said to Renquist.

The yapping stopped.

Harry released his end of the map. It rolled up with a snap. "We'll finish later, Jack."

Jack stroked his full auburn beard, looking unhappy.

"But sir," Renquist whined. "Your next appointment. What do I—"

"Have him wait. Mrs. Stannert," Harry indicated a plush chair on the far side of the desk, "please sit down." It was not an invitation, but a command. "I'll be back in a minute."

Harry gathered the map and papers. Jack finally spoke in a deep rumble. "I'll check those results again. We don't want to blast if there's any doubt. It'd be a waste of giant powder."

Harry shot a look at Renquist. "I need those figures before I leave tonight."

Inez twisted around and watched with satisfaction as Renquist scurried out the door to the reception area.

Twisting back, she saw Jack open a side door to a second room. She spotted an enormous safe inside before the door shut behind the two men.

Alone in the office, Inez sat back and allowed herself to look about more closely. Despite the large window, the room felt closed in with its ornate paneled walls. Harry's rosewood desk and a cluster of chairs, including the one under Inez, floated on a maroon Brussels carpet surrounded by a sea of inlaid wood floor. Inez marveled that, considering how many filthy boots probably tramped in and out, the floor and carpet looked clean. *I'll wager someone cleans it every day.* A brass parlor stove heated the room, and a large painting of the War Between the States hung opposite the window.

All and all, it fit Harry to a T.

Her attention focused next on the desk. He'd removed all the papers, leaving only a large blotter, several expensive pens, a silver-chased inkwell, and two standing leather photocases facing away from her.

Another rumor was that Harry had a wife, somewhere back East. A woman of delicate temperament, perhaps an invalid, who could not or would not face the rigors of the West. Yet, no mention of "wife and family" had ever entered their conversations.

Unable to rein in her curiosity any longer, Inez glanced at the side door, still closed, then used a gloved finger to rotate the larger of the two cases in her direction.

It did not yield the half-expected family portrait. Instead, a framed tintype showed two groups of uniformed men facing each other in front of a military tent. Shadows from a tree dappled the men in dark and light.

Inez reached for her reading glasses for a better look, then hesitated, looking around again.

Both doors were still closed. The only sounds were the ticks of the grandfather clock standing sentinel behind her and the subdued pulse and wave of heavy machinery outside.

Inez pulled her glasses out from her pocket, slipped them on, and leaned closer.

The officer in the dark uniform. Harry, without a doubt. The angular profile and erect carriage were unmistakable. He had his hat tucked under one arm, his dark hair reflecting in the ferrotype like a mirror. *I wonder where this was taken. Harry never talks about the War.*

The surrounding faces were somber. One, in particular, drew her attention. Close by Harry's side, a young fellow stared into the camera. His belligerent expression, coupled with a mustache of grandiose proportions, made her smile. *What a ridiculous mustache! Remove it, he'd look no more than sixteen. A boy impersonating the men around him.* Mustache aside, there was something familiar about the face and eyes, about the way the boy stood at military ease with hands clasped behind him.

A single footfall behind her was her only warning.

Chapter Twenty-One

Harry reached over her shoulder and snapped the photocase shut, nearly catching her nose. He rounded his desk and dropped the case into the top drawer as he lowered himself into his leather chair.

Inez snatched off her reading glasses, feeling like a child caught sneaking change from the church offering. "Why, Harry, I don't remember you ever saying you were an officer in the War. A colonel? A major? I could never keep the insignia straight." Inez listened to herself babble.

Harry sat back, fingers interlaced across his waistcoat. His tie was now straight; silver cufflinks winked at his wrists.

"I doubt you rode through the storm and burst into my office to hear war stories." His tone was mild, as if her transgression was a minor one. He didn't smile, but an expectant air about him unnerved Inez far more than if he'd taken her to task for snooping.

While Inez pondered how to begin, he added, "Given up living with your ghosts?"

She stiffened. "I also didn't ride all this way to discuss my son. Or my husband." She threw down the word *husband* like a gauntlet.

Harry let it lie. "So, Inez, why *are* you here?"

She cleared her throat, retrieved Emma's much-folded note, and opened it before pushing it across the desk toward him. She could reach only halfway across the wide expanse of rosewood.

"I'm here on behalf of Mrs. Rose. I'm certain you're aware of Joe Rose's untimely demise. She asked me to reconcile her husband's accounts. I have some questions about your business with him."

Harry shifted his gaze to the activity outside the window. Five ticks of the grandfather clock sounded in the silence. Finally, he opened a side drawer and extracted a cigar. He clipped the cigar and lit it. The paper lay, untouched, in the no-man's-land between them.

When he looked back at her, the expectant air had evaporated and his pale eyes were colder by degrees.

"You've enlisted help in your endeavors."

He must mean Elliston. Damn Jed and his "discreet" inquiries.

"Joe's books are incomplete, a mess," she improvised. "The last entry for Silver Mountain was two months ago. But there are gaps in the accounts, so I can't be certain who is waiting for assay results or who owes money to him. Or his estate."

"So you can't close the books." He rocked in the swivel chair and exhaled. A blue cloud of smoke obscured the air between them. "I might be able to spare Renquist Monday. He knows the mining businesses around here. Could help you tie up loose ends."

The very thought of Renquist in proximity to her twisted Inez's stomach. Her aversion must have been apparent, because Harry quickly lifted a hand, and said, almost wearily, "Do it your way, Inez. You're obviously set upon a course of action."

"Renquist is…" She couldn't think of a term appropriate for polite company.

"Renquist is exactly what he appears. A crack man with the numbers."

Determined to steer the conversation back to Joe, Inez said, "I didn't come here to beg for help. I'll be frank. It's clear something happened between you and Joe. You were his primary client. Until October. Then, there's the night he died. As you probably recall, I was present when he came into my saloon and shouted that you 'owed him.'" *And called you a son of a bitch.*

"So, what did you owe him, Harry? And why weren't you at his funeral this afternoon?"

Harry raised his eyebrows. "Is that what this visit is about?"

He glanced over at the grandfather clock, impatience filling his face. "You're wasting your time and mine. Silver Mountain has no outstanding business with Rose. His books are correct on that point. As for the funeral, I have a business to run. As you do." He began to stand, obviously expecting her to take the hint.

She stayed seated. *If I'm going to get anything from him, it's got to be now.* She leaned forward, tapping Emma's note for emphasis. "The Roses are destitute. According to Mrs. Rose and Nils Hansen that's in no small measure due to you."

Harry froze, half out of his chair, then sank back down.

She continued, "You met with Mrs. Rose. At your hotel. It must have been at your instigation. You threatened to ruin Joe and you reduced her to tears." Inez knew she was making tenuous connections, but she had to say something. Something that Harry would deny, or qualify, or—

"She said that?" There was the anger, at last.

Harry picked up the note, penned in Emma's delicate handwriting. He read it as if looking for clues. *Or trying to decide what to say next.*

He tossed the stationery on the desk and leaned back again. More smoke.

When he spoke, his voice was deliberate. "Joe Rose was a liar and a cheat. He falsified his assay reports. That's why we stopped doing business. I couldn't trust him."

"How..." Inez couldn't believe it. Couldn't think where to proceed from there.

Harry watched her steadily, as if he knew the directions her mind raced. "We had suspicions. Then Hansen came to me. I double-checked his story, split some samples, just to

be certain. When I got the results, I had a talk with Rose."
His colorless eyes had all the warmth of a glacier.

"As for this 'rendezvous' you're accusing me of, Mrs. Rose
requested that meeting. Her husband was out of town, she
was low on household funds and thought Silver Mountain
was delinquent. Rose'd apparently left her in the dark." Harry
extinguished his cigar. "I told her exactly what I've told you.
Without mentioning Hansen."

She closed her eyes. *This can't be true. But if it is, it explains
a great deal. Why Emma lied about meeting Harry. Why she
wants the books balanced with as little fuss as possible. And why
she wants to leave Leadville. It might even explain why Joe took
out the loan. Maybe he was trying to cover costs, so Emma
wouldn't find out.*

"Mrs. Stannert. If I might offer some advice." Harry's tone
made clear he thought the odds of her accepting it were low.
"You'd be doing Rose's widow a favor by dropping the matter.
If Rose had creditors, they would have found you by now.
The more you dig into his life, the more unpleasantness you'll
find, I guarantee. That's not to the family's benefit. And,
although you persist in thinking the worst of me, I did take
his family into account. Rose and I had a deal. He agreed to
leave town, I agreed to not press charges. How he explained
himself to other clients was," Harry shrugged, "not my concern."

He stood and escorted her to the door. "I'm expecting
other visitors."

Inez turned Harry's explanation over in her mind, as if it
were a line of music. She said faintly, "I just can't believe it.
Joe, cheating? Why?"

Harry reached past her and held the door closed.

"Why? Look around. Getting rich is everyone's preoccu-
pation in this town. Even yours."

She flinched, remembering the hopes and heartaches she
had confided. *I should have known that Harry wouldn't offer
information without exacting payment.*

He continued, "When the race to wealth is everything, some count integrity and honesty as liabilities."

He looked hard at her, as if trying to decipher if she was listening.

"Well, Harry, seems you're among the first at the finish line." She tugged at her gloves, making a show of her readiness to depart.

"With the saloon and your shares of Silver Mountain stock, you won't finish last, Inez." His hand lowered to the door-knob. "I hope you heed my words. But then," his voice held bitterness and something darker, "your terms seem to be the only ones acceptable."

"Then, Harry, we have something in common after all. We both prefer doing things our own way."

They stared at each other. His physical closeness felt like an invasion, but Inez, door at her back, was loathe to sidestep, retreat. *Full retreat and surrender. That's always what Harry demands—*

"Waaall who the Sam Hill's in there anyways? I got news for Gallagher."

She recognized that voice and, judging from his expression, so did Harry.

Harry gripped Inez's arm and pulled her close. "Next time we have a private meeting, we'll discuss other matters. You can't avoid me forever."

He threw open the door, revealing Renquist and Marshal Hollis. Hollis saw Inez and sneered.

"Renquist." Harry's voice carried the threat of a storm.

"The marshal just got here, Mr. Gallagher. He was late. I didn't have time to ask him to wait."

"Get Jack. Have him escort Mrs. Stannert to town."

"*Mr.* Gallagher," she pulled away, indignant. "I'm quite capable of—"

"*Mrs.* Stannert." Harry captured her arm again and pro-pelled her toward the entrance, away from Renquist and Hollis. He lowered his voice. "This is a matter of practicality, not gallantry. You were seen coming up here. You're going to be seen leaving and arriving safely back in town. I want no 'accidents.' No speculation."

Jack appeared.

Harry turned, still gripping Inez's elbow. "Once Mrs. Stannert is delivered to town, call it a day. We'll talk about the drift tomorrow."

Jack looked pained. "How about I get one of the militia to take her back. I was going over those maps."

"You see her back. Safe and sound." Harry's tone brooked no arguments.

Resigned, Jack pulled a winter overcoat and wide-brimmed hat off a row of pegs. He went out the front door, calling, "Bring up that horse and cutter!"

Renquist twitched Hollis' sleeve, indicating the office. "This way, Marshal."

Harry walked Inez to the entrance and waited until she was seated in the cutter. As she picked up the reins, he said, "Safe journey, Mrs. Stannert. See you tomorrow night."

Chapter Twenty-Two

Up in the saloon's dressing room, Inez smoothed the bodice of her chocolate-brown polonaise. Her funeral outfit was draped over the tops of the room screens, damp reminders of the afternoon and her trip back from Silver Mountain.

Inez lifted the lamp from its holder and carried it out of the dressing room. Abe was waiting in the office, with a cup of coffee. "Thought you could use this."

She set the coffee, untasted, on the rolltop desk and paced by the window while Abe opened the safe. Outside, traffic surged up and down State Street. Snow blew softly from the night sky.

"I wonder when State will get gaslights," she said aloud.

Abe sat on the loveseat, cashbox in hand. "Town's Improvement Association sure worked fast on Harrison and Chestnut. Guess they're thinkin' about investors. Money men won't gamble on anything but a respectable, first-class operation."

Abe watched as Inez continued to pace. "You gonna tell me?"

"Tell you what?"

"When you came back from Fryer Hill, I figured you must've shot Harry. It was the most likely reason for your murderin' face. So, is there gonna be an empty chair at the table tomorrow night? Or did you just wing him?"

"No, I didn't shoot him. But I wish to God I had." Inez clenched her fists. After a moment, she sat down beside Abe.

"Harry says Joe falsified his assay reports. Nils told him, and Harry's got proof. He also said Emma herself sought out a private meeting. Apparently, Joe didn't tell her that Silver Mountain was no longer a customer. No wonder Joe took out a loan. He was probably trying to cover the loss, for Emma's sake."

Abe set the box aside and settled back on the couch. Inez, head bowed, felt his dark eyes dwell on her for several bleak moments.

"So Harry just up and told you all this, and you weren't even holdin' a gun on him? Hmph. Don't seem like Mr. Gallagher, somehow. Even if you were bein' your usual charmin' self."

"I wasn't exactly charming."

"Thing is, you gotta certain flash and fire when you get all determined-like. I wouldn't discount its effect. Especially on Harry."

She shrugged.

Abe rested one long arm along the back of the couch. "Well, now. I don't rightly know what Harry's up to, but don't take his talkin' to heart."

"The marshal showed up. He's in Harry's pocket, I'm certain."

She leaned against Abe's outstretched arm and closed her eyes. The smell of sweat and smoke pulled her back to when it was just the three of them. Her, Mark, and Abe. No ghosts from the past. No worries about the future.

Abe shifted and withdrew his arm. "Inez, I've been meanin' to ask. Have you thought about goin' to California with Emma and Joey?"

She opened her eyes and stared out the window. The wind paused. White flakes appeared at the top of the pane and drifted down to vanish from sight beneath the sill. Something inside her froze. Like a small animal trying to escape notice through immobility.

"No."

"We cash out of Leadville, you'd have a considerable sum. You could get your young'un back. Move to Sacramento. Do something different."

And what about you? She didn't say it. What came out instead was "But if Mark comes back…"

The pain she'd fought to contain seemed to grow and envelope the room. Side by side, Inez and Abe watched more fat disks of snow splat into the window and slide down the glass into oblivion.

"And you're not here." Abe's gentle voice finished her sentence. "Well, just thought I'd ask. See which way the wind was blowin'."

He stood. "We can't leave Useless by hisself too long."

Inez felt weary to the bone. *Tomorrow night, Harry'll sit next to me while I deal the cards, not say a word about today. As if it never happened.*

Sometimes, the pressure of his presence combined with the ache of missing her husband and son made her want to walk out of Leadville forever. *Abe's right. I could say to hell with it and start a new life elsewhere.*

The thought pulled like the night sky. But like the sky, it shed no light or warmth.

<>< ><>

Bracketed by Abe and Useless, Inez locked up the Silver Queen. Useless shuffled his feet. "I appreciate you lettin' me be a bardog tonight."

Inez pocketed the key. "We couldn't have managed without you."

Useless snuffled into his muffler. "I always wanted to work the bar, y'know. Mrs. DuBois, she never gave me the chance." He headed down State.

Even though it was after two, men still milled about the twenty-four-hour music halls and saloons. Blasts of brass bands and the tinkling of pianos pumped out the doors as they opened and closed. The restlessness of the streets echoed Inez's disposition. Her mind turned over the events of the day, placing bits and pieces side by side, looking for a fit. *Nils told Harry that Joe fixed Silver Mountain's assays. How did he know? Is there something we overlooked in the laboratory?*

"Abe. Let's go to Joe's office."

"Now?"

"I want to take another look around, just for a minute. If Joe was falsifying assays, there should be some sign."

"Inez, we've been over every inch of that place."

"But we were after his records, Chet's samples."

"Do you have any idea what you lookin' for?"

"I'd like to look at what's left of his equipment. The furnace, especially. If Joe was cheating, how did he do it?"

"All right, all right. I say no, you'll go anyway. Too late at night for a woman t' walk around by herself."

"I don't need an escort. I'm armed. I can take care of myself."

"Armed, yeah, with a peashooter. Now, if you had a shotgun or heavy artillery." Abe sighed. "Let's make it fast."

As they approached the assay office, Abe put out an arm to stop her. "What's that?"

"What?"

A dim light flickered deep inside the building.

"That." Abe unbuttoned his greatcoat and pulled out his old Army Colt. "Someone's in there."

"For heaven's sake, put that away!" hissed Inez. "When was the last time you shot anyone?"

"Been years as you damn well know. Knife's more reliable. But I'll do it if I got to."

The ghost light wavered and vanished.

"Someone's in the back." A snake of tension twisted down her spine. She pulled her small revolver out of her cloak pocket and eased the safety off.

"Aren't we a pair of gunfighters," grumbled Abe. "Let's hope there's only one fella in there or we're in serious trouble."

Inez reached out. The door swung open at a touch. They eased into the front of the office, through the counter-gate, and into the narrow passageway to the laboratory.

The light brightened as they inched forward, Abe first. As they approached, Inez made out a kerosene lamp, turned low.

Inez identified the scraping of metal against metal at the same time that she recognized the broad back of the man bent before the cast iron stove.

"Hansen!" Her voice snapped like a whip.

Nils yelped and banged his head on the lip of the stove. A small shovel clattered to the floor, scattering ashes. He turned. Soot-blackened hands shot in the air. "F' God's sake, don't shoot!"

Abe dropped the muzzle of his Colt toward the floor. "Nils?"

Inez pushed past Abe. "Isn't it enough that you robbed Joe of his reputation and his life by going to Gallagher? Are you back to steal what's left?"

Nils' voice shook along with his raised hands. "What do you mean?"

Inez did not lower her gun. "Don't play games with me. Abe has a soft spot for creatures and human conditions. I do not. I could shoot you right now and claim we mistook you for a burglar."

Abe's voice came from behind. "We?"

Inez ignored him. "Now that Joe is in the ground and his family destitute, have you come back for whatever you couldn't find the first time?"

"It wasn't me!" Nils sounded frantic. "I started thinking on what you said about Mrs. Rose, how she's got no money. I still had a key to the office. I wanted to see if Joe stashed his assayed silver and gold in the ash pan. Most assayers do that. It's not stealing, just part of business. I even found some. Over on the counter."

In the flickering lamp light, Inez saw what looked like a small dusty pile of rice.

Nils rushed on. "I thought I'd give it to Mrs. Rose." A thought seemed to strike him like a hammer. "Does *she* know I went to Gallagher?"

Inez's trigger finger ached to squeeze the quarter-inch needed to fire. "You're no better than Judas!"

"But Joe *was* cheating," Nils whispered, staring at the small gun aimed at his chest, not six feet away. "I *saw* him. Shooting me won't change that, Mrs. Stannert."

Abe reached over and pushed down the muzzle of her gun. "What'd you see, son?"

Nils exhaled in a quivering sigh and slumped against the stove. "The bellows." He nodded at the large bellows hanging next to the assay furnace. "One of the last times I was working here, I saw him pump up the assay fire until it was hot. Too hot."

"You saw this?" Inez glowered, daring him to continue.

"I was in the office, saw down the hallway. He was in front of the furnace, but when he moved to shut the door I saw the fire. It's supposed to be orange yellow. He had it up to straw yellow, almost yellow white. Silver vaporizes when it's that hot. When that happens, the assay comes in low, showing less silver than there really is."

"Why would he do that?" Inez tried to puzzle out the profit in a depressed silver assay.

Nils rubbed his face slowly. When he dropped his hands, his face was streaked with soot and despair. "A seller wants the assay high. A buyer wants it low, to drive the price down. But I don't know who that assay was for. He was doing most of the chemistry himself, leaving me to haul bags around, crush the samples, take in orders. The last time he went to Denver, I looked for his assay notes, to figure out what he was doing to who. I never found them."

Inez glanced at Abe. He nodded to show he'd heard.

"And Silver Mountain?" Inez asked.

"Mr. Gallagher was buying up the claims around Silver Mountain. Everybody knew he used Joe for assays. Joe knew the area, could tell if someone borrowed a bucket of ore from somewhere more promising...y'know, salted a claim. Anyhow, Joe did all of Gallagher's samples himself. He said Gallagher wanted to be sure nothing was tainted."

Nils laughed bitterly. "If that's true, the joke's on him. I know for a fact, Joe inflated those assay results, made 'em run high. I figured he was in cahoots with the sellers. Maybe they thought Gallagher's so rich, what's the difference if he sinks a few thousand dollars in a worthless hole."

Abe walked over to Nils, grabbing a chair as he went. He set the chair beside him. "Better tell us the rest, son."

Nils fell into the chair. The muscles in his arms jumped beneath his worn blue workshirt as he kneaded his hands on the thighs of his jeans. "I looked at the final assay certificates." He wiped his nose with his sleeve.

"We'd assayed some of the claims before, early summer. These results were different. Joe was doing something, maybe pulling out dross after crushing the samples or splitting them." Despite the cold, Nils was sweating. "That leaves more silver per gram weight. Or maybe he added chlorine to the water in the parting process. There's lots of ways an assayer can cheat. Especially when no one's watching too close."

Inez spoke. "So you went to Harry with this story. You had no proof, outside of some previous numbers. How could you remember those from way back then?"

Nils hunched his shoulders. "I got a claim, I keep up with the news in the district. And I got a talent for numbers. I figured if I told Gallagher, he'd watch his back. But he already knew things weren't right. They were blasting and not finding what they expected. Gallagher'd split some samples and sent the matches to a Georgetown outfit, on the quiet."

"So you quit, got a job at Kelley's, and Joe died." Inez glanced at Abe, who was leaning on the opposite doorframe.

Nils bowed his head. "He did it to me too."

"What?" Abe straightened up.

With his hands clasped and head bowed, Nils looked like he was about to pray. "I staked my first claim mid-summer. It looked good, so I asked Joe to assay it. He came back sayin' I must've been mistaken, the area ran hot and cold, and I must've hit a cold spot." Nils shook his head. "He offered to set me up with a buyer. I sold that claim for a hundred. Just about covered what I put into it. When he was in Denver, I went to the Recorder's Office. Y'see, after Gallagher, I'd started wondering. Well, that hole in the ground had been sold again for three thousand dollars."

Abe exhaled and glanced at Inez. "Guess we found what we came for."

Chapter Twenty-Three

"Did you believe Nils last night?" Inez pushed her breakfast away, nearly untouched. Abe, feet up on a nearby kitchen chair, was rewrapping his knife handle with a new leather strip. The old leather curled on the saloon's kitchen table like a sluffed-off snake skin.

"Don't think he was lyin', under the circumstances."

"None of it sounds like Joe." Inez thought of the brass check for Mattie Silks' parlor house. She took a deep breath. "Abe, there's something else—"

Bridgette bustled in. "That painter of yours, I just gave him some biscuits, he's been hard at work all morning."

Inez pushed back her chair. "Abe, let's talk later. I want to see what Llewellyn's up to."

New caulking made white stripes on the planks of the bar's back wall. Llewellyn hopped off a short ladder, brushing biscuit crumbs off the canvas apron covering his ruffled shirtfront. He gestured toward the wall. "Once that dries, a couple coats of white, and the canvas is ready." He opened a satchel and pulled out *Paradise Lost*. "Thank you for the loan. Most educational."

"Ah then, a test. Satan's ultimate sin was?" She retrieved the book.

He shrugged. "I read mostly for the descriptions of Heaven and Hell."

Inez smiled. "The sin of injured pride."

Subdued light rippled across the room. Inez turned toward the entrance. "We're not open yet," she said to the backlit figure.

The figure took a step forward and materialized into Reverend Sands. "This is a social call, Mrs. Stannert."

Inez hesitated, remembering their conversation at Emma's doorstep, the veiled threat—and invitation—behind his words.

She realized he'd approached and now stood but a few feet away. "Please," he said gently. "I'd like a private word with you."

She wavered. *Oh, what possible harm could come of a conversation. He turns rude, I'll have Abe throw him out.*

"There's an office on the second floor. Let's go to the kitchen first. We can get some coffee and I'll introduce you to Mrs. O'Malley."

Reverend Sands paused by the upright piano and read the hand-lettered sign aloud: "Please don't shoot the piano player, he's doing his damnedest."

"We're trying out someone new," Inez said. "Thursdays through Saturdays. 'I'll Take You Home Again Kathleen' ad nauseam."

He tapped a high, slightly sour G. "What happened to the previous player?"

"Not everyone in Leadville can read."

On the way to the kitchen, Inez summarized the house rules. "No drunks served a drink. No married men allowed to gamble."

"Thought I heard about a Saturday night poker game."

"A private game. You're welcome to join us. You've met some of the regulars. Doc Cramer, Mr. Gallagher." She waited to see if Harry's name would bring a response.

He nodded politely.

Eyes up and center. No innuendoes. That's good.

Bridgette was rolling out pastry. Flour particles hung in the air like dust motes.

"Reverend Sands, Mrs. O'Malley."

"Reverend Sands!" The rolling pin paused, mid-roll. "What a pleasure. I've heard about you, I have."

"You have?" Reverend Sands raised his eyebrows at Inez.

Bridgette blushed to the top buttons of her wool overdress. "Oh no, not from Mrs. Stannert. Around town."

"Leadville was that impressed with my first sermon." A smile etched deep lines at the corners of his eyes.

"Well now, when a nice-looking and by all accounts unattached gentleman like yourself comes to town, ladies get interested and tongues start a-wagging."

"Bridgette!" Inez couldn't decide if she was amused or horrified.

Sands turned to Inez. "Quite all right, Mrs. Stannert. Truth to tell, it's flattering to find myself so noticed. I'll be on my best behavior."

"Abe, Reverend Sands and I will be in the office discussing church business."

Abe stopped wrapping the knife hilt and looked the reverend over. "Reverend. Got a piece of advice for you." He pointed the blade at Sands. "You want to stay healthy, you'd best carry a sidearm."

Sands spread his hands. "I'm a man of the cloth, Mr. Jackson."

"Don't make no nevermind. Even women go armed in Leadville. Ask Mrs. Stannert if you don't believe me." Abe returned to his task.

Inez realized with a start that Abe was right: The only thing interrupting the reverend's somber garb was a silver watch chain, looping across his black waistcoat. *No gun.* It was as unexpected as finding a man standing barefoot in a snowbank.

Once in the office, Reverend Sands strolled to the window. Mount Massive towered four thousand feet above Leadville's rooftops. "Impressive."

His gaze lowered to the desk and William's photograph. "Handsome little fellow. Do I detect a family resemblance?" He reached out. To Inez, the sight of his fingers on the glass-covered photograph felt like an invasion of her heart.

She moved quickly, picked up the case, and snapped it shut. He looked startled. "Pardon. I meant no disrespect."

She slid the palm-sized case into her pocket, reminded of yesterday and Harry's photograph. "It's a painful subject." She motioned him to the loveseat. "Now, you had something you wanted to discuss?"

Reverend Sands walked over to the overstuffed couch and remained standing. He removed his hat, ran a hand through his light brown hair. The light picked out gray at his temples. He appeared tired and somewhat chagrined. "It seems that I've offended you. I came to make a confession and offer an apology."

"A minister confessing to a member of his flock? Most unusual." She settled into the desk chair.

"Nothing about this situation is usual." He sat on the edge of the couch and leaned forward, looking her straight in the eyes. "To be blunt, I committed the sin of not practicing what I preach. 'Judge not, and ye shall not be judged: condemn not, and ye shall not be condemned: forgive, and ye shall be forgiven.' Luke six, verse thirty-seven."

She raised her eyebrows. And waited.

"I judged by what I saw. A woman, running a saloon, with a husband—pardon me, if I'm mistaken here—nowhere in sight. In my experience, that usually means the woman is...." He floundered, then proceeded doggedly, a man charging up a steep slope into the unknown. "I was taken to task by those who know you better. I apologize and hope you won't hold my previous behavior against me."

She let the silence hang. His face remained open, contrite. *How much is real, how much is bullshit? Well, he's asking for a truce. It would be heartless to turn him down. Not to mention rude. If he's after something else, I expect I'll find out before this conversation ends.*

"Apology accepted. I suppose we both erred, since I judged you as well." Inez smiled.

He leaned back against the couch, taking a relaxed posture at last. His eyes, however, were vigilant. "We have something else in common. A desire to help the Roses."

Ah. Now we'll see.

He continued, "I understand you're settling Joe Rose's business affairs. It would be best if you wrapped them up quickly."

"What's the hurry? Emma said she wasn't leaving until the new year."

"True. But if she can leave earlier, all the better."

He's not answering the question. Let's see what he knows.

"Reverend, Joe didn't leave Emma a cent. Even worse, he put his business up as collateral for a large loan. Now, I'll ask again. What's the hurry?"

"Joe Rose took out a loan? Do you know why?"

Now he's interested. She crossed her arms and remained silent.

The reverend studied her. "My turn to raise, call, or fold, hmmm?"

The flag of truce dipped. "You fold, so help me, I'll shoot you as you walk out the door and claim that you brought it on yourself. And it would be the honest truth."

Reverend Sands laughed in genuine amusement. "You'd shoot a man of God in the back? By Jove, I believe you would. Well, Mr. Jackson did say you were a dangerous woman." He pulled out his silver pocketwatch and flipped open the cover. "There's no time now for the kind of conversation we need to have. Forgive me, but I'm going to call your bluff on this one, Mrs. Stannert." He stood and held out his hand.

"In that case, Reverend Sands, I'll grant you a reprieve. But we must have that conversation. And soon." She took his proffered hand and rose.

He smiled. "I think we're beginning to understand each other. And I'm glad we had a chance to talk." His tone imparted more significance to that last word than she would have imagined possible. "Perhaps," his warm clasp tightened slightly, "since you extended the invitation, I will drop in tonight. Perhaps we could talk further, after your game."

The implied question hovered in the air between them.

Inez's flustered gaze fell on the desk and the blank assay certificate from Joe's office. A memory clicked. "I knew it!" She pulled her hand from his grasp and pounced on the paper. "There's one more person for you to meet. A painter, who's doing some work for us. I think he did work for Joe as well."

Downstairs, Llewellyn was covering his caulking tin and preparing to leave.

Inez set the certificate on the bar. "You did these for Joe Rose."

He looked at the paper as if it might bite him.

"It's your work. I saw this very design on a scrap of paper in your workshop."

"I'm sorry, Mrs. Stannert. Jobs come and go. Assay certificates, bank drafts, stationery—"

"May I?" Reverend Sands picked up the certificate. "Nice work. Very professional. So, painting and engraving. Printing too, perhaps?"

"And signs," Inez added.

"Hmmm." Sands' expression reminded her of his remark on sheep and wolves. "I need some marriage certificates. A design like this will do."

Llewellyn stuffed caulking tools into his satchel. "Engraving's only a sideline."

Sands leaned over the bar. "But you do it often enough to forget the clients, right? This," his finger jabbed the paper, "is exactly what I'm after."

Llewellyn shrank back, then regrouped. "Of course, Reverend, if you insist. But I probably won't get to your certificates right away. I've got Mrs. Stannert's project, I've got other commissions—"

"I'll come to your workshop. We'll talk business."

"I'm not always in."

"I'll find you."

Llewellyn paled at the ominous tone.

Sands addressed Inez. All courtesy. "May I keep this?"

"Suit yourself."

"Thank you." It disappeared inside the black overcoat. "Until later, Mr. Tremayne." He smiled at Inez. Winter retreated. "See you tonight, Mrs. Stannert."

Llewellyn watched Sands leave. "Who did you say that was?"

"Reverend Sands. The interim reverend for our church."

He shouldered his ladder and bag. "The less I have to do with him the better."

Inez leaned her elbows on the bar and watched Llewellyn hurry out.

Abe appeared and lifted the cat from her curled-up comfort on the bar. "What was all that about?"

"The reverend wants some marriage certificates done up. I think Llewellyn's got himself another customer. Not that he's very pleased about it."

"That's not what I meant."

She sighed. "Reverend Sands wants a truce. For the Roses' sake."

"Hmmph. You tell him about Nils?"

"No. Of course not."

"Glad to hear. Just because he packs the Good Book don't mean he's honest." Abe put on a clean apron. "Fella puts on some outfit that makes him into someone folks trust: an apron for a bardog, a black suit for a minister. Mix a bit of truth with the lies, real smooth, no one knows what's what. Just remember, he ain't here permanent. Six months, mebbe sooner, he's gone. He's got no real stake in the Roses, Leadville, or you."

The words unexpectedly stung. "Don't preach, Abe. It doesn't suit you. Besides, if we're going to sidestep all who aren't what they seem, that'd be nine-tenths of the town."

"Yeah, but pourin' drinks, fixin' wheels, or pullin' teeth is a damn sight different from doctorin' folks' souls."

"Well, we'll see if he's up to more than preaching."

"You can bet he is."

Chapter Twenty-Four

Inez adjusted the small silver butterfly perched on her chignon as she conducted a quick visual inspection of the spittoons in the card room. Her lapel watch showed a quarter to eight. Her players would be arriving soon.

She glanced around. Comfortable upholstered chairs snugged up to a round mahogany table, parlor stove spinning out warmth. The rug underfoot echoed the leaf pattern of the gold-flocked wallpaper. Ornate bronze lamp sconces cradled lamps set high to banish shadows. All reflected Mark's vision of elegant interior decorating, conducive to the masculine pursuits of whiling away time and money.

A staccato roar of voices cut off with the click of a closing door. Turning from the sidebar, Inez saw Useless holding a box of high-grade liquor. "Over here, Useless." She shifted the crystal glasses to one side.

When he didn't respond, she looked up.

He stood, trapped behind the box, staring at the square low-cut neckline of her dress. The words that finally ground out were innocuous enough. "You sure look nice, Mrs. Stannert."

Inez looked down, brushing the watered silk maroon bodice. "I haven't worn this since summer." *Since Harry.* Earlier that evening, she'd pulled the shimmering dress from the depths of the upstairs wardrobe on an impulse. An impulse engendered by the reverend's lingering hand clasp that morning and his promise to "drop in."

She continued, "This was one of my husband's favorites. He always said, the lower the neckline, the less attention men pay to the cards. I swear, if he'd had his druthers, he'd've had me prancing around looking like one of Cat DuBois' boarders."

"You're purtier than them girls," Useless choked out. "Before you hired me, I used to come and watch you work the bar. I remember seein' you in that dress. Makes your skin look like, like…"

Bottles of bonded Kentucky bourbon and Portuguese port clinked and tinked as his shaking hands gripped the rough corners of the box.

Inez frowned at the turn of conversation, his odd deportment. *Useless needs lessons in decorum. No wonder respectable women like Susan and Emma shy away.*

A shadow zipped out from under the sideboard and veered away from her. The rat zigzagged toward the door where a sizeable gap between sill and frame promised escape.

Inez gripped her skirts with both hands. For an insane moment, she visualized pulling out her gun and ending the rodent's mad dash to freedom. "Do something!"

Useless moved faster than she'd ever seen him move. He reached the rat and stomped with a force that shook the boards beneath her feet.

The rat's ear-piercing screech blended with Inez's shriek. "Useless! Jesus Christ!"

Useless looked down. He lifted his boot. Bits of gore dripped from the sole, plopped to the rug. The tail, the only part that remained unmashed, twitched once.

"Oh my God! What possessed you!"

"Sorry, sorry," he mumbled, shrinking. "I, uh, didn't want to drop the box."

Rat fur, guts, and splattered blood glistened on the carpet, imposing a mangled pattern on the maroon and gold wool leaves.

Inez thought she would lose the contents of her stomach on the spot.

The door cracked open and the cacophony of the saloon washed over her. Jed Elliston hesitated, looking first at Useless, who'd hastily hidden the rat remains beneath his boot again, then at Inez. "Mrs. Stannert, a word with you. It's about Joe Rose."

Inez forced out a response in a tone approaching normal. "Certainly. In the office."

Jed turned around and headed toward the stairs.

As she passed Useless, Inez hissed, "Clean it up. Now! The others will be here any minute. Good God, Useless. You really lived up to your name this time. If the carpet's ruined, you'll pay for it out of your wages."

Revulsion added intensity to her tongue-lashing. Useless ducked his head, but not before Inez saw a sullen anger in his eyes.

Climbing the stairs, she fought to bring her twisted insides under control. *I need a drink. Soon as this chat with Jed is finished.*

In the office, she turned to Jed, eyebrows raised in question.

Careful grooming aside, there was something beaten in his carriage. He looked like a dog that had been whipped and kicked into the street. Elliston coughed and addressed a point high over her left shoulder. "I'm dropping the paper's inquiry into Rose's death."

"You're dropping—" She stopped. *What would convince a bulldog like Jed to drop a story?*

Then she knew. "What did Gallagher say to you?"

Elliston jerked his head back, as if she'd whacked his nose with one of his own rolled-up newspapers. "Harry Gallagher? Ha ha! No, no. This is strictly a business decision. I asked around. But there's no story. It's..." He ran out of steam. "Miss Carothers has the ledger," he finished lamely.

Inez sighed, too drained to push him any further. She led him to the door, saying, "Well, you tried. Don't think any more on it. A nice evening of cards is what we need. And a drink. We both need a drink."

They found Doc outside the card room, brandy in hand. "Ah, a quorum is developing. And here's Bob."

Inez flashed her hostess smile at Bob Evan, owner of the biggest mercantile in Leadville. Evan had arrived early in town, hoping to strike it rich. Story was, while hacking through the rocky subsoil of his claim, he'd broken the shaft of his pickaxe. He'd vowed then and there to make his fortune not from silver but from shovel handles, drill bits, rifles, wool socks—whatever was needed by the miners. He played cards like he ran his business: with careful calculation, but without disdaining an occasional risk.

The four of them entered the card room. Useless stood at the sidebar, setting up the bottles. Inez glanced down at the rug. The stain looked innocent. As if it could have been caused by a spilled drink, a mis-aimed squirt at a spittoon.

Jed Elliston headed straight for the liquor. Useless picked up the box, which now held rags bunched around a suspicious lump. He hurried out, avoiding Inez, just as David Cooper arrived, brushing snow from his fur coat.

"I see I'm not late after all." Cooper smiled at Inez, every inch the East Coast lawyer. His successful Leadville practice rested on settling claim disputes. He had an uncanny ability to guess which way judge and jury would lean. His mannered speech didn't reflect an unfortunate tendency to yield to impulse on the cards.

"Pick your poison, gentlemen." She settled in her chair, feeling the bulky train of dress flatten beneath her. Glancing about the table, she noted Nigel and Harry were missing. The others took their seats as Inez broke the seal on the cards.

Evan adjusted his brown corduroy jacket. "You look very fashionable, Mrs. Stannert. Lovely, as always." He squinted. "New dress?"

"Thank you, but no. Just one I haven't worn in a while." Inez suspected that Evan's concept of women's fashion was hampered by his main customers, miners and roustabouts. She privately bet he had a wardrobe full of corduroy, his fashion mainstay.

"Ah, here's Harry." Doc beamed. "Business hold you in abeyance?"

Harry removed his overcoat, still dusted with snow. "An overturned sledge on Stray Horse Gulch held up traffic." His eyes settled on Inez. "Evening, Mrs. Stannert."

"We're waiting on you, Harry." Cooper waved at the empty chair by Inez.

Inez tapped the deck of cards on the table. With Harry seated, she shuffled the stiff cards with an expert hand. "Ante up, gentlemen."

Quarter eagles rained onto the table. All murmuring ceased as she dealt out cards, one at a time, five cards face down. The players picked up their hands.

As was her habit, before looking at her own cards she scanned the men's expressions and postures. To her immediate left, Elliston's grim face looked a shade grimmer. *Nothing there.* Next to him, Doc straightened up a bit, no longer so snoozy. *Possible pair? Doc takes even two deuces as a good omen.* Evan peered through metal-rimmed glasses at his hand, noncommittal. *Hard to say. We'll see when the betting starts.* Cooper eased back in his chair, getting comfortable. *Settled in for the long haul. He must have something worthwhile.* Nigel's empty chair. Then Harry.

Harry was watching her. His gaze traveled leisurely down to encompass her gown. The color flew to her cheeks. *Perhaps it was a mistake to wear this dress.* She examined her own hand. Pair of queens. Jack, seven, five.

Elliston said, "Pass."

"Time to get the evening rolling." Doc threw in a quarter eagle.

Evan's coin chinked onto the pile.

"Oh, we can do better than that." Cooper added a half eagle.

Everyone stayed in. Cards were discarded, replacements dealt. Inez found no improvement to her pair of ladies. When Harry doubled Cooper's twenty-dollar bet, Inez groaned inwardly and stared at Harry, trying to divine his mind. No nervous ticks or mannerisms showed. Just a knowing smile that irritated her beyond belief. She hated backing down to him. *However...*

"I'm out." She closed her hand.

"Well, my dear, the house wins every time, in any case." Doc's consoling smile lifted the loose wrinkles around his jowls.

She reached for her coffee cup. Doc was right. The house got its cut from each pot. Her personal objective was to neither lose nor win an extravagant amount. Lose too much, it wiped out the house's take. Win too much...well, the customers didn't like losing. Especially to the house. And, despite all their gallantry, especially to a woman.

Elliston threw down his cards. "Out."

Doc shook his head. "Until more citizens pay their medical bills—"

"Guess they're paying me first." Evan added forty dollars.

Cooper stroked his close-cropped beard, examining Harry as if he was a potential juror of unknown quantity. "Raise you sixty."

Harry didn't even bother to look at his hand. "Double it."

Cooper said, "Call, Harry, you old devil. What've you got?"

Harry spread out a king-high straight.

"I'd've sworn you were bluffing." Cooper chucked his hand. Evan followed.

Doc swirled the brandy in his glass, "So, Harry, I hear you're headed east this spring. Doesn't our Chestnut Avenue measure up to Philadelphia's? Or are you in search of more capital?"

Harry counted his winnings, slid the house's portion toward Inez. "Philadelphia for family business. Then New York, Boston. Eastern capitalists are all afire about Leadville. I don't want that heat to go to waste. As for Chestnut, Leadville will never be the Philadelphia of the West."

"I dunno." Evan laced his hands over his brown waistcoat. "There's talk that Leadville might steal the title of capital city from Denver."

Harry raised an eyebrow. "Leadville needs more than gaslights, a telephone exchange, and an opera house to qualify as a capital. More law and order, for example."

"But a railroad." Evan's face glowed, as if he contemplated the Holy Grail.

Cooper nodded. "The Supreme Court should decide on the Santa Fe and D&RG case soon. I'm betting we have a line by summer."

A murmur of agreement circled the table. Folks took a serious interest in the legal and occasionally armed disputes between the Atchison, Topeka and Santa Fe and the Denver and Rio Grande railroads. While the court debated which would have right-of-way up the narrow Royal Gorge canyon to Leadville, both railroads continued to sabotage each other's tracks.

Harry leisurely lit a cigar. "Once a railroad, any railroad, sets up business, freighting costs will drop. I'm betting on D&RG, myself."

Everyone present knew that Jed's family fortunes rode on the Santa Fe.

Jed's face darkened. "Now that you've consolidated the claims around Silver Mountain, with Cooper's help, I've heard you're opening an assay office at the mine. Guess local business wasn't up to your standards, Harry."

Silence descended. No doubt all were remembering, as was Inez, Joe Rose's accusations the previous Saturday. And that Rose now lay buried in Evergreen Cemetery.

Chapter Twenty-Five

Unperturbed, Harry rolled his cigar ash into a crystal ashtray. "The mine's big enough to support a company assayer."

"Sounds like Silver Mountain is prospering, if silver prices are any indication." Doc, like many others in town, bought shares in the local mines and avidly followed production figures and the silver market.

"I'll put it this way, gentlemen. And Mrs. Stannert. Don't sell your shares of Silver Mountain yet."

"The way real estate's appreciating, Mrs. Stannert's sitting on a bonanza right here on Harrison and State. Last I heard, business district lots were going for ten thousand dollars." Cooper's eyes crinkled as he smiled at Inez. "Had any buyout offers lately?"

Inez cut the deck and watched Jed deal. "The saloon's still not for sale."

At the midnight break, Inez stopped by the bar. Abe poured an inch of brandy into the bottom of a coffee cup and handed it to her, then glanced at a nearby knot of dark-skinned men with somber faces. "More Exodusters. Don't know what they expected to find here that isn't in Kansas. More snow. More cold. Only work is underground. Most were dirt farmers from the South. A damn shame."

He capped the brandy and nodded toward the card room. "You might have a taker for that empty seat."

Reverend Sands stood inside the room, surveying the décor. He turned at Inez's approach and nearly sloshed his coffee onto the carpet at her feet. "Pardon me, Mrs. Stannert. I was just admiring the room." His gaze, which he valiantly attempted to keep at eye level, kept straying to her dress. "Exquisite. The décor, I mean."

"It's meant to be," she said with a hint of a smile. "Are you here to watch or play?"

"What's the limit?"

"No limit. Quarter eagle ante."

"I'll watch."

Inez continued to the kitchen for coffee. Strong to begin with, after hours on the range it was as black and impenetrable as the night sky. Her return found Doc expounding on clergy in saloons.

"I've witnessed more sermons than I can number where the good man of the cloth raves about the evils of cards and the devil in drink. All from the floor of a saloon! Dilutes the message, if I may say so."

From a chair by the stove, Reverend Sands said, "It depends, Doctor. If the point is to preach to sinners, one goes where the sinners are. And that's rarely the church."

"What about you?" Jed filled his pipe. "You don't rave from the pulpit about the sins and moral weaknesses of men?"

The reverend swirled his coffee meditatively. "My religious philosophy leans more to the adage, 'All things in moderation.' Where sin lies, I believe, is when we begin to see everything and everyone in absolutes. Black or white. Saved or damned. Pure or stained." He smiled at Inez. "I strive for a more balanced, rational approach to saving souls. The good Lord himself said, 'Let your moderation be known unto all men.' Philippians, four."

Doc banged enthusiastically on the table with one ham-sized fist. The glasses shivered. "My philosophy exactly!"

Evan interrupted. "Excuse me, but I'm here to play poker. Not discuss religion. Begging the reverend's pardon."

Inez nodded and began to shuffle.

‹›‹›‹›

"Last hand, gentlemen."

"Next Saturday is the twentieth. Almost Christmas." Cooper pulled out a slim leather case and extracted a last cigar. "Will you be open on the holiday, Mrs. Stannert?"

Inez watched Harry deal the cards. "You'll have to find your Christmas cheer elsewhere. We'll be closed."

He lit his cigar. "The only saloon that will be. But I suppose you can afford it."

"It's a question of priorities, Mr. Cooper."

Cooper exhaled, watching the smoke curl and disappear into the room's haze. "And after Christmas comes the Silver Soiree."

Evan spoke up. "I hear the guest list is exclusive. So, Cooper, you made the cut?"

Cooper's white teeth flashed in reply.

The final hand played out uneventfully, with Jed the winner. The players prepared to leave. As Inez accepted Jed's portion for the house, Cooper approached Harry, who was savoring the last of his cigar. Inez caught Cooper's low voice: "...the last holdout?"

Harry's reply slid to her under the general symphony of masculine voices. "This has dragged on too long. Everyone has a price. Find out his and pay it. Otherwise—"

"How's that Smoot handling, Mrs. Stannert? Had an opportunity to try it on a moving target yet?" Evan's voice drowned out the rest of Harry's response. The merchant had wandered over, near-empty glass in hand.

One hand still on the strongbox, Inez patted the concealed pocket in her overdress. Her Remington Number Two Pocket Revolver, Smoot's Patent, nestled inside. "It's my constant companion. But I've only wounded tin cans and bottles."

"Cleaning it regularly?" Evan set his glass on the table.

"Religiously."

"Interesting term when applied to weaponry." Sands set his cup by Evan's.

Inez gave up trying to eavesdrop on Cooper and Harry. "Carrying a gun *is* a religious matter around here. Only a fool would go unarmed—" She stopped, glancing involuntarily at the reverend's waistcoat. Below the watch chain, she saw the heavy gleam of a gun belt.

He finished her sentence. "In Leadville. So I've been told." His smile didn't hide the exhaustion on his face.

She cocked her head. "Long day, Reverend?"

"It was. After our talk this morning, I called on the Roses." He took a breath as if preparing to plunge into cold water. "Mrs. Stannert, would you allow me to walk you home? We could continue our conversation of this morning."

Inez hesitated, looking into his tired eyes. *Not blue. Not gray. Hard to pin down. Just like he is.*

Behind her, Harry shifted. Turning her head slightly, she could just see his profile. He appeared to be lending one ear to Cooper's exposition and another in her direction. The chandelier lights glinted off a silver cufflink as Harry leaned over to grind out his cigar in the ashtray. She remembered his proprietary grip on her arm as he propelled her through the door of his mining office. And his words: *"Next time, we'll discuss other matters."*

She faced the reverend. "It would be a pleasure. I'll meet you by the bar. I need a few minutes upstairs."

Chapter Twenty-Six

With profits in the safe, her day clothes on, and her cloak over her arm, Inez paused on the landing outside her office and examined the milling multitudes below. The scent of whiskey, stale bodies, and cheap tobacco rose with the smoky haze.

Reverend Sands stood talking with the Exodusters, who huddled together, stoop-shouldered and underdressed for the harsh mountain winter. She wondered how long it had been since they'd had a regular meal and how many Leadville saloons and restaurants had turned them away with the curt statement "We don't serve coloreds."

Inez approached Abe. "Did they get something to eat?"

"Coffee, leftover stew. Coffee was pretty thick."

She nodded a greeting at the haggard faces. Not one nodded back. Tattered gloves and mittens—some no more than rags—gripped tin mugs.

She turned back to Abe. "Can you close tonight without me?"

"You're leavin' now?" Concern flickered over Abe's face.

"I have an escort." She inclined her head in Sands' direction.

Abe's eyebrows collided with wrinkles of disbelief.

She hurried on. "I'm meeting Nigel at the bank early. I can't stay much longer tonight. I'm exhausted. Can you manage?"

Abe gathered up the empty bowls and stacked them in the tub destined for the kitchen. "Those men, they've got no money, no place to stay. I told them they could sleep on the floor tonight and tomorrow. I planned on stayin' so's Bridgette won't have a fit in the mornin'."

"Ready, Mrs. Stannert?" The reverend was at her side, adjusting his hat.

"Yes, I am. Good night, Abe. I'm glad you offered them the floor." Feeling guilty, Inez walked toward the door. The pianist, seeing her leaving, swung into "I'll Take You Home Again, Kathleen." *He'll pay for that.*

Outside, Inez exhaled, watching her breath snake away into the light pouring from the doors closing behind her. The storm had passed. Half a moon limned ragged clouds with a cold, fierce light.

She slid her gloved hand around the reverend's proffered arm and they maneuvered through the crowds on State. She was aware of how her hand nestled between the reverend's arm and his wool overcoat. It felt so solid. Safe. She wriggled her fingers experimentally. He turned his face toward her. Even though the wide hat brim cast a deep shadow, she could still see his expression. Warm. Waiting.

"So, Reverend. Why did you leave the Golden State and come to Cloud City?"

"Cloud City. Yes, I've heard Leadville called that." He glanced up at the moon breaking through racing clouds, then focused on negotiating around the brass band in front of the Board of Trade Saloon. When the trumpeting had faded behind them, he said, "Leadville's closer to heaven than Sacramento."

Inez sniffed. Sulfur fumes from smelters mixed with sewer stink. "It doesn't smell much like heaven."

Sands acknowledged her remark with a smile. "My interim term was up. Besides, Sacramento was too tame. I prefer ministering where it counts."

"Ah yes, you like preaching to the sinners. In that case, you should be spending more time on State Street."

"How do you know that I'm not?"

Inez considered this as they walked up Harrison. Reverend Sands interrupted her thoughts. "I hoped we could talk about Rose. I know about the crooked assay results, about his office. When I talk with folks about him, I sense a man living two lives: straight and narrow on the top, in deep trouble beneath. You knew him. Did you see any of that?"

Inez thought back. "He seemed more...reserved the last few months. But I can't say for certain. Emma never said anything to me, though."

"Any idea what might've been the problem?"

"I've wondered myself. Perhaps a large gambling debt? He must have been desperate. I can't imagine Joe doing what he did except out of desperation."

The reverend was silent, as if dissecting her words. He then said, "The people who were in his office might not have found what they were looking for. The family may be in danger. That's why I'm pushing them to leave Leadville sooner rather than later." He looked pointedly at her. "That danger could extend to you, since you're settling his affairs. It might be safer for you to hand over this business to his lawyer or banker."

"I can take care of myself," she said with some asperity.

Sands laughed. "Mrs. Stannert, you remind me of someone."

Sands slowed his gait, then stopped under the gaslight on the corner of Park Street. Without Harrison's sheltering buildings, the west wind whistled upslope across the Arkansas Valley and tugged at their overcoats.

Looking down the unlit street toward the white, distant peaks of Elbert and Massive, Sands tapped his gloved fingers on the buttons of his black overcoat before reaching a decision. He opened his coat, pulled out his pocketwatch, and flipped the casing open, angling it for Inez to see. An ambrotype fitted inside the cover showed a young boy and a girl on the edge of womanhood. The fair-haired boy had some baby softness lingering in his face, but the determined mouth sang of Reverend Sands. The girl looked like a younger, feminine counterpoint to the man standing by Inez.

"My sister and me. Soon after this was taken, our parents died of consumption."

Inez swallowed past the sudden lump in her throat. "I'm sorry to hear. What happened to you and your sister?"

Sands caressed the ghostly image with his thumb. "Judith and I were shuffled from relative to relative. Judith was all I had. Mother and father to me for all those years."

"Is she in California?"

He closed the watch with a click and tucked it back inside his waistcoat pocket. "Judith died during the War."

The ache in her throat grew. Sands rebuttoned his coat and gently refolded her hand back over his arm. "It all happened a long time ago. The point is, you remind me of her. No one told her what to do. Not even me."

They turned away from the light and started down Park.

In front of her house, Sands stopped. "There's something else."

He fished through his coat pockets and extracted a square, formal envelope. "I wondered if you might accompany me to this." He fumbled with the envelope, then pulled out the enclosure.

Inez ran a gloved fingertip over the embossed lettering and tipped the invitation to the moonlight. She read aloud, "Your presence is requested on Saturday, December 27, nine o'clock in the evening—" She stopped. "You have an invitation to the Silver Soiree?"

He watched her waver between temptation and caution.

"I'd be honored if you'd say yes, Mrs. Stannert. You could consider yourself a guide of sorts. Point out the illustrious folks of Leadville, explain some of the town's history. I hear there's going to be fine food, music, champagne from France, dancing—"

"French champagne? I doubt that. At the most, it might be from California, dressed up to look imported."

The mischievous smile of a five-year-old boy crossed his face. "Only one way to find out."

He opened his hands up and away from his sides, the gesture of an unarmed man. "I'll be the most proper of escorts. A perfect gentleman."

She laughed in spite of herself. "Very well, Reverend. Since you seem in need of a 'guide' and promise to be on your best behavior. So you don't mind being seen in the company of a saloonkeeper?"

He grinned back and dropped his hands. "No more than you mind being seen in the company of a minister."

As Inez unlocked her front door, she hesitated. "Reverend, one question. Does it snow in Sacramento?"

"Almost never. Why?"

Inez thought of the sled she and Abe had picked out for Joey for Christmas, wrapped and waiting in her back room. "I just wondered."

As she opened her door, Sands touched his hat. "Thank you for allowing me to accompany you home. I hope we might do this again soon."

"Yes. Well, good night." She shut the door softly and stood in the dark, thinking.

Chapter Twenty-Seven

By morning, the clouds had returned in force. A gray ceiling pressed down on the town and obscured the mountains. Hurrying to the bank, Inez noticed that people and objects cast no shadows. *Like paper dolls.*

The flat lighting made everything appear dirtier than usual: the raw, peeling lumber of hastily constructed buildings, the garbage encased in the snowbanks between boardwalk and street, the grimy creases on passing faces.

The bank looked staid and East Coast in its brick solidity. The brass knob turned in her hand, and she walked into the dim bank foyer. Light spilled from Nigel's office behind the two teller cages. Her boots echoed on the plank floors.

"Nigel?"

Inez thought she heard a cough, a muffled response. Striding with more certainty, she skirted the teller area, pushed open the assistant bank manager's door, and entered.

"I'm sorry, Nigel, I detest being late."

At first, she thought maybe he was taking a short nap, head down on the desk by the loan papers. Weary, perhaps, from waiting or from too long an evening sampling the nighttime entertainments of Leadville.

Then, she saw—

A slow red river, soaking the blotter, oozing across the cherrywood desk, dripping to the carpet.

Comprehension, then horror gripped her, shook her bones. She took two quick steps forward. Stopped, suddenly realizing there was too much blood for hope. She turned—

A gloved hand from behind grabbed her throat, cutting off her breath. Yanked off-balance, she slammed backward into her assailant.

Panic washed over her. Labored breathing filled her ears.

Inez jabbed with an elbow, connecting with a coat-padded body. She stamped her boot heel on an unseen foot as she attempted to twist away.

The grip on her neck grew tighter.

"Bitch!"

The whispered word overflowed with rage and something close to triumph.

Black spots danced before her eyes. Her anger and fear rose on a last resolve: *NO!*

Her hands grabbed one of the fingers at her neck, bending it back. The grip loosened. A hiss of pain erupted in her ear as she gasped for breath.

The body pressed to hers shifted.

Sudden pain split her head like a scream. Her vision exploded into black, streaked with white fireworks. The streaks receded like an express train at night, carrying her away.

The light winked out.

<><><>

A black sound in her head would not stop. Ugly buzzing filled her body with pain.

The buzz separated into voices. The voices into words.

One voice, filled with alarm: "The blood!"

Another voice, calm, almost matter-of-fact: "Head wounds bleed a lot."

Familiar.

"Are you certain she's not dead?"

The voices dissolved in a roar. She was swallowed, turning around in sound, more nauseated with each revolution.

She resurfaced.

"Does she know about—"

"No!" The familiar voice was sharp. Then slow and tired. "I don't know what she knows."

What I know?

"Shouldn't we remove—"

"Leave it."

Leave?

"She's moving!"

A warm hand enclosed her throat. She gasped. Ammonia vapors assaulted her. Coughing painfully, Inez opened watering eyes on an unsteady image of wood-beamed ceilings. She grabbed at the hand and tried to roll away but was hopelessly tangled in her long cloak and skirts.

The hand withdrew.

"Easy, easy, Mrs. Stannert."

Two faces met, crown to crown, in her narrow view of the ceiling. One belonged to bank manager Morris Cooke, his round countenance like a worried cherub unprepared to welcome her to Heaven. He held a small bottle of smelling salts.

The other belonged to Reverend Sands. Relief flooded his face. He flexed his ungloved fingers and glanced at Cooke. "There's a definite pulse. You can cap those salts."

She grabbed Cooke's arm, tried to speak. All that came out was a croak. "Nigel!"

Cooke's dismay increased visibly. He glanced at Sands as his shaking hands tried to cap the small vial.

Inez tried to sit up.

"Easy." The reverend applied gentle pressure to her shoulder to keep her down. Her head pillowed onto something soft. The distant buzzing sharpened and grew. The ceiling wavered, shading to gray. She moaned. Coughed. Pain spiked her throat.

Reverend Sands turned to the bank manager. "Get Doc. And the marshal."

Cooke nodded, then looked at Inez. His eyes reflected panic. "Please lie still, Mrs. Stannert."

After he'd left, Inez tried again to sit up. Sands made as if to stop her.

"No! I must see!" she croaked. The words sent agony shooting up her neck.

Sands settled back on his heels.

She struggled to sit amid a tangle of cloak, skirts, and petticoats. Then she saw what held her clothes.

A knife skewered a dead rat through her skirts into the floor.

Her stomach twisted. She grabbed a handful of wool and yanked. The fabric parted around the sharp blade like butter.

Free to move, she barely had time to turn away before retching on the carpet.

Reverend Sands waited until she was done. Then, he said gently, "A blow to the head can do that."

He offered her two crumpled handkerchiefs. Both streaked with blood.

Inez gingerly touched the back of her head. She looked at the wet glove, then down at her splattered dress. *So much blood.*

"We tried to clean you up." The reverend moved closer and placed a comforting arm around her shoulders. "Thank God you're all right."

She felt his fingers gently touch her hair, exploring the wound. "You'll recover. Which is more than I can say for Nigel Hollingsworth."

Sands looked long and hard at the rat, still pinned to the floor. In a single swift movement, he stood, wrenched out the knife, grabbed the rat by the tail, and threw it into a dark corner. He turned toward her, knife in hand.

"You realize you're lucky. You got a warning. If he'd wanted to kill you, he would've used this." Sands held up the knife. "As he did on Nigel. Not that." He pointed with the blade to a fist-sized globe at her feet, reflecting shattered light from its crystal facets. Nigel's paperweight.

Sands dropped the knife to the carpet and returned to her side. Squatting, he searched her face. "Did you see who it was?"

She shook her head. Then, as the room spun around, wished she hadn't.

Sands hastily put an arm around her shoulders. Concern marked his features. "Don't move. Don't talk. From the looks of it, you were nearly strangled. I'll get Miss Carothers or Mrs. Rose to stay with you. I'll come by later, after the morning service."

Hazy questions surfaced in her pain-filled mind. *What are you doing here? On a Sunday morning, with the bank manager, who's a Quaker and no member of the church?* She opened her mouth. No sound escaped.

Far away, a door banged open. Footsteps and voices approached, Marshal Hollis' nasal twang a counterpoint to Doc's limping gait.

Inez closed her eyes, wishing she were anywhere but sitting on the carpet, covered with blood and vomit, with Nigel's body lying in mute accusation behind her.

<><><>

"Inez. Can you hear me?"

Inez stirred, feeling flannel at her fingertips, a roaring pain in her head and neck. She opened her eyes to the familiar lace curtains of her bedroom, Susan Carothers perched on a rocking chair by the bed.

"Oh thank goodness. You looked at death's door when Doc and the marshal brought you in. I was so worried. But Doc said you're going to be okay. Maybe I shouldn't have awakened you, but…"

Something about Susan's posture reminded of Inez of a race horse at the starting line—straining forward, ready to leap at the drop. Susan pawed through her reticule, searching.

Inez heard Doc expounding in her parlor. *Probably drinking my brandy as well.*

"I looked at Joe's notebooks and went to the Recorder's Office. I'll tell you more later, but I have to show you what I found in the notebooks."

Susan held up a paper, crisscrossed with creases. "The missing ledger page! And folded inside the page I found..." She held up a small key.

Chapter Twenty-Eight

A full twenty-four hours later, Inez fumbled with the buttons of her day dress. She finally left the top two undone to spare her swollen neck. Battling waves of dizziness, she opened the bedroom door.

In the parlor, Susan looked up from her book, then jumped to her feet. "You should be in bed! Doc didn't think you'd be up for another day, at least."

"Bank," croaked Inez. "Joe's papers."

"Papers? Oh, Joe's loan! That's why you went to the bank to meet…ah well."

Inez mimed writing, using her palm for paper.

"I'll get them. You sit down." Susan rustled out of the room.

Inez collapsed on the sofa. Susan reappeared with a sheet of stationery, a stubby pencil, an ink bottle, and a pen. Inez cleared the parlor table, dipped the pen's steel nib, and wrote: "Mr. Cooke, The bearer of this note is acting on my behalf for Mrs. Joseph Rose. Any information you have concerning Mr. Rose's loan—"

A knock sent Susan scurrying to the front door.

"No need to disturb Mrs. Stannert. How is she?" Reverend Sands' voice melted Inez's concentration.

Pushing aside the note, Inez stood and slowly walked to the entry hall.

"Mrs. Stannert." Reverend Sands whisked off his hat and smiled with a warmth that reminded her of summer.

"She should be convalescing," Susan interposed hastily.

"It's all right," Inez whispered. "Come in."

Susan wavered, then finally pulled the door wide. "I'll fix some tea. Reverend, please don't tax her."

"I wouldn't dream of it." The reverend took Inez's arm solicitously and guided her to the loveseat. "Although I'm happy to see you up, I'm also concerned. You should rest."

"Enough. Rest." Inez was glad that her skirts masked her unsteady gait.

Sands grasped the piano stool. "May I?" At her slight nod, he rolled it close. He sat, pulling a much-thumbed pocket Bible from his black frock coat.

"I'm not here to quote scripture. Marshal Hollis wants to ask you about Nigel's death. Doc and I talked him out of it, said we'd relay questions that couldn't wait. Then, I arm-wrestled Doc for the role of messenger."

He riffled the Bible pages like a deck of cards. "Just nod or shake your head if it's too painful to talk. Did anyone besides you and Nigel know about your meeting?"

She remembered. Nigel in the saloon, shouting date, time, and place from the surging crowd.

Inez lowered her aching head into her hands. *That's half of Leadville.*

"Nigel. Came to the Queen," she whispered. She remembered the marshal's shifty eyes, his sudden departure. "Hollis heard. He was there."

Sands leaned closer. "Who else?"

"Abe. Useless. A big crowd. The opera was just over."

Could I have prevented his death? Awash with guilt, she stared at the reverend's Bible. The gold cross on the cover was cracked, the gold leaf flaking off. He riffled the pages again, thinking.

"You were meeting about Rose's loan?"

"Nigel...had loan papers."

His hands stilled. "Nigel had the papers? Did you see them?"

"On his desk."

The reverend shook his head. "There was nothing in the office concerning Joe Rose." He rolled back the stool to stand. "We looked."

"We?" Her lips formed the word. She no longer had a voice for it.

"The bank manager and I. And Marshal Hollis."

Inez's gaze fell on her half-composed note to Morris Cooke. She crumpled it up, leaned back, and closed her eyes.

"Reverend Sands, you promised not to tire her." Susan appeared with Inez's modest tea set.

Sands retrieved the crumpled note and smoothed it out. A sharp look from those gray eyes followed. "Mrs. Stannert, were you intending to pursue this? After what happened yesterday? I don't think that's wise. Do you?" He looked over at Susan. "Miss Carothers, were you planning to play Pinkerton along with Mrs. Stannert?"

The china cups chattered against their saucers as she plunked down the tea service. "If we don't pursue this, Emma will be penniless."

The Reverend rubbed the nape of his neck and muttered.

"What," demanded Susan.

"I said 'a conspiracy of women.' I see you'll not be dissuaded by common sense." He debated a moment. "It appears I have no choice. Although I'd hoped to bring the news to Mrs. Rose first." He walked to the piano and turned, speaking as if he was making an announcement from the pulpit. "Through the efforts of the church, in particular through a generous benefactor who wishes to remain anonymous, the bank loan has been paid in full."

‹›‹›‹›

After Reverend Sands had left, Susan circled a spoon in her lukewarm tea and asked, "What do we do, Inez? Let it go at that? "

Using the stubby pencil, Inez wrote, "If we do, someone in Leadville gets away with murder. Do you still have Joe's records and that key?"

Susan jumped up and returned with Joe's assay notebooks, his ledger book and the key. Inez examined the key. The length of her little finger, it was too small for a door or a normal-size padlock or strongbox. Its grip was cut in the shape of an ornate horseshoe

"I don't know what to make of the horseshoe design. For good luck, maybe?" Susan twisted a strand of hair. "Could it be to Joe's desk?"

Inez visualized Joe's desk drawers, then wrote, "Possibly."

"Well, it's something to check. Now, we hit pay dirt with the ledger and the notebooks." Susan held up the loose ledger page. "This is the missing page: forty-seven. In the ledger, the forty-seven is really forty-nine, with a bit of the nine rubbed out. Look." She flipped the bound ledger page. The printed number on the back was fifty.

"The one he tore out is only half-filled." Susan's fingers danced over the pages. "Each job has a number that Joe used for tracking the process and results. The last ten jobs are for 'C.D.'"

Inez hooked her reading glasses over her ears. Five C.D. entries appeared in the bound ledger. She looked a question at Susan.

Susan continued, "Joe's very methodical, so it wasn't hard to follow which tracking numbers were which. Eight of C.D.'s samples show up in the assay notes. Of those, five are recorded in the bound ledger and three appear on the ledger page Joe tore out. I'd guess the last two jobs, which are entered on the torn page, were never processed. At least, they don't appear in his assay notebooks.

"The first five have a location. Fryer Hill. But the rest…" Susan shrugged. "No location mentioned. Well, to make a long story short, the Fryer Hill results are impressive, averaging nearly two hundred ounces of silver per ton. But the last three, with no location, came in over seven hundred!"

Inez stared at Susan in disbelief. *Figures like that would've been trumpeted from the rooftops.*

Susan nodded as if Inez had spoken aloud. "If this information had been recorded and made public, all of Leadville would be traipsing after C.D. and digging in his footprints. And Joe knew it."

She pointed in the notebook, where Joe had underlined the numbers 743, 739, and 709. Under that, Joe had written in precise script: "Cut a deal with C.D."

"It all comes back to C.D. Maybe we should go talk with that prospector, Chet Donnelly. Wasn't he missing some sample bags?"

Inez tapped the pencil against her lips and thought of the two bags of unassayed rocks in the saloon's safe. All of a sudden, she was less anxious to track down Chet and hand over the samples. Less willing to break the last, concrete link between Chet Donnelly and Joe Rose.

Finally, Inez set pencil to the paper. "Not yet. First, we talk to Nils Hansen. Then, we visit the City Recorder's Office. We start tomorrow."

〈〉〈〉〈〉

Tuesday morning, Inez and Susan advanced through the maze of sacks labeled "Breece Mine" to the counter of Jay G. Kelley and Company's Assay Office.

Inez nudged Susan, who said primly to the counterman, "Mr. Hansen, please."

The counterman peered at Inez, recognition chasing surprise across his face. She pegged him as one of Nils' companions at Joe's funeral. He disappeared into the back, shouting, "Hansen, you've got visitors."

Nils emerged, saw Inez, and stopped dead in his tracks. His aghast expression was easy to read; his tone merely confirmed his dismay. "Mrs. Stannert!" Catching sight of Susan, Nils controlled his voice, with obvious effort. "Miss Carothers."

Inez smiled. She'd counted on Susan's presence to defuse the situation and keep Nils on his best behavior. Inez nudged her friend. Susan jumped and said, "Mrs. Stannert has a question."

Nils approached slowly. "She can't talk for herself?"

"She's lost her voice." Susan thrust a strip of paper at him. "Here."

He took the note gingerly. Inez had kept it brief: "Who bought your claim?"

Inez watched as his fair Nordic complexion flushed from his stand-up collar through his blonde beard to his hair line. Nils crumpled the note and glared. Not at Inez, but at Susan. "Tell her to leave me alone! It don't matter anymore. Harry Gallagher owns it now." He flung the paper in a waste can.

Susan looked at Inez. Inez smiled sweetly at Nils before gliding toward the door with Susan at her heels. As they left, she heard the counterman say, "*Two* women! How do ya do it, Hansen?"

‹›‹›‹›

At the City Recorder's Office, Susan presented the case that she and Inez had agreed to put forth. "I'm writing an article for *The Independent* on recent mining property transactions and thought it would be interesting to follow the activities of one person. Chet Donnelly, for instance, always seems to know where to dig. We just wondered, as a matter of public record, what property transactions he's made. He's, ah, difficult to find."

The city recorder extracted a small leather tobacco pouch and a pipe from his waistcoat. "Yep, Chet Donnelly's been in and out of the office a lot this year. A busy man. When he's not in his cups, that is."

He grinned lopsidedly around the pipe stem. "You ladies know how it goes. Fella stakes a claim, sinks a shaft, if it looks good he takes samples to an assayer." He scratched a match with a fingernail and lit his pipe. "If it assays good, he gets the claim surveyed and recorded. That seals legal ownership. Of the surface, anyways. Legally, though, whoever finds the mineral first, owns it. So, even if you've recorded, someone with more men, moving faster, can dig right under your feet and beat you to the silver. Nowadays, when fellas like Chet make a strike, their best bet is to sell out or join a consolidated. Chet likes to sell and move on. Keeps him in liquor, I guess."

"Recording a claim means listing the location, doesn't it?" Susan pressed. "Suppose someone wanted to record a claim but not tell the world where it was."

He dropped the still smoking match into a tin mug. "If a fella found something promising late in the season, he might stake but not file. If the claim is in the middle of nowhere under twenty feet of snow, his secret's probably safe until spring." The recorder puffed on his pipe, sending smoke signals into the still air. "But let's see what we can find on Mr. Donnelly."

After two dusty hours, a picture of Chet's recent activities emerged.

"He's almost cleared off of Fryer Hill." The city recorder referred to the claim records they'd retrieved. "Sold five claims in that area, just this fall alone. Three bordered Gallagher's Silver Mountain Consolidated. Old Harry, he's got that side of the hill almost sewed up. There's one bit that, far as I know, hasn't changed hands."

He shuffled through the records. "Yep. That's Chet and the twins. Zeke and Zed. They must be holding out for a higher price."

Inez whispered, "Chet was in Roaring Forks area. Anything recorded from there?"

The recorder shook his head. "Kinda makes you wonder, doesn't it?" He drew on the dead pipe, then tapped the ash into the tin mug. "If I had the time, I'd go buy Chet a few beers and get him talking about his summer. Or," he grinned, "I'd go buy a few beers for his assayer."

"How about Nils Hansen?" Inez whispered. "He sold a claim last fall."

"Doesn't ring a bell. If he only made a couple transactions, it'd be like looking for a needle in a haystack."

Inez removed her reading glasses. *So Chet's the "holdout" Harry and Cooper were discussing. And there's no record of Chet's bonanza, except in Joe's notes. Could Chet have killed Joe to keep his find a secret until spring?*

She envisioned Chet, reeling down State at his worst. Meaner than a mad bear and roaring drunk.

Men have killed for less.

Chapter Twenty-Nine

Dusk did not come slowly; it slammed down like a fist. People didn't tarry on the streets. Most hurried home or to other places offering a drink, a meal, and some form of human companionship. No matter how meager the comfort, it was better than being caught outside in the dark where the cold pressed hard as iron.

Inez, walking as fast as the rest, stopped outside a window display of hats, fans, and other feminine accoutrements. The sign overhead, swinging slightly in near dark, announced: "Elisabeth T. Hoffman. Dressmaking and Millinery. By appointment only."

The previous day had fired her with a new resolve to set things right without delay. In the relative silence of the saloon office, Inez had reviewed Joe's books, missing ledger page in hand, and verified that Chet Donnelly's two ore samples were the only unfinished work. Once they were returned, she would have fulfilled her obligation to Emma.

It should have brought a sense of closure. Instead, Inez felt irritable, as if there was an itch she could not reach. Joe was dead and so was Nigel. The loan papers were missing. *Yet everyone wants me to just let things be.*

She focused on the light flickering from the upstairs shop window. *If I'm going to get something for the Silver Soiree, I'd better speak with Mrs. Hoffman tonight.*

Once inside the building, Inez shook out the hem of her snow-crusted skirts and ascended the stairs to the shop. A murmur of women's voices grew louder until she heard a contralto drawl: "I don't give a damn what you think, Mrs. Hoffman. I'm paying the bill."

Cat DuBois?

On the other side of the door, Mrs. Hoffman snapped, "It's completely inappropriate. It's worse than vulgar."

"To whom?" Cat sounded amused. "The gentlemen will approve. They're the only ones who matter."

Gritting her teeth, Inez twisted the knob and entered.

Elisabeth Hoffman stood against one wall, measuring tape draped about her narrow shoulders, arms tightly crossed. Cat DuBois stood at the opposite end of the room, arms also crossed. Between them, Angel stood motionless on the dressmaker's platform. A silver and cream evening dress hugged her from torso to toe, shimmering in the lamp light and accentuating her coffee-colored skin.

Upon seeing Inez, a flicker of surprise crossed Angel's face. The emotion passed, leaving her expression as remote as if she stood on a distant mountaintop.

Cat swung toward the open door. "Well, well, Mrs. Stannert. Good. I could use an unbiased opinion. This dress," she waved her closed fan at Angel, "is for the Silver Soiree." Her green eyes glinted. "I don't imagine you'll be there, given that the extended absence of your oh-so charming husband leaves you without an escort."

Inez bit back an acerbic reply. *I won't give her the satisfaction.* Instead, she turned to the dressmaker. "I'll come back tomorrow."

"Please wait." Mrs. Hoffman sounded desperate. "We're almost finished."

Cat watched Inez with the gaze of a feline predator scenting something tantalizing but not quite definable in the air. "Well, well," she murmured. "So you *are* going. Saloonkeepers and Cyprians. The respectable women will be absolutely horrified."

Cat glided up to Angel, grabbed her arm, and pulled her off the platform to face Inez. "I told that sorry excuse for a seamstress to make the bodice lower. Like so." Cat tugged down on the tight-fitting gown.

Mrs. Hoffman jumped as if Angel's breasts had spilled out the top. "That's indecent!"

"The idea, Mrs. Hoffman, is to display the wares to their greatest advantage so the buyer knows what he's getting."

Mrs. Hoffman's pointed nose quivered. "I will not tolerate—"

Cat laughed. "Oh, for the right money, you will." Her gaze shifted to Inez. "Money talks. Don't you agree, Mrs. Stannert? It buys a percentage in a silver strike or a choice lot in the business district. Without it, you better have something else. A highly prized face and body, for instance." Her gloved hand slid up the young woman's bare arm, lingered at the neck, brushed back the long black hair.

"That's enough!" Inez found her voice and her feet. She walked up to Cat, forcing her away from Angel. "You have no right to speak to Mrs. Hoffman or treat this girl that way. She's not your property."

Cat laughed in delight, a descending scale of notes. She snapped her fan open and closed, seemingly relishing the exchange. "Why, you're quite wrong. She *is* my property. Angel, why don't you tell Mrs. Stannert how I saved you from becoming meat for the maggots. No? Then I will."

Cat faced Inez with a vengeance. "I found Angel in a Denver alley. Fucking for crusts of bread."

Mrs. Hoffman sucked in her breath. Cat ignored her.

She lightly tapped Angel's breast with her closed fan. "That pile of rags in the gutter beside you. Your brat? You never did say. Well, it was dead. But you lived. Thanks to me and me alone. Oh yes, I own you, body and soul."

Cat slapped the closed fan against her open palm. The crack sounded like a whip in the dressmaker's shop.

"It works both ways, Mrs. Stannert. I give Angel shelter, food, beautiful clothes." She indicated the elegant dress. "Put her in a position to be adored by men of wealth, position, and power. And she gives me..." Cat tipped her head, red lips thinning into a smile. "We're back to money. Think, Mrs. Stannert, if your recently departed husband had left you with no bank account, no property, where would you be now? Who knows? You might be working for me."

"You're despicable!" Inez forced her still raw voice into service. "It's clear you take advantage of this girl and take pleasure in speaking in a particularly foul manner. You don't shock me. I've heard those words before and more. And, one more thing."

Inez moved forward into Cat's lilac scent, close enough to see the face powder caked into creases around her painted mouth.

"We're not the least bit alike, Mrs. DuBois," she whispered. "You don't know me. No more than you know what lies in Angel's heart."

Inez turned to Angel, who stood, lips parted, following the exchange. "Should you ever decide to leave the trade, remember the Silver Queen Saloon, corner of Harrison and State. I'll help you find another way, a way that allows you to keep your dignity."

Cat sneered. "Don't give her any grand ideas. Angel's just a whore, like the rest of us. Not worthy of your attention. Angel, get your cloak!"

Cat pulled bank notes from her purse and threw them down. The paper money scattered around Mrs. Hoffman's long skirts like leaves. "For the dress. At this price, I expect alterations with no whining. Ladies, we *are* the same, in this way: We provide services for money. Mrs. Hoffman, I suggest you provide those services with a smile."

The door slammed behind Angel and Cat. Mrs. Hoffman collapsed onto the platform and drew a handkerchief from her sleeve. Inez started forward, but Mrs. Hoffman held up a hand. "No, please, it's just that *woman*." She spat out the word as if it were spoiled food. "If pride goeth before a fall, she's headed straight for perdition."

"It's not pride that drives Mrs. DuBois," said Inez. "It's ambition."

Mrs. Hoffman dabbed at her eyes, then stooped to gather the currency. "I would never have taken her business, only most of the decent women left town for the winter and won't return until late spring. I need the money."

Inez recognized the tone of dread, the unspoken fear of not being able to cover the business costs and grocer's bills.

When Mrs. Hoffman returned from putting the money away, the handkerchief was back up the sleeve, and her face was composed. "I'm sorry you walked in on that. Now, what can I do for you, Mrs. Stannert?"

Inez also tried for a normal tone. "I'm looking for something suitable for the soiree. Nothing flashy," she added hastily, remembering Angel's skin-tight, revealing dress.

Mrs. Hoffman nodded. She ran her eyes over Inez's figure, as if extracting a mental file of pertinent measurements. "It's too late to sew up anything." Her face brightened. "But I have something that might do."

She hastened to one of three massive oak wardrobes and pulled out a dress. Laying it on her worktable, she said, "I made this for Mrs. Smythe, but she left town. It's a lovely mix of greens."

Mrs. Hoffman smoothed the satin insets on the velvet overdress. The material fairly begged to be touched. "And, if I'm not mistaken—" She held it up to Inez. "Perfect for your complexion." Her expression became thoughtful. "Ruffles at the hem and sleeves for length." She glanced at Inez's waist. "You'll have to lace tighter."

"Mrs. Hoffman, please, I want to be able to dance without falling over in a faint." Inez looked down at the dress, tempted, but still doubtful. "I'd like to be able to wear it on other occasions as well."

"The underdress with your black cashmere would work for Sundays and special occasions." She faced Inez, the underskirt bunched in one hand. "Given that the twenty-seventh is less than two weeks away, it's the best I can do."

"How much?"

She told her.

Inez swallowed hard. *At two hundred, I had better find many occasions for wearing it.* She removed a glove and ran a hand over the different textures and shades. "Very well. I'll pay half now. But I'll need one more alteration. A pocket. A little deeper than—" She held her hands apart, the length of her pocket Remington.

Mrs. Hoffman squeezed her eyes shut, looking like a child that had just been offered a spoonful of cod liver oil. "This, this is an *evening* dress."

"You're a marvelous seamstress. I'm certain that, when you're done, the pocket will be invisible. Now, when should I come in for a fitting?"

"The twenty-third." Mrs. Hoffman watched Inez count out coins and currency. "That gives me a few days if I need to make further alterations. I would have it ready sooner, but..." Her expression fell.

"The twenty-third is fine." *Cat will probably have her jumping through hoops until Christmas.*

Chapter Thirty

Sun slanted down Tiger Alley, lending a false warmth to the early morning air. At the back door of the Silver Queen, Inez scraped snow off her sturdy walking shoes. Her gaze traveled down the path where State Street's buildings revealed their less public aspects. For a moment, she imagined Joe walking the alley in the dead of night. She shook her head to banish Joe's ghost and went inside.

Abe was finishing off a fried breakfast steak.

"Good morning, Abe, Bridgette."

Abe speared another chunk of meat and offered it to the calico meowing at his feet. "Mornin' to you too, Inez. You're soundin' almost normal today." A quick snap of feline teeth, and the cat vanished into the storeroom with her prize. "Meant to ask, Inez, have you seen my knife past few days?"

"No." She dumped Joe's notebooks and ledger on the table. "Oh Abe, not your knife. You've carried that since the War. How long has it been gone?"

"Since Monday." Abe absently thumbed the edge of the cutlery knife. "Didn't want to mention it, you bein' so busy settlin' Joe's business."

"Those men, the Exodusters, slept here Saturday and Sunday. You were with them. Could one of them have…?"

Abe set the knife on the plate. "Well, if one did, he probably needed it more'n me. I'll just get another. How's it comin' with Joe's books?"

"Done." She sat down across from him. "I tried to return them to Emma. She said, 'What good will they do me in California? Throw them out.'" Inez sighed and flipped the ledger pages. "All I've left to do is return Chet's bags and the five dollars he gave Joe to perform the last assays."

"Reminds me, Chet was here last night lookin' for you. He's been holed up on his Fryer Hill claim with the twins. Turns out, they've broken through into one of Silver Mountain's drifts. They're hunkered underground, eyeball to eyeball with Harry's boys, shotguns at the ready. Chet figures Harry'll make an offer pretty soon. He wants to be there so's the twins don't give it away."

"I imagine Harry's not too happy about that."

Abe rocked his chair back on two legs. "Best thing in my opinion, not that you asked, is you hand over those bags to me and I take them on up the hill to Chet. Sounds pretty tense up there."

"I'll go. Lucy can use the exercise. Besides, I have questions for Chet." Inez poured coffee for herself and Abe, taking care to leave the broken egg shells in the pot.

"Thanks, Inez." Abe's chair thumped back down. "You heard about Emma's good fortune, the loan bein' paid and all."

"Mmm-hmm." She sat again. The heat from the stove warmed her back though her fingers still tingled with cold. "How did you hear?"

"Your reverend. He dropped by last night about midnight." Abe sipped his coffee. "I think he was a mite disappointed you weren't here."

Inez bristled. "He's not 'my' reverend."

Abe took his time brushing a few crumbs from his silver and black vest. "Sure he is, Inez. It's your church, right?" He looked at her, his brown eyes steady. "It's interestin', though. You get in trouble and he's right there, turnin' up at just the right time. I reckon he must have a direct line to the Almighty, so he knows just when to show."

Bridgette bustled over and grabbed Abe's empty plate. "A man of God's supposed to look out for his congregation. That's his job." She waved the plate under his nose. "Another steak? To keep some meat on those long bones of yours?"

"No thanks, Bridgette." Abe examined Inez much as Mrs. Hoffman had the evening before. "So, Inez, what about you? Gonna have somethin' besides coffee for breakfast? It'll just eat a hole in you, sloshin' around on its own."

"I'm not hungry." The thought of a heavy lump of meat grinding around in her stomach was not appealing.

"Hmmph. You still look a mite peaked from that knock on the head."

"Lack of appetite can be a sign of many things," chirped Bridgette. She swished a towel around the table and returned to the stove, humming.

Inez decided to ignore Bridgette's remark.

"Abe, about December twenty-seventh. That's a Saturday—"

"Right, I know it's Saturday—"

"She means," interrupted Bridgette, "it's the night of the big do. And Mrs. Stannert, she's going and will need the night off."

"Bridgette!" Inez sputtered. *How did she find out?* She faced Abe. "I plan on canceling the game unless you want to take my place."

"Come on, Inez. Those boys don't show up for the better part of a Saturday night to play poker with a nigger. And I can't leave Useless at the bar by hisself. Now, am I supposed to guess who asked you to this fandango?"

"No need to guess," interrupted Bridgette with the air of a satisfied matchmaker. "It's Reverend Sands of course."

Abe crossed his arms and watched Inez flush scarlet. "Like I said. *Your* reverend. You sure you know what you're doin', Inez?"

Inez stood with all the dignity at her disposal. "Don't start seeing things that aren't there, Abe. That goes for you too, Bridgette. I'm off for Fryer Hill. I'll be back by noon."

‹›‹›‹›

Once in the office, Inez pulled out the two burlap bags from the safe, opened one, and peered inside. *Rocks. Rocks that could signal a fortune.*

An inner voice, which sounded suspiciously like her mother's, demanded to know what she thought she was doing as she removed a couple of fist-sized chunks from each bag. *What if,* Inez argued silently with the voice, *Joe cut a deal with Chet and bought a percentage of the claim with the loan money. If I get these rocks assayed, and if they fit the results in Joe's assay notes, and if I can find proof of an agreement, Emma and Joey stand to benefit.*

A lot of "ifs" and a shaky legal position, at best. But the voice in her head had no doubt about the moral position of her actions. "Put those back!" it hissed. "Ladies do not steal! Ladies are the moral standard."

Inez had practice ignoring that voice. She placed the rocks in two small flour sacks, pushed the sacks into the safe, and clanged the door shut. *Now for a ride up Fryer Hill.*

‹›‹›‹›

Inez always marveled at the anonymity a set of clothes brought her. Wearing Mark's old sheepskin jacket and canvas pants, a slouch hat pulled down low and a neckerchief pulled up tight, she was just another b'hoy, shotgun slung by the saddle, riding up to Fryer Hill.

Once past the Silver Mountain turnoff, she veered onto a less traveled road winding around the shoulder of the hill. Evidence of mining activity appeared: skeletons of timber headframes black against the snow, mounds of tailings, and hastily constructed shanties, apparently empty. She puzzled at the inactivity, then remembered. *Ah yes. Harry owns all this now. He's probably busy extending Silver Mountain's underground workings.*

They rounded a snow-capped bend and Inez reined Lucy to a stop. They'd almost plowed into a rig, its horse hitched to a rickety shanty. Chet's roan and two shaggy ponies stood nearby. *Probably the twins'. Now where have I seen this rig before?*

Inez admired the sleek black horse before tying off Lucy by the rig. The wind shifted, and a voice from beyond the cabin said, "…last offer. Harry's being more than generous. His offer's twice what the claim's worth, even if the assay results prove valid."

Inez glanced again at the handsome horse, chewing on its bit. *Cooper's rig. He must be trying to cut a deal for Harry.*

"Haw!" That was Chet's characteristic snort. "I got Harry by the short hairs. Them assays are good. He can drag his feet all winter, takin' samples and splittin' assays. Our price'll just keep goin' up."

The wind shifted, swallowing Cooper's reply.

Inez inched around the back of shanty, squeezing between the log wall and a towering ice-crusted snowbank. *If I can reach the far corner, I might be able to hear better.*

Cooper's voice returned. "Thirty thousand. Take it or I wash my hands of this deal. I'll not be a party to what Harry's got planned for you and your partners if you turn it down."

"Haw!" This time, Chet's guffaw was triumphant. "Shake on it, Cooper! Hey Zeke! Come on down! We got a deal with that devil Gallagher!"

Inez almost missed the last sentence as snow avalanched down over her hat. That shower was nothing, however, compared to the heavy weight that hit her shoulders and drove her to the ground. She yelped, getting a mouthful of crusty snow for her efforts. She started to push herself up only to feel the unmistakable bite of a gun muzzle in the back of her neck.

"Don't move or I'll ventilate ya, ya varmint!" Zeke's nasal whine shook with indignation. He jerked her to her feet, then marched her out into the open. "Chet! Lookit this! Harry sends his fancy-pants lawyer to sweet-talk us into a deal, and one of his damn flunkies to bowdlerize us, if'n we don't agree."

Chet and Cooper swung startled faces toward Inez. Looking ready to explode, Chet snarled, "Talk fast, mister lawyer."

He reached for the gun under his tattered jacket. Cooper held out his hands—whether to show he wasn't interested in a gun battle or to show his confusion, Inez didn't wait to find out.

"You idiots!" she shrieked. "I am *not* one of Harry's flunkies!" The pressure disappeared from the base of her skull.

Zeke spun her around. His face, slack with surprise, showed white where sweat streaked the grime. "Jumpin' Jehosephat, he's a female!"

"Let go of me!" Inez spat.

Zeke let go and stepped back, gun hanging from one hand. She turned to Chet. "If I'd any intention of 'bowdlerizing' you, I would've come armed." She yanked open her coat to show that she had no gun. "My shotgun is on my horse. Along with the sample bags you've been hounding me about."

Cooper, who had regained his composure, bowed slightly and lifted his hat in courteous irony. "Mrs. Stannert. An unexpected pleasure."

"Huh. Pay her no mind," Chet growled. "Ya got your deal, Cooper. I'll even throw in the burro." He twitched his head toward the dispirited beast, which was nosing halfheartedly at the hardpacked snow by the windlass.

"I'll relay your generosity to Mr. Gallagher," said Cooper.

"Hey Zeke, go holler down the shaft to that no-account brother of yours. We're gonna celebrate, yessiree. So when do we get the money?" Chet zeroed in on Cooper.

Cooper shrugged, elegant in his fur-trimmed cashmere coat. "Today, if you wish. The paperwork's in the rig. I fill in the amount, you three sign, and I get Harry's signature. I'll complete the necessary paperwork for the property transfer in town. I don't imagine," he added, sarcasm sliding through his words, "that you'd agree to abandon your post before you have the finished documents in hand. And the money."

"Damn tootin'. Zed and his shotgun stay underground 'til we get the dough."

"Before sunset, then."

Chet's brown teeth snagged on a maniacal grin. "Thirty thousand smackeroos! Look out ladies of State Street!"

Cooper turned toward Inez. "Mrs. Stannert, would you like me to accompany you back to town after I get these gentlemen's signatures?"

Inez nodded. No way did she want to be left alone on that solitary hill with Chet and the twins. Particularly with her shotgun still hanging on Lucy.

They all crunched through the snow to the horses. Reaching into his rig, Cooper pulled out a portable writing desk, paperwork, pen, and ink.

After signing, Chet fingered his tatty gray beard, avarice lending a beatific afterglow to his face. "Now. Them bags, Miz Stannert?"

Inez returned to Lucy and pulled them out of her saddle-bags along with a five-dollar gold piece. "For the assays Joe never did."

"Hell, woman, keep it. Give it to Joe's widder. Come sundown, I'm ten thousand dollars richer." Chet hefted the bags, tender as a mother with a babe.

"A new stake, Chet? Anything you might sell at a later date?" Cooper's easy voice seemed to jolt him back to the present.

"Naw." Chet paused. "Just a piece-a-shit claim not worth spit."

His gaze slitted back to Inez, sly.

Ha! Piece-of-shit claim my foot. He's holding aces and trying to pass it as a worthless hand.

Chet's little red eyes suddenly bloomed with light. "Hey, Mrs. Stannert. What's it take to play in your high-falutin' poker game?"

"Take a bath," she retorted. "Get some decent clothes. Show up sober. And with cash. We don't take credit."

"Yeah, yeah, just like the whorehouses," he growled. "Okay, Mrs. Stannert. You and your fancy-pants players git ready for some real poker playin'." He hefted the bags again, his eyes gleaming brighter. "Tomorrow night."

Chapter Thirty-One

By ten o'clock Saturday night, Chet had not showed at the Silver Queen. At the poker table, Inez began to breathe easier.

The saloon had buzzed all day with talk about Chet's and the twins' sudden wealth. How they'd bought drinks for the house here, gone on a buying spree there. The three seemed to be spending their new-found fortune as fast as they could.

Some folks wondered aloud—but not too loud—if Harry had been played for a fool. Most kept their counsel. Time would tell if Harry had thrown away his thirty thousand or if he'd invested well.

The evening progressed at a leisurely pace. Cooper, ever the gentleman, uttered not a word about the embarrassing mishap of the previous day. Evan was in quiet good humor, being top man so far that evening. Doc imbibed brandy at a rate directly proportional to his small but steady losses. Jed was absent. As for Harry...

He certainly doesn't act like he signed a check yesterday for thirty thousand dollars.

She caught herself wondering if Sands might stop in at midnight.

Her musings were interrupted by a ruckus outside the door. Useless poked his head around the corner, greasy hair plastered over his ears, eyes wide. "Ma'am, Chet Donnelly's here and—"

Useless was yanked from view from behind. A figure filled the doorway.

"Howdy. Is this the high-rollin', no-limit poker game?"

Inez's first thought was: *Chet has a chin.*

His scraggly, to-the-navel beard was gone, replaced by a short-cropped grizzled fuzz. Gone, too, were the baggy corduroys, worn jacket, and shapeless hat. Instead, his enormous belly strained at the pearl buttons of a scarlet and gold waistcoat peeping out from under a formal, black evening suit the size of a small tent. A silk top hat perched atop hair cut short and pomaded to within an inch of its life. Of the original Chet Donnelly, only three things remained: bloodshot eyes, scarred leather gunbelt cinched tight under the swallow-tail jacket, and worn-out boots crammed on over the black dress pants.

Except for boots and belt, he'd have done the opera crowd proud.

"Lessee if I got it right. Bath. New clothes. Sober." He dug out a roll from his pocket and thumbed it with a snarky smile. "Money. And you've got an empty chair waitin' for me."

Inez took stock of the table. Cooper and Harry appeared bemused. Doc's eyebrows were raised so high they disappeared into the wrinkled topology of his forehead. Evan sat frozen, cigar raised halfway to his mouth.

She faced Chet. "This is a hard money game. Just like every other game in town. That means gold. Silver. No paper."

"Hell's bells, ma'am. That wasn't what ya said yesterday. Money's money. Asides, luggin' double eagles in my pockets'd ruin these fancy duds." He patted the waistcoat and spoiled the sartorial effect with a loud burp.

She faced her players, seething. "Gentlemen?"

Harry and Cooper shrugged.

Doc sighed. "I think the game just escalated beyond my means in any case."

Evan, the only one to look doubtful, simply said, "Your call, Mrs. Stannert. It's your game."

"Congress passed the law resuming specie payments last January," Cooper pointed out. "Those notes are as good as gold at the bank."

She deliberated, then finally addressed Chet. "Give your gunbelt to Useless. No weapons allowed in the room."

While Chet fumbled with the buckle, Inez beckoned to Useless, who hovered by the door. "Have Abe bring me all the paper money we've got. I'll not put up good gold against that many greenbacks, no matter what the government promises."

Her attention returned to the table. "Gentlemen." She pulled out Jed's empty chair. "We have a sixth."

Chet bowed, catching his hat as it tumbled off. He passed behind her chair, the sharp minty scent of hair tonic trailing in his wake. *Wonder what the barber doused him with. Hope it kills lice.*

Inez steeled herself to play cards with a madman. And Chet obliged her.

He threw his money down as if he had the touch of Midas. He bet so high and often that, very soon, he was winning little beside the ante simply because no one would raise or call him. Doc, who had dropped out of the game entirely, watched by the sidebar, brandy close at hand.

At the midnight break, Evan approached Inez. "I'm out. See you on the first Saturday of the new decade."

It was Inez's turn to deal.

"Damn!" Chet looked at his cards, eyes bulging. "Ya call this a hand? A couple these here fifties oughta change my luck."

Around the table, the players silently matched his bet.

Chet shoved his cards toward Inez. "Five new ones."

Inez exhaled hard.

"Four's the limit. Standard rules."

"Hell, ma'am. A hunnert in the pot says I want five, I get five." He hooted. "Just joshin'. Two."

Gritting her teeth, she sailed two cards his way. Cooper and Harry stood pat. She took two.

When she saw what fate had dealt her, she knew:
I've got him now.

The door swung open, and the roar of the saloon thundered in with strains of "What a Friend We Have in Jesus." Inez turned with a smile. "Evening, Reverend Sands."

He paused, halfway to the stove, and removed his hat. His returning smile warmed her to her toes. "Evening, Mrs. Stannert. Hope you don't mind if I watch."

"Not at all. Gentlemen?"

Murmurs from around the table. Chet, chewing on his bottom lip, didn't even look up from his hand. "Naw. Just no God-talk."

"No God-talk." Sands saluted with his coffee mug.

Inez nodded at Chet. "Your call."

"Fifteen hunnert smackeroos."

Cooper tossed his cards on the table. Harry followed with "I've contributed enough to your retirement, Donnelly."

"Haw!" exulted Chet, on whom the sarcasm was lost. "Now you, Mrs. Stannert."

Inez looked long and hard at Chet, then said, all sweetness, "Double it."

She counted out fifties and pushed them into the center.

"Now we're playin' poker!" Chet slammed the table with a hairy hand. The coffee sloshed in Inez's cup. "Raise ya, 'nother thousand."

"Up another thousand, Chet. You do have the money, don't you?" She leaned over to retrieve the strongbox from the floor. As she did, Harry asked in a low voice, "Are you sure about this, Inez?"

She covered her bet with a mix of paper and gold. The men looked at her as if she'd gone crazy. Except for Chet. Chet's lower teeth were attempting to consume what was left of his mustache as he pondered his options.

Inez said loud enough for all to hear, "I've no intention of contributing to Chet's retirement. I guarantee, however, that he will be contributing handsomely to the saloon's expansion fund."

Her words had the desired effect. Chet dug into his pocket and extracted the now-slim roll of bills. He looked a trifle glum. "Aw, hell. I wanted to save somethin' for Cat's whores."

"I don't mean to cut into your fun, Chet." She tapped her chin in a show of deep thought. "I'm willing to accept an asset in place of the cash."

He looked suspicious. "Asset?"

Inez tore a sheet from the tablet she'd been using to keep tab of the winnings, and printed: "Your 'piece-of-shit' claim by Roaring Fork. The one you and Joe cut a deal on."

She folded the paper and held it out to him.

Chet snatched the note, scanned it, and crumpled it in a fist.

He then turned and spat on the carpet before counting out his thousand. There were only a couple of bills left when he was done.

"Lay down them cards."

She did.

Cooper murmured. Inez was gratified that he could look surprised. She glanced sideways at Harry and detected a smile lurking beneath his mustache. Doc leaned forward to see and pursed his lips in a silent whistle.

Chet examined the four aces and queen of diamonds peeking coyly from behind.

He heaved to his feet.

His chair toppled to the carpet with a thud.

Harry and Cooper tensed visibly. Inez slid a hand into the pocket that held her gun.

Chet kicked the chair out of his way and stalked out the door, slamming it hard. The framed Civil War print shivered on the wall.

Reverend Sands walked forward and flipped over Chet's cards.

Inez realized that, sometime during the last exchange, the reverend had unobtrusively positioned himself against the wall behind the prospector.

Chet's abandoned hand showed a full house, kings and a pair of jacks.

"No wonder he emptied his pockets," remarked Cooper.

Harry looked at her with admiration. "Now that, Inez, is playing poker."

She stacked the money neatly before her. "Like taking candy from a baby. Now, if I'd duped *you*, Harry, *that* would be playing poker. Gentlemen, any objections to breaking up the game early?"

No one objected.

Doc came over and clasped Inez's hand. "Congratulations, my dear. I suppose after this, you'll be leaving town. Surely you aren't serious about the expansion. Why, with this windfall and a sale of your property—"

Feeling flush with victory, Inez extracted her hand from Doc's grasp. "The windfall belongs to the saloon's partnership. And Abe and I have plans for the Silver Queen."

She carried her winnings to the sideboard. "We may turn the upper level into a gentleman's club and hire professional dealers. These private games would, of course, continue."

While talking, she poured a generous brandy to celebrate.

The first sip, golden and smooth, settled with a glow in her stomach. As she set down the snifter she noticed, with a flash of irritation, that Doc had been careless while helping himself. Puddles of brandy showed here and there on the polished wood.

She lifted her stack of bills, exclaiming in annoyance. The bottom note was soaked. She pulled it off to examine the denomination. And blinked.

The complex whorls and lines on the back of the fifty looked smeared and melting. As if...

She stared at her fingertips, coated with ink.

Chapter Thirty-Two

"Sweet Jesus," Inez said under her breath.

On cue, Reverend Sands stood by her elbow. She clenched her hand into a fist to give herself time to think.

"What's this?" Reverend Sands picked up the discarded fifty. The ink smeared further, making the back of the bill nearly unreadable.

His smile of congratulations disappeared. He turned the bill over to examine it further and straightened up, his stance changing subtly. When his eyes met hers, he seemed to be taking her measure anew. His deliberate gaze reminded her of a player trying to sniff out a bluff. "It's counterfeit."

"I can see that," retorted Inez. She lowered her eyes to the thick wad of paper money in her hand. *That one and how many others?*

She felt ill.

The reverend set the bogus fifty on a dry section of the sideboard. "You'd better have your bank look at those notes."

"I wonder who passed this?" *And if they did it on purpose.* The term for deliberately passing counterfeit floated to consciousness, from long-ago bits of conversation between Mark and Abe. *Shoving.*

"Could have been anyone."

It could have even been me. The paper money she'd used for the game had come straight from the saloon's safe.

Harry, Cooper, and Doc clustered about her and Sands.

"Coney money, hmmm?" Doc bent to view the worthless piece of paper. "Saw lots during the War. Inferior stuff, for the most part. You could usually spot it right off. That is, if it wasn't handed to you in some poorly illuminated drinking establishment."

"This one looked pretty good," said Sands.

The note of authority in his voice caused Inez to turn and stare. As she did, she caught a glance, fleeting as a sigh, traded between him and Harry.

Doc's jowls creased upward in a sympathetic smile. "Coney floats around. Just bad luck, my dear, that it ended up with you."

Inez nodded, mute. She wondered if she could pretend nothing had happened. Take it all to the bank on Monday. She locked up the money in the box, except for the wet counterfeit. "I must talk to Abe. Help yourselves, gentlemen. If you leave before I return, Merry Christmas. Remember, we won't be playing again until the third of January."

She moved through the crowded barroom, making an effort to smile and nod graciously at the congratulatory comments. It seemed everyone knew how she'd slipped the last of Chet's fortune from him.

Once at the bar, she beckoned to Abe.

"Inez." Abe came over, towel in one hand, brandy bottle and snifter in the other. "Heard you took the wind out of Chet's sails and the money from his pocket. With a handful of aces, too. Wish I could of seen that." Abe began to pour her a drink. She grabbed his arm to stop him and leaned over the bar. "That's the good news. We're now about six thousand dollars richer. The bad news is, at least one greenback is bogus."

She handed him the soggy bill.

Abe set the brandy bottle down, overly careful, and took the fifty from her. "Coney? Passed durin' the game?"

She nodded.

Abe examined the note, grim. "Damn. Wonder if someone's been shovin' regular. All the money passin' over the bar, we haven't got time to check it."

"This looked genuine. At least, until it was soaked in alcohol. We certainly can't douse every bill that comes our way. Let's talk more, before we make the Monday deposit." She surveyed the room. "Chet gone?"

"Reckon so. He took a bottle of rotgut to dull the pain of losin'." Abe took the strongbox from her and slipped the counterfeit inside. "If the reverend's walkin' you home be sure he's totin' somethin' more powerful than the Good Book. This'd be a bad time to bump into Chet."

Inez returned to the card room to collect the empty glasses.

Sands left off talking with Cooper and Harry when he saw Inez gathering the glassware. "I'll walk you home when you're ready." Commiseration tempered his smile. "Don't let the phony money ruin your evening. Counterfeit circulates through boom towns, cities, any place where money flows freely. As Doc said, it was probably just a matter of time before it happened here."

"Probably." Unconvinced.

She carried the tray of glasses into the kitchen and paused, just inside the passage door. One lamp, turned low, hung by the back as a signal to befuddled customers. The back door was closed. *Good.*

She had had visions of Chet lurking by the door to the alley, waiting for her. The lamp cast wavering shadows on the range, where the fry pan and oversized iron pot sat. The tin washtub filled the corner of the kitchen table, visible in the light pouring in from the saloon's main room.

She walked to the table and began stacking glassware into the tub.

The slice of light from the saloon narrowed and disappeared as the kitchen door swung shut behind her.

"How'dja know?"

Startled, she turned. Chet's bulk separated from the shadows next to the closed passage door.

Adrenaline pounded through her body. She carefully set a shot glass into the tub with her left hand and slid her right into her pocket. She pitched her voice calm, burying her fear. "How did I know what, Chet?"

He moved forward, a shambling bear. "Joe and that piece-a-shit…How'dja know?"

"Seven hundred ounces per ton is hardly a piece-of-shit claim." The words flew from her mouth before she could reconsider.

Chet was quick on those enormous feet, suddenly only an arm's length away. "Joe flap his gums afore he kicked the bucket? Naw. He said, keep it quiet 'til spring thaw."

She didn't want to pull the gun on him while he was thinking aloud. Besides, he stood at the wrong distance. *If he were only closer. Or further away.*

"Lady Luck?" he ruminated. "Naw. She don't talk to the likes of you. I got it." A ham-sized hand shot out and shoved her against the rear wall. The lamp above her head flickered. "Joe's widder. Bet Joe told his old lady, she told you. Damn palaverin' women."

No one would hear her yell over the racket in the saloon. If she pulled her gun now…*I'd never make it. Best keep him talking until he backs up or moves closer.*

"Is that what this is about?" She strove for a conversational tone. "You had a deal with Joe and now that he's dead you don't want to give the widow what's legally hers?"

"Haw!" A snarly laugh. "We shook, but he never coughed up the money. No money. No deal. And I got somethin' else to tell you, Mrs. High-n-Mighty Stannert."

He moved closer until his face filled her vision. Lit by the lamp above her head, he looked like a denizen of the underworld. She held her breath to avoid the bouquet of mint tonic and firewater that enveloped her.

"I don't like folks messin' in my business. And. I. Don't. Like. You."

He grabbed her shoulder, pinning her to the wall. "Thought it'd be fun playin' in your high-falutin' poker game. Fun, haw. I been to funerals more fun. Everyone looked like they was bettin' their last dollar. Hell, I don't care about the money. More where that came from."

He's close enough.

She began to ease the small gun out of her pocket. Chet squeezed her shoulder tighter, focused on her face.

"Think you're so goddamned smart." His spittle sprayed her. "No wonder your old man lit out on you. One word to anyone about that claim, I swear I'll—"

Chet froze midsentence, his eyes registering sudden sobriety and the fact that Inez had the business end of her revolver jammed into his crotch.

"Chet Donnelly," she spoke softly as a black rage hissed in her ears. "If you still want to save something for Cat's whores, step back three paces. Now."

She cocked the hammer, punctuating her intentions with the click.

A shadow flickered behind Chet. Suddenly, Chet was not stepping, but flying backward. The reverend, hand twisted into the back of Chet's collar, spun Chet away and released him.

Chet careened into the kitchen table, going down in a crash and tangle of chairs. He staggered to his feet, then roared forward.

Sands cracked him in the jaw just as Chet's foot snagged in an overturned chair. The prospector's sheer bulk and momentum sent them both to the floor. The two men flailed, each struggling to get on top.

Inez looked about desperately for a weapon less lethal in close quarters. Her eyes lit on the stovetop. *The fry pan!*

She shoved the gun back into her pocket and grabbed the long-handled pan. A tinny crash announced that the fight had just unbalanced the full washtub on the table.

The men grappled amid glass shards and wrecked chairs. Sands gouged Chet's eyes. Chet growled and hit Sands in the ear with an elbow.

Inez hopped around the action, hoping for a clear shot. Then, Chet was on top, roaring inarticulately and banging the reverend's head on the floor.

Seeing her chance, Inez swung the iron pan hard in a wide, two-handed arc. She whammed Chet on the skull just as Sands managed a knee to Chet's groin.

It was like the final axe blow to a giant tree. With a creak and a groan, Chet toppled on top of his opponent.

"Reverend! Are you all right?" Her hands stung from the contact of the blow.

Sands shoved Chet's body off and stood up. He staggered, cradling his right hand. "Ho-ly sh—"

He stopped, gasping for breath, then eyed Inez.

Rage and relief poured over her. "I should have blown his balls off."

The reverend's eyes widened. He managed a pain-twisted grin. "That last remark. Not exactly ladylike."

"That last kick. Not exactly Christian."

"I was desperate." Sands massaged his knuckles, staring at Chet. "God helps those who help themselves. Jesus, it was like hitting a rock. Glad you had the fry pan." He nudged Chet with an ungentle foot. "What now?"

Together, they regarded Chet's still form, arms outstretched on the floor as if for crucifixion. Inez knelt and began rifling his pockets.

The reverend regarded her in the murky light. "What are you doing?"

"My first inclination is to roll him out into the alley." Her voice was tight and furious. "But if he's got any money now, he'll have none by morning. Normally I wouldn't care. However I don't want him saying I stole the last of it. If he remembers any of this. Which I doubt. Ha. About a hundred dollars." She rose to her feet, clutching the bills. "I'll give this to Abe to put in the safe. *Then* we'll roll him out."

Chapter Thirty-Three

After leaving to the accompaniment of "My Heart at Thy Sweet Voice," Inez and Sands walked arm in arm for two long, silent blocks. Sands spoke first. "Win a few thousand. Uncover counterfeit. Stop a mountain man from dismembering a man of the cloth. Busy evening, Mrs. Stannert."

"A typical Saturday night."

His deadpan expression relaxed and she felt him grip her hand tighter with the crook of his arm.

As they approached Park Street, Inez ventured, "Abe is right. You always show up in times of trouble."

"You were gone a long time for dirty glassware. When I walked in, it looked like Chet had you by the throat." Sands glanced at her. "Could it have been him at the bank?"

Inez thought. The night air whispered past her cheek. "I'd say not. The man in the bank didn't...smell...like Chet. But from now on, I'm checking behind doors. Both times, someone hid behind the door and caught me unawares."

"Well, when I came in, I thought you needed help. Little did I know you had it all under control. Just what were you holding on him?"

She unpocketed the revolver. He examined it lying across her palm. "Remington. Stood you in good stead. What was the disagreement about?"

"No disagreement. Chet hates losing."

"That's all?"

"Isn't that enough?" She heard a small crinkle. When he pulled the paper out of his pocket, she knew immediately what it was. *My note to Chet.*

.nez bit her lip. "And a few other things," she finished lamely.

"The Joe in the note." He wagged the paper at her. "Joe Rose?"

Before Inez could decide what tack to take, Sands added, "No more lies, Mrs. Stannert. Lies can be deadly."

"No lies?" She warily took the proffered note. "This works both ways, of course."

"Of course."

On her porch, Inez pulled out her key, weighing its heft and her words. "Would you like some tea?"

"I would enjoy a cup, as long as it includes your company. And I'd rest better knowing that no one's lurking inside. If that wasn't Chet at the bank, your attacker is still at large."

Reverend Sands prowled through the house, checking behind doors and testing windows, while Inez prepared the tea.

"No uninvited guests." He sat on the loveseat and accepted a cup, waving away her offer of sugar. She perched on the piano stool, grateful for the warmth of the parlor stove and the hot liquid. Two globe lamps spilled light over familiar furniture and softened the reverend's countenance. Her gaze settled on his hands, which looked strong and capable— *Capable of what?* murmured an errant inner voice—and out of place holding a delicate porcelain cup. She remembered how warm his clasp had been in the office.

The reverend set down his cup. "So. Are you going to tell me what that note's about? No lies."

She toyed with her spoon. "I wanted Chet to put his money on the table, of course. Four aces and a fortune don't coincide every day. I was gambling that he and Joe had some kind of agreement or that Joe grubstaked him on a prospecting trip. Either case might mean added income for Emma. I thought if I goaded him, he'd give himself away with a word or gesture. Chet said he and Joe had a gentleman's agreement but that no money changed hands. He could be lying. Now, it's my turn to ask a question." She watched him closely. "When did you shave off your mustache?"

He half-raised a hand to his face, then smiled ruefully. "Old habits die hard. I shaved it off right before coming to Leadville."

He's telling the truth on that.

"My turn, Mrs. Stannert." She felt her shoulders tense. "Where did you learn to play the piano?"

She stared. "How did you know?"

"The night after Joe's death. Remember? I came pounding on your door. I don't think you heard me at first. But I heard you."

"Oh." She remembered: *The sonata. And my green-striped stockings.*

"I know very little about music, but it seemed you played uncommonly well. Expertly, even."

"My mother taught me when I was young. Later, I had instructors."

"Your mother played piano?"

"Played is not the right word for it." Inez chose her next words carefully. "Her life moved through music." For a moment, Inez could see her, dark head bent over the piano in the conservatory at dusk, creating lyric tapestries out of her pain, her anger, her isolation.

"Moved through music." Sands considered the phrase. "Is she living?"

Inez thought of her mother's existence with her father. "No," she said flatly. "Now, it's my turn." She rose and went to the sideboard for brandy for her tea. Looking down at Sands, she asked, "Where did you learn so much about counterfeiting?"

He started to smooth his nonexistent mustache, then laughed and sank back against the cushions. "So I strike you as an expert?"

She kept silent, watching.

Sands shook his head and looked away. She could almost see him weighing his answer.

Is he going to lie?

Finally, his gaze returned to her. "From Frank Vintree."

"Who's he?"

"A counterfeiter from back East. He's in prison now." The reverend tapped his empty teacup. The porcelain sounded a small, shiny note. "Our acquaintance was short. After the War. A brief interlude during the more dissipated years of my youth. The way I view it," he smiled slightly, "I'm a better minister for having seen the dark side of human nature up close. You'll never find me casting the first stone."

He stood and set his cup on the sideboard. "Now that I know your home is secure, I'll rest all the better." With his back to her, he asked, "Who taught you to play poker?"

She stood also and felt her shoulder blades loosen. It was only then she realized how tense the truth-telling game had made her. "My husband, Mark. And Abe. Good teachers, both."

In the same neutral tone, Sands asked, "What kind of a man is your husband?"

She ran a finger along the ivory keys of the piano. For comfort. "He's charming, has a way of putting everyone at ease. A good father." She heard the quaver in her voice and stopped.

Sands watched her struggle for control. He said gently, "Forgive me if I seemed to pry. I should go." He moved forward and took both her hands in his. "Bless you for using that fry pan."

He caressed her palms with his thumbs. The sensation shot to the pit of her stomach with a ferocity that took her by surprise. She felt as if the parlor were shrinking, pushing them close together. Too close.

She slowly pulled her hands away.

"No calluses to speak of. You're no farm girl from Kansas, are you, Inez?" His voice was seductive, inviting confidences.

"You could have asked. No lies, remember?"

"I could have. I wonder what you would have said."

They seemed poised in a balance, scales nearly equal in weight, tipping ever so slightly one way, then the other.

Inez bit her lip, willing herself to silence. He finally moved away, gathering hat and gloves from the sofa. The walls of the parlor eased back.

At the door, Sands paused. "Someday, I'd like to hear what brought you to Leadville and why you stay." He adjusted his hat. "See you at morning service in a few hours. And I'm looking forward to the twenty-seventh."

⟨⟩⟨⟩⟨⟩

That night, a memory stole past the guard of Inez's consciousness, under the guise of a dream.

Early September. The end of a brief alpine summer that is more like spring. She and Harry, returning to Leadville from Twin Lakes. Harry turns off the main track, saying, "I want to show you something."

Their rig climbs through aspen forest mixed with small fir. The track opens into a grassy meadow. Waves of lupine and paintbrush ripple in the breeze. Beyond the meadow, the land dips into a view of the Arkansas Valley and distant snow-covered peaks. Her breath catches. "It's beautiful, Harry. I wish I could stay here forever."

"Inez." Her name is a verbal caress. "That could be arranged."

Her heart thuds as he leans toward her. After their kiss, she opens her eyes to see him watching her. His eyes, which can be so cold, seem to glow with an intensity that might burn if she doesn't look away. Without shifting his gaze, he removes his hat, sails it into the back seat of the rig. They move toward each other again.

Inez opens her eyes after the embrace to find not Harry, but Reverend Sands. He tosses a fifty-dollar bill on her lap: "You're no better than the rest."

Inez woke, gasping.

She threw back the covers. In the pre-dawn cold, she groped her way to the washstand. Grabbing her hairbrush, she used the silver back to crack the ice sealing the water from the surface. The water stung her face, froze her fingers, but couldn't freeze the memory. Loosened by the dream, it poured over her like glacier water.

Inez trapped her face in icy hands. "It's over," she whispered to the empty room. "It's over!"

Chapter Thirty-Four

"We've got to, Abe. We have no choice." Inez strode toward the Carbonate City Bank, a watchful eye on the varying elevations of the boardwalk.

"I still think we oughta sit tight on this." Abe clenched the satchel with the coins in one hand, the shotgun with the other. Inez carried the satchel with the paper money under her cloak.

They'd gone round and round about the counterfeit, Inez wanting to notify the bank as soon as it opened Monday, Abe dragging his heels. On Wednesday, he'd finally caved. Now, here they were, on the bank steps, carrying three days' take between them, still arguing.

"Inez, suppose they check the whole deposit? Maybe there's more of the same."

"What of it? Others saw the bogus bill. If we say nothing, we're breaking the law. I'm not willing to go to jail for passing counterfeit."

Inez entered the bank, Abe an unhappy shadow behind her. In the bank manager's office, she lined up bundles of paper currency on his desk. "Mr. Cooke, before we begin, Abe and I have an issue of some delicacy to discuss with you."

Cautious alarm flitted across Morris Cooke's round face, made rounder by bushy muttonchops. "Of course, Mrs. Stannert. You and Mr. Jackson can rely on my discretion. I know your accounts were handled by Nigel. I hope nothing was amiss in that regard."

Inez pulled an envelope from the satchel and extracted the smeared bogus note. "Someone passed us a counterfeit fifty. We only discovered it when the bill became wet. Soaked with high quality brandy, actually."

Cooke withdrew a pair of small, round spectacles from a drawer and hooked them over his ears. He picked up the bill fastidiously. "When did this happen?"

"Late Saturday," said Inez. "After the poker game."

"I see." Cooke's response was cool. The days since Sunday hung in the air. "Have you seen anything like this before?"

"No, of course not!" A touch of guilt added to Inez's indignation. "If we had, we would have notified you, the marshal, or the proper authorities."

Cooke held up a placating hand. "I'm just trying to get an idea of the breadth of the problem." The hand lowered to the stacks of bills. "We'll have to examine the total deposit. How much do you have, by your reckoning?"

"Eight thousand three hundred sixty. Not including that fifty," she added belatedly.

Cooke's eyebrows popped up. "I've not handled your accounts in the past, but that sounds extraordinarily high."

"Big win Saturday night," said Abe shortly.

Cooke bobbed his head several times like a turtle. His chubby hands gathered the stacks together. "We'll let you know of the outcome."

"What do you plan to do? Soak the lot in a vat of spirits?"

Cooke winced. "There are other ways. It will take time, is all." His coolness cracked into something like an apology. "Of course, we won't be able to credit a total to your account until we're done."

Inez sighed and looked at Abe.

Abe seemed to be studying the floorboards. But when he raised his dark eyes, Inez could see he'd been listening as carefully as herself. "Mr. Cooke. Two questions."

Cooke turned attentively to Abe.

"First, you seen evidence of any other counterfeit around town? Second, you plan on talkin' to the Treasury or Secret Service?"

Cooke removed his glasses, and pulled out a linen square. He polished the lenses, saying, "I can't comment on other possible activities. I'm certain you understand, Mr. Jackson." He raised watery eyes to Abe. "As for notifying the authorities…We'll see."

Abe nodded, as if it was exactly what he'd expected. Inez stood, and Cooke popped up from behind his desk, suddenly obsequious, and ushered them out. "We won't raise any alarms until we know the situation. I'm as concerned about this as you are."

Back on the street, Abe removed his hat and wiped his brow with his sleeve. "So much for bein' good citizens."

Inez pulled her cloak close as the cold curled about her long skirts. "Well, what's the worst that can happen? Say the fifties are bogus. How many did we have? Twenty?"

She fastened her cloak, snapping each button through its hole. "What I *don't* understand is Cooke's reception. The minute I mentioned counterfeit, I got the distinct feeling he held us at least partially responsible. Like we were common thieves. Criminals."

"Come on, Inez, this ain't the first time we've tangled with counterfeit. At least this time, we're on the side of the law."

Inez froze on the last button at her throat. "What?!"

Abe was scrubbing his hair, looking at the busy intersection, distracted.

At her exclamation, he volleyed back a look of surprise to match her own. "What do you mean 'what'? Don't tell me you didn't know what Mark and I were doin' in New York when you two met. There I was, haulin' coney all over upstate, while he was waltzin' you out the back door of your daddy's home."

Brown eyes met hazel. A strange look descended on Abe's face, just as the bottom of Inez's stomach dropped out.

"Damn." He dropped his hat into place. "Inez—"

She seized his arm. "Not here." Pedestrians flowed around them, chins tucked, coats pulled tight against the cold.

Abe was still staring at her as if she, not he, had dropped the bombshell. "Jesus H. Christ," he muttered.

Chapter Thirty-Five

When Inez and Abe entered the saloon, Useless and Llewellyn stood heads together. Llewellyn straightened up as a blast of cold air brought in the two saloon owners.

"Mrs. Stannert, what do you think?" He gestured toward a painted army of headless angels with flaming silver swords. "All ready for the faces."

"Not right now." With hardly a glance at the painting, she started toward the stairs with Abe beside her.

They didn't exchange a word until they were seated in the office, Inez at the desk, Abe on the overstuffed lovescat.

Inez spoke first. "Mark never mentioned being involved in counterfeit. Abe, *you* never told me."

Abe sighed, looking older than his forty-five years. "All this time, I thought you knew."

She leaned forward. "Tell me."

"After the War, Mark and me rambled up and down the coast, playin' cards, bettin' at races. When our luck ran bad, we carried boodle for a couple coney brokers, mostly distributin', sometimes shovin'. Last time was New York. That's when he met you, at some high society party, right? Well, while you two were makin' eyes at each other, I was hoofin' bogus bills upstate." He rubbed his eyes. "Until I got caught."

"You got caught?" She stared at Abe's face. A face she thought she knew as well as her own. "But I remember meeting you after…" *After I eloped.*

"Yep. I was lucky enough to get caught by a marshal who wasn't averse to takin' money, good or bad, and lookin' the other way. Just like local law around here." Abe hiked his head in the direction of the city marshal's office. "Anyhow, I gave him a couple names and handed over the boodle. He turned his back long enough for me to leave town. That and your daddy gave us all plenty reason to head West."

Inez leaned an elbow on the desk and looked down at the framed photograph of her son. She couldn't stand the sight of his innocent face. She closed the photocase and pushed it into a pigeonhole.

"I had no idea, Abe."

Abe exhaled hard. "The only way you could of not known was if you didn't want to. Mark and I, we talked about the old times, the coney gangs, the shovin'. If you didn't hear, it was because you turned a deaf ear."

"But, counterfeiting. That's illegal!"

"Inez, come on." He sounded exasperated now. "Even us three weren't always on the right side of the law. Remember New Orleans? St. Joe? Hell, what about Dodge, that business at the Lone Star—"

"Stop." She looked out the windows at the mountains.

"You dealin' seconds under Bat Masterson's nose. Damn near gave me a heart attack. I mean, he was runnin' the place and undersheriff of Ford County, no less. You might of pulled the wool over those cowboys' eyes, but I still believe he was on to your shenanigans. Think he just let it slide, since you were smilin' sweet at him and he was supplyin' the brandy. Not to mention later that night, when you both disappeared—"

Inez rounded on him ferociously. "I said *stop!*"

"Look, I'm not layin' blame. I'm just sayin' you didn't mind livin' life on the edge of the law while we were on the move. Then, we got here and stopped movin'. Got the saloon. You and Mark started a family." Abe shook his head. "Everything changed."

Inez stared at the business ledger on the desk and forced her thoughts back to the present, away from the Lone Star Dancehall and Bat Masterson. She could not, in good conscience, enter concrete numbers in the deposit and profit columns until she heard back from Cooke. *What a mess.*

She drummed her fingers on the ledger. "Well, what difference could all that coney business make now. It was ten years ago. I can't imagine Cooke or anyone else in Leadville knows."

Abe sat back. "You're right, it was long ago. But Cooke did give us the cold shoulder. And him sayin' he might, might not get the Treasury or Secret Service involved. That's bull. No banker's gonna sit on a pile of coney. He's got to notify the government. I don't like this a-tall."

I don't like it either. Cold fingers slid up her spine. "Abe, does the name Frank Vintree mean anything to you?"

Abe's brow furrowed. "Vintree. Jesus, that was Philadelphia. Big-time coney ring. Where'd you hear about him?"

Vintree. Philadelphia. Sands. And there was another connection, one she couldn't remember. Something else about Philadelphia. A measure still missing, the tune half done.

Abe waited for her response. She realized, having said that much, she couldn't very well wiggle out of answering. Inez took a deep breath to overcome her reluctance at betraying what felt like a confidence. Or a confession. "Reverend Sands said he knew Vintree after the War. Briefly."

Abe grunted. "I suspected somethin' but wouldn't've picked him as a coney man. Don't it strike you mighty strange that all this comes up and your reverend admits he was mixed up with a coney ring?"

"No stranger than finding out my husband and my business partner, both people I thought I knew fairly well, were dropping counterfeit money up and down the East Coast. Perhaps at the same time as Sands."

"Let's not fight about it," said Abe tersely. "The big question is, were we just unlucky or were we targeted?"

"Targeted?"

"Saloons are a good place to pass bad bills. Lots of money changes hands. No one looks too close. Sometimes, the saloon owners are part of it."

"Not us." Inez was indignant.

"Yeah, but Cooke's suspicious. Maybe someone wants it that way."

"Who? Why?"

Abe spread his hands on his knees. "Who'd profit if we went down for passin' bogus?"

She thought a moment. "We'd have to sell the saloon. Who's eager to buy?" She ticked them off. "Harry Gallagher. Cat DuBois. Jed Elliston? I don't know. He loves the newspaper business. Cooper acts interested. I always assumed he was inquiring for Harry, but maybe not."

"Straight-and-narrow Cooper? He don't seem the type to run a gin mill."

Inez stood and straightened her skirts. "At this point, no one is what they seem." *Not even you and Mark.*

‹›‹›‹›

Downstairs, the saloon had opened for business. While Abe and Useless provided early arrivals with the means to toast the coming holiday, Doc swirled the brandy in his glass and meditated on the faceless mural.

"Magnificent, my dear." He wrinkled a smile at Inez. "Your artist," he indicated Llewellyn, who sat nearby devouring a bowl of Bridgette's stew, "told me you're selling spots in Elysium. As well as in the underworld. Of course, any battle, celestial or otherwise, should have a physician in attendance. How much to paint my visage on the fine fellow at the far right? And change his sword to a caduceus?"

Inez, bemused, examined the muscular physique of the warrior angel on the wall, so at odds with Doc's stooped form. "So you'd like to be field physician to the Lord's battalions? An eagle buys you immortality."

Doc dug out the ten-dollar gold piece and dropped it on the bar.

Inez pocketed the eagle and led the physician to Llewellyn's table. "We have our first taker. Doc Cramer has chosen the angel on the far left, with a few modifications."

Llewellyn wiped his mustache on the sleeve of his painter's smock and jumped up to shake Doc's hand. It looked like a formal introduction between an aging Paul Bunyan and an elf. "You'll not be disappointed." Llewellyn gestured to an empty chair and picked up a sketch pad. "I need a three-quarters view, so if you'll turn your chair a bit to the left."

Doc adjusted his chair and bow tie, before raising his chin to strike what, Inez assumed, was supposed to be a heroic pose. Llewellyn sketched in rapid, flowing strokes. "A quick likeness now, and I'll begin painting after Christmas. By New Year's you'll be in Paradise for a mere ten dollars."

Another gold coin arced through the air and plunked onto the table.

"Were it truly so easy to enter Heaven." The reverend smiled amiably at Doc and touched his hat in greeting to Inez.

Llewellyn froze in place, pencil stilled. "Talk to Mrs. Stannert if you want a spot in the mural, Reverend. She has final say on its design. I'm merely the artistic executor."

"Are you." The reverend regarded him with little warmth before grabbing a nearby chair, pulling it to the table, and straddling it. "How are those marriage certificates coming along? A crack engraver like yourself should have them done by now. Especially since the design is nothing new to you."

Llewellyn's pencil point wavered above the paper. He stared at Sands, dislike and unease chasing across his face. "I warned you that I had other commissions before yours."

"So you said." Reverend Sands stood his ten-dollar gold piece on edge and gave it a spin. It gyrated merrily across the table. "It appears you'd rather be painting Mrs. Stannert's epic picture."

What's going on between these two? Inez leaned over and stopped the spinning coin. "Reverend Sands, since you're interested in being portrayed, do you choose to fight on behalf of darkness or light?"

She'd asked the question in jest, to lessen the tension. When Sands looked up, his eyes, shadowed by his hat, looked gray and somber. They lightened briefly as he smiled. "I choose to fight by your side of course, Mrs. Stannert. So tell me. Which side is that?"

"I wasn't intending to be in the mural."

"I see. Like most generals, you remain apart from the battlefield, plan the strategy, and direct the troops."

The reverend abandoned his chair to survey the painting. "Hell looks like a cold, uninviting place. Heaven doesn't look much warmer. The Garden is the only hospitable spot on the wall." He glanced at Inez. "Where did you get this vision?"

"From John Milton and Leadville."

Doc twitched in his chair. The noble pose vanished. "Surely you don't need to ponder, Reverend. You're a man of God *and* you fought on the side of might and right in the War. Pick the winning side, man."

"In my experience, even the winners end up losing something." Reverend Sands strolled to the bar to inspect the painting up close. "Right or wrong. Win or lose. Black or white. Life's seldom so simple. In my experience, most choices end up shades of gray."

Inez moved to stand beside him. "In this case, though, there are only two possibilities. Heaven or Hell. No shades of gray."

He walked back and forth, examining the scene. "I'll be Abdiel. Always faithful to God, yet followed Satan. At least until he defied Satan in the heavenly war."

Llewellyn interjected, "An angel who sneaks into the enemy's camp? Sounds like a common spy to me."

Sands looked at him. "I see him as delivering the Word to those most in need."

Doc harrumphed. "During the War, those who infiltrated the secessionists' camps and won their confidence provided an invaluable service to their country." He craned his neck to look at the sketch. "Finished, Mr. Tremayne? I must resume my rounds."

Reverend Sands retrieved his ten-dollar gold piece and returned to Inez. He took her hand, dropped the coin into her palm, and closed her fingers around it.

Still holding her hand, he added, "A pity you won't consider gracing an angel with your likeness. I can imagine you as one of God's chosen, sword in hand, secure in your convictions. You'd be most persuasive. I, for one, would follow you without question." He lowered his voice. "Recovered from Saturday?"

The pressure of his hands sent a delicious warmth shooting about inside her and encouraged unangelic thoughts.

"Quite, thank you." She cocked her head, eyeing his face for bruises. "And you?"

"Never better. Well, my head is still sore from the pounding on the floor. But I've been worse." His hands tightened a moment, before letting go.

She slipped the coin into her pocket. *At least it's gold and not paper.*

Sands continued, "It shouldn't interfere with the Christmas Eve service. Will you be there?"

Inez nodded.

"Excellent." He rubbed his face where the mustache had once resided, then stopped, mid-gesture. "Remind me never to play cards with you. I'd give myself away in a second. What I was working around to, is, I hope you'll allow me to walk you home afterward."

"I'd be delighted."

He tipped his hat and turned to Llewellyn. "It's settled then. Abdiel has a face, and Heaven will have one of her own in the enemy camp."

Chapter Thirty-Six

The Christmas Eve service was a tapestry of candlelight, joyful voices raised in familiar song, and the sharp scent of pine boughs. Through it all, Reverend Sands' smooth voice wove in and out, speaking of the promise the next day would bring.

After the service, Susan Carothers turned to Emma, Joey, and Inez. "Are you sure you won't come caroling? There are plenty of armed and sober men. It should be safe."

Inez waved her away. "Have a good time, Susan. See you tomorrow."

Reverend Sands strolled up, looking genial and thoroughly in the spirit of the season. He winked at Inez before addressing Emma. "Mrs. Rose, do you need an escort? Mrs. Stannert and I are walking your way."

"No, thank you, Reverend. Mr. Gallagher offered to drive us home."

"And you accepted?" Inez interrupted incredulously.

Emma's hand strayed briefly to the lap of her coat. "I've no energy for walking tonight." The skin around her eyes looked bruised, as if sleep eluded her. Inez remembered her own exhaustion in the early stages of pregnancy and refrained from further comment.

Emma turned to Sands. "Will you join us for supper tomorrow? It will be our last with our Leadville friends. Inez, Susan, and Mr. Jackson will be there."

"I'd enjoy that. Thank you."

Harry approached. "Are you ready, Mrs. Rose?"

Joey spoke, sounding petulant. "I want to walk home with Reverend Sands and Auntie Inez."

A few words into his protest Emma's hand fell on his small shoulder. Inez could see those gloved fingers tighten in a tactile rebuke, even as she spoke to Harry. "He's tired and forgets his manners, Mr. Gallagher. We are, of course, grateful for your offer."

Harry's cold gaze lingered speculatively on Inez before moving to Reverend Sands. It was as if he was summing up earnings and liabilities, expecting a profit, and had discovered a disturbing debit instead.

With worshippers gone, candles extinguished, and church doors locked behind them, Inez and the reverend stepped to the street. "Silent Night" drifted to them, along with the distant tootle of a brass band. Reverend Sands looked up at the ink-black sky, pricked with light. "A beautiful night with a million stars. Any of them bright enough to be the star of Bethlehem."

Inez raised her face to the night, more aware of the vastness of the sky than its beauty. "I'll miss Emma. I worry how she will manage."

"It's hard to see friends move on. Rest assured, friendly people await Mrs. Rose at the end of her journey. California will be good for her. A new start." His voice sounded comforting in the dark.

As they stepped into the Harrison Avenue intersection, Inez bent her head to concentrate on her footing. The smooth soles of her Sunday shoes skated on the treacherous ice, throwing her momentarily off balance. She was more than willing to lean on Sands while negotiating the uneven terrain.

With her eyes lowered and the hood of her cloak muffling her ears, she didn't see or hear the horse careen around the corner at full speed.

"Look out!" Reverend Sands shouted.

He tried to yank Inez across the intersection. Her shoes slipped and she fell to one knee, cushioned by petticoats and skirts.

Inez looked up.

For a heartbeat, she saw the horse rearing above her, moonlight glinting off the pointed studs of winter horseshoes.

Sands wrenched her across the jagged surface, sharp as broken glass. Her shoulder felt as if it was being pulled from the socket. She regained her footing, and they scrambled to the safety of the boardwalk. Sharp cracks rang out behind them. The peaceful spell of Christmas Eve shattered along with the ice in the streets.

"You nearly killed us, you damn fool!" The reverend's voice was rough with anger.

"Reverend Sands, is that you?" Cat DuBois' distinct contralto slid across the night air. "My apologies. I'd hoped to run into you after the service, but not quite this way." She reined in the large horse as it pranced in excited circles, smashing broken ice to slush.

Inez gasped freezing air into her lungs, her limbs trembling with a tardy surge of adrenaline.

The horse danced sideways and blew clouds of condensation. Mrs. DuBois, covered neck to ankle in a long fur coat, peered out from under a matching Cossack-style hat. Her eyes reflected the nearby street lamp. Inez was reminded of a winter forest creature—*A fox. Or a weasel.*—peering from its den and sizing up another animal as a possible meal.

"My, my, is that Mrs. Stannert with you? She looks shaken." Cat leaned forward. "You're not going to *faint*, are you, Mrs. Stannert?"

How I loathe that woman.

Cat returned her attention to the reverend. "I'm sorry the girls and I missed the service, but we're very busy tonight. All the poor men so far from wives and sweethearts on the holiday. We do our Christian best to offer them comfort and solace." She pulled a small white envelope from her coat and held it out to Sands. "For you."

He didn't move. "What is it, Mrs. DuBois, a Christmas card?"

"A Christmas card? Oh, how droll!" Cat's laughter climbed up and down the scale. "No, no, my dear Reverend Sands. It's a special invitation, extended to a very select few. A small party's planned for midnight tonight with refreshments and entertainment. We hope you'll attend. Special rates for the clergy. And, I should tell you…" Her tone dropped, becoming as intimate as the touch of a satin sheet. "After your last visit, the girls were so impressed they voted you their most favorite man of God."

"If I impressed all you ladies so much, I hope to see more of you at church services in the future." His tone walked the line of studied courtesy.

"Join us tonight and I promise you'll see much more of us." Her eyes measured him approvingly, as she tapped the envelope against her lips. She finally tucked the invitation back inside her coat. "Well, no need for this. When you come, say that I extended an invitation to you. In person."

With a final glance at Inez, Cat DuBois reined her horse about and trotted back down Harrison.

Inez couldn't help but think of the bedraggled appearance she presented next to the elegant Mrs. DuBois, who was riding away as sedately as an Englishwoman to the hunt. She finally became aware that Sands was repeating "Are you all right?"

"I am not about to faint, if that's what you're thinking." Her palm stung. She flexed her gloved hand, trying to dispel the twinge.

"I wasn't thinking that at all. I was concerned about your shoulder. Sorry about dragging you across the road. But I figured that was better than the alternative. Did you hurt your hand?" He took her hand in his.

Inez pulled away. "Her carelessness nearly killed us."

"Is that what you're angry about?"

"She's an expert in the saddle, or so I hear." Inez gritted her teeth at the unintended double entendre and then identified the deeper source of her fury.

She took a couple of steps. Her shoes were scuffed beyond repair.

Sands kept pace with her, watching her intently. "I won't be taking her up on the invitation. That goes without saying. So, does that tight-lipped expression I see have to do with my 'previous visit' with Mrs. DuBois?"

"It's none of my business."

"No lies between us, remember? Ask, and I'll answer."

She focused on her shoes.

Sands put both hands on her shoulders and turned her toward him. "Mrs. DuBois wields words like a weapon. Now, my visit. It was a courtesy call, same as I've paid to all the parishioners. Well, almost the same. I turned down her offer of 'refreshments and entertainment.' My interest is in the state of their souls. Nothing else."

"You don't have to tell me any of this."

He looked her in the eye. "Yes, I do. If I don't, her words will hang between us, destroying any chances we have of getting to know each other better. Now, let's get you home."

Chapter Thirty-Seven

Abe held up the ivory-handled bowie knife. "Mighty fine, Inez." He turned it this way and that, admiring the wicked blade etched with "AJ".

"I gambled that your old one was still missing. Merry Christmas, Abe." Inez eased back into Emma's window seat, glad that her choice pleased him.

The fire in the parlor's small fireplace popped behind the painted screen. Next to Emma's rocking chair, a small fir tree stoically shouldered candles and strands of cranberries. The black crepe, which had draped the mantel and few pictures in the parlor since Joe's death, was nowhere to be seen. Inez had been surprised that Emma proposed a Christmas gathering, given the circumstances. But she had insisted. "Joe always said we should look to the future, not to the past." Tears had veiled Emma's eyes, but did not fall. "He would have wanted us all together. Wanted us to carry on."

She did, however, keep the curtains drawn.

Joey bumped Inez's elbow as he wiggled around and pulled back a corner of the heavy curtain to peer out the window.

"Joey." Emma's voice carried a mother's verbal nudge. "Why don't you open your gift from Aunt Inez and Mr. Jackson."

Joey pulled the ribbon and foil wrapping paper off the box on his lap and handed them to his mother for later reuse.

He lifted the top off the box. Inez was gratified to see his eyes go wide.

"This is how it works." She took out the pocket telescope, showing him how the inner tube could be extended from the larger brass cylinder.

He nudged the curtain aside again, allowing a shaft of sunlight to pierce the room, and pointed the telescope out the window, training it up the street.

"What do you say?" Emma prompted.

"Thank you Auntie Inez, Mr. Jackson."

Abe handed a flat rectangular package to Inez. "For you, Inez."

Inez removed the wrapping paper and stared with bemusement at the book on her lap. *Leaves of Grass.*

"I took a chance that you don't have it." Abe leaned forward, watching her face. "Leastways, I don't remember you ever talkin' 'bout it. When I asked the bookseller for somethin' for a highly literate lady, he recommended this one. It's mighty fine poetry, he said."

Inez remembered reading Walt Whitman's sensual poems aloud from an edition that had been smuggled into her boarding school by a classmate. *It seems like a century ago.*

She flipped the pages until she came to a remembered passage:

> *"But the expression of a well-made man appears not only*
> *in his face;*
> *It is in his limbs and joints also, it is curiously in the*
> *joints of his hips and wrists;*
> *It is in his walk, the carriage of his neck, the flex of his*
> *waist and knees—dress does not hide him... "*

"Poems?" Emma's voice jolted Inez out of her reverie. "How thoughtful, Abe. We all know how Inez loves her books. Would you read one for us, Inez?"

"Ah—" Inez paged quickly, looking for something less flammable than "I Sing the Body Electric."

The lens of Joey's telescope thunked against the windowpane. "Uncle Mark! It's Uncle Mark!"

The book thudded to the rug as Inez rose from the seat and turned. She wrenched the curtain back. Light flooded the room, momentarily blinding her. Placing a hand on the cold pane, Inez leaned close to the glass, her breath twisted in a knot around her heart. Abe, Emma, and Susan rushed to the window.

Joey's voice climbed in excitement. "I knew he'd come back for Christmas!"

With confident strides and hands buried deep in pockets, he stepped sure-footed between the hollows and humps melted and refrozen in the old snow. His head was bent, the black hat shutting his face from view.

Dear God.

He paused two doors away and removed his hat to smooth light brown hair. Inez's world slid sideways as he glanced up in their direction.

"Oh—" A chorus of exhalations told Inez that she wasn't the only one who'd stopped breathing.

Reverend Sands replaced his hat and continued toward Emma's house.

"Joey. How could you?" Emma's reproof was directed toward her son even as she patted Inez's shoulder consolingly.

Inez sank back on the window seat and shut her eyes to bring her world back in order. "Don't scold him." She squeezed Emma's hand. "When I saw...but how could I have even thought..."

"Well, Reverend Sands does look like Mark. I, I mean just a little," Susan stammered.

Abe smoothed back his own hair, looking curiously at Inez. "He's a dead ringer at a distance. You didn't see it before now?" He winced, perplexed, Inez supposed, that she'd been so blind to the physical similarities.

A rapping at the door sent the group flying in different directions: Joey to hide, Emma to greet Reverend Sands, Susan to retrieve a cup of eggnog for the new arrival.

Sands entered the parlor just as Susan barreled out of the kitchen. "Merry Christmas." She handed him the cup.

"Thank you." He nodded to Abe, smiled at Inez. "Merry Christmas." He shifted to peer down the hallway. "Where's Joey?"

Whitman's words whispered through Inez's mind like a tree in a breeze. *"You linger to see his back, and the back of his neck and shoulder-side."*

"I'll get him," Inez said hastily.

Glad to escape the suddenly stuffy parlor, she hurried to the small bedroom. Pushing the door open, she saw Joey folded over his rocking horse, torso and head hidden from view. All she could see were the soles of his shoes, his Sunday-best pants, and his rump sticking up above the horse's saddle.

"Joey, Reverend Sands is here." She sat on his bed. From there, she could see his upside-down head, face turned away. "For a minute, I thought he was Uncle Mark, too."

"Mama told me Uncle Mark's with the angels. I forgot."

"That's all right, Joey."

Joey turned to face her. "She says Uncle Mark's with papa in Heaven. I miss papa. Do you miss Uncle Mark?"

"Yes. Very much."

"Do you get so sad that you cry sometimes?"

She hesitated. Then, "Yes. Sometimes."

Joey sighed and righted himself on the horse. "Me too."

He rocked a moment, the rockers thumpeting on the plank floor. She could almost see the wheels turning. "Maybe..."

"What, Joey?"

"Maybe you could marry Reverend Sands. Then you wouldn't be so sad anymore." His face brightened. "And mama and me could visit."

Bemused but irritated, she put out a hand to stop the horse. The elaborately carved eyes and nostrils gave it an astonished expression. "Getting married and all, that's not a subject for children. Don't repeat it to Reverend Sands. Or anyone else."

He looked at her, dark eyebrows knitted in a frown that reminded Inez of his father. "Don't you like him, Auntie Inez? He likes you. I heard Miss Carothers say so to mama."

"There you are." Reverend Sands leaned on the doorjamb, overcoat still on. "Joey, your mother gave us permission to go to the corner and back before supper. So, are you riding that horse to California or would you like to throw a few snowballs?"

Joey perked up and slid off the rocking horse. "Snow won't pack."

"I've got something else to show you then." Sands wiggled his eyebrows in a mock show of seriousness. "Hurry. It's a secret."

Joey grabbed a cap from the floor and a long, tangled scarf before heading toward the kitchen for his jacket.

Inez stood and looked around the near empty room. A small trunk stood in the corner, half-filled with Joey's clothes, waiting to receive the last few items. *By this time next week, they'll be gone.*

She turned to find the reverend still leaning in the doorway, watching her. He moved aside to let her pass, then caught her arm. "I asked Mrs. Rose to save me the chair next to yours. I hope you don't mind."

"Mind? Not at all."

"Good. Wish you'd come walk with us. You look as if you could use a bit of fresh air as well." He slid his hand up to her shoulder. An answering shiver ran down her spine.

"I'm half afraid of what will happen next if you and I go strolling down the street."

He smiled and raised his eyebrows.

"I mean," Inez added hastily, "given the near miss we had last night." She edged past him. "Emma probably needs help in the kitchen."

Reverend Sands dropped his hand, still smiling. "I understand. You two have just a few days left. We, on the other hand, have time."

In the kitchen, the aroma of a roasting wild turkey filled the air. Joey jittered from one foot to the other by the back door in barely contained excitement. "I've got a surprise too. Mama says I can show you outside." Inez caught the glint of the pocket telescope behind his back.

"A surprise, eh? Let's go. Looks like we've got lots to do." The reverend winked at Inez and Emma as he opened the door.

The women watched the two figures—one tall, one small—negotiate the footpath through the snow-filled backyard to the alley.

Emma wiped her hands on the towel looped over her apron. "Reverend Sands is a good man, Inez. He helped us through the worst of times and is getting us started on a new life. And now, Joe's debt is taken care of. I only wish I knew who paid it off so I could thank them in person or at least in my prayers. Reverend Sands says he's passed along my gratitude and not to think on it any more."

She started back to the stove. "It's a miracle, when you think about it. Five thousand dollars. I can't think of anyone with that kind of money who'd do something like that."

"Speaking of people with that kind of money," Inez drifted over to the stove with her, "how was your ride home with Harry last night? Did he behave himself?"

Emma froze a moment, her face still. She then shook her head, dipped a spoon into a canister, and sifted a spoonful of flour into the drippings. "Mr. Gallagher wished us a pleasant journey to California. And he apologized."

"Harry *apologized?*" The notion boggled Inez.

"For any distress he might have caused." She added canned milk to the bubbling gravy. "He also wants to buy Joe's lot downtown. Building and all. I told him to work it out with you and the bank. Ironic, isn't it. Harry Gallagher ruins our lives, buys what's left, and finances our new life in California."

"Harry's buying Joe's business?" Inez leaned against the kitchen table. Baffled. "Why?"

"Location, I suppose. It's on Chestnut, after all."

Inez thought of something else. "Too, there's the assay equipment. I heard he's hiring a company assayer. Maybe he'll cart Joe's furnaces and so on up to Fryer Hill."

Emma stirred the gravy. "He said he'd pay eight thousand dollars. Eight thousand. Is it really worth that much?" She shook her head. "I'll leave it to you, Inez. I don't want to think about him or Joe's business any more."

She filled the gravy boat. "Would you tell Abe and Susan that supper's ready? Then, you can help me put it on the table."

Inez smoothed her skirt. A bump in her pocket reminded her: *The key.*

"I have a quick question for you first." Inez pulled out the small key. "We found this among Joe's papers in his office. Does it look familiar?"

Emma's eyebrows drew together in a frown. She took the key from Inez and examined it briefly. "No. Maybe it opens his desk."

"We tried and it doesn't. The design and size are unusual. Maybe it belongs to something here at home. A strongbox or—"

The key made a decisive *tick* as Emma slapped it on the kitchen table. "I've never seen it before. And unless it's the key to a fortune, I don't care. Joe's gone. Right now, I'm doing what he would have wanted and trying my best to look forward, not back. To make some kind of future for myself, Joey, and…and the baby."

Her mouth began to tremble. She brushed the back of her hand across her eyes before tucking a strand of carrot-colored hair behind one ear. "We've packed nearly everything in the house. You helped us. Did you see anything that might fit that key? I didn't. Give it to Mr. Gallagher. It must belong to something in the office, and he's going to own it all anyway. Let him figure out what it unlocks. Now, please bring the gravy to the table."

She swept out of the kitchen into the small dining area.

Inez looked at the orphan key and swallowed the lump in her throat. *Maybe I'll get lucky and see something I've overlooked.*

She slipped it into her pocket as boots rattled up the back steps. Joey burst into the kitchen, eyes shining, cheeks ruddy from cold. "Auntie Inez! Watch!" He set two fingers in his mouth and let loose with a piercing whistle. Emma, who was just entering the kitchen, clapped her hands to her ears. "Not inside!"

"'Scuse me." He didn't look particularly contrite. "I can whistle! Reverend Sands showed me how!"

Another, heavier set of boots clomped up the stairs, and the reverend walked in, looking pleased. "I heard you all the way to the shed, Joey."

Joey beamed.

Reverend Sands crouched low, his face level with Joey's. "Now tell your mama. What's the signal?"

Joey looked up at his mother to be sure she was listening. "Three whistles means help, mama. You blow three times, I'll come rescue you."

She smoothed his rumpled hair. "I'll remember that. Now go wash your hands."

Chapter Thirty-Eight

Evening gloves in hand, Inez examined her reflection in the mirror over her bedroom washstand. In the lamplight, the ivory lace bled white, tracing the décolletage of her new evening dress and falling in a straight line down the front of the bodice. Inez stroked the dark green velvet, marveling at its softness and trying to ignore the turmoil in her stomach.

You'd think I was fifteen, preparing for my first dance.

She felt for the strand of pearls wound through her intricately knotted hair and checked that the countless hairpins were all in place.

Inez twisted the two bands, gold and silver, on her ring finger, debating whether to remove them. At the knock on the front door, she hastily pulled on her gloves and quenched the light.

She opened the door to find the reverend in full dress. He stared, then doffed his top hat. "Mrs. Stannert. Words fail me completely."

Inez finished buttoning her gloves and smiled. "Well, this is a first. Thank you, Reverend."

He helped her with her evening cape and escorted her to a waiting buggy.

"You brought a rig." She was pleased she wouldn't have to navigate through snow and slush on foot.

"Much as I enjoy walking with you, I didn't want to chance more ruined coats and shoes. Or worse. I intend to deliver you to and from the dance in one piece."

"You sound like Abe." She settled against the cushioned seat, her satin skirt making a satisfying rustle. "When I took the money to the bank Wednesday, he insisted on coming. Said he didn't want me to mysteriously disappear along the way."

The reverend turned up the collar of his overcoat and shook the reins. The buggy jolted into motion. "That's one thing that Mr. Jackson and I agree on. No disappearances allowed. Which means I'm your constant companion tonight." He paused, and his tone lightened. "Your dance card is full, Mrs. Stannert. Too bad for the other fellows, lucky for me."

He clucked to the horse, which obediently picked up the pace, turning onto Harrison's gas-lit street. In front of the Hotel Windsor, a confusion of rigs and enclosed buggies angled for space.

The reverend guided the buggy around the corner. He sat for a moment, scanning the area. Whatever he saw, or didn't see, seemed to satisfy him. "We shouldn't have any problems walking this short distance."

"I think you're making way too much of this." As he eased out of the rig she caught the dull gleam of a gun belt beneath his tail coat. "You came armed to a soiree?"

"As I said, I'm taking no chances." His face softened as he helped her down the steps and they began to walk. "I'm looking forward to a pleasant evening in your company. With no complications. So, you mean to say you don't have your little Remington tucked in a secret pocket?"

"I left my gun at home."

They ascended the steps to the brick-sided hotel. A wreath of pine boughs framed the heavy oak door while the leaded glass insets twinkled with shifting lights and colors from within. Reverend Sands turned toward her, eyes crinkling at the corners, reflecting her own anticipation. "Ready?"

He released her elbow for a moment to retrieve the engraved invitation from inside his dress-coat. A few tentative snowflakes fell as the reverend opened the door.

The first thing to hit her senses was the unexpected warmth, heavy with the scent of vegetation; the second was the color and light. Flowers of an astonishing variety perched in crystal vases on tables. Fragrant winter garlands twined around the banister of the grand staircase that led to a balcony overlooking the crowded floor below. Potted ferns and small trees, some ten feet high, stood in silver urns along the walls. Their branches held brilliant crepe paper and birdcages with multicolored birds.

These hues couldn't even begin to compare to the vibrant reds, oranges, and pinks worn by the women who twittered on the arms of their more somber, black-coated escorts. Amid such brilliant plumage Inez felt almost invisible in dark green.

Stepping forward in full evening wear, a stiff collar pinching his long neck, a poker-faced fellow took the reverend's invitation. "Evenin' gov'nor, ma'am. Welcome to the Garden of Eden. Not bad for midwinter, eh?" He turned and waved a white gloved hand. "Drinks an' victuals upstairs. Dancin' will commence shortly afore everyone partakes o' too much after-Christmas cheer."

He swayed gently, having apparently partaken already, and added, "Gentlemen are asked t' leave firearms wi' th' overcoats."

After checking overcoats and the reverend's gun, they headed to the banquet tables on the second floor. Sands gingerly sidestepped the sweeping trains of women engrossed in conversation on the staircase. Down on the dance floor, the string quartet enthusiastically mangled Vivaldi.

Upstairs, the scent of food overwhelmed the flowery perfumes. An army of tables offered chickens with oyster dressing, sugar-cured hams with champagne sauce, and venison with red currant jelly at one end, then marched through all the various courses to halt at mince pies, marble cakes, cream kisses, and chocolate macaroons at the other.

They found a vacant table near the balustrade. As they ate, Inez remarked on Leadville's illustrious citizenry on the floor below. "Jed Elliston's with Angel. That fellow with the bristling mustache to the left of Harry Gallagher is Horace Tabor, the richest man in Leadville. Jerome Chaffee and David Moffat are to Harry's right. They're major stockholders in the Little Pittsburg Consolidated. Probably all discussing silver prices." A shock of color caught her attention. "Well, well. There's Mrs. DuBois."

Cat, looking like a flame in red and gold silk, glided up to the knot of men and linked her arm through Harry's. The men seemed to fade to shadows as she gleamed.

The quartet finished butchering Mozart and began a rousing waltz.

Reverend Sands stood and bowed. "May I have the first dance, Mrs. Stannert? As well as all the rest?"

Inez smiled back and stood. She held her skirts close as they descended the stairs along with other couples bent on the same destination. On the dance floor at last, Reverend Sands pulled her to him with a flourish. As their bodies made contact, a jolt passed through her as if his very proximity was electric. Inez knew from the sudden widening of his eyes that Reverend Sands felt it too. Without a word, he eased his grip on her waist to allow a measure of space between them.

Several quadrilles, lancers, and schottisches later, the musicians announced their intention to break for liquid refreshment.

"Sounds like a good idea." Reverend Sands led her to a chair nestled between two silver potted palms, which met in a kiss overhead. "I'll find you some of that French champagne." He leaned forward and said in a voice as intimate as a touch, "Don't disappear."

"And miss dancing more with you?" She smiled.

She watched him wind his way to the bar, greeting others on the way.

Fanning herself lightly, Inez twisted in her chair to gaze out the window behind her. In spite of the brilliant lights within, she could still make out a nearly full moon. At the front of the room, the violins settled into the smooth lilt of another waltz.

"Mrs. Stannert. May I have this dance." It was not a request but a command.

Inez shifted about and eyed Harry Gallagher's outstretched hand. "This dance is taken, Mr. Gallagher."

He smiled the merest of civil smiles. "Sands is detained. Trapped in conversation with Mrs. Titweiller. He won't begrudge me one turn on the floor with you."

Without waiting for a response, Harry captured her hand and pulled her out onto the crowded floor.

Chapter Thirty-Nine

Inez found herself smashed against Harry's starched white shirt front. He held her tight, as if she might run away if held at a polite distance.

She addressed her remarks to the shoulder of his elegant swallow-tail jacket. "Just what do you think you're doing?"

"That's exactly what I intended to ask you." He spoke close to her ear. "It appears your fancy has shifted to men of the cloth."

The bitterness that threaded his voice seemed to spread from his body to hers by contact alone, like a contagion.

She looked up into his distantly polite face, mere inches from her own, and tried to rein in her responding ire. "It appears yours, Harry, has shifted to well-heeled madams of State Street."

He looked over her head, nodded to someone behind her, and continued as if she hadn't spoken. "You know nothing about him. What kind of man he is."

"Of course, I forgot. You were on the church selection committee that considered interim candidates and extended the offer. So, tell me, what kind of man did you bring in to lead the church?"

She watched his jaw tighten as he gritted his teeth. "This is preposterous," he muttered.

Perceiving an advantage, she pressed on. "And, further-more, if we're going to compare the moral standings of our companions, Mrs. DuBois hardly strikes me as a paragon of virtue."

He pulled her almost viciously aside from an imminent collision with another circling couple. "At least she states her price up front and doesn't renege on a deal."

"Price, oh yes. You're a great one for saying everyone and everything has a price." Inez shifted her attack. "Emma said you offered to buy Joe's property for eight thousand dollars. The place is worth half that. What are you trying to buy, Harry? Peace of mind?"

She felt him take a deep breath. He glanced around at the spinning couples as if to remind himself of where they were. When he looked back down at her, his eyes were as cold as a Colorado winter sky. "Save the business discussion for the bank, Inez."

"Oh, that's right. We discuss only matters on your agenda. So, what is it about the Roses, Harry?" Inez felt his hand clench in the small of her back. "Was it just the assays? The fact that Joe pulled the wool over your eyes, but now he's dead and you're sorry about the bad blood between you? Or," she searched his face for clues, "is there more?"

"My business with the Roses is a closed book, Inez. And none of your concern."

A sudden thought struck her. "Harry. Are you Emma's anonymous benefactor, the one who paid off Joe's bank loan?"

His face revealed nothing. Making her all the more certain that her hunch was correct.

"You are! Why?"

Those pale eyes were fixed on her, watching and giving nothing away.

Inez's mind began to race like the wind, chasing connections like scattered leaves. "You're after something, Harry. You only throw money at those things you can't get any other way. Chet's claims, Marshal Hollis' loyalties, Mrs. DuBois'... services." She spat out the word. "Just like you tried to buy the Silver Queen. I told you I'd not sell, not at any price. So, you wooed me. And, when you thought I was yours, you went to Abe and tried to buy his share of the business behind my back. What have you done that you need to buy forgiveness from Emma Rose?"

In the midst of her accusations, a flash of astonishment crossed his face followed by a calculating expression. She could almost see him sorting through her speech, focusing on what interested him, throwing the rest away. The room whirled about as Harry turned her in a tight circle.

"So that's what was going on last fall when you refused to talk to me." Harry lifted his eyes to steer her between two swaying couples. When he looked back down, his expression had settled into amused irritation, like a parent tolerating a pampered child's outburst. "Inez, you're a fool."

She jerked and began to pull away. "This dance is over, Harry."

"It's over when I say it is," he responded, his eyes focused over her head again. "Sands has been rescued from Mrs. Titweiller by Mrs. DuBois."

He turned so Inez could see Cat DuBois standing close to the reverend. As Inez watched, Cat tapped him lightly on the chest with her closed fan and shifted her weight to one hip. Her red and gold dress shimmered.

"They suit each other." His voice dismissed them as irrelevant. "I have a carriage outside. When the music ends, we'll leave and go where we can talk privately."

"We have nothing to discuss."

"Yes we do." Harry spoke as if all was decided. "It's a conversation long overdue."

He absentmindedly caressed her back like a rider stroking a favorite thoroughbred. She stiffened.

"Harry, if you do not escort me to a chair immediately, I will leave you standing right here in the middle of the floor."

"Wouldn't that set people talking." There was definite amusement in his tone now. "And whose reputation would suffer from such an episode, Inez, yours or mine?"

"That's poor coin to buy my acquiescence with, Harry."

A small smile hovered beneath his mustache. She could feel him relax his guard, confident that she was merely bluffing.

Inez twisted out of Harry's grasp and pushed through the crowded dance floor without looking back. Startled stares and speculative murmurs rolled behind her like a spindrift avalanche. She kept her eyes fixed on the far wall, praying that the velvet curtain straight ahead hid an empty window alcove.

Reaching the drape at last, she yanked it aside and entered a cool sanctuary surrounded on three sides by mullioned windowpanes. Inez walked to the furthest window and pressed her forehead against the freezing glass to collect herself.

A shaft of light and a rustle announced that she had company. Inez turned quickly, expecting Harry or Reverend Sands.

A ghostly figure stood just inside the curtain, shades of silver and pearl spilling in a column of silk to the floor. Only one person wore a gown that ethereal tonight.

"Angel?"

Angel held a finger to her lips: Wait.

She tweaked the curtain back to survey the dance floor, then closed it tight. She hitched up her long narrow skirts, revealing a length of white silk stocking topped by a wide silver garter banded with rosettes. Angel fussed with the garter, retrieving an object tucked into the band. She released her skirts. Waves of silver and pearl cascaded back around her shoes. Angel glided forward and thrust the object—flat, round, and hard—into Inez's palm. Inez could just make out the initials "JR" engraved on the dustcover.

"Joe's pocketwatch," Inez whispered.

Angel turned to go.

Inez seized her wrist. "Where did you get this?"

Light stabbed across the alcove as the curtain was wrenched back.

"What have we here?" Cat DuBois held one corner of the velvet drape up, her narrowed eyes darting from Inez to Angel.

"The oh-so-imprudent Mrs. Stannert and my very own Angel. What an odd pair."

Inez slipped the watch into her pocket while Cat gazed at Angel.

"Is Mrs. Stannert describing the moral advantages of a virtuous life or some such drivel? It so happens she just cast her own dubious reputation into the mud by insulting one of the most powerful men in the state." Cat raised her penciled eyebrows at Inez. "That was quite entertaining, watching you stalk off the floor. I daresay Harry won't soon forget being publicly spurned by a State Street saloonkeeper."

"Pardon me, Mrs. DuBois." Relief weakened Inez's knees as Reverend Sands squeezed past Cat.

"They're temporarily out of champagne." He handed Inez a brandy goblet.

With her fan, Cat DuBois traced the swell of her breasts above her low-cut neckline. "I so enjoyed our conversation, Reverend. Let's continue another time, shall we?" She held out a hand to Angel. "Come, Angel. It's not proper to leave Mr. Elliston cooling his heels."

The curtain fell as the two women disappeared into the noisy ballroom, leaving Inez and the reverend in a muffled space of moonlight.

Inez tossed down the brandy. She sighed once, as the fierce and familiar warmth loosened the knot in her stomach.

Reverend Sands, who'd been lounging against one of the windows, hands in trouser pockets, straightened up. "How was it?"

"Couldn't say. I didn't taste it." She held out the goblet. "Let's try again."

The reverend took her glass, paused, then spoke as carefully as a man stepping out onto a frozen lake, testing for thin ice. "One minute, I saw you dancing with Harry Gallagher. The next minute, you'd disappeared. Mrs. DuBois was right about one thing—he did not look happy out there. Tell me, is there something between you and Gallagher? I don't want to step on any toes. At least, not without knowing who they belong to."

Inez traced a line down a frosty pane. "Once, there was. But it's over. And I really don't wish to discuss it."

She turned back to Sands, who had moved a couple of steps closer. "Now I have a question for you. Did Harry pay off Joe Rose's bank loan?"

He tipped her empty glass back and forth. The moon slid across the bulbous surface. "The benefactor demanded anonymity."

"Demanded." She faced the window again. "That sounds like Harry."

Chapter Forty

Several brandies, two glasses of champagne, and half a dozen dances with Reverend Sands later, Inez succeeded in drawing a mental curtain over the whole wretched waltz with Harry. Even the sidelong glances and whispers from other revelers didn't touch her.

Close to one in the morning, Inez and the reverend paused to recover from a fast-moving schottische. Inez was thinking that the musicians weren't so bad after all—as long as they steered clear of Mozart—when she spotted Harry watching her from across the room. Once their gazes locked, he turned away, grasped Cat DuBois' bare arm, and pulled her toward him. As he murmured into her ear, she leaned against him. Her vivid dress shimmered against the dark silhouette of his evening clothes, a fire about to be engulfed by the night. She nodded acquiescence. They moved toward the entrance.

"I think," Inez announced with careful precision, "more champagne's in order."

"Your wish is my command. Only this time, you're coming with me." Reverend Sands steered her toward the bar. "No more disappearances."

"Noooo. Won't happen." Inez tripped, then concentrated on her feet. As she walked, the toe of one green dancing slipper then the other peeked out from under the satin ruffle hemming her skirt. Those feet seemed far, far away.

He handed the glass to her. "So, is it French, as advertised?" She sipped and thought a moment. "It's been a while since I've had real champagne, but it tastes heavenly."

The extended notes of an open A announced that the musicians were tuning up for the next set. She quickly finished her drink. "Let's dance. You move so exquisitely, I hate to stop."

He took her hand and they moved to the floor for another waltz. As he drew her close he said softly, "Who knows when I'll have another chance to hold you this close. We'll stay as long as you like."

<><><>

When Reverend Sands helped Inez down from the rig two hours later, it was still dark. Standing before her small frame house, Inez looked up. No stars, no moon.

"Clouds. Storm's coming." She swayed slightly. The reverend slipped an arm around her waist and she leaned against him, grateful for his steadiness as they mounted the two steps to the porch.

"Tired?"

Inez smiled, fumbling in her pocket for the key. "No, not really." Her fingers touched Joe's pocketwatch. "Oh." The fuzziness in her head evaporated like her breath in the cold dry air.

She pulled out the watch by its chain. "Joe Rose's pocketwatch." *And the perfect excuse to invite him in.* "Would you mind coming in a moment? I'd like to talk with you about this."

She opened the door, and they entered. He stopped her by the entryway. In the near darkness, she could see him cock his head, listening.

"What?" she asked.

"Probably nothing. Wait here, I'll look around." He melted soundlessly into the unlit interior. She shivered and pulled the door closed behind her. A moment later, a shape reformed from the darkness and touched her sleeve. "No one lurking behind the doors. Everything's fine."

Inez lit a parlor lamp while the reverend coaxed the still warm coals in the fireplace back to life. After adding a few chunks of wood, he came over to the piano where she waited. She opened her hand and they both looked at the watch, gold and silent, lying on the palm of her glove.

"Whoever's had it all this time hasn't bothered to wind it," he noted.

"Angel gave it to me. In the alcove, before Mrs. DuBois appeared."

She flipped open the dustcover. A photo of Joe, Emma, and Joey was mounted on the inside of the casing. A small bit of folded paper fell out and tumbled down the skirts of her dress to the floor.

Sands retrieved the paper and handed it to Inez. Unfolded, it seemed a small rectangle ripped from a larger sheet. A finely engraved border ran along two edges with a blank space at the corner. The border's design was vaguely familiar to Inez, but it was the penciled message that drew her attention. In careful, child-like printing, it said: "Joe knew."

"Joe knew," Inez repeated in puzzlement. "Knew what?"

"Can I see that?" The reverend carried the paper to the lamp. He turned it over, examining the other side.

"Interesting." He refolded it and set it on the end table. "So, what are you going to do about the pocketwatch?"

"Return it to Emma, of course. Oh dear." Inez looked down at the family portrait, an echo of happier times. "I can't tell her who gave it to me. I guess we know how Joe spent his last hours."

She closed it with a snap and carried it to the sideboard. The gold chain slithered through her fingers to coil in a shining heap between the pocketwatch and the brandy decanter. The golden liquid in the decanter glimmered. Inez righted a clean glass and poured herself a healthy dose.

"He's not the first married man to stray, Inez." The reverend stood by the loveseat, hands in trouser pockets. "I know it's small comfort, but on the large scale of things, it's a small sin."

"That may be your view, but it's not Emma's. Or any married woman's, for that matter."

"Inez, you can't tell me women—married or otherwise—don't sometimes suffer from the same human frailties as men." He gathered his hat and gloves.

"No, please." She set down the glass. "Don't go."

The reverend slowly tossed his hat and gloves back on the sofa.

The room felt charged with an understood, but unspoken potential. In the fireplace, a piece of wood snapped loudly as it disintegrated in a leap of orange flame. The reverend took one deliberate step toward her. She drew a breath, almost gasping, "Would you like me to play something for you? On the piano?"

He halted as if she'd suddenly slapped a line of fortifications between them. He considered her curiously, then smiled. Glancing over to the pile of books and sheet music heaped haphazardly on top of the parlor grand, he asked, "My choice?"

"Whatever you want."

"Whatever I want." He studied her a moment. She felt the room begin to whirl slowly around them, in a strange approximation of a dance.

He walked to the piano and began leafing through the stack. "Mozart, Mozart, Bach, Bach, Bach...hmmm. No Stephen Foster. No hymnals. Ah, how about Mendelssohn?"

Inez took the dog-eared music book from him and flipped through the pages. "'Lieder ohne Worte.' Songs without words. Some of the first pieces my mother taught me."

"She didn't force you to memorize 'Battle Hymn of the Republic'?" His gentle teasing gave her the space she needed to breathe normally again.

"What do you expect from a woman who wanted to name her first two daughters Harmony and Melody?"

"So you're the third? Is that how you escaped becoming Melody Stannert?"

"No, I'm eldest of two. Only two." She clasped the music to her a moment, as if hugging a baby. "Aunt Agnes let it be known in no uncertain terms that the first daughter would be named after her. No one ever gainsaid Aunt Agnes. Inez is a form of Agnes."

"Aunt Agnes sounds formidable." He flipped up the tails of his evening coat and sat on the small sofa. "Pick whatever tune you fancy, Inez."

She sat at the piano and slowly unbuttoned her gloves, aware that he watched her every move. She continued talking to fill the silence. "Mendelssohn said these songs were meant to arouse the same feelings in everyone. Feelings that can't be expressed in words. My mother often said that music begins where words end."

She laid the gloves on the piano top and opened the keyboard cover. "When I was young, she would test me by giving me the opus and the number. I learned to play them all on demand and to her satisfaction." Inez smiled wryly. "I can still play them by heart. Some things, when you learn them young, stay with you forever."

She opened the volume and scanned the first score. "Opus nineteen, number one." She closed the book, positioned her hands on the keyboard and—just as when she was a child— held the silence inside herself for three heartbeats. With the first liquid notes, her own private universe opened to receive her. Her heart greeted each chord like an old friend.

When the last notes shimmered and died, a wave of completeness settled over her. Inez kept her eyes closed to savor the moment.

The reverend's voice, directly behind her, broke the silence. "I've changed my mind, Mrs. Stannert. In that mural of yours, you should be painted with a piano instead of a sword. Hearing you play, Satan's legions would lay their weapons at your feet." His tone was light, but hesitant, searching for the proper balance for the moment.

She sensed that, if she leaned back, he would be near enough to touch. It was as if they teetered on the edge of a cliff, a cliff from which neither dared to jump.

The cliff.

Inez remembered. Her small, stubborn toes digging into the ledge above the swimming hole, stockings and shoes lying in a heap nearby. Below—far below, in her ten-year-old estimation—boys from neighboring summer estates splashing, screams of "Jump! Jump!" piercing the humid air. Then, one voice above the rest: "She won't jump! She's just a *girl!*"

She leaped. The exhilarating fall was supplanted by the sudden impact, the cool water foaming about her. Boys' screams, birds' songs, all ceased. Opening her eyes, she saw her hair curling through the water in snakelike undulations. Her white lawn dress billowed in a green world of filtered sunlight and muffled sound. Triumphant, she pushed off the muddy bottom, rising toward the light.

Ascension.

Anticipation.

The promise of release.

Inez rose from the piano stool and turned to face Reverend Sands.

He retreated a step, as if the boundaries had shifted beneath his feet, leaving him in foreign territory. She followed and placed her hands on his shoulders. Inez could feel that he too was holding his breath. Waiting to break through the surface to the light.

She took his face in her hands and moved closer still.

Their kiss, tentative at first, intensified.

After a while, he gripped her arms and, with visible reluctance, pulled her away. "Inez, are you sure?" His voice, pitched low, held an edge of warning.

She placed her fingers on his lips. *No words.*

He took her hand, kissing each finger before drawing her to him.

Lost in the passion of their mutual embrace, Inez dimly heard—as if from underwater or far away—faint musical notes, plinking out tinny and small. She realized her elaborate knot of hair was coming undone under his hands and the steel hairpins were falling, hitting the piano keys, the stool, the floor.

Taking a shaky breath, Reverend Sands ran an exploratory hand along the back seam of her dress. He lifted a loose lock of hair from her shoulder and murmured into her ear, "This isn't one of those outfits with a hundred hooks and eyes up the back, is it?"

Inez placed his hand on the neckline of her dress, and guided it down the front of her bodice, along the fall of lace concealing the dress fastenings.

His eyes never left her face.

Lacing her fingers through his, she turned to extinguish the single lamp before leading him out of the parlor and across the hallway to her room.

Chapter Forty-One

Inez rolled to the side, sleepily aware that Reverend Sands had slipped his arm from beneath her head. The feather mattress shifted as he rose from the bed.

Outside, the wind moaned and drifted into silence.

"Wind's rising," Sands observed.

Inez sighed and rolled back, curling into the warm hollow he'd left behind. She watched him prowl about the bedroom, gathering his clothes. He pulled the undervest on over his head with an elegant economy of movement. He dressed like he danced—complete attention on the task at hand, physical grace in action. *And not only when dancing and dressing.*

"You may dance with me anytime, Reverend." She smiled in the semi-dark.

He sat on the edge of the bed, buttoning his dress shirt. "Just let me know when the music starts. I'll be there." He was smiling as well.

He glanced toward the window, now a gray rectangle behind the drawn shade. "It's almost dawn, Inez. I've got to get the rig to the livery and be at church in a few hours."

Reverend Sands draped the white necktie about his collar, then gathered one long strand of her hair, letting it slide between his fingers to the pillow. "Even though I'd rather stay," he added.

She watched him through half-opened eyes. "Won't do to have that rig sitting out there at first light. Your reputation as an upright man of God might not survive an all-night visit."

"Next time, I'll walk." There was enough of a question in his voice to cancel the presumption of his words.

"Next time. I like the sound of that."

"Me too." Still smiling at her, he began maneuvering the complicated loops and twists of the cravat.

"I think," Inez ventured, with a stretch, "that we're at the stage where first names are appropriate. You know mine. What's yours? I can't keep calling you Reverend Sands."

He reached over her to retrieve his cuff links from the nightstand. "It's on the church sign."

"Reverend J. B. Sands." She meditated a moment as he worked the cuff links into the link holes. "What does the 'J' stand for?"

"It stands for itself." Reverend Sands snapped the last link into place.

"Surely you have a birth name," she persisted.

He leaned forward, tracing her eyebrows with one finger. "Very well. But this is just between us. Justice B. Sands. First part's a bit heavy-handed for the ministry, I thought. Suits a man of the law, not of the cloth."

"Justice B. Sands." She tried it out. "Nice. And the 'B' is for...?"

He smiled and ran his finger down the side of her face, from temple to cheek to jaw.

"Another secret, Justice Sands? How many do you have?"

"Probably enough to match yours, one for one."

"Hmmm." She curled her fingers into his shirt front and tugged. "So, will you tell me? Or do I have to coax it out of you?"

He lowered his face and their lips touched, lingered. Inez took his hand and moved it down to her breast.

Sands sat up. "That's enough," he said with mock gruffness, tucking the flannel sheet firmly under her chin. "We keep doing this, there'll be no minister to receive the congregation."

She smiled lazily, watching him pull on his shoes. "So what's the sermon for today, Reverend?"

"New beginnings." He stood and uncovered his black waistcoat from a tumble of stockings, petticoats, and drawers. "Appropriate for the coming decade. For Mrs. Rose. For us too, come to think on it. Will you be there?"

"Of course." She turned to one side, propping herself with an elbow. "And while you're preaching at the pulpit, you can imagine what I'm thinking about in the pews."

"And you can imagine what I'm thinking about during the hymns."

He finished buttoning the waistcoat, glanced around, and spotted his gun belt on the cedar trunk. After buckling on the heavy leather belt, he returned to the bedside and sat once more, adding, "Number one-oh-six is for you, Inez." His eyes lingered on her lips a moment, then he bent down and swiftly kissed her nose.

As he stood and shrugged into his evening coat, he asked, "Do you have an extra key?"

"Extra…" She blinked. "In the table by the front door. Why?"

He laughed at her cautious tone. "I don't want to leave your door unlocked when I leave."

"You're making too much of all this."

"No. Just being careful. There's too much at stake. Especially now." He paused by the bedroom door. "The get-together for the Roses is after the service."

"I remember." She started to drift off.

"I'll walk you and the Roses home afterward." He closed the bedroom door behind him.

She rolled onto her back, listening. The front door squeaked open and shut. A key turned and the bolt shot home.

Inez floated in a pleasant surfeit of warmth, remembering her first encounters with Reverend Sands and her initial suspicions, which now seemed so distant, so foreign. *How long ago? Not even a month.*

A month.

Her smile faded. She counted backward, trying to recall the last day...

"Damn!" Inez leaped from the bed. She grabbed the wrapper hanging on the bedpost and snugged it tight around her as she hastened to the cedar chest. Throwing it open, she began feverishly tossing out items of clothes, searching. *It must be here. I haven't used it since—*

Her hand closed on the small case holding her female syringe. Relief surged through her. But the various nostrums she had used with it were gone, casualties of her empty marriage bed.

The pantry.

She flew barefooted to the kitchen and fumbled along the pantry shelves, pushing aside tins of milk, coffee, and tea and almost knocking over the bottle of vinegar. Inez hugged its dusty brown glass with the fervor of a drowning man grabbing a life line and tried to recall whether vinegar was an effective douche or not.

I don't remember. But it's this or water.

Back in the bedroom, she filled the syringe with shaking hands and lay back on the bed, steeling herself for the cold liquid intrusion. Afterward, she moved off the bed and crouched over the chamber pot.

From this bleak position, she stared through the tangled snakes of her loose hair, trailing to the floor, and remembered the aftermath of her plunge to the swimming hole twenty years earlier.

A groom from her family's stables had discovered her and hauled her back to the main house and her mother's wrath. Her mother, bedridden for months, had stood before her, one hand clutching her dressing chair, the other supporting her swollen belly.

"Inez! Look at you!"

Inez bent her head to hide defiant eyes, dark hair dripping pond water onto the inlaid mahogany floors.

"If your father were here, he'd whip you so hard you wouldn't sit for a week." Her mother paced with a heavy, rolling gait, her fury building. "A lady does *not* jump into a swimming hole. Or ride astride. Or whistle. Or argue with her betters." She winced, gripped her belly, and sank onto the bed. "A lady must, above all, protect her virtue and reputation. If you continue this way, you will have neither."

She rocked, hazel eyes boring in on her unrepentant daughter. "Your father and aunt want to send you to boarding school. Your Aunt Agnes says you've too good a mind to waste. Your father," her voice sank, contemptuous, "thinks the discipline will break your spirit. He doesn't see how much like him you really are. Made of iron and steel, both of you."

Inez looked up from her muddy toes to see her mother weeping. Terrified at last, Inez ran to her, promising she'd be a lady from now on.

"Inez, the baby's coming soon—please God, a son—and I can't handle you anymore." Her mother smoothed back Inez's tangled hair with a tender but despairing touch. "When your father returns, I will tell him he may send you to board in the fall. Dear child, if only you'd been born a boy."

Inez's sister Harmony was born soon thereafter. The last of seven children, the only other besides Inez to survive childbirth and infancy.

Two decades later, Inez opened her hand and watched the empty syringe roll across the floor. She covered her eyes and listened to a far-away roar grow closer.

The approaching gale howled across the broad Arkansas Valley in the high Rocky Mountains and hurtled itself upslope to Leadville, rattling windows, setting unseasoned wood planks creaking, insinuating itself through thousands of unchinked cracks.

The storm had arrived.

Chapter Forty-Two

Dawn increased toward morning while Inez yanked the snarls out of her hair and listened to the winds wail. By the time she left for church, the gales had diminished to occasional gusts and the snow fell in earnest. The dark gray sky seemed in mourning, promising only sorrow.

She stepped into the sanctuary of the church. The service was yet to start; Reverend Sands was nowhere to be seen. She moved up the pews and slid in beside Susan, Emma, and Joey.

"How was the dance?" Susan's cheeks shone red from the cold.

Inez searched for the right word. "Wonderful," she said faintly.

"Wonderful?" Susan prompted.

"Yes. For the most part."

Susan looked disappointed at her brevity.

Inez suspected she didn't present the appearance of a belle returning from a ball. Her eyes felt gritty from the stinging snow, and the alcohol and lack of sleep were catching up with her. She folded back the hood of her cloak and scanned the pews.

No Cat DuBois. No Angel. None of Cat's girls.

Harry.

Impeccably groomed as always. Yet there was something slightly out-of-focus about him. Haggard shadows around his ice blue eyes led her to believe he had also spent a sleepless and dissipated night. He glanced toward her. Inez turned away, not willing to read his expression any further nor let him read hers.

In the front pew, Mrs. Titweiller whispered to a gaggle of women. In unison, they turned toward Inez, noses pointing like hunting dogs flushing out game.

Inez lifted her chin and glared back, daring them to find easier prey.

"Good morning! Today we greet the last Sunday of the year and the decade, and prepare for the next." Reverend Sands mounted to the pulpit and sorted his notes as whispers and coughs faded to silence. He appeared as refreshed as if he'd had a full night's sleep.

"We have a change in our order of service. We'll begin with hymn number one hundred and six." Above a sea of heads bowed over hymnals, Reverend Sands smiled at Inez.

The stinging in her cheeks intensified. She thumbed through the pages until one-aught-six jumped out. The voices of the congregation rose in chorus. "Through all the tumult and the strife I hear the music ringing. It sounds an echo in my soul. How can I keep from singing!"

Outside, snow and wind hissed. Inside, music enveloped Inez. "What though the tempest 'round me roars, I know the truth, it liveth. What though the darkness 'round me close, songs in the night it giveth. No storm can shake my inmost calm while to that rock I'm clinging. Since love prevails in heav'n and earth, how can I keep from singing!"

<> <> <>

The somber social over, Reverend Sands escorted Inez, Emma, and Joey out behind the church to a lean-to that sheltered the same buggy as the previous evening, but hitched to a different horse. The reverend climbed into the front seat next to Inez, remarking, "It seemed a good day to hold onto a rig."

His arm brushed hers as he reached for the reins. Despite the layers of wool between them, it might as well have been his skin sliding across hers. He clucked to the horse, then glanced back at Emma and Joey in the rear seat. "Looks like a big storm. Hope it doesn't delay your departure from Leadville, Mrs. Rose."

"As long as the passes stay open, the sleigh-coaches drive through all but the most impossible weather." Emma tugged Joey's cap over his ears.

Mid-afternoon was surrendering to early dusk by the time they reached Emma's home. As the reverend set the brake, the curtain of snow thinned long enough for Inez to think she saw something not quite right about the front of the house.

"I'll come with you." She descended from the rig. The snow fell harder.

She was nearly to the porch when the driving snow and wind paused. The curtain lifted. Behind Inez, Emma gasped.

Dead center in the mourning wreath splayed the frozen form of a barnyard rat.

Chapter Forty-Three

The rat's brown fur was picked out with flecks of snow. Rivulets of frozen blood painted small red streaks down the door. A knife hilt protruded from the pinned rat. Silent punctuation to a deadly statement.

The reverend's hand closed on Inez's shoulder. "Give me your gun." His voice, next to her ear, sounded foreign in its abruptness.

Inez turned. His mouth was a tight line. Snow clung to his eyelashes and patterned his hat.

She slowly pulled the Remington out of her pocket. Emma gasped again. "Inez! You brought that into church?"

Reverend Sands spun the cylinder to inspect the chambers.

"It's fully loaded," Inez said belatedly. Then, "You're going in? Alone?"

"Mrs. Rose, your key."

Emma opened her reticule and handed him the key.

"Ladies, Joey, back into the rig."

"I'll walk them to my house. It's just two doors down," said Inez.

Reverend Sands swung around. "No." His voice was flat. "Take them to the rig."

She bristled and opened her mouth to retort. His expression caused her to reconsider. Strangling a stifled protest, she took Emma and Joey by the hand and hurried them away.

At the rig, Inez turned in time to see the ghostly, snow-obscured figure of Reverend Sands push open the front door. He slipped into the dark interior.

"Was that a rat on the door?" Emma's teeth chattered as she huddled with Joey on the back seat. "This must be some kind of horrible prank."

Inez gathered the reins, remembering the dead rat in Joe's office and the rat pinned through her skirt at the bank. "I think it's a warning, Emma."

"What kind of warning?"

Inez said nothing, but gripped the reins more tightly, feeling unprotected with her empty pocket.

If he's not out in five minutes, we're straight off to the marshal's office. I'll drag Hollis back by his nose if I must.

Sands reappeared at the door and strode to the rig.

"No one's there or even been inside, as far as I can tell. Inez, I'm going to hold onto this for a while longer." He set the safety on the pocket revolver. "This is what we'll do. We'll all go inside. Mrs. Rose, gather what you need for two days. Then we'll go to the Clairmont Hotel and get you a room. Inez, you should probably take a room, too."

Harry Gallagher's hotel.

Protests rose simultaneously from Emma and Inez.

Reverend Sands shook his head through the blizzard of words.

"Listen to me!" Inez shouted over the storm. She threw down the reins and climbed down to Sands, clutching her cloak as the wind gusted and threw snow in her face. "With this weather and the holidays, there won't be a free room anywhere much less at the better hotels. You think a hotel room is safe? Think again. One door. No other avenue of escape. What do you plan to do? Post yourself as sentry?"

"If necessary."

"No." Now her voice brooked no argument. "The Roses will stay with me. I've an extra room. And a shotgun."

Reverend Sands glanced from Inez to Emma and rubbed his face as if missing the absent mustache more than ever. "Done."

Inez blinked, thrown off-balance at his unexpected capitulation.

He continued, "And I'll stay as well. The parlor floor will suit me fine."

"You can't." Inez was speechless.

"Can't what? Spend the night on your parlor floor?" Reverend Sands sounded as if, under different circumstances, he'd find her protest comical. "There are plenty of chaperones to go around, if that's what you're thinking. Discussion's over. Now, let's be quick."

The four hustled back up the walk and into the house. The banked stove eked out a thread of warmth that barely raised the temperature of the parlor. Trunks and boxes, packed and ready to go, lined the nearby walls. The house felt empty, cold, abandoned in spirit.

In her room, Emma handed Inez a carpetbag and threw open a trunk. They were stuffing a quilted petticoat into the bag when a scratching noise drew them to the hallway. Joey was tugging his rocking horse down the hall toward the front door. Long gouges trailed behind in the polished planks.

"Joseph Lawrence Rose!" Emma sounded beside herself. "*What* do you think you're doing?"

"Papa said my horse's our ticket to freedom. Papa said it's my res...respon...job to watch over him. I'm taking him to Auntie's house." Joey tugged. The gouges lengthened.

"You are not! You heard Reverend Sands. We take only the necessities."

"NO!" Joey shouted.

Emma moved swiftly. Her hand cracked against his cheek like a small gunshot. "You will *not* speak to me that way!"

Joey screamed and started to cry. Even in the face of his mother's fury, he wrapped his arms around the horse's wooden neck, prepared to go down with the ship.

Emma stared at her hand, then at her weeping child. Inez moved between mother and child, too late. "He meant no disrespect, Emma."

Reverend Sands emerged from Joey's room, carrying a small carpetbag. A red flag, the leg from a set of flannels, trailed out of the hastily closed top. He took in the sobbing child and the two women.

Emma, still staring at the fire-red imprint of her hand on Joey's fair skin, whispered, "He shouldn't talk that way to his elders."

The reverend strode forward, pried the horse from Joey's grasp, and hefted it under one arm. He turned to Emma and Inez. "Ready? Let's go."

Back out on the porch, Reverend Sands locked the door and handed the key back to Emma. "Same key works the back door?"

She nodded.

"Good. It's locked up tight as we can make it."

The small parade worked its way back to the rig, stepping into the vanishing impressions of their footprints. Sands hesitated. "We might as well walk. It's just a few steps."

They bent their heads toward Inez's home. The snow fell unrelenting, encouraged by gusts, as they waded through ankle-deep powder.

The reverend had them wait on the porch while he entered and made a quick sweep of Inez's house. As they shivered outside, Inez realized, with the slowed-down reactions of one completely exhausted, that he had opened her door with the key from his pocket. She glanced at Emma, wondering if she'd noticed. Emma's eyes were closed. She held Joey's carpetbag in one hand and clutched Joey to her cloak with the other.

Sands reappeared at the door. "All clear."

He stoked the fires in the parlor stove and fireplace while Inez went to her bedroom, rolled up her comforter and sheets, and put fresh bedding on her bed for Emma. She slid out a little-used trundle bed and added blankets for Joey before retrieving her own bedclothes. Up close, they emitted a faint, musky odor that reminded her of Sands.

She spread her bedclothes on the braided rug of the second bedroom and gathered extra blankets for Sands to layer on the parlor floor. While Emma and Joey settled their meager belongings in the bedroom, Sands drew Inez aside. "You said you have a shotgun?"

"In the pantry."

"Let's see it."

Inez retrieved the twelve-gauge shotgun and handed it to Reverend Sands. As she pulled a box of shells from the pantry's top shelf, he asked, "Can you use this?"

She turned to face him, box in hand. "Fourteen months ago I stood off two lot-jumpers with that shotgun."

He looked up sharply from his examination of the gun. "No, Inez. Can you *use* this? Not just wave it in someone's face, but point it at them and pull the trigger."

She extended her hand for the gun and said frostily, "Oh ye of little faith."

He gave it back to her. "I don't want to leave you with something you won't use. I'm going out for a while. To talk to the marshal, return the rig, and get a few things from the hotel. Including my gun. I'll also check for open seats on tomorrow's coaches to Georgetown and Fairplay. If it were up to me, I'd send the Roses packing tonight. And you too. I don't like the situation." Grey eyes sized her up. "You could go with the Roses to Denver for a few days. Maybe I can get someone to ride shotgun on the three of you."

"New Year's Eve is Wednesday. I can't leave Abe with only Useless for help." She hesitated. "Once Emma and Joey are out of town, they'll be safe, won't they?"

"I'm not placing bets either way. Are you?"

"When will you be back?" she finally asked.

"Two, three hours. I'll knock, so don't shoot me." He began to give Inez her key.

"Keep it for now. You'll be staying tonight, at least."

He pocketed the key. "I don't have to tell you to keep the doors locked."

"No, you don't."

After he left, Inez returned to the parlor where Emma and Joey sat close to the fire. Joey's eyes went wide at the shotgun.

"You've seen one of these up close before, haven't you Joey?" Inez lay the gun across her lap and opened the box of shells.

"Papa had one at the office, but I wasn't allowed to touch it."

"Well, you can't touch this one either." She broke the breech of the side-by-side and loaded one shell. It slid in with a cold metallic click.

Emma squeezed Joey's shoulder. "Go get ready for bed."

"I'm not sleepy."

"Joseph—"

He walked reluctantly across the room, giving his rocking horse a shove as he passed. The rockers clickety-clacked against the plank floor as he went into the bedroom and closed the door.

Emma grabbed Inez's wrist. "Promise me something."

Inez looked up, startled. Emma's blue eyes bored into her like the double barrels of the shotgun.

"If anything happens to me, I want you to take care of Joey."

"Don't say that! Nothing will happen. Tomorrow, next day at the latest, you'll both be heading to a new life in the Golden State."

Emma shook her head, not to be placated. "Promise me you'll raise Joey as your own. You've a strong spirit. You'll protect and love him. Let no harm come to my son."

"Emma, don't talk such foolishness."

"Promise!"

"All right, all right. I promise."

Inez looked down at her friend's freckled hand and noticed how Emma's pale wrist was as bony as her own. Events of the last month combined with the high altitude were eating away at them both, leaving them shadows of their former selves. Inez had seen it happen to others in Leadville. Faces became gaunt, necks thin.

The only ones who stay sleek and prosper are Mrs. DuBois and the rats.

"Mama!"

Emma released her grip and straightened with a sigh. She went into the bedroom, then returned a moment later. "I can't believe I forgot it."

"What?" Inez sorted through the shells in the box.

"My Bible." Dismay etched lines around her mouth. "I must have put it on the bed while we were packing and got distracted by that horse."

"We'll get it tomorrow morning." Another metallic click as the second shell entered its chamber. Inez closed the action with a decisive snap. *If anyone tries anything, I'll blow a hole through him and any nearby walls big enough to walk through.*

"We read verses last thing every night and first thing every morning. We've never missed a reading. Not even the day Joe—" Emma covered her mouth with a hand.

"Use my pocket Bible. It's on the sideboard."

At the sideboard, Emma froze. "Inez?"

Oh no. Inez pictured Joe's watch by the decanter, exactly where she'd left it last night.

Inez placed the loaded shotgun under the sofa to give herself time to think. When she straightened up, Emma was waiting, Bible in one hand, Joe's pocketwatch in the other.

"I was going to bring it to you after church. But then all this happened." Inez's tired mind raced, not prepared with a ready lie. "Someone dropped it off at the Silver Queen yesterday."

"At your saloon?"

Ignoring the implicit "why?" in Emma's question, Inez said, "Useless told me he turned around and it was on the bar. He didn't see who left it," she added lamely.

Emma opened the dustcover and stared at the family portrait inside.

"State Street. It ruined our lives." Her bitterness spoke volumes.

Chapter Forty-Four

A soft knock wrenched Inez from a doze on the loveseat. She retrieved the shotgun from under the sofa and listened as a key turned in the lock. Her grip eased as Reverend Sands entered, black hat and coat dusted with snow.

Inez held her finger to her lips, indicating the closed bedroom door across the hall.

He nodded to show he understood. She slid the shotgun back under the sofa and rose to fix him a cup of tea. "What did Marshal Hollis say?"

Reverend Sands set down a small carpetbag and walked to the fire, removing his gloves. "The marshal said dead rats nailed to doors don't amount to much when he's got live cutthroats and footpads to deal with."

Inez sniffed. *About as much help as I expected.* She poured hot water over the tea strainer and watched the liquid darken to sepia. "Any room on the coaches tomorrow?"

"There may not be any coaches tomorrow. They're talking avalanches in the passes. The Georgetown trains to Denver might not even run."

He set Inez's revolver on the sideboard before accepting the cup.

Inez lowered herself onto the loveseat, leaving the end closest to the fire for Reverend Sands. He sat down, a polite distance away. "I stopped by Mrs. Rose's house coming back and double-checked the windows. Everything is as we left it. My guess is," he stretched out his legs, flexing his ankles, "someone's after something in that house. If Mrs. Rose is the target, I don't see why they would bother with the rat. I think they wanted to scare her away. I considered spending the night there." He sipped his tea, meditatively. "See if I could ambush them. But that would leave you all here alone. I don't like that. Household goods can be replaced. Human lives cannot."

Firelight flickered over the polished rosewood of the piano. Inez looked longingly at the covered keyboard, wishing she could lose herself in music, for just a while. Nervous fatigue had her strung tight as a piano wire. Sighing, she rested her head on the sofa back. The square nail heads in the planked ceilings appeared like so many orderly notes on a musical score. Too tired to think, she closed her eyes. "Who is doing this? And why now? Joe's dead. Emma's leaving. What are they after?"

From the small darkness behind her closed eyelids, she heard the click of porcelain cup on saucer and felt his hand, warm from the teacup, smooth back hair that had escaped from her plaited knot. "I'm going to find out."

She was too drained to question why he should be so involved in what were essentially law enforcement matters. Nor why he sounded so absolutely convinced that he would succeed in unraveling her questions.

"I just wish it was all over," she murmured.

"It will be. Soon. Then, we can concentrate on other things." In the pause that followed she heard the crackle of horsehair as he moved closer. "Our chaperones are asleep."

Inez knew, in a moment, she would feel his lips on either her mouth or her throat. Once that happened, she would be swept into currents not of her own making.

"Please don't," she whispered.

She sensed him shift away on the sofa. When she opened her eyes, he was watching her. Waiting.

She took a deep breath and straightened up. *I suppose we must deal with last night's events now.*

Clenching her hands into fists, she said a low voice, "Last night. I was…unprepared."

He seemed to shuffle through and examine the possible interpretations of "unprepared"—spiritually, emotionally, physically.

She attempted to clarify. "Unprotected."

Slight frown lines appeared between his eyebrows.

"I'm a married woman. My husband disappeared eight months ago. I was foolish to take a chance that, that—"

The frown became more pronounced. "But I thought… When I tried to…" He stopped.

They were dancing around words to describe what took place in the dark intimacy of her bed less than eighteen hours ago. At the very last possible moment, he'd tried to separate from her. The twisted flannel sheet, their tangled arms and legs, their passion—all had worked against him. *As I did.* She'd pulled him closer, deeper. With immediate and overwhelming results for them both.

Inez forced herself to face him squarely. "I thought it was safe, but I miscounted the days. I took steps after you left. But I don't know how effective they were."

He looked as if he couldn't quite believe their conversation.

Inez hurried on. "Even in Leadville there are situations that are beyond the pale. Not tolerated. I cannot chance that. And neither can you. Not in your position. Even if your stay is temporary."

She rubbed her tired eyes, desperate, yet determined. "In the future, we must take precautions. I don't know what I'll be able to do, what I can purchase or where. But we just can't…can't…"

Reverend Sands lifted her chin, forcing her to look at him. His eyes were warm. Warm and the color of storm clouds.

"Inez. We won't."

He glanced at the shut bedroom door across the hall before drawing her close. She buried her face in the shoulder of his damp jacket.

"There are other methods besides counting days," he murmured into her hair. "But you must trust me."

Reverend Sands settled her gently against the sofa and kissed her forehead, her eyelids. He covered her mouth with his, drawing her into a world where his touch and the pressure of his body filled her mind. A world of no thoughts, no words. A while later, he freed her mouth and began a slow descent down her throat.

Inez shivered and twined her fingers through his hair to anchor herself. It was as if she floated on the surface of a whirlpool, circling closer to the center. Upon entering that spiral, Inez knew she would go under without a struggle.

His lips brushed the hollow at the base of her throat. She felt him whisper again:

"Trust me."

<> <> <>

Scritch, scritch. The timid noise dragged Inez from a deep sleep. From the floor of her son's room, Inez blinked, disoriented by the lack of familiar landmarks and the scant hours of sleep.

The sound continued, fingernails on wood. Joey's voice outside her door finally penetrated the fog in her brain. "Auntie Inez. Where's mama?"

"What? Just a moment, child." She scrambled about, gathering the minimum needed to be decently clothed. In less than a minute, she flung open the door, still buttoning a dress over her chemise. "She isn't in the room?"

Inez heard a thump from the direction of the parlor. Reverend Sands appeared in the hallway, minus jacket and shoes, waistcoat hanging loose over his half-buttoned shirt. With his hair rumpled and the sleep still clearing from his face, he looked only slightly less disoriented than she felt.

"Could she be in the kitchen?" He started to the back of the house, buttoning up his shirt and waistcoat.

Joey jumped from one foot to the other, a small red grasshopper in flannels. "I just woke up. She's not here."

Inez finally registered the ancillary source of his discomfort.

"Do you need a chamber pot, Joey?" At his nod, she led him back into the room and pulled the container from under the nightstand. A quick examination showed the big bed slept in, but the sheets no longer warm.

Sands appeared, terse. "The back door's unlocked." He headed to the parlor for his boots. "Looks like footprints outside, heading to the alley."

Inez hurried Joey into pants and jacket and into the kitchen. She pulled on Mark's old sturdy boots over her wool sleeping socks and tied Joey's shoes.

"Stay here." Sands came through the kitchen, buckling on his gun belt, his overcoat hanging on his shoulders.

"We're coming. Two of us can search twice as fast." She shoved her arms into Mark's old greatcoat, ripping the lining in one sleeve in her haste.

Sands shot her a dubious glance, which she ignored. Inez stuffed her waist-length braid under the coat and searched pockets for gloves. He yanked open the back door.

It still snowed. Soft, silent, fast. Faint, regular depressions advanced to the alley.

"Any reason she'd go back to the house?" Reverend Sands pulled on his gloves.

"Her Bible." Inez's heart beat hard, a hammer pounding the same nail over and over. "She left it in her bedroom. I lent her mine, told her we'd come back in the morning."

Reverend Sands started down the steps. "I never should've returned her key."

Inez gripped Joey's mittened hand and hastened after the reverend.

The journey to the alley and past the intervening lots was silent and cold. Inez heard only her own ragged breathing as she and Joey floundered through drifts, struggling to catch up with Sands, and thought only her own silent prayers: *Please God, let everything be all right. Please God, not Emma.*

At the back fence to Emma's house she saw, through the scrim of falling snow, the back door hanging open like the broken jaw of some gaping beast. The shadow form of Reverend Sands hesitated on the back porch, drew his gun, and vanished inside.

Inez wavered, considered the wisdom of taking Joey any further. Dark apprehensions crowded, whispering like the falling snow. She could not retreat. Her fears for Emma forced her toward that dark doorway.

She picked up Joey, pushing his face against her shoulder. "Hold on tight," she whispered. "And don't look." Burdened with his weight, she wallowed through the shrouded yard and up the back stairs.

Blundering into the kitchen, blinded after the dead-white world outside, Inez screamed as she collided with an unseen form. The form materialized into Sands, who crowded her into retreat. "Out. Get him out of here. Get a neighbor. Doc. The marshal."

Inez caught a whiff of something sour, metallic.

A smell she identified with panic. With blood.

Her sight adjusted to the dim interior. The kitchen was a chaos of overturned boxes, smashed china.

Inez pushed Joey toward Sands, forcing him to grab for the child. Freed of Joey's weight, she dodged around the reverend and ran through the kitchen into the dark hallway.

To the right, she saw a slice of the parlor, trunks upended, clothes and personal objects spilling into the hall. Immediately left, Joey's bedroom. Beyond that, the half-closed door to Emma's room.

She shoved the door open.

A broken china washbasin, scattered books, linens.

A slashed bedtick, spilling out a wasteland of feathers.

At the foot of the bed, what looked to be crumpled bedclothes.

Until she saw the tangle of red hair and a blood-splattered, outstretched arm, fingers almost touching the Bible just beyond their reach.

Chapter Forty-Five

"Emma. Oh, Emma."

Inez cradled Emma's head in her arms.

Blood, everywhere.

A particularly ominous patch soaked through Emma's thin dress and petticoat, pooling about her hips and legs. Inez touched the woolen stocking hanging from Emma's neck. The fabric, now cut away, had left angry red marks impressed on her throat.

Inez tried to untie a second stocking knotted around one of Emma's wrists.

"Who did this to you, Emma? Who?"

Emma's eyes were half-shut, her face blue and mottled with bruises. Inez could barely detect the rise and fall of her breath.

A thunder of footsteps pounded up the back steps and grew louder in the kitchen and hallway, accompanied by the urgent baritones and tenors of masculine voices. Inez tugged the dress down over Emma's pale, blood-streaked calves, attempting a small measure of modesty for her unconscious friend.

The company of men descended on the room like a cloud of ravens, dark winter coats swirling about them. Gloved hands lifted Inez from the floor, away from Emma's limp body. Inez struggled to stay, clutching Emma's unresponsive hand.

"Mrs. Stannert." Doc's calm rumble called her back from the edge of hysteria. "Let me do my work. There's no place for you here right now." His voice rose to include the others. "Please leave the room."

Doc delivered her to other waiting hands and crouched by Emma. He rapidly shed his coat and began to peel off his gloves.

Reverend Sands herded everyone toward the parlor. Curly Dan and another deputy, faces apprehensive under their hat brims, ushered Inez to the parlor's threshold and released her as if their duty and nerve ended at the doorjamb.

Marshal Hollis snaked past them and walked slowly around the room examining the shambles and pulling at his tobacco-stained mustache. When he'd completed his circuit, Inez stepped forward to block his path.

"You." She jabbed him with a finger covered with blood. *Emma's blood.* "You find out who did this. Because if you don't, I will. And I'll kill him."

Hollis scratched one end of his ragged mustache. Inez's finger had missed his coat lapel and left a small red blotch on his sheepskin vest next to the badge. His tight green eyes focused beyond her. "Reverend. You was first on the scene, right?"

"That's right." Sands skirted an overturned box to stand by Inez.

"So what's *she*," Hollis jerked his chin toward Inez, "doin' here?"

Inez spoke up. "Since your response to our request for help yesterday was less than overwhelming," she could hear the deputies behind her shifting uneasily on their feet, "Mrs. Rose and her son stayed at my house last night. We thought it would be safer. When we awoke this morning, Mrs. Rose was," she faltered, "gone. We came here looking for her."

"Uh-huh." The marshal's narrow face thinned further with contempt. He chewed harder, glancing from Reverend Sands to Inez and back again.

Inez realized that her undefined *we* invited any number of speculations. Some, no doubt accurate.

Marshal Hollis looked around, as if searching for a place to spit. He finally brushed past Reverend Sands and muttered, "We're talkin' later. Alone."

The marshal went out the front door. A moment later he was back, wiping tobacco juice off his chin. "You take that outta the room?" He pointed.

Inez looked down at Emma's Bible, clutched in her hand. The leather cover of the book was splattered with dark spots. "She came back for this."

He snapped his fingers and held out his hand. Inez reluctantly gave it up, adding, "She reads to her son every morning—" She broke off, aghast that Joey hadn't even entered her mind until that moment.

Reverend Sands squeezed her shoulder gently. "He's at the saloon with Abe and Bridgette."

Hollis flipped through the pages perfunctorily then handed it back to Inez. "Guess the young'un might need this," he said gruffly. "Curly, take Miz Stannert home. And Miz Stannert, I've got questions for you, too, so stay there 'til I come lookin' for you."

The thought of sitting alone in her house was more than she could bear. "Marshal," she said with equal coolness, "I'll be at the saloon with Joey."

Hollis grunted. Inez took that for consent and began to pull on the gloves she'd hastily stuffed into the pockets of the oversized jacket.

Reverend Sands made a move as if to leave with her.

"Nope, Reverend. You stay. You an' me, we gotta talk."

Sands squeezed her shoulder once more. He and Hollis then moved to the far side of the room, hands clasped behind their backs, voices low, shutting out everyone else.

<>< ><>

Bridgette sat next to Joey at the saloon's kitchen table. "Tish. Eat. Your mother would want you to keep your strength up."

Inez watched by a tray of clean dishes, shot glass in one hand, towel in the other.

Joey looked at the fingers of dry toast stacked log-cabin style on the plate before him, his silent misery plain for all to see.

"That's right," Bridgette said, as if by merely looking at the food he could draw sustenance from it. "Eat one, there's a lad."

Inez shook her head, picked up the tray, and carried it to the barroom.

Abe turned from counting whiskey bottles. "The boy eatin' yet?"

"No. Nor talking. He hasn't said a word since he asked..." She bit her lip too hard, then rubbed it with her knuckles. "'Is mama going to die?'"

Abe's pencil paused above the inventory list. "What'd you say to that?"

"I told him, 'If there's a God in heaven, she'll live.'"

"Let's hope you're not settin' him up to be a nonbeliever."

"Emma's got to live." Inez began arranging the glasses on the shelf under the bar. "Do you know what her last—well, almost last—words were to me?" She didn't wait for his response. "She made me promise to look after Joey if something happened to her. To raise him as my own. Not that I've done such a bang-up job with William." Panic rose in her throat. "I can't do it, Abe. She's got to live."

"You'll do what you got to do and when you've got to do it, Inez."

"Emma's at the hospital. Doc said he'd come by tonight after Joey's asleep. I've never seen him look so grim. Oh Emma. Oh God. Abe, if you'd seen her." Inez flinched from the memory of Emma crumpled on the floor, smeared in blood. "I can't imagine who would do that. Some animal. Worse than an animal. A monster."

Crouched below the level of the bar, she rested her forehead on the smooth mahogany edge. The dark hollow underneath smelled of wood polish, whiskey, and dust. "That dolt of a marshal better catch who did it. And they better string him up."

Abe's footsteps echoed on the raised plank floor. "Hope he catches the right man." His tone was dark. "Emma's no fallen flower of State Street. Folks'll be hollering for a necktie party, the sooner the better. The town is still all riled up over Stewart and Frodsham, and they were just a footpad and a lot-jumper. The law won't have a chance."

Inez remembered the midnight lynchings that had occurred a block away just before Thanksgiving. "In this case, Abe, I'd cast my vote with the vigilantes for swift justice at the end of a rope."

Justice. The glasses lined up on the shelf, touching lip to lip. "Reverend Sands will be by later."

"Hmmph." Abe's footsteps approached and stopped.

She turned her head. "What?" At that level all she could see were the knees of his brown worsted pants and his brown boots.

His voice drifted down to her. "Thought you'd be on first-name basis with your reverend by now. After the dance and all."

And all.

Inez suddenly felt warm all over—her wrists, the back of her neck, behind her knees. She rearranged the glasses, staggering the line to make space for the last ones. "Where's Useless? Today, of all days. We need his help if we're going to be ready for New Year's."

"Sorry, sorry," Useless' apologetic voice fumbled in from the kitchen. "Sorry I'm late. I can finish that inventory, Mr. Jackson. Or I can do the storeroom, if you haven't yet. Jeez, it's storming out there."

Inez popped her head above the counter. "You look terrible. Are you all right?"

He ducked his head, pulling his hat down. "Yes'm." His face looked frozen and raw. He snuffled and pulled the threadbare muffler tight about his neck, glancing back toward the kitchen.

"Don't get sick on us." Inez picked up the empty tray. "Mrs. Rose has had a terrible accident. I'll be taking care of her son. So, you can't count on me for a while, particularly nights."

His head swiveled toward the kitchen. "That her boy?" His head swiveled back. "Jeez. I didn't know she had a kid." His complexion mottled, like meat turned bad. "What, uh, happened to her?" His ungloved hands twisted in the muffler. Fresh scabs oozed on his knuckles.

"I can't talk about it. But someone will pay. If the law doesn't see to it..." She gripped the edges of the metal tray until they bit into her fingers. "I will."

"Now, Inez, leave the shotgun under the counter and let the marshal do what he was hired to do." Abe moved to unlock the front door. Early customers filtered in, along with the weak afternoon light.

Inez lost herself in the routine of taking orders, pouring drinks, accepting money, making change, making small talk. Her half-trance and Useless' increased bumbling caused more colliding behind the bar than usual. Abe finally sent Useless to the wholesale liquor dealer to place an order and extract a promise of next-day delivery. Inez checked the kitchen frequently to see how Joey was doing.

Late afternoon, Inez exited the kitchen from another brief foray and almost bumped into Abe, who was looking for her. "Marshal's here, Inez. Wants to talk with you."

She removed her apron, smoothed her hair, and scanned the crowded saloon room. Marshal Hollis slouched by the bar, pants and coat crusted with snow, small icicles hanging from his frozen mustache. He clutched a tumbler in his hand, a bottle of Red Dog at his elbow.

"We can talk in the office, Marshal Hollis." She led the way upstairs, posture as erect as if she was escorting him to the family drawing room.

Once in the office, Hollis threw himself onto the small sofa without waiting for her to sit. He gulped down half the tumbler of Red Dog and cradled the glass as if the high thermal power of the remaining firewater could warm his hands through the soaked gloves.

She sat in the office chair and waited. She didn't have to wait long.

"You think I'm stupid, don't ya."

Startled, she narrowed her eyes and said nothing.

He banged the glass down on the end table. "Stupid and crooked. I seen it on your face, every time I open my mouth. Waall, don't think that your friends in high places are gonna pull you or Jackson outta the fire, if you-all turn out to be the ones I'm after."

Her mouth dropped open.

He leaned back, fingers intertwined over his rough sheepskin vest. His coat and pant hems dripped onto the rug. "I know all about the coney from Saturday last. And I know about you sniffin' around after Joe Rose's dee-mise, in his office, the bank, the Recorder's Office. You won't back off. Waall, maybe what happened to Miz Rose is a dee-rect result of your meddlin'."

"How dare you!" Inez half rose from her chair.

"Siddown." He stretched out his legs. His coat fell open further, revealing a Colt .45, holstered for a cross-draw and only inches from his laced fingers.

She sat down.

"I haven't figured it all out yet," he continued. "But I know the coney's part of it. Old Harry, he and his buddies want the town cleaned up, but they won't listen to me, especially now that they got an 'expert' in town." He glared. Furious, excluded. "Gallagher thinks it's all your husband's and that nigger's doin', that you've been duped. Not me. Wouldn't surprise me to find out you're in it deeper than pig shit in a wallow. You're a piece of work, Miz Stannert." His contempt was clear as rainwater. "Actin' so proper when you and that *reverend*—" He stopped, jaw working. He looked around, stood, walked over to the spittoon, and spat. "He don't look so lily-white to me neither."

He returned to the sofa and sat, removing his wet gloves and squeezing them in one hand. Dirty water ran down his fingers and dripped onto the rug. "I'm here to make you a deal. I don't like it, but I've been told to." His green eyes locked onto her. "Tell me who's in the coney racket. What Joe Rose did for them. What he got that everyone's so all-fired eager to get their hands on now, and what you're lookin' for. Tell me about that blackleg husband of yours and Jackson. You talk to me, right now, and you don't get charged."

She was stunned beyond belief. Nearly beyond response. "My husband has been missing for months! I had nothing to do with the counterfeit. How dare you make these accusations? And what do you mean about Joe?"

"You deny bein' involved?"

"Deny it? It's preposterous! You can't arrest me. For what? On what proof?"

"Okay. You had your chance." Hollis heaved himself out of the seat and towered over her, hooking his thumbs over his gun belt. "I'm lookin' for a murderer and a coney ring. I'm sayin', official-like, I want you and Jackson to sit tight. Not that this blizzard gives you any choice. You leave town, I'll take it as a right-straight admission of guilt. And I'll hunt you, Jackson, and that no-account Mark Stannert—wherever he is—to the Colorado state line." He tipped his hat, heavy on the sarcasm. "I can find my way out."

Inez remained in the office, staring at the half-empty tumbler of whiskey by the sofa. The marshal's defrosting outerclothes had left wet spots on the velvet upholstery and the braided rug.

He must know about Abe and Mark's past. If Hollis and Cooke know, so do others. Abe's right, someone's stacked the deck against us. Joe in with a coney ring? How absurd! Harry's behind this, that's clear. And what did Hollis mean by an 'expert'?

She couldn't bring it together. But this much was clear: She and Abe were under suspicion. Marshal Hollis thought Mark was still alive. And someone was looking for something.

Someone who'd searched Joe's office and the bank, nailed a rat to the Roses' house, and searched Emma's belongings. *They found it or didn't, and Emma showed up at the wrong time. Is Harry after the same thing? Is that why he bought Joe's office, why he's so close-mouthed about his dealings with Joe and Emma?*

She finally got up and left, locking the office door behind her. Descending the stairs, she felt weighed down, as though fifteen pounds of lead shot were sewed into the hem of her dress.

Chapter Forty-Six

She grabbed Abe's arm, stopping him mid-pour. "We've got to talk."

"Inez—" The front door swung open. A group of miners entered, heavy bootsteps shaking the planks. "Shift's changin'. It's gonna be hell for the next hour or so. Useless not back from errands. It'll have to wait."

One of the group halted before Inez and Abe and tossed a folded newspaper on the countertop. A Cornish lilt underlined his words: "Mrs. Stannert. Are you the lady what gave Gallagher the devil evening last?"

Intense brown eyes quizzed her from a face still streaked with gray, glittering dust. The speaker tapped the folded newspaper, the grime of long hours underground leaving a smudged fingerprint on the printed page. She picked up *The Independent* and swiftly scanned the indicated column. An elaborate description of the Silver Soiree including food, music, and who was and wasn't there flowed on and on in Jed Elliston's trademark turgid prose. The smudge marked two overlong sentences, twelve narrow lines of small type:

"The magic strains of Strauss' waltz apparently did not succeed in soothing at least one savage breast as this reporter observed a subdued, yet heated exchange on the dance floor between a well-known State Street saloon proprietor of the feminine persuasion and Silver Mountain owner H. C.

*Gallagher. The exchange culminated in said proprietor
abandoning said owner mid-twirl, leaving him bereft of
dancing companion and stewing in his own juices amid
the many couples dipping and turning to the joyous musical
circumlocutions of the orchestra."*

Inez dropped the paper. Not happy. *Harry must be livid. Why
did Jed do this?*

The answer came to her, as clear as the remembered
rhythm of the waltz: *Revenge. For the browbeating Harry gave
him before Christmas.*

The speaker swung around to his mates. "Told you 'twas
Mrs. Stannert. Had to be her or that other." He jerked his
thumb downstreet toward Cat DuBois' saloon and parlor
house. He faced Inez again. "My money was on you. You
seem the type to outstare the devil." He gazed over her
shoulder. "I hear you're selling faces on the wall."

Not one miner had come forward to buy a drink. A
tenseness about the group radiated like ripples on a pond.
The noise level in the saloon gradually decreased as others
became aware of the conversation.

Inez nodded. "Ten dollars a face. Interested?"

"Maybe. But not for me." He set his tin lunch bucket on
the counter and leaned forward. His posture said, "This is
just between us." But his voice reached to the corners of the
room. "How much to put old Harry's face on Satan?"

Inez drew back.

He pursued. "You need someone for the Devil. Who better
than Gallagher? A man who grows rich off the sweat of those
who toil in his workings. A man who won't pay a living wage
or agree to a reasonable shift." His voice rose. "Four dollars a
day wouldn't make a dent in his pockets. An eight-hour shift
is only human. But then, old Harry isn't the human sort, is
he." He winked at Inez, conspirator to conspirator.

Suddenly, she recognized him. She recalled the accusations
of the Silver Mountain militiamen: *Agitator. Organizer.*

Inez looked down at the newspaper. The idea of painting Harry as the Great Deceiver was unbelievably seductive. "I don't believe Mr. Gallagher would sit for the portrait."

One of the other miners spoke up. "I've seen his likeness at the Carbonate City Bank. In that new painting of the money men. The picture's done by the same jack-a-dandy that's workin' on this one."

Harry and the Carbonate City Bank. She stepped through the facts carefully, as if they might blow up and bury her. *So, Harry owns my bank. He owns Joe's business. He owns the marshal and half the town. And, if he could, he'd own my soul and the souls of these men as well.*

Her hand balled into a fist, crumpling the newspaper. "Can you pay?" Her voice sounded abrupt and harsh to her own ears.

The mining organizer grinned, opened his tin bucket, and pulled out a small leather pouch. He dumped the contents on the counter. Shiny pebbles of smelted silver rolled out on the mahogany wood.

Inez examined them. "From highgraded Silver Mountain ore?"

"We give our daily ten hours to Harry Gallagher. We pay ten times over, riskin' life and limb." His eyes challenged her to say different.

She cupped the pure silver beads in her hand. Weighing. Considering. "This pays for more than Satan. Where would you boys like to be painted?"

The smile broke through, teeth made brighter by the surrounding dirt. "On the side of justice, Mrs. Stannert. On the side of justice."

‹›‹›‹›

"Damn it, Inez. What are you tryin' to do, sink the business and get us thrown out of town?" Abe faced Inez in the unlit poker room.

Inez could see Useless tending bar through the gap in the half-open door. She and Abe stood just inside, near enough to keep an eye on things, far enough away so no one would overhear them argue—she hoped.

"What's Harry going to do? Burn our place down? Sue us?"
"He could."

"He won't. After that newspaper article and our...discussion...Saturday night, he'll probably never show up here again. Why didn't you tell me about Jed's article? You must have seen it this morning."

"I did. But with what happened to Emma, it kind of slipped my mind."

"Emma." She brushed her hand across her eyes. "Now that Useless is back, I've got to take Joey home. Doc'll be by soon."

"Yeah. Doc and that reverend. Wouldn't want to miss him, now, would you?" Abe switched gears, back to their original disagreement. "Inez, I'm gonna ask—no, beg—that you not paint Harry as the Devil. Jesus, a portrait paid for with highgrade from his own mine. It'll get back to him, Inez, and it'll be nothin' but trouble. The worst. Give those boys their silver back, let's throw in a round of free drinks, and forget about it."

"No." Inez felt her stubbornness rise. "If Harry doesn't fancy himself as the Prince of Darkness he can pay to have his face removed."

Abe stared. All she could see of him in the dusky room were the whites of his eyes, shirt sleeves, and collar. His waistcoat, skin, hair, all faded to shadow. "You're not gonna turn away from this. Even though I asked."

She crossed her arms. "The painting is mine. I can do with it as I please. You said so yourself." Even to her ears, it sounded childish.

Abe shook his head. "I don't understand the hold Harry's got on you. You've pegged him as evil as Old Scratch, but he's just a man. You say you want nothin' to do with him and then you pull him back into our lives through the rear door. Paint him on that wall, he'll be lookin' over your shoulder every minute. Think about that, Inez. Think about what that means before you give any orders to that painter of yours."

She tried to grab his arm. "The marshal said that Harry—"

Abe pulled away. "Not now. I gotta calm down before we talk more. And you got some serious thinkin' to do."

He turned and left her standing in the dark room. Alone.

Chapter Forty-Seven

"Then, Hollis accused me, Mark, Abe, and Joe of being party to some counterfeiting scheme."

Dusk crept through Inez's parlor as she gripped the reverend's hands. Her own, icy with fear, searched his for warmth.

"He said that Joe had something that 'they' wanted. I didn't get the impression that Hollis even knew what it was."

Sands squeezed her hands encouragingly, then put an arm around her, drawing her close. "What do you make of all this?"

She thought, resting her head against his shoulder. "I think Harry is in a race with the counterfeiters to find something Joe hid before he died. Someone must have been searching Emma's house when she walked in. It must have been the counterfeiters. Unless Harry hired some scum to do his dirty work. Harry might." Inez thought of Hollis and the Silver Mountain militiamen.

The reverend's face was inches from hers. Up close, the color of his eyes, always on the line between blue and gray, seemed to shift subtly, becoming more colorless, more shadowlike. "Did Hollis say anything else?"

"He pretty much said Harry's trying to break the ring. It makes sense. Harry's outspoken about ridding Leadville of the lower element. Then, Hollis said that Harry's brought in an expert. Who do you think he means? Someone from the Treasury?"

Sands looked over her head. "Ready for bed, Joey?"

Joey stood uncertainly at the parlor threshold, dressed in clean flannels. "Auntie, will you tuck me in?"

She pulled away from Sands. "Absolutely. Now into bed with you." She noted Joey's unkempt hair and thought with dismay that she hadn't combed his hair all day.

As they stood, Reverend Sands added in a low voice, "Hollis said he'll have a man patrol your neighborhood tonight. Whether to make sure you don't bolt or to protect you, it hardly matters. They'll be close in case of trouble. Do you want me to stay?"

She shook her head, avoiding his eyes. "I need to sleep. But come by the saloon tomorrow before we open. We can talk then. Perhaps you could take Joey out to the livery or the ice rink. Sitting in the kitchen all day can't be much fun for a five-year-old."

"I'll be there." He glanced at Joey, then lifted one of Inez's hands to his lips. A compromise. The light kiss, barely brushing her skin, made her heart race. "You're both safe. Nothing will happen to you. I promise on my life."

Inez locked the door after him and turned to Joey. He looked so small and pitiful, her heart went out to him. She gave him a ferocious hug. "To bed, young man."

"Will you read to me? Like mama does?"

She grimaced over his head, thinking of the Bible and all the trouble it had caused. "Of course, Joey."

As she bundled him under blankets, he asked, "When will mama be better?"

"As soon as Doc tells me, I'll tell you." She picked up Emma's Bible from the washbasin stand and paged through it, her back to Joey. A neatly folded piece of paper, scented of violets and wedged between pages, caught her attention. As if from a distance, Inez watched her fingers unfold the single sheet. The note was written in a careful and feminine hand:

Dear Emma,

I just read of Joe's passing in an old copy of The Independent. I'm probably the last person you want condolences from, but I give them anyway, along with the following information.

Joe left a locked box with me that I will hand only to you or someone you trust. It requires a key, which I do not have. If you decide to send someone, have them bring this letter as proof. You can seal the letter if you do not want to share its contents with the bearer. I will be discreet.

With greatest sympathy,
M. Silks

P.S. I understand that your old admirer is a frequent visitor, if not resident, of Leadville. I trust he has been gentleman enough to keep the past to himself.

"One moment, Joey." Inez hastened to the entryway and yanked open the drawer of the spindle-legged table. There, in the very back, was the brass check she'd palmed from Joe's wallet. The check stamped "Good for one free screw. Mattie Silks, Prop. "

"What can this mean?" She spoke aloud, perplexed.

"Auntie?" The tone was querulous, tired.

She grabbed a leather-bound book from the drawer and brought it into the bedroom.

"I won't be reading from the Bible, Joey." She spoke in what she hoped was a calm voice. "Your mother can do that when she's better. I have something else here, one of my books. It, too, is about God and the Devil, heaven and hell, good and evil. I'll read some to you every night until your mother is well."

Inez opened to page one, Book One, of *Paradise Lost* and in a sleep-inducing cadence began: "Of Man's First Disobedience, and the Fruit/Of that Forbidden Tree, whose mortal taste/Brought Death into the World, and all our woe,/With loss of Eden, till one greater Man/Restore us and regain the blissful Seat,/Sing Heav'nly Muse…"

‹›‹›‹›

Inez and Doc sat in the parlor, brandies hardly touched. Outside, all was dark and soft with falling snow. Inside Inez's heart, it felt like midnight. Doc tented his fingers as if in prayer. "So, my dear, to summarize, Mrs. Rose is in a bad way. She may not make it."

Inez twisted the paired rings on her left hand, reviewing Doc's interminable explanation: *Lost the baby. Internal bleeding. No response. In God's hands.* "I must see her."

"Give her a few days. Then we'll see."

"The marshal says I'm to blame."

"Nonsense, my dear."

"He said," Inez took a deep breath, "that Joe was involved in some counterfeiting scheme. And he pointed a finger at me, Abe, and even Mark. He said Joe had hidden something before he died. These people must have been in Emma's house when she came in, and that's why she—" Inez stopped herself from saying *died.*

"Now, now." Doc patted her hand.

She flexed her fingers and looked over at the piano. "This whole situation is incomprehensible. It reminds me of when I was a child, learning the scales. I would look at my mother's sheet music. I could pick out a note here and there, but mostly it looked like a page filled with random scribbles and dots. I feel like that child right now. All this is just squiggles on a page. I've got to find a way to hear the music, to put it all together."

Doc looked distressed and stopped patting her hand. "Leave it to the professionals who know about these things. You have Joey to take care of. And, you ought to prepare him and yourself for the worst."

The worst. Her mind absolutely refused to think on it, preferring to dwell on other matters instead.

"Doc, when you say professionals…Hollis said Gallagher has brought in an expert."

Doc was now patting his waistcoat. He finally pulled out his pocketwatch. "Professionals. Experts. Treasury people are probably in Denver looking into this, I assume. Denver has a Pinkerton office too, I believe."

"No. It sounded like he meant someone up here." She caught his eyes at last. "Do you know who it is?"

He took a breath and let the air out between rubbery lips in a frustrated *ttthppp*. "My dear, I'm your family doctor. Take this old man's advice and don't think about this other business. It will all work out. The suggestion that you're involved is preposterous. I don't believe anyone but the marshal takes it seriously."

"But why would anyone think Joe is involved? And Abe? As for Mark, that's truly strange. He's been gone since May."

He stood. "Pray for Emma. She's the one who needs your help."

<><><>

Inez soft-pedaled the Bach partita, holding back, focusing on the waterfall of notes and the interaction of melody and harmony, left hand to right. With another, more distant part of her mind, she examined the facts and surmises.

When the piece was done, she sighed and covered the keyboard, music dying in her ears. *I still don't hear it.*

She reached into her pocket for the key with the horseshoe worked into the handle and turned on her stool. Joey's rocking horse sat nearby, her only audience. "Let's assume, for a moment, Joe was involved in counterfeiting." She wagged the key at the horse. "Storing the bills, providing a conduit for distribution from Leadville to Denver, something. He must have been under duress. I can't imagine he would be involved of his own free will."

The horse was silent.

"Maybe," she continued, "he found a way to buy his freedom. Maybe he had some evidence that he was going to hand over to the Treasury office in Denver, after he, Emma, and

Joey left Leadville. Suppose, on his last Denver trip, he left this evidence with someone he trusted. Suppose, what everyone is looking for is really in Denver. In the strongbox with Mattie Silks."

The carved eyes of the horse looked vaguely astonished at her line of reasoning.

"Then this," she held up the key, its wrought iron handle for the horse to see, "must be the key to the box in Denver."

She looked at the horse's blank eyes. "Then again," she said slowly. "Maybe not."

She got down on her knees before the rocking horse and ran her hands over the polished wood as if blind. There, in the carved bridle, her fingers found a wooden echo of the key handle's horseshoe-shaped design. Feverishly, her fingertips ran over the rest of the horse—the saddle, the legs. She finally turned it on its side and looked at the belly.

The seam outlining the hidden panel was nearly invisible. But she saw the keyhole, between the back legs.

Holding her breath, she placed the key in the lock and turned. A small click, and the panel pulled away.

She plunged her hand into the hollow body of the horse. Her fingers touched rough straw, stuffed in for padding, and something else. Paper, a small bundle, tied with what felt like thin rope or twine. She pulled out the bundle. A fifty dollar bill stared from the top.

She righted the horse and rocked it violently. With a thumpety-thump and a flutter of straw, the horse gave birth to bundle after bundle of greenbacks and finally, a small unadorned silver key.

Chapter Forty-Eight

After a restless night with the money under her bed and her revolver under her pillow, Inez greeted the first light of sun with dawning realizations. She hustled Joey to the saloon early. Bridgette clucked and fussed and fixed them breakfast while Inez prepared to go to the bank.

"Can I come?" Joey asked, without much hope.

"No, Joey. This is business." *And it might get unpleasant.*

Inez anchored the saddlebags full of counterfeit under her cloak and grabbed the shotgun she'd brought from home. She turned to Bridgette. "While I'm gone, keep Joey with you. No one takes him anywhere."

"Not even the reverend?"

"If he shows up, ask him to wait. I shouldn't be long."

At the Carbonate City Bank, Inez greeted the teller and gazed at the portrait mounted over his head. The smell of paint and linseed oil lingered in the air. A gathering of dark-coated, somber men stared down. Harry, she thought, was well captured, from the silver gleam in his hair to the intensity of his expression.

"I'm curious about the painting, it looks new. I recognize Mr. Gallagher. The other gentlemen are...?"

"It went up last week when the portraitist finished adding Mr. Harry." The teller said "Mr. Harry" reverentially, as if referring to God. "Shows our board of directors. Most are from Philadelphia, related to the Gallaghers in some way. We're lucky Mr. Harry takes such a personal interest in the family's businesses and investments out West. Most of the Gallaghers won't set foot outside Philadelphia, New York, or Boston."

"So, Mr. Gallagher recently joined the bank's board?"

The teller twisted around to look at the painting. "His father stepped down. His health. Mr. Harry's turn now, I suppose. We'll probably be seeing less of him in Leadville, what with the added responsibilities."

But he'll be watching from the wall. Inez gazed at the painting a moment longer, thinking on what Abe had said the day before.

She finally turned to the teller. "Thank you. I'm here to see Mr. Cooke, no need to announce me."

"Of course, Mrs. Stannert. You know the way."

Inez moved around the teller's cage, picking up speed as she neared the manager's office. She opened the door without knocking and walked in.

"Mrs. Stannert!" Cooke rose, eyes fixed on the shotgun.

Without a word, she set the shotgun down, unslung the saddle bag, and dumped half of its contents over his blotter and papers.

He looked at the bundles scattered on his desk. "A deposit?" He sounded uncertain.

She threw the half-empty saddlebag on the visitor's chair. "Counterfeit."

He glanced at her over half-spectacles. "All of it?"

"Probably." Inez thought on the previous night: Bringing her china washbasin to the parlor. Pouring in the leftover glasses of brandy. Picking a random stack of fifties, taking a note from the middle, and dropping it into the brandy. Watching the bill float, the printing on the surface blur. Stirring with a finger and watching the ink swirl off the paper like smoke in the air. Five notes from five different stacks.

"Where did you get these, Mrs. Stannert?"

She placed her hands palm down on his blotter and leaned forward, nearly touching his nose with her own. "Let's trade, Mr. Cooke. You tell me what you know about the coney ring in Leadville and I'll tell you where I found these."

"I can't do that."

"Yes, you can."

He hesitated. "We don't know the ring is centered in Leadville. There's some evidence it's being run from Denver, that certain materials are shipped from here and finished bills are shipped back."

"What materials?"

Stubborn silence.

"All right. A deal's a deal. I'll tell you where I found this. In a rocking horse."

"In a what?"

"A toy. A gift from a loving father to his son."

Understanding dawned on his face. "Joe Rose."

"Correct. Now, shall I guess who's part of this treasure hunt? Let's start with you. Harry Gallagher. Hollis, but on the periphery. Maybe Cooper, with ready advice on what one legally can and cannot do. Who else?"

Silence.

"Who's the expert Harry brought in?"

Cooke started, then regained his voice and composure. "I think we've traded enough." He gathered the bundles, avoiding her eyes.

"In that case, here's a bonus." Inez held up a brown paper packet. She unwrapped it, and with exaggerated care set the stack of crisp twenty-dollar notes on Cooke's blotter next to the bogus fifties. On the top twenty, Alexander Hamilton faced away from the neighboring stack, as if affronted to be in such company.

"My God!" The words burst from him before he clenched his jaw shut.

She watched Cooke with interest. "You're surprised. So, no bogus twenties before now? The ink didn't run. But I found them in the same place."

He cleared his throat, as if testing his powers of speech. "In the horse?"

"Perhaps your ring is diversifying, hmmm? First fifties. Now twenties. With better ink."

Cooke pulled out a linen handkerchief and dabbed his forehead as if the very thought caused him to break out in a cold sweat.

"Remember, Mr. Cooke, I brought these bogus notes to the bank's attention. I've cooperated fully. Pass that along to Mr. Gallagher, the marshal, your 'expert,' and whoever else is part of this merry chase. And tell them this. Abe and I are not counterfeiters or shovers."

He paled. "Mrs. Stannert, I never thought—"

"Of course you did. But you won't any more, will you." She retrieved her gun. "Tell Mr. Gallagher to put his energies to better use. Tell him to find the person or persons who attacked Emma Rose."

She walked out of the bank, feeling Harry's painted eyes on her back.

‹›‹›‹›

Inez entered the back door of the Silver Queen. Bridgette, Joey, and Reverend Sands looked up expectantly.

She took a deep breath. "Reverend, may I have a word with you."

He turned to Joey. "When Mrs. Stannert and I are through, we'll go to the stables and visit Mrs. Stannert's horse. Deal?"

A very small smile quivered on Joey's face. "Deal."

Inez gritted her teeth, hating what she was about to do.

In the office, she sat on the sofa. No sooner had Sands settled beside her than she jumped up and began pacing. "Last night, I found Joe's legacy—bundles of counterfeit hidden inside Joey's rocking horse. So, you were right. Joe was involved with a bad element. Maybe he stole the bogus notes from them and that's what they're after." She looked out the window at the snow, arms crossed, holding herself and her questions in.

"What did you do with it? Is it here?"

"I delivered it all to Cooke this morning."

"Did you find anything else?"

She thought about the plain silver key. "No."

She turned to see him settle back on the sofa. "Good. You did exactly what I would have done."

"There's more." She moved forward, stopping in front of him. "This hunt for the counterfeiting ring. Cooke is in on it. Harry too." Her mouth dried. "Now, I must ask. And you must tell me the truth. Are you part of this in some way? Part of the ring?"

He reached up and extracted a hand from her crossed arms. "I can set your mind at ease. I am not a member of a coney ring."

Having him deny her worst suspicions left her feeling weak with relief. But she wasn't finished. "Are you on the side of the law, then? Harry's 'expert'? A Treasury agent? Pinkerton, maybe?"

He pulled her onto his lap. "Not Treasury. Not Pinkerton."

She sagged against his chest, allowing herself to relax at last. "I remembered you mentioned Vintree, from Philadelphia. The bank and Harry have Philadelphia connections. When I came to on the bank floor and there you were with Cooke…It seemed like too many coincidences."

"I was at the bank because Cooke had arranged for me to talk with Nigel about Joe's loan. I thought the church could help. I have a professional interest in Mrs. Rose and her son, and I have a very personal interest in you." His hands moved slowly up and down her back. "As for coincidences, life is full of them. For instance, Abe, your missing husband, this current situation. Looks odd, don't you think? Which, of course, is how the marshal sees it. Then again," he lowered his voice, "some of life's events are nothing short of miraculous. For me, meeting you was one of those." He hooked a finger under the velvet ribbon circling her neck and brought her face down to his.

They kissed. She slid her arms under his coat, picturing the layers separating her hands from his skin. Waistcoat. Shirt. Undervest. *Three too many.*

He pulled back, keeping his arms around her. "Why don't I arrange for Bridgette to take Joey. I'll be at the church, working on next week's sermon. Meet me when you're done. Afterward, we'll pick up Joey with the rig."

She took his face in her hands. "How could you have become so much a part of me in so short a time?"

He drew a line down her bodice, echoing the trail of fastenings from her evening dress of Saturday. "Another of life's miracles."

Her lips brushed his. "We must go down." She stood and tightened her hairpins. *One kiss and they all seem to loosen of their own accord.*

‹›‹›‹›

Useless was late. Again.

Where the hell is he?

Inez poured drinks, smiled, chatted, and kept checking the kitchen door. Reverend Sands took Joey on the promised visit to the livery. Bridgette took orders for stew, biscuits, mince pie, and coffee. Abe was not due in until later, when the changing shifts at the mines and the dinner rush would swell the saloon's crowd.

Doc arrived from the hospital. "Her bleeding's stopped. Your prayers must have been heard. Have you seen Reverend Sands today?"

Inez wiped up a spill. "He took Joey Rose out for a while."

"Fine, fine. I'll wait." He accepted his brandy and limped to a table by the kitchen door.

Jed Elliston came in, with an appetite for something besides biscuits. He set his pad and pencil on the bar. "I heard you're adding new faces to your mural. I might start a running piece on this in the paper. Free publicity for you, human interest for me. We both profit. Any truth to the rumor you're going to put Harry Gallagher up there as Lucifer?" His eyes shone with anticipation.

"You can just wait and see with the rest." She tossed an empty bottle under the bar and retrieved a new one. "After that piece about the dance, you have some nerve coming in and asking me anything."

He looked surprised. "I thought you'd get a kick out of it. Puts Harry in a bad light, and I know there's no love lost between you two. I didn't even identify you by name. Kept it anonymous."

"Cat DuBois and I are the only two women who own saloons on State. Any idiot knows that Cat's not going to bite one of the wealthiest hands that feeds her."

"I thought you'd like it." Jed took his drink to a side table to sulk. Inez stared at the back door. Mentally willing Useless to appear.

A voice from a distant time and place broke her concentration. "Well, if it isn't my favorite lady gambler. Long time no see, Mrs. Stannert."

Inez turned in shock. There was no mistaking the good-looking, compactly constructed man leaning on the bar. Under the derby hat, distinctive, heavy black eyebrows arched upward over pale gray eyes that were keen, intelligent, perceptive. Beneath the black mustache twitched a barely suppressed smile.

"Bat Masterson!" Her heart skipped a beat. "What are you doing here? Last I heard, you were recovering from the Ford County sheriff's election."

The smile faded a little. "Damn Kansas politicians. Pardon my French." He spat into a spittoon. "Thought I'd hit the gambling trail and see if Leadville lives up to its wild reputation."

"When did you arrive?"

"Late last night. Been catching up with old friends. Jeff Winney at California Concert Hall, Bailey Youngston and Con Featherly at Texas House. Heard your husband's gone missing, Inez." His voice shaded into sympathy.

"Yes, well." She set a bottle and shot glass before him, "Mark's been gone a long while now. Abe Jackson is part owner, so it's not as if I'm running the place by myself. Do you remember Abe?"

Bat nodded. "Steady sort. Straight shooter at the tables. Leastwise, I never caught him dealing seconds. So, was I slow or he honest?" He winked, excusing her from answering. "Sure, I remember Abe. Mostly though, I remember you." His gaze brushed her mouth, traveled down her bodice—as if counting the buttons—then returned to her face. He smiled. "Heard you've got a game on Saturday nights. Any chance I'd be welcome?"

"Absolutely. Poker, no limits, high rollers with deep pockets. You'd like it. Profit from it too, I'm certain." An idea emerged from a welter of chaotic emotions. "Bat, are you thinking of settling here a spell?"

"Anything's possible now that I'm not wearing a badge."

"Come work for me."

"That's the third offer today."

"Well, I'll double whatever anyone else says and throw in an extra percent of the house take. Come spring, we plan to finish the second floor for games of chance—faro, poker, the usual. We'll need someone to run it."

Bat laughed. "You sure know how to tempt a gambling man, Inez."

He turned and scanned the barroom. As he did, Reverend Sands came out of the kitchen. Doc caught his sleeve. Sands smiled at Inez and nodded at Bat in a polite half-salutation before sitting down with Doc.

"I'll be damned." Bat stared. "I thought Leadville gave its low life the heave-ho in November." Bat's gaze shifted to Inez, his dark eyebrows drawn together in a frown. "That being the case, what's the Sandman doing here?"

Chapter Forty-Nine

Mystified, she looked where Bat Masterson was staring. "Reverend Sands? He's our new minister. What did you call him?"

"Reverend. Ha." Bat didn't sound amused. "If Justice B. Sands is a reverend, then I'm Jesus Christ. I remember him in Dodge in seventy-seven. Worst of the worst."

"What do you mean?"

"Well, his moniker says it all. The sandman in kids' fairy-tales puts them to sleep, right? You can run, but the sandman catches up with you sooner or later. Justice Sands was the same way. If he had your number—you got on his bad side or he was paid to hunt you down—there was no escape. Only the sleep he brought was the permanent kind. No waking until Judgment Day."

Inez gripped the edge of the counter to hold herself upright as Bat downed his drink. *This can't be true.* Her heart felt as though it had been used for target practice.

Bat wiped his mustache. "The other reason he's called Sandman—" he stopped, as though suddenly remembering to whom he was talking.

"Go on."

"Well." Bat coughed and had the grace to blush. "Sands had a way with the ladies. He'd just tip his hat and they'd, ah, fall into bed. With gusto." Envy tinged his words. "Anyhow, that charm was his downfall in Dodge."

Her knuckles turned white. "In what way?"

"Oh, it's old news, Inez."

"You've told me this much. Tell me the rest."

Bat hesitated. "Let's just say that 'lady-killer' fits him more ways than one. And I'm talking about a decent, married woman. Not some dance hall girl. Sands'd do well to leave Dodge off his preaching circuit. Folks there still remember." He stared at Inez's drained face. "Inez, am I talking out of turn? You haven't, I mean you and Sands aren't—"

She gripped the bottle and poured Bat another shot, not daring to look toward Doc's table. "What else do you know about him?"

"Well, I know more than a few so-called 'bad men.' Some friends, some not. But Sands is nastiest bastard I ever met. Especially when drunk." His jaw worked as if he'd bitten into an apple, only to discover it rotten to the core. "Gotta confess, when I saw him walk into your place I almost didn't recognize him. He used to have a—" he described a vague arc above his upper lip, "bodacious mustache."

Inez sank against the bar, grabbing the corner for support. A far-away crash and the pungent odor of expensive whiskey told her she'd knocked the bottle to the floor. When she dared look toward the back table, Sands and Doc were gone.

Bat appeared alarmed. "Well, now, men do change. If Justice Sands is your reverend, proper credentials and all, maybe he's had some sort of spiritual conversion." The doubt in his voice shouted out, loud and clear.

He bent to pick up the larger pieces of bottle glass, voice drifting up to her. "After all, you haven't had any lonely wives turn up dead in Leadville since he's arrived, have you? No murdered husbands?"

He missed the expression on Inez's face as he straightened and placed the knifelike shards on the bar top.

"Uh, Mrs. Stannert, uh, I'm sorry I'm late, y'see—"

"Useless!" She whipped around, fumbling with the strings of her apron. "You're in charge. I've something to do that cannot wait."

She turned to Bat. "Could you stay for an hour or so? Abe will be here by then or I'll be back. I'll feel better knowing Useless has backup, especially if it's you. While we're at it, let's get you some free publicity. Have you talked to any newsmen since you arrived?"

"Can't say that I have."

"Well, I'll introduce you to the editor of *The Independent* and make sure everyone in town knows you're here and anxious to test the gaming skills of the best." She steered him toward Jed Elliston's table. "Jed—" He looked up, a sulky pout still lingering at the corners of his mouth. "Meet Bat Masterson of Dodge City and Ford County fame. He hasn't been interviewed yet and might consent to an exclusive if you buy him a drink."

Jed leaped to his feet and pumped Bat's hand with boyish enthusiasm. "What's your pleasure? And what brings you to Cloud City?"

Masterson shot an amused glance at Inez. "You mean besides old friends?"

Jed looked at Inez with awe. "You know Mrs. Stannert?"

"Met her when she came through Dodge with her husband and Abe Jackson. I remember when she—"

"Keep me out of this. No telling tales out of school."

As Jed hastened to the bar for a bottle of the best, Bat asked in a low voice, "You all right? You're not taking on Sands alone, are you?"

"I can take care of myself. It's the saloon that concerns me. If you'd stay a while, I'd appreciate it."

"No problem, Inez." He adjusted his chair for a clear view of the room.

Jed came back with a bottle, two glasses, and writer's lust in his eye. "So tell me, Sheriff Masterson—it is Sheriff, isn't it? What brings you to town?"

Before the kitchen door closed behind her, Inez heard Bat say, "...damn Kansas politicians."

She grabbed her coat and shotgun. Bridgette and Joey had already left.

Two hours ago, I thought I had all the answers I needed. Turns out, I was asking the wrong questions.

Chapter Fifty

Inez stopped in front of the church, looking up at the white spire thrusting into the low, gray sky. The blizzard had paused. Desultory snowflakes drifted past. They seemed in no hurry to meet the ground where they would be crushed and molded into ice beneath boots and wheels. A few fell on her upturned face, feeling like the cold gentle taps of angel wings.

She felt empty. Bat Masterson's words had blown clear through her, like the high Colorado winds, leaving her numb.

Clutching her shotgun, Inez trudged to the minister's office in the rear of the church, stepping in the reverend's footprints.

When she entered, Sands looked up from the notes and books on his desk. A warm smile spread across his face. All that smile did was increase the icy feeling of betrayal in her heart.

"I heard Emma's doing better." His smile faded, concern taking its place. "Is something wrong?" He rose from his chair.

Inez stepped back. "I just talked to someone who remembers you. From long ago."

Concern disappeared, replaced by a flicker of caution. "Who?"

"Bat Masterson."

"The Kansas lawman?" His voice stayed steady. "Never met him that I recall."

"You're lying. He knew your full name. And he called you something else."

Sands looked down at the open Bible and hymnal, and flipped them shut. He walked to the window, back to Inez. "What was that?"

"Sandman."

She saw him lift a hand to where his mustache would have been. He muttered, "Jesus Christ." It did not sound like a prayer.

After a moment, he added, "What did he say, exactly. If I may ask." He was excruciatingly polite, as if inquiring after the weather.

She willed him to turn around so she could see his expression. He didn't. "Bat said you were a hired gun in Dodge."

She saw him flinch, as if she'd hit him between the shoulders. He finally turned to face her. "I won't deny it, Inez. I'm not proud of that time in my life, but I'm not that person any longer."

"He also said you were a thoroughly nasty bastard. And a lady-killer." She bit her tongue, wondering if she'd gone too far.

He picked up a letter opener, toying with the blade. Eyes on her. "For years, alcohol was my poison. It brought out the worst in me. It erased months from my life. Months where I can recall nothing."

How convenient.

"So, Reverend. Tell me about this decent woman in Dodge. The one that'll earn you a necktie party if you return. Is that something you don't recall?"

He finally moved toward her. "Inez—"

His eyes were pleading. The numbness within her shimmered, threatening to fall apart like a mirage.

She retreated another step and brought the shotgun up. Not pointing at him, but close enough. "Stay behind that desk!"

He stopped, spread his hands wide. "Inez, let me explain—"

"Stop! I don't want long, involved explanations. I'll ask the questions. You answer yes or no. And I want to see your face while you do so."

Slowly, he lowered his hands behind his back and waited.

"Justice Sands. Did you kill a woman in Dodge? Yes or no."

He struggled visibly and said at last, "She was shot with my gun. But I didn't pull the trigger."

"No? That's not the way it sounded to me."

He lowered his eyes, as if it was easier to look at the desk than at her. One hand came out from behind his back and began stacking papers. "Can I tell you what happened? It was a complicated situation. More than yes or no can handle. I'll make it short."

He glanced up. She nodded. Reluctantly.

He looked back down at the desk. "I was with the woman. Her husband came home unexpectedly. I'd left my gun and holster on a chair." He hesitated, as if debating over his next words. "With my clothes." He looked up, to see if she understood.

Inez gritted her teeth. "Keep going."

"He grabbed my gun and said it'd serve me right to die by my own weapon. The bullet meant for me caught her instead. I wrestled the gun from him. He was on the floor. I pulled the trigger. Twice. I meant to kill him and I did. I won't lie to you, Inez."

Her numbness vaporized, like her breath in the cold air. "How can you say you had nothing to do with her death? You had everything to do with it! You killed them both."

"I know I'm responsible. I've paid for that episode every day of my life since." Sands looked at her, almost sympathetically, as if he understood why she was throwing words at him like knives. "I made a mistake, Inez. A big mistake. I should have told you sooner about my past. But to be honest, the past didn't seem to count for much here. People rush in—from the East, from the West—and collide at the top of the Rockies. They're looking for riches or looking to escape. And running. Everyone's either running from their past or running toward some elusive vision of the future. What about you, Inez? Are you running from the past or toward the future?"

"We're not discussing me!" She felt control of the conversation slipping from her.

"I thought," he said, "we'd get to know each other gradually. That, over time, I'd tell you more and you'd come to trust me. It didn't happen that way, though."

"No, it didn't. You didn't tell me anything. Bat said you're a lady-killer, that you prefer married women. I remember how you first looked at me and how you acted—as if I was a whore. Then, when I rebuffed you, it was all politeness and apologies. I fell for that, didn't I. For every step you took back, I took one forward. When your appointment ends in June, you'll probably shake my memory from your mind as easily as you shake Leadville's snow from your clothes. You preyed on those other women when they were vulnerable, took them when they were weak. You're no man of God!"

His voice hardened. "Don't paint yourself the victim, Inez. You're just as responsible for bringing us to where we are now, strangers to each other in some ways and in other ways very decidedly not. Whose decision was it to jump headfirst into a—let's see, what euphemism would best suit your sensibilities—an *affaire d'amour*. And 'unprepared' at that?"

His words hit with deadly aim.

She clenched the shotgun. "It takes two. And you hardly objected!"

He picked up the letter opener again and flipped it once, catching it neatly. "You set the tune. I merely followed in the dance."

They stared at each other.

"I don't know you," she whispered. "What kind of person you are."

"I could say the same about you, Inez."

The desk stood like a dark, impenetrable barrier between them. Sands circled the desk slowly, as if expecting her to order him back at any moment. He stopped a few feet away, and cocked his head, examining her with the deliberate expression she recalled from their first encounters. "I wonder. Was it just a way to keep your distance?"

"What do you mean?" She retreated another step.

"Up close, it's hard to see someone. Particularly if you don't know him well to begin with. That, of course, leaves you free to imagine him any way you want." Moving faster than she would have believed possible, he knocked the shotgun from her hands.

Then Sands was holding both of her arms, without an inch of space between their bodies. "Look at me," he whispered. "Do you see me? Do you even want to?"

His face filled her vision, blurred at that intimate distance. She shoved him away. He released her and backed off. "That's it, isn't it. You pull close, then push away when reality no longer fits your vision. It's an old game, one I've played myself. It works, sometimes. You stay in control. But you always end up alone."

She pointed a shaking finger at him. Angry. Feeling that, in some way, he'd managed to strip her to the skin. "You do this every time. Twist the conversation, twist the words to suit yourself. This is not about you and me."

"Oh?" He lifted his eyebrows with mild sarcasm. "I thought it was."

"What about you. You and Harry."

He blinked. "Me and Harry?"

He stood, hands behind, balanced on his feet: soldier at ease.

"Bat said you had…" her fingers lifted to her face, an echo of the earlier gesture, "a 'bodacious' mustache. I saw you with that mustache in a photo on Harry Gallagher's desk. A photo from the War. He's an officer, you're hardly more than a boy. You're Harry's man. His counterfeit expert. You lied to me!"

His expression stayed closed. "I've answered each and every question you put to me honestly, even the painful ones. But here, I draw the line. I will not discuss Harry Gallagher."

"Why not?" She held out her hands, palms up, almost pleading. "I'm right, aren't I? If I'm wrong, what do you gain by not explaining? Is this your idea of being a 'good soldier'?" She hurled the term at him like a curse. "Why are you protecting Harry?"

"You weren't in the War, Inez. You have no idea what it was like."

"Then tell me!"

Silence.

She crossed her arms. "Then, Reverend Sands, we have nothing more to discuss."

He looked her over as if trying to decide whether she was serious or bluffing.

I should turn on my heel, stalk out, and slam the door. But her traitorous body refused to budge.

He leaned against the desk, rubbing his forehead in partial surrender. "I shouldn't even say this much, but give me a week. One week. Take Joey. Go to Denver. It should be safe there. When you come back, we can talk. If you want to."

He stopped and glanced around the office as if he'd forgotten where they were. "Well. That's that, isn't it. I'll get the rig. We'll pick up Joey at Bridgette's, and I'll take you both to your home." He sounded proper, polite, the minister offering aid to a church member.

"Don't bother. I'll walk."

Her body jerked into motion, obedient to her will at last. Inez turned on her heel, picked up the shotgun, and slammed out the door. As she walked to the street, she told herself that the freezing tears on her face were due to the icy wind, nothing more.

Chapter Fifty-One

At the corner to her street, Inez wavered.

Denver.

Sands had said, "Go to Denver."

Her impulse was to head anywhere but.

However, Denver had Mattie Silks. Mattie had the box. Inez, in the saloon safe, almost certainly had the key. She thought further of the two bundles of counterfeit she'd withheld from Cooke—one of fifties, the other of twenties—also in the safe. If the counterfeiting extended to or emanated from Denver, Denver would surely have Treasury agents or others looking into it. The melody ran true: It would have to be Denver.

Inez neared her home with a yearning she hadn't felt in a long time. The small frame house waited, offering safety, sanctuary. She unlocked the front door with a sigh, stepped inside, and stopped.

Something was different. Something was wrong.

Leadville's clamor, normally muted by the walls, sounded more distinct than it should have. The chill air inside felt alive, stealing toward her from the rear of the house and curling about her ankles. She gripped the shotgun tighter and moved forward.

The bedroom doors stood open. A quick glance revealed no intruders, no disturbances. She flattened herself against a wall and scanned the kitchen. The back door gaped, wounded wood showing white around the lock. The kitchen appeared untouched, unoccupied.

Holding her breath, she strode into the kitchen, paused by the pantry, and approached the broken door, fully expecting to find a dead rodent impaled on the boards.

Nothing.

Everything else was as it should be, which unsettled Inez more than if the house had been in disarray. It was as if someone had come to violate her, then disappeared, deed undone, with a whisper: "I'll be back."

The parlor.

On entering the house, she'd noticed the piano was intact, her furniture standing. She'd not walked in.

Inez rushed to the parlor.

The splintered, dark wood was kicked into a corner. She stared, not quite sure of what she saw. The curve of broken rockers was her first clue. Then, she picked out a bit of saddle trim, a fragment of wooden mane.

Joey's rocking horse.

"Damn them!" she screamed. "What do they *want?*"

A white square sat like a stranger on her piano stool. Holding the shotgun in the crook of her arm, she ripped open the envelope.

Spring assailed her nose. Dried rose petals drifted to the floor. The note was on plain paper, folded twice. She opened it and more petals fells out. In block letters, the note read: "One Rose left."

Underneath, underlined: "We want it all."

‹›‹›‹›

Old habits of packing fast and lean returned, along with the words Mark would say as they hastily prepared to slip from nameless towns turned ugly: "Take only what you need. What fits in one bag."

For Denver, that meant her winter traveling suit, charcoal gray and uncomplicated, and a change of clothes for Joey. The note from Joe's pocketwatch. *Paradise Lost.* She stuffed it all in the carpetbag. The Remington was in her pocket. No extra bullets. No second hat.

Inez stole precious minutes to nail the broken door shut. Each slam of the hammer was accompanied by the vehement exclamation: "Bastard!"

She locked the house, after a final glance at the smashed rocking horse and her unscathed piano.

On Harrison, she hesitated. *Stop at the bank for money?* No.

Cooke knew about the rocking horse.

The saloon's safe had cash, the silver key from the horse, the samples from Chet's bags, two bundles of counterfeit, and Mattie Silks' token and note to Emma. Inez silently thanked God she hadn't left the token or note in her entryway table. Then she cursed Him for not providing guidance on what to do next. Across the street on Carbonate Avenue was a livery stable. She walked toward it, haunted by the smell of roses, formulating a plan.

Chapter Fifty-Two

The hired livery driver looked doubtful when Inez gave him directions to Abe's house. "After that," she said, "I'm going to Chicken Hill."

The horse pulling the cutter shook its mane as if disapproving. The driver, a well-swaddled beanpole of a man with a bulbous nose and sorrowful eyes, seemed to share the sentiment. "Now what's a lady like you wanting with the colored and the Irish?"

Inez held up a quarter eagle. "When you deliver me to Chicken Hill," she said.

His doleful air vanished.

Inez hadn't been to Abe's cabin since Mark's disappearance. Rough hewn logs faced the street, but she remembered the interior as being as warm and comforting as the owner.

The horse busied itself with a feed bag and the driver with his pipe while she mounted the porch and pounded on the door. An eternity later, vibrations in the porch boards heralded approaching footsteps.

Abe opened the door in shirtsleeves. "Inez!" His eyes widened. "What're you doin' here? Who's mindin' the saloon?"

"Useless."

"By himself? Damn it, Inez—"

"Bat Masterson's there in case of trouble," she added hurriedly.

"Masterson!" His eyes narrowed. "What's he doin' in Leadville?"

"Visiting. He'll wait until you arrive. But that's not why I'm here."

Her teeth were chattering so she could hardly talk. "Abe, listen. Bat remembers Reverend Sands from Dodge. Sands was a hired gun. Oh Jesus, Abe. He killed a woman and her husband. A respectable woman, not some sporting girl. And there's probably more. Bat wouldn't say."

She set the carpetbag and shotgun on the porch. "When I confronted him, Sands denied nothing. He's Harry's man too, but refuses to discuss it. Yesterday, I tried to tell you what Hollis said about Harry and this counterfeiting business, but you wouldn't listen. Now, let me in. We've got to talk." She shouldered her way past him and froze.

Crouched in a chair by the stove, Angel peered up, fingers fixed on the disjoined buttons and buttonholes of her half-closed bodice. Papers, pencils, and a dog-eared primer were scattered at her feet.

Inez found her voice. "What is *she* doing here?"

"Inez." Abe's tone warned her. "You know Angel. She attends your church, remember?"

A complicated jumble of emotions crashed over Inez. "It's not enough you take in stray cats and orphans. Now, it's stray whores as well!"

"That's it! We do our talkin' outside, Inez." He turned to Angel. "It's okay, honey. Mrs. Stannert and I, we're gonna have this out right now."

He grabbed Inez's arm and his coat, forced her out on the small porch, and slammed the door behind him. "That was downright rude."

"What is she *doing* here?"

"I'm teachin' her to read and write."

"And what is she teaching *you*, Abe?"

He ignored her question. "She's bright. Like you. Wasted in Cat's place."

"So you're rescuing her? Abe, you're crazy. She's young enough to be your daughter. Your granddaughter!"

Abe buttoned his coat, glaring at her. "What goes on between Angel and me is none of your business. And, if we're gonna start like that, let me tell you how it's been the past eight months bein' your 'business partner.'" He tossed the words at her like they were counterfeit coins. "When Mark left, I thought you'd just give up. I worried, didn't know what to do for you and your boy. Then, Harry started comin' round and you sent your boy away."

Her face burned as if she stood before an open furnace. "It didn't happen like that!"

He ignored her outburst. "It was Harry and his flowers, his letters, his fancy gifts, his takin' you out on Sundays." He shook his head. "You acted like he was the Savior, arrived for the Second Coming. Harry suited you, y'know. More than Mark ever did. It's how you and Harry stride around. Like you own the ground you walk on, a cut above us mortals. Comes from bein' born to a life of privilege, I'd guess."

"I don't have to listen to this." Inez moved forward to grab her shotgun and carpetbag. Abe laid a hand on the muzzle and blocked her path.

"No runnin' this time, Inez. We never talked about this, and it's festered like a boil between us. Time to air it and be done. Now, when Harry wanted to buy my share of the saloon, I was willin'. Maybe, I thought, it's time. Time to move on, open my own place. But when I tried to talk to you about it, all of a sudden you cast him into the sulfury pit. And there he's been ever since. Not only that, I gotta hear about Harry on a regular basis as you rake him over the coals. Like I said, you slammed the door, but never let go."

"Send my things to Bridgette's." Inez said through her teeth as she sidled toward the porch steps. "I'm done with this conversation."

Abe stretched his arms from porch post to post. The only other way out was over the railing.

"And Harry wasn't the only one. Next was Reverend J. B. Sands." Abe sounded like he was identifying some vermin that crawled out of the trash. "He started hangin' around, eyes all over you. Two, three weeks later—" He smacked a post. "Big surprise, he's got feet of clay too."

Inez opened her mouth to respond.

"I ain't done. Now Masterson's in town. Jesus H. Christ. I remember you two carryin' on in that dance hall of his. Lord only knows what happened afterward, but I can guess."

"How *dare* you throw that in my face!" She clenched her fists.

"I'm gonna finish. As I was sayin', at the time, I figured it was none of my business. But, I always thought, privately, you know, that it was a good thing for you and Mark that we left Dodge when we did."

She swiped a hand across her face trying compose herself so she could speak without crying. "If you remember Dodge that clearly, you'll also recall why Mark wasn't there that night. I forget her name. Some actress. At least that was her stated profession. Blonde." She turned her head away and said bitterly, "They usually were."

There was a moment's silence.

"I never said Mark was a saint." Abe's voice was tired, his anger gone. "Or that you or I were. What I've always said, and believed, is that Mark loved you. And your boy."

He slumped against a post, looking as spent as she felt. "So, here we are, Inez. I'm lookin' over the terrain, and what do I see? Harry on the saloon wall. Sands with a gun. And Masterson. I swear, I don't want to be anywhere near when this all explodes."

Abe stuffed his bare hands into the armpits of his coat. "I can't keep goin' through this with you. I'm not your father. And I'm not," he took a deep breath, "your husband."

"We're partners," Inez whispered. "We're friends."

Abe shook his head. "I can't take bein' yanked up, down, and sideways with your problems. I'm worn out. Besides,

I've got needs too. You get my drift? Bein' with you, Inez, the lines get blurred. Are we friends? Well, sometimes, the way you look at me or brush against my arm…It's too damn confusing."

Inez clutched the porch railing, trying to assimilate his words. The livery driver, not twenty feet away, puffed studiously on his pipe, gazing at the distant mountains.

Abe continued, "Now Angel, she's good for me, and I'm good for her."

Inez turned back. He looked at her, steady. "I didn't bring this up before today, thinkin' first, it wasn't your business anyhow and second…well, I just didn't know how we'd weather that storm. But if you and I are business partners, *friends*, then you gotta accept her and give me some breathin' room." He finally moved away from the steps. "I'm done. Said all I'm goin' to say."

Past ghosts and present pressures crowded around her on the porch. A woman with a small child and two men in ragged overcoats walked past, eyeing them curiously.

"Abe, I can't think on all this right now. Sands said some of the same things."

Abe raised his eyebrows. "The man just rose a mite in my estimation."

"But I must tell you about this coney business. Hollis as much as said that he knows about you and Mark, your past. He's working for Harry to uncover the ring in Leadville. Before he left, Hollis gave me a chance to 'confess' and avoid arrest."

Abe raised his eyebrows further.

"I told him that there's nothing to confess. Angel," she nodded toward Abe's house, "knows something about Joe Rose. She gave me his pocketwatch at the soiree, and I'll bet you a dollar to a dime she wrote the note inside that said 'Joe knows.' Last night, I found bundles of counterfeit inside Joey's rocking horse. It's a lot, Abe. Thousands. I turned it over to Cooke this morning, figuring it'd prove we were innocent."

She picked up her carpetbag. "After I spoke with Sands, I went home. Someone had broken into my house. No dead rats, but Joey's horse was smashed. They left a note, threatening Joey and saying they 'want it all.' The only ones I told about the horse and the counterfeit are Cooke and Sands."

"Jesus, Inez. You gotta tell Hollis."

"I don't trust him. You're the only one I'm telling this to. I'm not dragging Bat into this mess either." She looked hard at Abe. He shrugged, as much as admitting that the thought had crossed his mind.

"I'm leaving for Denver with Joey tomorrow. I'll find a way out besides the usual coaches. Do the best you can with the saloon. As for the other business," she started to put a hand on his arm, then drew back. "I didn't realize I'd dragged you so deep into my troubles. I never meant to…confuse you. I'll think on what you said. You consider my words as well. Angel knows something. If she can clear the Roses—and us, I might add—maybe she will. For your sake, if no one else's."

Chapter Fifty-Three

When Bridgette opened the door, her face went from welcome to worry in a flash. "Arriving with shotgun and luggage, ma'am? And looking very peaked. Come in, come in. The boys are having supper."

"Bridgette, I must ask some favors of you." Inez stepped into the sudden comfort of the cabin. Curtains across the one large room divided sleeping from living areas. Along one side of a long, rough-hewn table, four tow-headed boys sat from tallest to smallest, like notes descending a scale. Joey's dark hair provided the closing note at the end of the line. Joey dropped his spoon and raced over to grab Inez's iced-up coat in a hug.

Inez set gun and bag down and hugged him back while addressing Bridgette. "Joey and I need a place to sleep tonight. If we could take a spot on your floor—"

"Joey can sleep with the two youngest. You take my bed."

"Oh no, I couldn't."

Bridgette bustled to the stove. "Ma'am, you've kept a roof over our heads and food on the table. So, not another word. Now, what else?"

Inez led Joey back to his seat before joining Bridgette. "This is a little more difficult." Inez lowered her voice, glancing at the boys. Spoons rose and fell from bowls to mouths. Five sets of blue eyes regarded her. "I need a driver with a sleigh. Someone who knows the roads out of town and who can leave before dawn tomorrow. I'll pay well, but he must keep his mouth shut."

Bridgette stared, a half-filled bowl of soup forgotten in her hand. "Leaving town in this weather? Where would you be going?"

"Bridgette, the less I tell you the better. This way, if anyone ask; where I am, you can honestly say you don't know."

Bridgette tapped her ladle on the iron stove, thinking. "Finding a man who knows the roads, now, that's not hard. They all need the money. It's finding someone who won't drink it all up and start a-wagging his tongue." She brightened as her eldest brought in a blast of cold air and an armload of firewood. "Michael, fetch Mr. McMillan. Tell him there's the prospect of a good paying run from town." She addressed Inez. "He's your man. Hard-working, sober. Wife's been poorly for months, he can use every penny."

"Thank you, Bridgette. One last thing—paper and pencil?"

Fortified with writing tools and a scrap of paper, Inez pushed the soup bowl aside. She twisted the double rings on her left hand, pondering what to say and how to say it. She finally picked up the stubby pencil and wrote:

Dearest Emma,

If you're reading this, it means our prayers have been answered and you are recovering from your trials. I have Joey with me. I promise to protect him with my life and bring him back to you, safe and sound.

Affectionately, Inez

She wrote slowly, thinking that anything addressed to Emma would reach Reverend Sands, and probably Harry and Hollis. Inez sealed the note in an envelope, wishing she could say something more to calm a mother's fears.

"Bridgette, I need this delivered to Mrs. Rose when she's better. Or you can give it to Abe or Susan Carothers. No one else."

"Not even," Bridgette dangled the envelope between thumb and forefinger as if it were scalding, "the reverend, ma'am?"

"Especially not him." She picked up her spoon.

Bridgette looked crestfallen.

Michael returned, snow on his hat and shoulders, along with Mr. McMillan, a man so tall he had to stoop under the lintel. Inside, he remained slightly bent as if constantly wary of banging his head on low ceilings.

After quick introductions, Inez said, "We'd best talk outside."

Once the door closed behind them, Inez continued, "Mrs. O'Malley says you can be trusted to be discreet. I need to get to Georgetown tomorrow."

"A-yep." McMillan scraped a thumb across his bearded cheek. "Take me two days. One t'get you there, another to get meself back. Cost you a pretty penny, as I've nothing to haul down right now. Can always find folks in Georgetown heading to Leadville, though. You've trunks? Household goods?"

"Just me, a boy, and a carpetbag."

He nodded, as if accustomed to women fleeing Leadville with little more than the clothes on their backs. "Traveling light, we'll make good time. We leave five in the morning, you can probably catch the last Georgetown train to Denver. Denver's your destination?"

She sidestepped his question. "Be here at four thirty, then. I need to make a stop on our way out of town."

Later, she sat on the edge of the "small boys" bed to say goodnight to Joey. Lying head to toe like sardines gave the three a little extra turning room. Joey, being a guest, got the foot of the bed to himself.

Joey's eyes were dark in the lamplight. "Where are we going, Auntie?"

She smoothed his hair. "We're going to take a sleigh and then a train."

"If we don't say goodbye Mama won't know where we are." Joey's lower lip trembled.

"I wrote her a note. It's just a short trip, Joey. Then we'll come back."

He yawned. "Will you read me more about the angel wars?"

Inez opened *Paradise Lost* at the ribbon and whispered Satan's first words to Beelzebub in a Hell where fire shed not light, but dark: "If thou beest hee; But O how fall'n! how chang'd/From him, who in the happy Realms of Light/Cloth'd with transcendent brightness didst outshine/ Myriads though bright…"

<>‹›<>

It was pitch dark when McMillan arrived with a sleigh pulled by two sturdy bays. It was one of the few times that Inez was grateful for Leadville's "get-go," twenty-four-hours-a-day style. With the main streets overflowing with pre-dawn traffic, they were just one more nondescript vehicle.

She directed McMillan to wait at the corner of Harrison and State. "I'll be five minutes." She tucked the buffalo robe around Joey. "This will be a great adventure, Joey." She tried to sound encouraging.

She unlocked the front door of the Silver Queen and entered, shotgun in hand. The place appeared deserted. Inez hurried upstairs to the office.

Opening the safe in the near dark, she took out two envelopes: one held Mattie Silks' letter and brass check, the other held Angel's note and the silver key from the rocking horse. She pulled out the two bundles of counterfeit, then counted out two hundred in hard money from the saloon's cash reserve and tucked money and envelopes into the pockets hidden in the lining of her travel coat. Finally, from the safe's depths, she pulled out the two bags of rocks liberated from Chet's samples.

After securing the safe, she debated leaving her shotgun under the bar with the office key. When he saw the gun, Abe would know she'd found a way out of town.

At the top of the stairs Inez stopped, thinking that she'd heard something besides her own footsteps. She waited. Listening.

Nothing but the usual street noise, honky-tonk music, and inarticulate shouts.

Then, a thump. Almost beneath her feet.

The cat jumping off a box?

Inez padded silently downstairs and into the kitchen. A weak light escaped from the open doorway of the storeroom. She set the sample bags down, breathing fast and shallow as she tried to identify the sounds: Wood scraped on wood, a heavy footstep.

She set her finger on the trigger and swung around the doorframe.

"Useless!"

Useless, crouched behind a row of crates, turned.

They stared at each other. In the weak lamplight, his eyes glittered, feral, cornered. When he spoke, however, it was just Useless, stuttering and nearly inarticulate. "Muh—Muh—Mrs. Stannert. What're you doing here?"

Without lowering the gun, she stepped around the crates to see what he hunched over. She gestured with the gun, a short jerk. "Move."

He straightened and stepped aside, eyes on the muzzle.

The half-shuttered lantern threw ragged shadows over a crude wooden cage lashed together with small poles and leather straps.

Something dark skittered inside.

In the confined storeroom, Useless' labored breathing provided a counterpoint to her own rapid heartbeat. Scritching, scrabbling emanated from the cage. Light glanced off a small beady eye. Inez's breath caught as she identified the shifting form inside.

Rat.

She stared, horrified, at Useless. He looked as trapped as the rodent.

Useless held up his gloved hands, palms out. His nose dripped as he snorted out his words, "Oh Lordy. I promised

Mr. Jackson I wouldn't tell. Oh jeez, he's gonna kill me. Please, don't tell him you caught me."

Babbling, he reached into his coat pocket. She pulled back the hammer of the shotgun. It sounded like the snap of a dry bone. "Stop."

He looked confused, hand in pocket. "My nose, ma'am. I, I gotta..." Inch by slow inch, he pulled out a grimy red handkerchief.

She eased the hammer back into place, bracing the gun stock against her hip so he wouldn't see how much her own hands shook.

Her cold voice filled the cramped room. "You'd better have a very, very good explanation for this."

He blew his nose with a liquid honk, folded the large square of damp cloth, and patted his forehead with it. "You sure put a scare in me, ma'am. I thought you were a thief looking for liquor. Mr. Jackson said no one's ever here this time of morning." He looked at the cage and crumpled, hunching his shoulders in and his head down. He peered up at Inez, mournful. "It was Mr. Jackson's idea, y'see. On account of the cat."

"The cat." Her trigger finger ached with tension.

"Yeah." He hunched his shoulders further, looking as if he wanted to duck his head into his collar like a turtle. "Mr. Jackson thought if we trapped the mice and rats every once in a while, you'd think the cat was doing her job and let her stay. She'd die if you turned her out. And Mr. Jackson, he's got a soft spot for animals." Useless snuffled, stepped away from the cage as if to distance himself, and barked his shin on a crate.

"Ow!" He grabbed his shin. "Mr. Jackson won't even let me kill them rats. I'm supposed to catch them and let them go somewheres else. Durn things probably freeze to death. Better to put 'em out of their misery, I figure. But, no, Mr. Jackson said..."

Inez watched Useless blather. He seemed genuinely distressed. But the image of the rat and the look in his eyes when he'd first seen her lingered.

A meow sounded behind her. The calico squeezed past Inez and moseyed over to Useless, barely glancing at the captured rodent. She twined around Useless' legs, directing a hungry complaint to his shaking boots.

Inez's finger eased off the trigger.

"Durn cat. Doesn't even *want* the rats," moaned Useless. "I swear, she's been spoiled on all the table scraps Mr. Jackson and the customers sneak to her. We had an old mouser back home on the farm. Boy, was she good. She'd catch them rats, spread their guts all over the ground."

"That's enough, Useless." She deliberated, still wavering.

I was wrong about Reverend Sands. Blind and deaf to Abe and Mark. Can I trust what I see now?

"Well jeez, ma'am, what're you doin' here anyway?"

Inez started, her allotted five minutes long gone.

"I'm leaving town." She stopped, reluctant to say more. Picturing the rats nailed to Emma's door, to her dress at the bank, in Joe's assay office.

Useless isn't that devious. And he hasn't got that sort of blood lust. Abe and I, we would've seen it in him before now. The cat, the rats...that sounds like Abe, right down to letting the rats go free.

The trapped rat squeaked, driven to frenzy by the cat's nearby presence. Tiny claws scrabbled at the cage's confines. Inez's skin crawled. Her desire to escape increased.

She retreated to the threshold. The four small panes of the kitchen window, high above the stove, showed gray. *The answers are in Denver. If I linger here, Joey and I will be trapped by the daylight.*

Useless snuffled and honked into the handkerchief again.

She pulled up the gun. "We'll discuss this when I return. If I return."

Inez gathered the sample bags, rehung the office key, and kept the shotgun. After locking the front door, she ran to the waiting sleigh.

"Thought we'd have to come looking for you." McMillan barely gave her a chance to settle under the robes before the sleigh started moving. Inez wrapped her wool scarf around her face and her arms around Joey.

The runners squeaked and hissed over the snow as they left town, an echo of the frantic, imprisoned rat.

Chapter Fifty-Four

Inez awoke in the hotel room, frowned at the clanking radiator, and tried to remember where she was. Rolling to the side, she spied Joey in a trundle bed, blankets covering all but the very top of his head. From the light leaking in around the shades, she estimated that it was mid-morning on December thirty-first. The Denver business district would close early. The red-light district, on the other hand, would be open all night.

With stops to make in both areas, Inez didn't want to be caught in the unfamiliar streets of Denver after nightfall. Propelling herself out of bed, she staggered to the wash basin and splashed cold water on her face. Not as cold as Leadville, but cold enough.

Toweling off, she shook the lump in the small bed. "Joey, wake up. We're going to an assay office this morning."

He yawned and sat up, rubbing his eyes. "Like Papa's?"

"Yes, like your papa's." She re-examined the business address scribbled down by an obliging hotel clerk.

After breakfast in the hotel's dining room, they hailed a carriage. Inez gave the assay office address to the driver. "How much?" she inquired.

"Two dollars, ma'am."

"I'll make it five if you wait. We have another stop before returning."

Entering the office, Inez was struck by its silence until she remembered it was close to noon on New Year's Eve. A man sat behind a desk, reading the *Denver Post*. He popped up as Inez and Joey approached.

"Can I help you?" He unrolled his shirtsleeves hastily, as if caught in a state of undress.

"I have samples I'd like assayed. I need the results tomorrow." She plunked the two bags on top of the counter formed by the half-wall. Rock dust in the air stung her nose. The man eyed the bags without enthusiasm and turned a polite face to her. "Sorry ma'am. We're closed New Year's. Soonest we could get results to you is Monday."

She switched on her most engaging smile. "What's your fee, Mr.—?"

"Helt." He belatedly removed his derby. "The fee depends on how much you've got." He peered past her, as if expecting to see a wagon waiting to be unloaded outside the door. He reversed his gaze to the bags on the counter. "This all?"

She nodded.

He scratched his upper lip, hidden beneath a smartly waxed mustache, and looked doubtful. "It's a mighty small sample. A fiver for the two."

Inez reached into her coat pocket and extracted a ten-dollar gold eagle from a coin purse. "Mr. Helt." She slid the coin across the counter, keeping hold of one edge. "I really must have those results tomorrow. We're only in town for a day. Are you certain there isn't anyone available to do them?" She tapped the gold with a gloved fingertip.

Helt looked at the money, then, for a long moment, at Inez. She held the smile and the eagle, eyebrows raised questioningly.

He finally hefted the bags onto his desk. "Guess I could run your assay tonight, being it's just these. I'm not much of drinking man anyway."

She released the gold piece. "Thank you. What time tomorrow?"

"Oh, say noon. I'll need the morning to finish the analysis." He returned to the desk and retrieved a ledger. "A couple of questions, and we'll be set. Your name?"

"Mrs. Stannert."

He scribbled, then opened one of her bags and took out a fist-sized specimen. "These are from?"

"I'd rather not say."

"Leadville?" He grinned. "That's okay, Mrs. Stannert. I'll assay for the usual." He scribbled a bit more. "You looking to buy or sell?"

"Neither." She took his receipt. "I'm looking for the truth."

<>‹>‹>

The driver pulled up to an imposing brick house on Holladay Street. "You sure this is the right address?" he asked for the third time.

"This is Mrs. Silks' boarding house, is it not?"

"Madame Silks." He shifted in his seat. "Yeah, but it ain't exactly a boarding house, if you get my drift. If you and your boy are looking for a place to stay—"

"I'm looking for Mrs. Silks." Inez handed him a quarter eagle. "The rest is yours when we return to the hotel. It may be a wait."

"You pay, I'll wait."

She grasped Joey's hand and they climbed the steps to the entrance. By the door, Inez stooped down, eye level with Joey. "I need to talk privately with the woman who owns this house. You will need to wait while I do that. You must be on your best behavior. Don't touch anything, be polite, don't speak unless you're spoken to. And, Joey, we'll not mention this visit to your mama."

He nodded, looking more intrigued than alarmed.

Inez lifted the brass knocker and let it fall. After a long minute, the door creaked opened. A man with a face of discretion carved in brown mahogany raised his eyebrows.

"I'm here to see Mrs. Silks on a matter of some urgency."

"Who is it, George?" A soft voice floated to them.

George turned. "A visitor, ma'am. She says it's a matter of some urgency."

"*She?*" Amusement shaded the voice as it came closer. "We usually don't have women arriving on urgent business."

George drew back, and the owner of the voice appeared in the doorway.

Inez, who had been prepared to look straight into the speaker's eyes, found herself gazing down instead. A diminutive version of Lily Langtry gazed up, all blonde, blue eyes, and porcelain skin. A good six inches shorter than Inez, the woman carried herself as if she stood at equal height. A diamond-encrusted cross sparkled on the bodice of a dress as blue as her eyes. Those eyes raked Inez, head to toe, as if she stood upon an auction block.

Pity followed by dismissal crossed those baby-doll features. "No boarders with children. Find a suitable place for him. If you're still looking for work, come back then."

Inez halted the closing door. "Mrs. Silks? I'm not looking to 'board.' I'm here on behalf of Emma Rose, the wife of Joe Rose." She handed Mattie Silks the folded letter.

Mattie opened it, glanced at it, and handed it back. "Emma must trust you a great deal. Whoever you are." Suspicion was plain in her face.

"I'm Mrs. Stannert. A friend of the family." Inez placed Joey before her. "This is Joey. Joe and Emma's boy."

Mattie leaned down in a rustle of silk and tipped Joey's chin up. "You look like your father. I know your parents, but I don't know this woman. Who is she, love?"

"Auntie Inez, ma'am." Joey responded, obviously mindful of Inez's advice to speak when spoken to.

"Your real aunt?"

"Not really. But almost."

"Almost." Those blue eyes flashed up at Inez then returned to Joey. "And what, pray tell, does Auntie do in Leadville?"

He didn't hesitate. "She rides horses. She plays piano. She plays poker. She shoots guns, sometimes. And she owns a... drinking establishment." He pronounced the last two words one careful syllable at a time, with Emma's studied cadence.

"Well, well." The suspicion was now tempered with amusement.

"A business woman," said Inez. "I'm a business woman."

Mattie Silks nodded. "As I am." She turned to Joey. "Where's your mama and papa?"

"Papa's in heaven. Mama's," he reached for Inez, "in the hospital."

Mattie's face softened. After a pause, she moved aside. "Come in."

Inez and Joey stepped onto a crimson carpet so deep it threatened to bury their shoes. The reception hall could have swallowed half of Inez's house. Crystal chandeliers tinkled as the cold air stole in through the front door. Straight ahead, a walnut-banistered staircase led upstairs.

Mattie glided ahead, tossing over her shoulder, "George, have tea prepared for Mrs. Stannert and myself." Halfway down the hall, a brunette with the face of a madonna appeared in an arched entryway.

"Alice." Mattie stopped in front of her. "Would you watch this young fellow while I speak with his 'aunt'? Go ahead, Joey. There's a piano in there that you can bang away on. Maybe Alice will teach you some scales."

As they proceeded past the stairs, Mattie said, "Alice has a son about his age. He'll be fine."

They entered a long dining room, now vacant. Passing chair after silent chair, Mattie remarked, "Forgive me for questioning him. But children that age don't lie. Or, if they do, they lie badly." She opened a side door. A cozy parlor looked out over back gardens crusted with snow.

Mattie waved Inez to a chesterfield covered in crimson plush and took a matching chair. "So." She lit a thin brown cigarette and dropped the extinguished lucifer into a silver ashtray. "You know the Roses."

Inez nodded.

"I find it hard to believe Emma Rose would be friends with—much less confide in—a woman who runs a saloon," she said half to herself. "What is the name of your…drinking establishment?"

"The Silver Queen. Do you know Leadville?"

Mattie lifted one shoulder.

"It's at the corner of State Street and Harrison."

"I know the area." An enigmatic smile. "You sell…only liquor?"

It was Inez's turn for a cryptic smile. *Let her think what she wants. It might work to my advantage if she believes we're in the same business.*

"Emma's ill?" Mattie brushed invisible crumbs from her silk day dress.

Inez decided to be frank. "She was beaten, nearly killed."

Mattie exhaled a cloud of smoke. "Poor girl." Her tone implied Emma might as well be a child of ten, even though Inez estimated Mattie to be in her late twenties, early thirties, the same age as Emma and Inez. George appeared at Inez's elbow with a silver tea service. He set it on an occasional table and vanished.

Mattie approached a well-appointed sideboard. "We'll need something for our tea. This looks to be a painful conversation." She held out two bottles. "Mrs. Stannert?"

Inez indicated the less ostentatious bottle. *No contest between French cognac and donkey piss.*

Mattie nodded approval and poured a dose in each cup. "You have the key?"

Inez placed the small key on the table by the sterling teaspoons.

Mattie's shoulders eased down; the vigilance in her posture vanished like her obedient butler. Inez decided to go one step further.

"When Joe died, I found this in his wallet." Inez set Mattie's token next to the tea service.

Mattie picked up the brass check, turning it idly. The afternoon light shone through the heart-shaped cutout. "We go back, Joe and I. This was our little joke. I gave him one for my Georgetown house too, in seventy-four. Told him he could redeem it anytime." She tossed it back on the table beside the key. "The only time he tried was for Emma."

Inez set her cup down. "Emma never told me that she worked for you."

Mattie arched one eyebrow and remained silent.

Inez leaned forward. "I'm not judging Emma. I just wondered, could someone from her past be carrying a grudge against the Roses?"

"You mean her Georgetown admirer? I doubt it. That was all long ago." Her light brown eyebrows drew together. "Tell me again. What happened to her?"

"We found her, wrists bound, nearly strangled with one of her own stockings. Violated. Beaten. She's not regained consciousness."

Mattie's red-painted nails tapped on the exotic wood armrest of her chair. Finally, she spoke. "I never take a girl into my house who has had no previous experience of life and men. Most of the girls were married and left their husbands or at least had been involved with a man." The tapping stopped. "I broke that rule only once. With Emma. She showed up on my doorstep in Georgetown. A runaway, like so many others. Someone had told her that I treated my girls well. She was so lovely, with all that red hair. So I took her in, despite her inexperience and my misgivings."

Mattie looked toward the small fireplace. The firescreen, painted with a scene of cattails and herons, glowed with the light from behind. "Silver and money flowed through Georgetown then, just like in Leadville now. Investors, mine owners, speculators. Emma had many admirers. Too bad the one who offered the most had certain requests."

"Requests?"

Mattie pouted, blew out a thin stream of smoke, and eyed Inez for a moment, as if debating whether to continue. She finally set her cigarette in the ashtray and with a graceful motion, thrust out her arms, crossed at the wrists. A diamond bracelet winked at Inez.

She watched with amusement as comprehension dawned and set Inez's face ablaze.

"How entertaining you are, Mrs. Stannert. You must only sell liquor after all." She picked up the cigarette again, remarking off-handedly, "It's not an unusual request. Men of influence and money buy approval, agreement. After a while, all that bowing and scraping gets old, I suppose. Sometimes, they like a girl to resist."

She continued, "We have rules, of course. Silk ties only. No bruising. No gags. And nothing," she drew a line at her own white throat, "around the neck. Too easy to have something go wrong."

Inez clutched her teacup convulsively, picturing the ugly red marks around Emma's neck.

Mattie blew a stream of smoke at the ceiling. "Some girls would consider it a game, a chance to play the actress. Not Emma. She hated it. And, I think she was a little afraid of him. But he paid well. Very well. One night with him covered room and board for a week, plus incidentals; he insisted she take no other customers. I told her that if she didn't want to continue to just lie there. Don't fight. Don't struggle. He'd lose interest and I'd find him someone else. Of course, that meant she'd be back in the parlor every night."

The smoke curled around her head. Her tea remained untouched.

"Then Joe dropped in one day. He saw Emma and..." Mattie dramatically lifted one hand to her heart. "He tried to use his check, but I told him she was spoken for. So they talked in the parlor. After that, he came by every afternoon. Two weeks later, they married. Just as well. Emma wasn't cut out for the sporting life. Her customer wasn't happy, but he got over it eventually. They usually do." Mattie half-smiled through the smoke.

"Who is he?"

Mattie weighed the question. "No," she decided. "I've already said more than I should have. But I will tell you this." She snubbed out her cigarette. "He's extremely influential. And not just in Leadville. Now, I'll get you Joe's box."

Chapter Fifty-Five

Mattie returned with a strongbox, gun-metal gray, about the size of two stacked books. She pushed the tea tray to one side and set the box before Inez.

Inez realized she was holding the key so tightly its edges were biting into her palm.

She fit the key to the lock and turned. The top released with a snap. Both women leaned over, heads almost touching, to see what was inside.

"No diamonds," Mattie remarked. "No pearls. No silver bars. Pity."

Inez smiled wryly. She'd expected another bundle of bills, negotiable or otherwise. Mattie removed a small rectangular object wrapped in leather and tied with a thong. A thin stack of folded papers lay beneath.

As Mattie picked at the tight knot, Inez unfolded the first paper. She scanned neatly penned words before zeroing in on three signatures.

Joe's precise hand, Chet's shaky scrawl, and—

"Oh Joe," Inez said under her breath "Whatever possessed you to dance with the devil?"

Mattie stopped tweaking the recalcitrant knot. "Who?"

"Catherine DuBois." Hatred squeezed through her words. "The bitch."

When Inez looked up she saw her loathing mirrored in Mattie's face.

"Calling Cat a bitch," drawled Mattie, "is an insult to all female dogs."

Inez laid a hand flat on the paper. "You know Cat DuBois?"

Mattie's eyes narrowed. "She waltzed into town and tried to set herself up as queen of Holladay Street. I ran her out of Denver with her tail between her legs. Her and that little *artiste* of hers. She had the nerve to take one of my girls with her. Flo had been with me since Kansas." She gripped the leather package as if to strangle Cat by proxy. "What business did she have with Joe?"

Inez read the paper again. "This is an agreement witnessed by Joe between Cat and Chet Donnelly, a local prospector. It says that, in return for grubstaking Chet's efforts last summer, Cat is half-owner of any claims."

Inez looked up. "Grubstaking is common enough. That's how Tabor made his first million. He gave a couple of prospectors seventeen dollars in provisions and ended up with the Little Pittsburg."

Mattie waved her explanation away. "I know how it works. But Cat DuBois? I can see her running a parlor house, but what does she know about prospecting or mining? And what's Joe doing in the middle of it all?"

"Joe performed a lot of assays for Chet." Inez stopped. A melody line was forming. It wasn't clear yet, but she could almost hear it. And she didn't like the sound.

She stared at the other two pieces of paper, still folded. White, inert, they seemed only to promise insight into disaster. "I'm not certain I want to know what's on these." Slowly, she unfolded the second sheet.

It was one of Joe's assaying certificates filled in for the Lady Luck claim. Even to Inez's untrained eye, the results looked disappointing: a minor amount of silver, no gold. At the bottom, a brief notation indicated Cat had sold her half of the claim back to Chet for fifty dollars. The report was signed by Joe. Inez examined the numbers on the certificate again. She wished she had Joe's ledger or assaying notebook with her. Had she seen this particular set of assays listed? She couldn't remember.

Her eyes kept wandering off the numbers to the intricately engraved border surrounding the information like a stockade.

She turned to Mattie. "This is one of Joe's assay certificates. Looks like Chet didn't find much on this claim, the Lady Luck. He bought back Cat's half for what she'd grubstaked him on. Well, let's see what the coda is."

The last page was crumpled, hastily scrawled. It featured a crudely sketched map. Inez picked out Independence Pass, some directions, an "x" marked "Lady Luck." At the bottom were two signatures: Chet's and Joe's.

"Well?" Mattie sounded impatient.

Inez laid the three papers side-by-side, checking the dates. "This last one is dated the day after Cat sold her half of the Lady Luck back to Chet. It shows the location of the claim and states that, upon receipt of eight thousand dollars, Chet and Joe would be equal partners."

Chet's words from that dark night in the kitchen whispered back at her: *Lady Luck don't talk to the likes of you.*

"Why would Joe buy into a worthless hole in the ground?" Inez said aloud. "It doesn't make sense. Unless—"

"Shit!" Mattie examined her broken fingernail. "I'm getting a knife. Hold this." She dropped the package in Inez's lap. Inez was surprised at the weight. *This is far too heavy to be currency, counterfeit or otherwise.*

Mattie rummaged through a drawer at the sideboard and returned with a lethal-looking knife. "This should do it."

The thong didn't stand a chance.

Mattie pulled the wrapping away. "What was Joe doing with these?"

Exposed, in all their glory, were two engraving plates for a United States of America twenty-dollar bill.

‹›‹›‹›

Mattie handed Inez the metal plates. Inez ran a finger over the reversed figures and numbers, and the fine whorls and curlicues of the border. Then she rubbed the sheen of oil and ink between two fingers.

Claims and counterfeiting. One is the melody, the other the harmony. Together, they form a piece of music. A song without words.

Inez spoke cautiously, "Did Joe ever mention being involved in a coney ring?"

Mattie looked aghast, as if Inez had accused her of running a charity. "Joe? You're talking about a man who wouldn't cash in on a free fuck from the best parlor house in the West. Joe never drank, never played cards—"

"Joe changed. He may not have had anything to do with poker, liquor, or ladies of the line before, but Leadville was a different story. And, I'm afraid my husband was partly to blame."

She briefly told Mattie about Joe and Mark's mutual admiration society. How Mark took on the mannerisms of a respectable businessman, how Joe put on the gambler's mien.

"That's not all," Inez said bleakly. "Joe falsified some assay results, and the customer found out. Joe also mortgaged his business to the hilt. God knows where that money went. Maybe he paid Chet with it. Maybe he gambled it away." The plates on her lap seemed to grow heavier. "I also found a stash of counterfeit he'd hidden before he died." She decided to forgo mentioning that he'd been familiar enough with one of Cat DuBois' women to lose his watch to her.

Mattie sat motionless, her full lips tightly compressed. Inez realized that, whereas she'd seen Joe Rose transform over time and had had a month to uncover, absorb, and accept his sins, Mattie was having to deal with Joe's disintegration all at once.

Mattie finally sighed, lit another cigarette, and said, "Everyone wants to strike it rich, one way or another. But Joe?" She shook her head and exhaled.

Inez leaned forward. "There's apparently a coney ring in Denver with ties to Leadville. I must bring these plates to the attention of someone who can help me. Do you know whether Treasury agents are investigating locally? I must find someone I can trust, and I haven't much time."

Mattie stood and went to the window. She caressed the maroon velvet drape, gazing out at the black and white garden where sticks and bare trunks slumbered until the sun's warmth could call them back to life.

She finally spoke. "Gus Brown. He's posing as a drummer, selling paper to printers, engravers. I think he would be interested in the plates and whatever you have to say. I'll write down the address of his hotel."

She turned, blue eyes the color of spring. "Don't tell him I sent you."

Inez finished her tea while Mattie found a blank sheet of paper, a pen, and a bottle of ink in another drawer of the bottomless sideboard. As she wrote, she said, "So, your husband's a gambler. Mine too. George Silks. Last I heard, he was in Leadville. Ever come across him?"

An image flashed through Inez's mind: A tall, dark man with cavernous eyes and long mustaches. A dealer at the Board of Trade Saloon. "Hard to say," she said cautiously.

Mattie gripped the pen so tightly, Inez could see her knuckles through the skin, white on white. "He took off to make good on the silver rush without so much as good-bye. I don't give a damn. I've got a man now who's better than he ever was or will be."

Inez paused, then said, "My husband disappeared last May. I've...indications...that he might be in Denver. Does the name Mark Stannert sound familiar?"

Mattie waved the paper in the air to dry. "Can't say it does." Her eyes revealed nothing. Poker player's eyes. "If I hear something, should I send you a message?"

Inez hesitated.

"Sometimes," Mattie said, folding the paper, "when they get lost, it's best not to find them."

She leaned over the table to hand Inez Gus Brown's address. Her flowery perfume mixed with the darker scent of cigarette smoke. "When it's all done, and you've found the bastards who did this to the Roses, let me know."

Chapter Fifty-Six

The morning of New Year's Day, Inez and Joey rode the horse-drawn streetcar through downtown Denver. Joey eyed the closed candy shops with disappointment. Inez eyed the gray shroud hanging over the distant mountains with dread. The weather window for clear travel to Leadville was closing rapidly. She hoped Gus Brown had received the note she'd left at his hotel the previous day:

> *Mr. Brown,*
> *A mutual friend told me in confidence that you are a paper expert. I have some unusual samples that may be of interest. I suspect they are not genuine but require someone of your expertise to say for certain. I'll be in the dining room of the Wentworth Hotel at one tomorrow afternoon. Look for a tall woman in gray and a young boy with dark hair.*
> *Mrs. Stannert*

She'd decided not to mention the plates. They were her ace in the hole, and she would not play them unless absolutely certain about Gus Brown.

<><><>

Noon found Inez and Joey outside the Helt Brothers Assaying Office. Inez ignored the "Closed" placard in the window and opened the door. They entered a world of dust motes and sharp chemical smells. Helt appeared from the back, wearing a sooty leather apron. His sleeves were, once again, rolled up, but this time he didn't bother to unroll them. He was wiping his hands on a rag. "Finished up early and figured I might as well get started on another set since I'm here." He slipped the apron off and straightened his functional worsted waistcoat.

He went to the desk and opened the top drawer, remarking, "I've got to give you my usual speech about assay results on small samples, Mrs. Stannert. An assay's usually considered to be representative of a ton of ore on a given orebody. With small samples like yours, I'll not go on record saying that's the case here. So, I noted on your assay certificate that the results apply only to what you brought in. Now, all speechifying aside, I believe I understand why you're in such a hurry."

He set an assay certificate on the counter. "Seven hundred and forty-nine ounces of silver per ton, no gold, and fifty-two percent lead. Trace of copper." He leaned back against the desk, crossed his arms, and grinned. "Tell Mr. Stannert to dig up some more tonnage and get it assayed. If it proves out anywhere near these numbers, he's a rich man."

‹›‹›‹›

"Are you rich now, Auntie?" Joey spooned vanilla ice-cream into his mouth.

"No more so than I was before. Considering all I've spent here in Denver, I'm probably a good deal poorer." Inez glanced about the hotel's dining room. The baritone rumble of the mostly male clientele filled her ears.

"Then why did Mr. Helt say you were?"

Inez sighed and looked over at the ornate wall clock by the dining room's entrance: one-thirty. "Those samples weren't mine, Joey, so neither's the fortune." *It might be Emma's if I can find proof that Joe gave Chet eight thousand dollars. And that the samples came from the Lady Luck.*

She stirred her lukewarm soup.

A square-set man hesitated at the entrance, eyes sweeping the crowd.

Inez sat up straighter. *If this is Gus Brown, he fits his name.* Brown suit, shoes, overcoat, derby hat. Middling brown hair streaked with gray and a mustache to do a walrus proud. His gaze crossed Inez's, then came back. He waved the maitre d' away and approached her table.

"Mrs. Stannert?" His eyes were the color of copper pennies. He lifted his hat and bowed slightly, a question in his voice, ready to apologize and retreat if necessary.

"Mr. Brown." She indicated the empty chair. "I was afraid you wouldn't show."

"So sorry. Business at the other end of town slowed me down." He sat and removed his hat, patting his hair as if he wanted to be sure it was still there. He turned toward Joey, and the weather-beaten skin of his face pulled into a smile. "This is?"

"Joey Rose." She watched to see if the name made any impression.

He held out a hand. "Pleased to meet you, son."

After a glance at Inez, Joey took the proffered hand. They shook solemnly.

Brown turned to Inez. "You from Denver or just passing through, Mrs. Stannert?"

"We're from Leadville."

He signaled a waiter. "Coffee, please." His voice had the jovial overtones Inez associated with those who sell wares for a living. He turned back to Inez. "Interesting place, Leadville."

"Have you ever visited?"

"No reason so far." His gaze didn't even flicker. "Am I to understand that you have something that might change my mind?"

She slid an envelope over the tablecloth to him. "The samples I mentioned." She hesitated and glanced at Joey, who was concentrating on his vanilla mountain. "I only question their authenticity due to the ink's, ah, incompatibility with alcohol."

Brown lifted the flap of the envelope and, without removing the contents, squinted at the fifty and twenty that Inez had placed inside. He then closed the envelope again. "Ah yes. I'm familiar with this particular brand of paper. Seen the expensive one floating around. The other's new to me." His copper eyes regarded her thoughtfully. "Leadville, you say. And where'd you get these, if I may ask?"

"Before I say any more, I would like to see some proof of your employer."

He laced his fingers and rested the edge of his square hands on top of the envelope. The crisscrossed fingers jutted out like fortifications. "For my part, I'm curious as to who our mutual friend is. And what part you play in all this, Mrs. Stannert."

Impasse.

"I promised our mutual friend that he would remain anonymous." She changed the gender, to cloak Mattie Silks' identity. "As for me, I own the Silver Queen Saloon in Leadville. I hope the fact that I brought these samples to you of my own free will—indeed, at some trouble and expense—will assure you of my intentions, Mr. Brown."

"There are intentions and there are intentions, Mrs. Stannert." His smile widened, to reveal square tobacco-stained teeth. "You said these are samples. There are more?"

"Hundreds more of the expensive brand. Of the lesser, maybe sixty in all. I've been led to believe they all originated in Denver."

"Hmmm." He regarded her, then nodded as if she'd passed a test. "I'm going to give you the benefit of the doubt, Mrs. Stannert. Normally, I'm not a gambling man. So I hope you don't prove me wrong."

Brown reached into his waistcoat pocket and extracted a small leather case, which he slid across the table to her. She opened it in her lap, out of Joey's view.

A U.S. Secret Service badge nestled inside.

She closed the case and returned it to him.

"How do I know you are the valid holder of this? That you're not..."

"Some imposter?" Brown tucked the case back into his waistcoat. "You don't. But we're both taking a chance here. You've an advantage, though, in our 'mutual friend,' whoever he may be. If you trust him—and you must or you wouldn't have contacted me—then I suppose you'll have to trust that I am who I say I am. I have no such guarantee about you." He grinned again, reminding Inez of a jovial uncle. "Now, who passed you these bits of paper?"

Inez turned her eyes significantly to Joey. "Joey's father, Joe Rose. A precious metals assayer."

His eyes narrowed. The breastworks of fingers reformed on the envelope. He turned to Joey. "Your pop's an assayer in Leadville?"

Joey looked at Brown as if he were stupid. "He's an angel in Heaven."

"In early December, Mr. Rose met with an unfortunate accident." Inez stressed the last word.

"Ah." Brown's eyes flicked back to Joey. "Sorry to hear about that, son."

Joey stared at the ice cream slush in his dish.

"Son, did your pop come to Denver a lot? Every month or two, say?"

Joey nodded. "To get supplies. He said I could go when I get older." He bit his lip.

Brown asked Inez, "You know the name of his supply house?"

"Is it important?"

"Could be."

She closed her eyes and pictured Joe's office desk. *There's the stack of certificates. There's the ledger. I opened it and...*She opened her eyes, relieved at dredging up a memory of the bill of lading. "Denver Mining and Smelter Company?"

"Denver Mine and Smelter Supply Company," he corrected. "But that doesn't tell me how you came by this." He tapped the envelope.

"Surely, you know, Mr. Brown. Surely Morris Cooke or Harry Gallagher said something about—"

Brown held up a hand, square as a shovel, and glanced at Joey.

Joey's eyes were fixed on the two adults as he licked off an ice cream mustache. Inez dug into her handbag, fingers skimming over the wrapped plates, and found her coin purse. She handed Joey a nickel. "Joey, please get two newspapers for us. There's probably a hawker by the hotel."

Joey wiggled out of the chair and, puffed up with his new-found responsibility, swaggered across the dining room.

Inez turned to Brown. "Several weeks after Joe Rose's death, bogus fifties turned up after a large stakes poker game in my saloon. I reported it to Morris Cooke, manager of the Carbonate City Bank. He implied that he was in touch with the proper authorities. Before he died, Joe cached a large amount of fifties and two bundles of twenties. I found them last week and turned them over to Cooke. You didn't know?"

She could almost see him make a mental note. But all he said was "Interesting."

Inez decided to plunge ahead. Joey would be back any moment, and it was her last chance to extract information from Brown. "Now, I have a question. Have you ever conducted your trade in Philadelphia?"

"I've been all over, Mrs. Stannert." His laced fingers remained inert.

"Is the name Frank Vintree familiar?"

"Vintree from Philadelphia? Sure."

"How about Sands. Justice or J."

He didn't blink. His expression of polite interest remained intact. But Inez saw his fingers tighten convulsively, then relax. "Vintree and Sands are retired from the paper business. I don't see what they have to do with what we're discussing."

So he lied after all.

The bitter taste in her mouth had nothing to do with the creamed soup. "Would it surprise you to know that Sands is in Leadville and seems quite involved in these goings-on?" She tossed down the information like she would throw away a winning hand. "Perhaps he's decided to 're-enter' the paper business."

Brown's copper eyes finally registered something besides courtesy. "Sands in Leadville, yes, that is a surprise. But I think you misunderstood me. Sands didn't work for Vintree."

Inez sat back. "What do you mean?"

Joey approached the table, looking proud and lugging two sets of the *Denver Post*. "This fellow you just mentioned," Brown continued smoothly, "we worked for the same employer. He was good. Better than most while he lasted. Like I said, he's been out of the business a long time."

He took a newspaper from Joey. "Thanks, son. Now, here's something for you." With a smooth sleight of hand, Brown plucked a nickel from Joey's ear and gave it to him.

Joey grinned, enchanted.

Brown opened the paper, glanced at the headlines, then laid Inez's envelope on top and refolded the paper. He set a battered case on the table and opened it. Inez glimpsed strips of newsprint, foolscap, parchment, and other kinds of paper mounted on boards. He set the newspaper inside, and closed and locked the case.

"Thank you, Mrs. Stannert, for taking a chance on me. I'm sure it wasn't easy. Now, I have a last question for you." His eyes strayed pointedly to the double rings on her left hand. "Your husband is…?"

She put her hand in her lap. "He died some time ago," she said stiffly.

Joey said, "Does Mr. Brown know Uncle Mark?"

Brown smiled indulgently at Inez. "Mark Stannert, dead? Guess that was a ghost I saw the other night. My condolences, Mrs. Stannert. It's tough losing a loved one." He signaled the waiter. "Allow me to pay for the meal."

Shock hammered her. She wanted to grab Brown's waist-coat and scream, "Where? Where did you see him?" Instinct cut through the impulse. *Leave. Now.* "Oh no, Mr. Brown. I have no desire to be in your debt."

"No problem, Mrs. Stannert. Maybe you can stand me a drink at your place in Leadville. Say, how long you staying in Denver?"

"A few days," she lied.

Brown handed the waiter a ten-spot, then refocused on Inez. "You know, after our little talk, I've a hankering to see Leadville. Might be a good place to chase down some business. Maybe we could hook up in a couple days when the weather clears and I'll go back with you."

"That would be fine. We're staying here at the Wentworth. You can leave a message at the desk if we're out." Her heart pounded triple-time.

Brown stood and tipped his hat, sample case in hand. "Enjoy your stay in Denver, Mrs. Stannert."

Chapter Fifty-Seven

"You lied." Joey sat in the trundle bed, watching Inez brush out her hair in a long, rippled wave.

"Joey, not now." Inez stared at his reflection in the mirror.

He flopped down under the blankets. "You told Mr. Helt we were leaving today. Then you told Mr. Brown we're not."

She set her silver-backed hairbrush on the nightstand, among a jumble of papers, the two stacks of bogus bills, and the counterfeit plates. With swift, practiced fingers, she began braiding her hair for the night. "When you're older you'll learn that the truth isn't fixed in stone. And, in some cases, it can be dangerous. Believe me Joey, no one is truthful all the time."

She glanced back up at the mirror.

In the reflection Joey picked his nose absently, staring at the ceiling. "Mama always tells the truth." Some of Emma's moral superiority leaked through his voice.

Inez thought of Emma denying her meeting Harry Gallagher and of Mattie Silks' revelations. "Your mama's different, Joey," Inez said tiredly.

She unfolded her copy of the *Denver Post* and began stacking items on the open spread. Helt's assay certificate, Joe's certificate, the plates, the counterfeit bills, Angel's note, and Mattie Silks' letter to Emma. *I must remember to put it back in the Bible.*

In the emptiness of her tired mind, an impression uncurled and nudged her. Then nudged again, like a rise of octaves. She slowly unstacked the items, lined them up on the newspaper, and pulled the gas lamp chain to brighten the flame.

Joey's voice broke into her concentration. "I want to go home."

She examined the items, one by one, looking for what had captured her wandering attention. "We'll be home tomorrow night."

Before Brown comes back. Better the devil we know than the devil we don't.

Her eyes followed the border on a twenty-dollar counterfeit bill, then switched to the border of Joe's assay certificate. She sucked in her breath.

Like close cousins.

She took Angel's note, torn from a piece of paper. There, on the back, was an empty shield reclining in a bed of engraved flourishes. Inez covered the shield with her thumb. Her mind instantly provided the missing element: A two, followed by a zero, lying on a diagonal band across the shield.

In a fever, Inez unwrapped the counterfeit plates. On the top one, Alexander Hamilton's profile faced Victory advancing. Above Victory's head: the same flourishes and shield. Slanting across the shield: 20.

"Auntie? Will you read to me?"

"In a moment. I must finish packing our things." As she rewrapped and restacked everything but the counterfeit bills, she remembered what Mattie had said about Cat's *inamorato*. An artist. Someone small. Dandified.

Llewellyn.

Inez remembered his workshop. The table. The items that had caught her eye. Half-etched copper plates. Double-Xs, one pair plain, one rococo: Roman numerals for a twenty-dollar bill.

Llewellyn is engraving counterfeit plates! And, if he's Cat's man, I'll bet she's square in the middle. Cat and Joe, tied to counterfeiting and the Lady Luck. Angel gave me the note on one of Llewellyn's scraps. She must know about Joe and the bogus money.

Inez wrapped the package in the newspaper and stuffed it inside Joey's well-worn long johns for good measure. The bogus bills went under the false bottom of her carpetbag, the ball of fabric on top.

She opened *Paradise Lost* at the satin ribbon and told Joey, "It's late. I'm just going to read a bit where Satan is reviewing his troops of fallen angels."

As she read, Joey's eyelids lowered, his breathing slowed. Inez closed the book and moved to the gas light, whispering Satan's last words to his troops: "Peace is despair'd,/For who can think Submission? War then, War/Open or understood, must be resolv'd."

She extinguished the light.

‹›‹›‹›

All of Denver seemed to be crammed into the depot at four in the morning on the second day of the new decade. Inez squeezed through the crowds, gripping Joey's hand and her carpetbag. She bought two seats on the early morning Colorado and Central to Georgetown and two sandwiches for later: tough beef and too much mustard. But Inez figured that in a few hours, she and Joey would be so hungry that it wouldn't matter.

‹›‹›‹›

Five hours later, still feeling every bump and jostle from Denver to Georgetown, Inez argued with the ticket seller of the coach line to Leadville. "I absolutely must get to Leadville tonight."

He shook his head sympathetically. "The sleigh-coaches are full up, today and tomorrow. You'd best buy tickets for day after next, get a room, and come back in the morning. Maybe something will open up."

Inez clenched the handle of the carpetbag tighter. She felt trapped, the high canyon walls of Georgetown squeezing her like a pair of hands. The claustrophobia intensified her sense of urgency.

The man behind her harrumphed impatiently. She ignored him and addressed the dispatcher again. "How much for two seats on the first available run?"

"Ten-spot apiece."

"I'll take them."

No sooner had he handed her the tickets than she turned to address the room at large. "Gentlemen." She held the tickets high.

The rumble of voices dwindled and died. Inez continued, "Most of you are probably heading to Leadville hoping to make your fortunes. Well, a couple lucky souls can start right now. I need two seats on today's coach. I will trade these tickets, good for the day after tomorrow, and throw in fifteen dollars apiece to make your prolonged stay in Georgetown more enjoyable."

There was silence while the men in the room absorbed her proposal. The first man to jump to his feet pulled two tickets out of his coat pocket, saying, "These are for my partner and me, but heck, ma'am, for thirty and a ride out later, we'll stick around."

"Done!" Elated, Inez extracted thirty dollars, being careful to hide the money roll from prying eyes. The narrow canyon walls of Georgetown eased back; she could almost see the wide open vistas of Colorado's high country. She told Joey, "We'll be home by midnight."

‹›‹›‹›

It was nearly one in the morning when the sleigh-coach from Georgetown hissed to a stop on Leadville's Chestnut Avenue. As the driver climbed down from the box, Inez took a deep breath of sharp mountain air, tinged by the sulfur of the smelters. Snow blew in through the coach window and landed on her coat sleeve. Lights from late-night businesses twinkled through the falling snow, highlighting figures on the crowded boardwalks and the passing traffic.

Home.

The passengers gathered hats and bags, lit pipes, and prepared to disembark. Joey remained in the deep sleep of the young.

"May I offer you a lift to your destination?" The Easterner who had introduced himself as Isaac Eisemer settled an expensive beaver hat on his head and buttoned his fur-lined coat.

She shook Joey awake and gathered her single bag. "That's not necessary, Mr. Eisemer, but thank you. Enjoy your stay in Leadville. I hope it proves profitable." Inez hailed one livery rig among the many that hovered nearby hoping to catch fares from the late-arriving coach. She gave the driver directions to Bridgette's.

"I wanna go home!" Joey was now fully awake.

"Joey, I can't take you home until we know how your mother is. And we can't go to my house tonight." She thought of the smashed rocking horse in the parlor.

"But I wanna go home!" He began to cry. Thick snot oozed from his nose, traveling down to his upper lip.

Distressed and exasperated, Inez pulled out her linen handkerchief and tried to sop up the liquid leaking from his eyes and nose. "It's only for tonight, Joey. Now stop. This is going to freeze on your face."

Inez was relieved to see a dim light in Bridgette's front window. She paid the driver. "Could you wait? We may need to go to a hotel, I'll know in one minute." She and Joey pushed through the blowing snow.

After some insistent pounding on the door, it cracked open revealing Bridgette's eldest son, Michael. He lowered the shotgun. "Mrs. Stannert. You're back."

"Heaven's above!" Bridgette pushed Michael aside, flung her arms around Inez, and then did the same to Joey. "Come in, come in."

The frantic look she threw Inez belied her mother-hen tone as she clucked and pushed Joey inside. "Michael, take Joey to the stove and find some dry clothes for him."

Bridgette grabbed a shawl off a peg inside and stepped outside, head wrapped like a nun. "Oh, ma'am, such terrible things have happened!"

Inez's heart began to race. "Emma."

"No, no, the poor woman is holding on. Oh, if she'd only come around and say who did this to her."

"Have they found him yet?"

"It's not to be believed." She gripped the shawl tighter around her face, agony drawing lines deeper around her eyes.

"What?" Inez glanced at the still-waiting sleigh and driver, then turned back to Bridgette. "What's happened?"

"Mr. Jackson's in jail. They've arrested him for the attack on Mrs. Rose."

Chapter Fifty-Eight

Inez felt as if the ground had cracked open leaving a gaping crevasse at her feet.

"That's preposterous!" she said fiercely.

"The marshal says he's got proof." Bridgette wiped an eye with the shawl's fringed edge. "He doesn't need much when it comes to jailing the colored. Still fighting the War he is. And he never liked our Mr. Jackson."

Inez put a hand against the cabin wall to steady herself. "When did this happen?"

"New Year's Eve. The marshal and his men burst into the saloon, accused Mr. Jackson before the multitudes, and took him away. The marshal closed the place down."

Her thoughts turned black. "The *snake!*"

"He asked me where you were. I told him I didn't know." Bridgette twisted the shawl between her fists. "Oh ma'am, what are you going to do? You can't stay in town."

"Where's Useless?"

"I haven't seen nor heard of him these two days past."

Inez sank her face into her hands, thinking. "What's the town's mood, Bridgette?"

"Hung over and surly. There's talk of the committee, ma'am."

"Keep Joey tonight. I've got to see Abe. And the marshal."

"No!" Bridgette grabbed her sleeve.

Inez shook off her hand. "I want to see his evidence. What is he going to do? Arrest me as an accomplice? I refuse to run, hide, leave Abe to be strung up by know-nothings who can't accept that the South lost fifteen years ago. Did McMillan bring back my shotgun? Good. I'll take it. If I'm not back by morning, tell Reverend Sands—no, get word to Harry Gallagher—that what he's looking for is in the Silver Queen's safe."

<><><>

The driver dropped Inez, her carpetbag, and shotgun in front of the city jail. Built of brick in a town mostly slapped together with green planks, the jail looked sturdy enough to hold the most determined desperado. Yet, only a month earlier, forty-odd masked men had forced entrance and departed with two prisoners: a footpad and a lot jumper. The next morning found the two unfortunates dangling from a half-constructed building. An accompanying note warned all "lot thieves, bunko steerers, footpads, and thieves" that the vigilante committee would not tolerate further misbehaviors.

Inez took a deep breath, ordering herself into calm. At her knock Curly Dan opened the iron-reinforced door. The deputy marshal's well-worn face betrayed his reaction on seeing Inez.

She offered him the shotgun. "Hello Curly. I'm here to see Abe."

"Mrs. Stannert." Curly Dan looked back over his shoulder. "I don't think it's a good idea, you being here."

"Why? Is Hollis there, ready to throw me in chains?" She gripped the carpetbag handle with one sweaty glove.

"No, he's not. But he's been looking for you. We thought you'd skipped town."

"Well, here I am." She pulled out her pocket revolver with two fingers, slowly, and handed it to him grip first. "There. I'm unarmed. And I'm not leaving until I see Abe."

Curly Dan took a deep breath, then opened the door wide. "This is probably a big mistake. Leave your bag over there.

I'll take you to him. But only for a minute." He locked the front door behind her and headed for an inner door, sorting through his ring of keys. "I've got nothing against you or Mr. Jackson. But what Hollis found sure looks bad."

She set her bag in the shadow of a scarred desk. "What did he find?"

He looked at her mournfully, jangling the key ring. "I can't be discussing the evidence, Mrs. Stannert."

He opened the inner door and escorted her through. Two figures on the other side stirred, the gold buttons of their uniforms catching the guttering lamplight.

"Well boys," she didn't bother to hide her disdain, "pulling double shifts at Silver Mountain and the city jail?"

One of Harry's militiamen looked away. The other pulled up his rifle and glared.

Curly Dan hastened, "Gallagher offered his militia to help keep the peace."

Inez hardly heard, her eyes drawn to the cell in the center of the room. Inside, Abe rose from a straw pallet.

She moved forward and touched the cold metal bars.

Curly Dan was instantly beside her. "You gotta stand back. Rules."

"Abe." She tried to keep her shaking voice under control. "What happened?"

"They found my knife, Inez."

"No discussin' the evidence." Curly Dan sounded firm. He turned to Inez. "You see, he's all right. We're here to make sure justice gets done."

"And will you put your lives on the line if forty men come with a rope and their own notions of justice?" Inez turned back to Abe. "One question. Did you order Useless to trap rats at the saloon?"

His perplexed expression was all she needed to confirm her suspicions. She closed her eyes, then opened them to refocus on her business partner. " I made a big mistake when

I hired Useless away from Cat DuBois. In truth, I don't think he ever left her employ."

"What're you talkin' about?"

She gazed into Abe's dark brown eyes, then pressed her palms together as if in prayer. "Your guardian angel can help us."

Abe walked to the cell bars, wrapping long ebony fingers around the metal. "Inez, no. She don't know nothing."

A sudden banging at the inner door ricocheted off the brick walls, the echoes intensifying to a syncopated din. Through the racket, Inez heard Marshal Hollis shout, "Curly, open the goddamned door! I know she's in there." A thump from a vicious kick vibrated in the tense air.

Curly Dan sighed and pulled his hat off to scratch his bald head. "Now all hell's gonna bust loose. I knew this was a bad idea. Time to go, Mrs. Stannert."

Abe gripped the bars, staring over Inez's head. "Useless. He's been there since the start of all this trouble. My new knife disappeared at work two days after Christmas. I didn't want to tell you."

"Save it for the judge," Curly Dan warned.

Abe focused on Inez. "You should've stayed away. No one short of God Almighty's gonna find proof of my innocence now. This train's rollin' down the track too damn fast to stop. I've seen it happen to others." He sank tiredly onto the pallet.

"Damn your hide, Curly!" The door rattled.

"Hold your horses, Bart." Curly Dan pulled out the ring of keys. "Locked inside and out," he told Inez. "There won't be any lynchings while I'm here."

The door opened onto Hollis' face, purple with rage. "No lynchin's. Waalll, you ain't been in town, hearin' what I've been hearin'."

Back in the office, Curly Dan locked the door and the marshal's attention zeroed in on Inez. "Where've you been, Miz Stannert?"

"Around." She surveyed his iced-up clothes. "Where have *you* been?"

He spat on the plank floors, narrowly missing her skirts. Curly Dan nudged a spittoon toward Hollis with the toe of his well-worn boot.

Hollis ignored the hint. "We got your nigger but good." His voice rang with malicious triumph.

"All that rotgut you've been drinking must have pickled your brain if you really believe Abe hurt Emma Rose," she snapped. "You've arrested an innocent man. You can't possibly have any proof."

Hollis clenched his teeth so hard she could hear his jaw pop. He turned to Curly Dan. "Open the safe! Show her what we got. Maybe we'll catch her lyin'."

Curly Dan glanced at Inez, then knelt to open the black safe. He handed Hollis two cloth bundles from its maw. Hollis slammed the first bundle on the desk and yanked the cloth loose.

"Recognize this, Miz Stannert?"

Inez's stomach lurched in dismay. Lying on the desk was Abe's new knife, its engraved blade rusty with dried blood.

"I gave Abe that knife for Christmas. Where did you find it?"

"Under Mrs. Rose's bed."

She took a step toward Hollis. "Emma Rose will deny it."

Hollis snorted. "Doc says it could be a week maybe more before she comes around. Think Jackson's gonna last a week around here?"

Without waiting for her response, he turned to Curly Dan. "You heard her say it was Jackson's knife. Now, let's try this."

The second cloth yielded up Joe Rose's pocketwatch.

"Where did you get that?" Inez was dumbfounded.

"Jackson's overcoat." Hollis sounded almost gleeful. "I recollected it was missin' when we found Rose's body. Guess Jackson wanted a little mo-mento after he killed Rose. Maybe he kept peekin' at that picture of Miz Rose, thinkin' what he'd do to her when he got a chance."

"You've the mind of a worm, Marshal!"

For once, her words didn't faze him. "Now, let's see what we got on you. The other, Curly." Curly Dan reached into the safe and dragged out—

"My saddlebags!" Inez stared at the scarred leather bags, feeling confusion wind about her like a rope. "I left them with Cooke at the bank!"

"Uh-huh," said Hollis. His mustache twitched in contempt. He plunged one hand inside a bag and pulled out a bundle of fifties. "And this is just a reg'lar deposit. And you probably have 'no i-dee' how it got buried in a crate of Taos Lightning in your storeroom." He leered. "Lookit her face, Curly. She's guilty as sin."

"This, this evidence is a complete fabrication. Abe and I, we've been set up!"

"You're real fond of Jackson," taunted Hollis. "Maybe what they say 'round town about the two of you is true."

She gasped, the urge to hit him burning away common sense.

"Bart!" Curly Dan's voice was urgent. "Remember what Gallagher said."

Hollis tipped his grimy hat back from his forehead. "When I find the proof that hangs her, ain't Gallagher nor anybody else gonna stop me from throwin' her in the calaboose too."

Curly Dan turned to Inez. "Go home, Mrs. Stannert. You aren't bein' held on any crimes. But don't take any more trips out of town."

Fighting her anger, Inez grabbed her carpetbag from beside the desk. Hollis' eyes swiveled to the bag, suspicious. The counterfeit plates seemed to scream from their swaddling.

Curly Dan opened the door for her. "You want to help Jackson, hire him a lawyer. A good one."

Chapter Fifty-Nine

After Curly Dan closed the jailhouse door behind Inez, she stood on the boardwalk, motionless. Clouds obscured stars and moon while the wind and snow pushed her from behind.

Heavily bundled figures hurried past. Eyes slid to the shotgun in her hand and then away. Suddenly aware of her vulnerability on the street, Inez started toward her last sanctuary.

The notice on the door of the Silver Queen read "Closed Until Further Notice by Order of the City Marshal." *At least he didn't padlock the door.*

Once inside, she dropped the carpetbag to the floor where it landed with a puff of sawdust. Flexing her hand, she walked around the silent bar to retrieve the office key. Llewellyn had added to the mural while she'd been in Denver. Inez walked its length, examining half-faced armies clashing between cities of silver and ice. She paused before the winged figure of Lucifer, sterling sword pointing toward preordained defeat. Penciled lines drafted the contours of Harry Gallagher's face.

The chill that invaded her had nothing to do with the cold.

Once upstairs, she unlocked the office door and pushed it open.

The first thing she saw were the papers. Covering her desk, scattered across her chair and the floor. The door to the safe yawned open. The murky lights of State Street and the snow racing past the large window gave the room a strange under-water glaze.

She took one step, muttering, "Damn them all."

"Why did you come back?" Harry's voice reached her a second after his cigar smoke.

Dressed for the opera, he sat on her loveseat beside a bottle of brandy and a half-empty glass. The smoke curled through the air, disturbed by her entry. Harry's overcoat was folded over the back of the small sofa, white gloves crossed neatly on top like a pair of ghostly hands.

"Harry, what are you doing here?"

"Waiting. For you."

She finally moved inside. "How did you get in? How did you know I was in town?"

He stretched out his legs to reach into a pocket. The buttons on his waistcoat gleamed.

He held up a key to the saloon's front door. "Jackson's." The key went down beside the glass. "My driver recognized you at the coach stop."

Inez thought on Isaac Eisemer's expensive gloves and hat, the well-brushed overcoat, the cultured intonations. "He was picking up Eisemer."

She noticed the bottle at Harry's elbow was nearly empty. "How long have you been waiting? Was that a new bottle?"

"I'm good for it." He poured another measure in the glass. "I thought you'd be by sooner. Did you stop at the jail first?"

"Hollis has the wrong man. Abe wouldn't ever hurt Emma."

Harry lifted the glass but didn't drink. "And counterfeiting? Is that something else he wouldn't ever do?"

The corner clock ticked into the silence.

He continued, "It doesn't look good, Inez. What makes it worse are the saddlebags found in your storeroom."

"I gave those bags to Morris Cooke along with the counterfeit I'd found. Joe had hidden it in his son's rocking horse. But Cooke didn't tell you, did he. After I left those bags with him, someone broke into my house, axed the horse, and left a note threatening Joey Rose. I'll bet once I left town, Cooke just stuffed the bogus money back in the bags and had Useless plant them where they'd be found by…Hollis? Sands? You're right. It looks bad. But Cooke and DuBois set it up that way."

Harry looked at Inez as if she'd announced her intention to sprout wings and fly out the window.

Inez hurried on. "If you want counterfeiters, start with Cooke and Cat DuBois. And Llewellyn Tremayne."

Harry held up a hand. "Tremayne. The artist of your mural." He gazed at her quizzically. "Were you really going to paint me as Satan, Inez?"

I need Harry to believe me. No one else can stop this madness.

"I was angry." She moved to her desk chair and shifted the papers off the seat, avoiding his gaze. "I'm sorry, Harry."

He raised his eyebrows. "A little late for apologies."

She rolled the chair closer to him. "I can explain. If you'll listen."

He emptied his glass and refilled it. "So you're willing to deal with the devil to save Jackson and your own skin. All right. I'll listen to your story. Whether I'll believe is another thing."

She set the carpetbag on her lap. "I was going to put this and an explanation in the safe for you. Bridgette was going to contact you about it." She unfastened the latch.

He quickly leaned forward and gripped her wrist. "Slowly. I have no desire to be shot with that pocket revolver of yours."

Inch by inch, she reached inside and withdrew the knot of flannels. While unwrapping the plates and papers, she said, "These were Joe's trump card. He left them with someone he trusted." She handed him the plates. "Is this what you've been searching for, Harry? What you asked Sands, the ex-Secret Service operative, to find?"

Harry examined the twenty-dollar plates briefly, then rewrapped them. "How did you know about Sands?"

"Someone in town recognized him. And there's the picture on your desk. You were in the War together. Is he really a man of the church? Or is that another subterfuge?"

Harry's pale eyes glinted in the murky light. "Still interested in Sands? Do you want to know what the good reverend did for me during the War? He hunted. Information, deserters, spies, he'd bring them back. Or not. As ordered."

"You brought him here. Why? Why not go to the Secret Service or the Treasury Department? Isn't catching counterfeiters their business?"

He tipped his glass, watching the level of the brandy change. "What do you think goes through the minds of men like Eisemer when they visit places like Leadville?" He didn't wait for her reply. "They look around. At the businesses, the price of real estate, how well the town is run. Then, they estimate the profits from possible investments. If they see bodies swinging from half-finished buildings and hear tales of labor troubles, crooked assayers, murderers, and counterfeiters, they think anarchy. There's no profit in anarchy." He relit his cigar. "Do you think these men are gamblers?" More smoke hazed the air between them. "They play only when the odds are in their favor. Here in Leadville, we improve those odds through law and order. No lynchings, no vigilantes, no slippery mine deals. No counterfeiting."

"But the coney ring is based in Denver. Surely working with the authorities—"

"Denver is not my concern," he interrupted. "Trouble in Denver may even work in our favor, give Leadville a shot at becoming the capital. Now *that* would be good for business. I needed someone to take care of the counterfeiting activities here in town quietly, swiftly. Sands was to find those involved and send them packing. "

"How did you even know about the ring?"

"Bad bills started circulating last spring. No one wanted that kind of publicity for Leadville, so we tracked the money ourselves. We narrowed it down to State Street before your husband conveniently disappeared. I made inquiries. It didn't take long to uncover some interesting information about your husband and Jackson." He looked at her a long time. "All summer, I debated whether you were a part of it or not. You're hiding your past. You stayed in Leadville after your husband left. Sent away your son. What holds you here? Still, I was inclined to give you the benefit of the doubt. Your grief seemed genuine enough. As did your affection. At least, until I returned in October."

He idly ran a finger around the rim of the glass, making it hum. "Once Sands arrived, everything got far too complicated. Then, you disappeared. Like your husband. The bottom line is, counterfeit was found hidden in your saloon and Jackson has a lot of explaining to do. Nothing points to you directly. Not everyone agrees. Cooke and Hollis think you're part of the ring. Sands and others are convinced you're innocent. However, I'm not certain I can credit what Sands says about you."

"What about you, Harry?" Her chair squeaked as she leaned forward. "Do you think I had anything to do with this? Other than wanting to help Emma and find who killed Joe Rose?"

Harry looked at her, wearily, then glanced at the plates. "Sands ran Tremayne to ground some time ago. You're not telling me anything new."

I'm losing him. He doesn't believe me. Her desperation increased. "But do you know about Llewellyn Tremayne's connection to Mrs. DuBois? How Chet Donnelly and Joe tried to double-cross her?"

He narrowed his colorless eyes and said nothing.

"She and Llewellyn were an item in Denver. As for Chet—" She smoothed out contracts, the map, and assay certificates. "Mrs. DuBois grubstaked him this summer and Joe did the assays. When Chet found something big, Joe probably saw his chance. He played down the results to DuBois, planning to buy her stake in the claim once she sold it back to Chet.

I'm certain Joe saw it as a way to escape the coney ring. He couldn't have been more than a go-between. You knew Joe. He wasn't an bad man."

Harry examined the papers. "You went to Denver."

"It would take too long to explain all the reasons why. I found Chet's sample bags after Joe's death and kept a few pieces." She tapped Helt's assay report. "Those are the results. The real results."

"Donnelly." Harry spoke the name with resignation and distaste, then tossed the papers on the loveseat. "You spin a good tale when you're desperate, Inez. Like Joe Rose."

"Why would I lie? Why would he?"

He leaned forward. "Let me tell you about Joe Rose. After I cut him off for cheating, he crawled back. He'd heard I was tracing the counterfeit activity in Leadville. He named names, same as you. He wanted money. I wanted proof. He showed me the bills, but that was nothing. He could have picked them up anywhere. He said he could get a plate on his next trip to Denver."

"What happened?"

Harry's voice slowed. "Sands was coming to Leadville. I didn't need Joe. When he returned, he offered to give me a key and a location in Denver where the plates and other information were. I told him the deal was off, it didn't include a wild goose chase to Denver." He looked away, out the window. Inez thought she detected a bitter twist to his smile. "You recall the row he started the night before he died. Joe obviously thought I should pay him for his trouble, even though he didn't follow through on his part of the bargain." Harry's gaze returned to her. Flat. Final. "I owed Joe Rose nothing."

"Did Joe mention Cat DuBois?"

"Mrs. DuBois is a convenience. You give her too much credit."

"You don't give her enough. No wonder she's hidden her activities so successfully. She's invisible to you. When she's not being a 'convenience.'"

"Defending Mrs. DuBois? That's a first for you, Inez."

"What about you, letting Joe off the hook when he offered proof. And bailing out his widow. Those are firsts for you, Harry." She wheeled back on the chair's casters, distancing herself. "Joe had the answers, but you didn't pursue it. Why not? What really changed while he was in Denver? What happened during that time—"

Inez stood abruptly. The chair rolled backward, bumping the desk. "You met with Emma Rose."

Smoke rose like a screen. "She had nothing to do with it."

"I always found it hard to believe that Joe managed to keep such a big secret from Emma. I'll bet she found out, somehow. I'll bet she begged you not to pursue it. What payment did you exact from Emma?"

Silence.

Inez stepped through the smoke. Mirroring Mattie Silks' gesture, she thrust her arms out, wrists crossed. Holding Harry's gaze, she said softly, "Did you use silk so she wouldn't bruise? Or were you in too much of a hurry. Or didn't you care."

He sat, eyes half closed, as if mulling over her words. Inez held her pose, wondering if she'd made a mistake, read the music wrong.

His hand shot out and imprisoned her right wrist before she could blink.

"We were having such a civilized conversation, Inez. The first in months. Then, you had to cross the line." He stood, forcing her backward. "Emma's not the one I want."

"Emma was pregnant when she was attacked." Inez felt the wall at her back. "She lost the baby. She told me weeks ago she didn't want this child. Maybe she thought it yours."

She gasped in pain as his grip tightened.

"None of this would have happened, Inez, if you'd responded differently when I returned last fall. I wouldn't have been tempted. I would have turned Joe's offer away, out of consideration for you. He might have lived. But you slammed the door in my face. Refused to talk to me. Returned my gifts. Sent my letters back. With no explanation." He stepped closer, pressing her against the wall. His voice lowered to a caress. "My mistake was treating you like a lady instead of like Cat DuBois."

The moonlight flashed on the double rings of her left hand as she slapped him hard.

He jerked back without letting go.

She stared, enraged and aghast at the parallel gashes on his right cheek.

His mouth twisted below the dark mustache. He grabbed her left wrist and captured her mouth with a kiss that echoed of past passion tangled with rage and determination. Her anger rose to meet his, kindling a response between them that burned like a dark invisible fire.

Inez felt as if she was melting, her anger incinerated to ash, leaving a core hot and pure as liquid silver after the intense fire of the assay furnace has burned all else away. Her carefully erected defenses wavered and collapsed. She grasped the lapel of Harry's evening jacket, pulling him closer.

Harry pulled away. The rage in his face was gone. He looked at her almost tenderly, before placing one thumb on her cheek and wiping it hard. He rubbed the blood that had smeared from his face to hers between thumb and forefinger.

"As I said, I should have been less of a gentleman in October. It could have saved us all." His gaze lingered over her, a hungry man facing a feast he is denied. "I don't have the time or patience to wait while you make up your mind. You yourself don't know where you stand." His hand closed over hers.

She let go of his jacket as if it were on fire.

Harry smiled sadly, then released her. He pulled out a linen handkerchief to stanch the wound and returned to the sofa. "I paid Joe's bank loan. Bought his building for more than it was worth. Had Sands arrange a new life for Emma and the boy. Emma Rose and me—there's nothing more between us." He gathered his overcoat, gloves, and hat.

"By first light, Sands will have taken care of the engraver and smashed whatever elements of the ring remain in Leadville. He's ruthless. Efficient. I have every confidence in him. Justice has never let me down. At least, in that regard." Harry settled his hat with careful deliberation. The gleam of moonlight on his silver hair extinguished.

"I'm leaving Leadville soon. Pressing responsibilities have languished while I waited, foolishly as it turns out, for you to come to your senses. I know when to cut my losses." He sounded indifferent, as if talking about selling off a worthless stock.

He buttoned his evening jacket, eyeing Inez dispassionately. It was as if having brought her to her knees for a brief moment, he'd regained his confidence and his balance.

Inez rubbed her mouth on her sleeve, hating her momentary surrender.

"I give you and Sands six months." Harry shrugged into his overcoat and pulled on his gloves. "By then, you'll know what he is. Men like him are invaluable in war, dangerous in peace. And they never change."

He tipped his hat in mock farewell. "When the railroad arrives and Sands is gone, I'll return. Then we'll see. Goodbye, Inez."

As Harry walked away, Inez groped blindly through the papers on the desk. Her hand curled around the stoppered ink bottle. The door closed behind him just as the bottle hit the fine-grained wood. Ink, dark as blood in the night, splattered across the panels.

"Go to hell, Harry!" she whispered. Too soft, too late.

A single glance at the sofa showed that he'd taken the plates and papers with him.

Chapter Sixty

They'd searched her dressing room too.

Her most expensive gowns, saved for Saturday nights, were tossed on the floor in a welter of petticoats and underclothes. She held the oil lamp high and discerned a muddy footprint on a satin corset. The thought of Hollis handling her intimate apparel made her want to burn it all.

Mark's evening clothes still hung inside the armoire; Hollis had vented his ire on her things alone. She ran a hand over her husband's gold and black brocade waistcoat, recalling, with mixed emotions, the body that once gave it shape.

Everything I need to gain entrance to Cat DuBois' parlor house is here.

Inez yanked off her outer clothes, adding travel-stained skirts and petticoats to the pile on the floor. Skin prickling to gooseflesh, she pulled a roll of linen off an inside shelf. She stripped off corset and combination and bound the linen around her breasts. She unpinned her hair, letting the braid fall down her back. Ten minutes later, dressed in Mark's clothes, she held the lamp up to the mirror. With her face shadowed by the deep-brimmed black hat, Inez felt confident she'd pass on the street or in a crowded room.

Then, she removed the hat.

The tense, androgynous face sprang into feminine contours, betrayed by tendrils spilling about her temples and ears. *Not good enough.*

The furthest she'd ever taken her masculine impersonations was in the high-class parlor houses of New Orleans. She and Mark had fleeced the moneyed clients who, distracted by the feminine wares, dropped money like trees shedding leaves in the fall. Then, it had been a lark. But now—

She fumbled in the pockets of Mark's greatcoat for his short bowie knife and sheath. "Insurance," he used to say when strapping it to his ankle.

Inez tugged her hair from its hiding place under the dress shirt and gripped the knife, setting the blade under her braid at the nape. She hesitated. Remembered Mark unbraiding her hair in some nameless hotel, Justice letting one strand slip through his fingers to the pillow—

Her hair parted with little ripping noises under the knife's edge.

Weight transferred from her neck to her hand. She dropped the heavy braid to the ground where it coiled like a dead serpent around her boots.

Peering into the mirror, she examined the straight swing of hair ending at her jaw line. *Not short enough.*

She ruthlessly pared it around ears, parted it in the middle, and slicked it down with water. The face in the mirror would now blend in with any of the better-dressed men in town, hat or no.

As she straightened her tie in the mirror, a telltale glimmer brought her up short. Inez stripped the two rings from her left hand and set them on the washstand alongside the hair-pins she no longer needed.

Mark's gunbelt and Navy Colt hung on the peg beside the wardrobe. She buckled it on, making sure the gun was visible. Walking the block to Cat's parlor house would not be a Sunday stroll.

The small Remington went into her trouser pocket: a backup. Then, she knelt and fastened Mark's knife under her pant leg. His teasing rang in her memory. "A knife's not for you, Inez. You don't know how to handle it, it'd be more a danger than a help to you in a bad situation. Stay with the weapons you know best. Guns and words."

Insurance.

Inez fumbled through the pockets of Mark's winter overcoat until she found Frisco Flo's card. Flo's remembered voice whispered: *You'll need this to get in.*

One more thing was vital to ensure her welcome at Cat's doors. Inez checked her dress pockets and found five dollars. She went back to the office and checked the safe—empty.

She upended her carpetbag and pried out the false bottom. Counterfeit twenties and fifties fell to the floor.

Reflecting on the irony of using Cat's own counterfeit to topple her house of cards, Inez rolled the money tight into her waistcoat pocket.

Extinguishing the light, she opened the ink-streaked door and took a last look around the office, wondering when and if she would return. She thought of Abe, behind bars, their lives and reputations in shambles. Inez squared her shoulders. *Time to find a guardian angel.*

<>< ><>

Negotiating the block to Cat's high-class boarding house meant passing a half dozen saloons of various sizes and temperaments, a dancehall, a restaurant, and two lodging hotels of dubious repute. In near blinding snow, Inez circumvented five horizontal men—three puking on hands and knees, two lying inert on the boardwalk—and shoved her way through the surging throng. As she passed one murky saloon, she heard a woman scream just as a tangle of men boiled out onto the walk. Shouts were followed by the sharp report of a handgun. She pushed hard against the crowd that suddenly stopped to gape at the man bleeding and scrabbling across ice-encrusted boards. A policeman knocked her aside, shouting to others to clear the way. Inez hastened through the vacuum created by his wake. She spared barely a glance at Cat's saloon. All her attention focused on the three-story brick structure next to it: the parlor house.

Her hand finally on the door, Inez wheezed, trying to catch her breath and her equilibrium. At her knock, a man the size of a mountain answered the door and uttered one word: "Card?"

Inez handed him Flo's business card. He examined it, then peered at her. "Don't recall your face. New to town?" Inez nodded. "Let's see the color of your money, then."

She extracted her bankroll, and as an afterthought, peeled off the five. Forcing her voice down into the tenor range, she said, "Keep it."

He raised eyebrows that looked like fuzzy sausages and tucked the money into his waistcoat. "Stranger, you picked the best place in town to spend your money." He opened the door wide and Inez entered the foyer.

Inside, the clamor of State Street was as damped as the lamplight. She could barely see the wallpaper, maroon with swirls of gold above walnut wainscoting. Ten paces away and on the left, an arched entry led to what she guessed was a parlor. Beyond that, stairs ascended to the upper floors.

From the parlor room floated masculine murmurs and feminine laughter. A halting "Für Elise" stopped mid-measure, and the unseen pianist swung into a polished version of "Silver Threads Among the Gold."

The scents of flowery perfumes—gardenia, violet, rose—combined with those of burning tobacco and wood. Over all lay the subtle spoor of musk and sexual commerce. The place smelled like a hothouse on fire.

The doorman thrust out a ham-sized hand: "Your coat. And gun."

Inez unbuckled the heavy belt, thankful for her hidden weaponry. Frisco Flo in a lilac Worth gown drifted out of the parlor, patting her peroxide curls. She spotted Inez and flashed a welcoming smile as bright as her hair.

At the outer edge of her vision, Inez caught the doorman rubbing thumb and two fingers together meaningfully. Flo's eyes flicked toward him and away; her smile and eyes widened as she sized up Inez.

"Hello, honey. I'm Frisco Flo. Welcome to the best and cleanest parlor house in Leadville. The madam is busy," she batted her eyelashes, "so I'll show you around. We've twelve boarders. Lovely, cultivated girls, every one." Her coy expression wavered. "You look familiar. Have we met?"

Inez said hoarsely, "Georgetown. Mattie's house. You and a red-haired woman. She here too?"

Frisco Flo's demeanor shifted from suspicion to panic. "Oh my." She looked nervously toward the parlor and grasped Inez's arm with fluttering fingers. "Best not talk about those days. Past is past." Her smile rekindled as she drew Inez down the hall, but she avoided looking directly at Inez again, much to Inez's relief.

A familiar voice boomed from the parlor. *Eisemer.*

Through the arch, she could see a portion of the parlor. Morris Cooke lounged in an overstuffed armchair, a beatific expression pasted on his solid Quaker face. A brunette sat on a nearby ottoman, languidly fanning herself. Cat's distinctively musical laughter rose over the piano. Harry Gallagher strolled past Cooke, stopped, and pulled out his handkerchief, pressing it to the wounds oozing on his cheek. Inez stepped back, alarmed.

Flo tugged on her arm. "You're lucky. Some of Leadville's most influential gentlemen are here. Being new in town and all, you'll make some good contacts in addition to having a good time." She drummed restless fingers on Inez's sleeve. "What's your name and business?"

"Smith," rasped Inez, too busy thinking of ways to avoid the parlor to come up with a clever name. "Freighting."

Harry turned as she spoke. His eyes raked Inez. He frowned.

Flo reached up and removed Inez's hat. "Honey, that's Harry Gallagher. A good man to have on your side in Leadville. Come on."

Movement on the stairs caught Inez's attention. She almost whooped in relief. Angel descended, dressed in white lawn more fitting for sultry weather than the dead of winter. Inez recognized the man behind her, straightening his cuffs, as a prominent Denver politician.

"Her." Inez stepped away from Harry's scrutiny.

Flo's gaze flew to Angel; her full red lips turned down in a pout. "What's the hurry? I thought we'd get to know each other better."

Inez dug into her waistcoat and extracted a fifty. "Is this enough for…" *How long do I need?* "A couple hours?"

Flo's eyes riveted on the money. Realizing that the fifty was probably overly generous, Inez added quickly, "Keep the difference. For your trouble." She tucked the bill into Flo's ample cleavage. "Maybe next time."

Flo emerged from her trance and twinkled, clutching the banknote.

"Honey, you've got a date with a girl who can't say no." She winked. "Angel's no talker, so I hope you weren't looking for conversation. But she'll take good care of you. Angel," her voice turned businesslike, "treat Mr. Smith here nice for the next couple of hours so he'll come visit again."

Angel nodded. Flo turned and fluttered her fingers a last time at Inez. "Bye, honey. Nice seeing you again. Maybe next time, we'll do more than talk." She sashayed back to the parlor.

⟨⟩⟨⟩⟨⟩

Inez followed Angel upstairs to a dark, narrow hallway punctuated by doors. Angel opened the last door and beckoned. Inez halted.

Angel beckoned again, impatient. Inez stepped over the sill and looked around while Angel lit the one lamp. The small room was neat, but simply appointed: a horsehair-covered trunk, a cheap lithograph of nymphs in a forest, a bed covered with a brown shawl, a braided rug, a washstand, and a small heating stove. Inez walked to the window and lifted the curtain. Angel's room had the same view as Inez's office, minus one block.

Inez turned to see Angel loosening the pearl buttons of her dress with a professional smile and distant eyes.

"No!" Mindful of thin walls, Inez whispered, "It's me. Inez Stannert."

Recognition chased confusion from Angel's face.

"Abe and I need your help. You know he's been arrested—"

Angel covered her mouth, shook her head.

"You didn't? But, that was two, three days ago! Where have you been?"

Angel gestured angrily about the confining room, then pantomimed locking and throwing away a key.

"Here? Who's holding you prisoner?"

She swept her fingers across one cheek: feline whiskers.

"Cat DuBois?"

She nodded.

Inez moved forward and clutched Angel's soft brown hands. "Abe's accused of attacking Joe Rose's wife and being part of a counterfeit gang. But if we can prove he's not part of the bogus money game in Leadville and, better yet, reveal who is, I'm certain the charges will be dropped."

Angel gazed at her, no response.

Inez pushed on. "Llewellyn Tremayne and Cat came together from Denver. He engraves plates when he's not painting portraits. Cat's got her fingers in this too, I can smell it. You gave me Joe's watch at the party—"

Angel looked away.

"Your note was written on one of Llewellyn's scraps. You live here. You must have seen Llewellyn and Cat together, seen shipments come and go. There must be *something*. Something that will free Abe."

Angel withdrew her hands and grabbed the shawl from the bed, wrapping it tight around her. She took two hatpins from her washstand. Turning the lamp low, she cautiously opened the door and drew Inez across the hall to the backstairs. Angel put a warning finger to her lips: Quiet.

They crept down the stairs and entered a dark and silent kitchen. Angel flitted over to a door and set down the lamp.

She inserted the two hatpins into the lock. A tense moment later, a click announced her success.

Inez smiled. "Reading and writing isn't all Abe's taught you." A shy smile bloomed in answer.

They crowded into a long, narrow storeroom, Angel pulling the door closed behind them. She made a beeline to the back wall while Inez followed more slowly past crates of foodstuffs and liquor. She paused to marvel at a label identifying the contents as twenty-four bottles of very expensive brandy. *Business must be good if Cat buys this by the crate.*

She hastened to Angel, who pointed at a crate stamped *Denver Mine and Smelter Supply Company.* Inez slid Mark's knife from her boot top and pried at a board while Angel busied herself with a locked metal trunk.

The nails loosened with a squeak. Inez pulled up the end of the board and groped through straw, finally finding the wrapped banknotes. *This is why Gus Brown was so interested in Joe's Denver supplier.*

Angel tugged Inez's jacket. The trunk was open; piled higgledy-piggledy inside were sheets of foolscap, bits of penciled drawings and etchings, four half-etched copper plates, and cans of ink.

Inez looked at Angel. "Cat has finally run out of lives. She can't wiggle out of this. Now, we've got to close it all up and make sure someone else finds it. And soon." She paused, her triumph draining away. *Who?* For the first time, she regretted bolting from Denver without a word to Gus Brown.

Angel relocked the trunk. Inez pounded the sprung board back into place with the knife hilt, then slid her insurance back inside the boot. Back at the door, Inez stopped and laid an ear against the wood, listening.

Not a sound.

She gripped the handle, turned it slowly, and cracked open the door, intending to look around and check behind the door.

The handle was ripped from her hand.

Useless loomed on the other side, fist drawn back.

Inez hardly had time to throw up an arm before the blow crashed into her face. Pain exploded, followed by darkness.

Chapter Sixty-One

Inez awakened in another eruption of pain as her face and body slammed into the ground.

She groaned and opened her eyes to complete blindness. The only sound a heavy breathing overhead. A tug—and a burlap sack was ripped off her head. A none-too-gentle foot rolled her onto her back.

Staring down at her from what seemed an enormous height, Useless fumbled in his pockets. He finally extracted his filthy red kerchief and stuffed it into her mouth. It tasted of dirt, sweat, and mucus. She gagged and tried to tear it from her mouth, only to discover her arms were trussed up tight behind her.

Another kick rolled her face down again. Useless' footsteps and heavy breathing receded.

A door slammed.

Silence.

Inez sniffed, identified the liquid dripping from her nose as blood, and wondered if her nose was broken. Then, she realized that escaping her current predicament with only a broken nose would be a blessing.

Where am I?

She concentrated on what her senses could detect.

A ticking clock. The ornate legs of a chair or table. The wooly nap of a rug beneath her ear. The subdued flicker of an unseen fire behind a screen.

It's too deserted to be in the parlor house.

A rustling caused her to turn her head gingerly. Angel, arms similarly restricted, rolled against Inez in a soft whisper of linen. She sat up and scooted out of sight, toward Inez's feet.

Inez wiggled her right foot: *The knife is here.*

A tide of voices warned them of approaching company. Angel flattened herself to the floor and rolled away from Inez. Listening, Inez discerned Useless' urgent tones and Cat's musical ones.

"This better be important." Cat's words grew clear as the door opened. "I don't like to be dragged away from clients on trivial matters."

Footsteps, the clatter of a lamp glass, and a sputter of light came into being.

"What have we here," Cat drawled, her shoes coming into Inez's limited ground-level view.

With a slither of silk, Cat sat down, her feet and the hem of her skirts not two feet away from Inez's face. One satin shoe disappeared and reappeared as she crossed her legs. The shoe in the air seesawed, inches from Inez's nose. "Angel, Angel, is this your doing? What am I to do with you."

"She stabbed me with a damn hatpin," Useless interjected.

"What is she doing with a hatpin and no hat? And why did you drag them both across the alley and into my home? Was this gentleman trying to take unpaid-for liberties? If so, you should have thrown him in the alley."

"Ain't no gentleman, Mrs. DuBois." Useless' hand curled into Inez's hair and he jerked her head up. "Look."

Inez's eyes watered from pain. Through shimmering tears, she saw Cat twirling opera-length pearls with a closed fan. Cat frowned and leaned closer.

Her plucked and penciled eyebrows shot up. "Mrs. Stannert? What have you done to your hair? And what are you doing here? I thought you'd left town." She leaned back. "Tell me, Useless. Don't leave out anything."

Useless dropped Inez nose first onto the floor. Red stars streaked across her vision and nearly sent her back to oblivion.

"Flo wanted me to check that Angel was okay. Her room was empty, so I went down the backstairs, heard Mrs. Stannert, and saw a light under the storeroom door."

"That door was locked. How did they get in?" Cat sounded irritated.

A nearby door squeaked open. "Catherine? Is it safe?"

"Yes, love. Come in. You should hear this."

Quick, furtive steps approached. Inez turned her head and saw Llewellyn transformed. Long hair exchanged for short, extravagant mustache replaced by the merest line above his lip. He circumvented the rug in rough and simple clothes, looking completely miserable without his ruffles.

Llewellyn squinted at Angel, then Inez. "Who…?"

"Your patroness, my love. She of the epic painting."

"Mrs. Stannert?" His face paled. "In the storeroom? Did they find—"

"Since they managed to unlock the storeroom, I think we'd better assume they unlocked your trunk as well."

Llewellyn collapsed in a chair, staring at Inez.

Cat's voice turned brisk. "She left her sidearm at the door, of course. What else might she carry, Useless?"

Useless rolled Inez onto her back. Inez could now see Cat and Llewellyn to one side, Angel to the other. Useless hovered above her.

"She carries a pocket pistol."

Cat gestured impatiently with her fan.

Useless located the gun and handed it to Cat, who inspected it before setting it on the fireplace mantel. "Anything else? Knives or what-not?"

"She don't use a knife."

Inez kept her eyes steady on Cat and tried to breathe as normally as possible around the stinking kerchief.

Cat tapped her lips with the fan, eyes narrowed in thought. "Search her. We'll leave nothing to chance. Nothing."

Grumbling, Useless patted Inez's shirt sleeves and worked his way down her waistcoat. He extracted the bankroll from her waistcoat pocket and handed it to Cat.

Cat flattened the money on her lap. "Fifties and twenties." She passed the bills to Llewellyn, who examined them.

His breath erupted in an exclamation. "These are ours! Even the twenties, and I only did a sample run of them. Denver never got the samples or the plates from Rose." He gazed at Inez, eyes wide and dark. "*You* have them. Where are my plates, Mrs. Stannert?"

Cat waved his words away impatiently. "The plates, the counterfeit, it's all small potatoes. It means she must also have…" Cat leaned forward and said, deadly soft, "The map. Where is it, Mrs. Stannert?"

Inez blinked twice in what she hoped passed for surprise.

"Ask her about the plates!" squawked Llewellyn. "They took me a year to make. They're flawless. Denver was ready to pay us a thousand apiece for them."

Cat laid a soothing hand on Llewellyn's shoulder. "When the map and title to the Lady Luck are mine, you'll never need to engrave another set of plates or letter another saloon sign. Useless will work the claim, then we'll sell to Harry or the highest bidder for tens of thousands, as planned. After that, you can paint to your heart's delight. We'll travel to Paris, London, visit all the grand salons where your art will be appreciated."

Cat glared at Inez with a look that, if a knife, would have ripped out her heart. "All I need is that goddamned map."

Llewellyn wrung his hands, a gesture more fitting to ruffled sleeves than rough homespun. "Catherine. It's not so simple now. What about that prospector? The one you made the deal with? He still owns half the claim and won't reveal the location. And he's still gallivanting around. Somewhere."

"Chet Donnelly? We won't need him if we have the map." She talked as if to a child. "Next time Chet visits, I'll provide a bottle of spirits laced with snuff and—" she snapped her fingers. "He'll be found stiff and dead in Tiger Alley. Like Joe Rose. And the claim will have one owner. Me."

Her gaze slashed at Inez. "I suppose in all your skulking about you discovered that Joe was our Denver courier. On his last run, he was supposed to deliver the new plates and samples and bring back counterfeit for distribution. His contact was found dead a week later. No plates. No samples. No money." She leaned back in the chair, tapping her knee with the closed fan. "At first, Denver thought it was one of their own. Joe swore he'd given the man the plates and samples. He also insisted that there was no counterfeit in his shipment from the Denver Mine and Smelter Supply Company. Joe lied. He lied about a lot of things. His downfall was, he lied to me."

She turned to Useless. "Take that thing out of her mouth." He did so. "Now, I promise you, Mrs. Stannert, one yell, the gag goes back in, and Useless will lead you to a lingering and painful death. Where's the map?"

Inez took a deep breath. "Did you kill Joe Rose?"

Cat smiled slow. "Poor Joe. I was riding the same brute of a horse that almost trampled you Christmas Eve. Only Joe didn't have a fleet-footed minister to pull him to safety."

She shrugged eloquently, white shoulders smooth as satin.

Llewellyn's eyes were riveted on Cat in horror. "You *killed* Rose?"

Cat patted his hand absently. "An accident, my sweet. I didn't see him in the dark. The alleys are so treacherous." Her eyes glinted. "Well, Useless, she won't answer, she only wants to ask questions. Gag her again. Maybe you can convince her it's much, much better to tell us where the map is."

"But I heard the marshal found Rose's watch in Jackson's pocket!" Llewellyn sounded as if he was arguing with himself.

Cat looked at Angel. "Yes…I wondered how Joe's watch wandered from my home to Emma's pocket. Seems Angel can walk through locked doors. From Emma's pockets to Jackson's merely took a little sleight-of-hand on Useless' part. Clever,

Useless. With that maneuver, you redeemed yourself from that previous mess." She glowered at Useless, who writhed.

"But, but she caught me in the house!"

"And you had to take your pleasure before leaving her for dead. But not dead enough. Emma Rose," Cat sneered, "acted as if she was above us, when all along she'd turned out in the sisterhood. Joe was such a willing dupe, what with his gambling debts and his wife's reputation to protect."

Llewellyn buried his face in his hands. "As soon as the storm breaks, I'm leaving, Catherine. You should come too, fortune or no." His voice was muffled. "It's all closing in. First, Sands destroys my workshop. It's a good thing Cooke warned me, I barely escaped with that trunk. Now, this. Maybe Mrs. Stannert's talked to Sands, maybe he knows about us, my love. Sands sneaks around like, like a wolf. Who knows where he'll turn up next."

"I know where he'll be in an hour." Cat almost purred.

Llewellyn looked up. "You don't mean—"

"Oh, I do. He's coming here. The good man has been yielding to temptation, inch by inch. He's finally ready to take the plunge and succumb to the sins of the flesh. Not that he's any stranger to those pleasures, right, Mrs. Stannert?" She smiled sidelong at Inez, then tapped Llewellyn's clenched fists with her fan. "Don't be jealous, love. It's only business. And when I'm done, a little something in the coffee will ensure that he never preaches another sermon." She sighed. "Too bad. At least, I'll have the last of him."

"Huh. Bet she wishes it were her." Useless made a grab at Inez's crotch. Furious, she kicked his shin.

Useless jumped back. "Bitch!" That one hate-laden word told Inez all she needed to know about the identity of the killer in the bank.

He raised a hand to strike her.

"Stop!" Cat's voice froze him to the spot. "She's bleeding all over my rug as it is. Save it for later, Useless."

She snapped her fan open and lazily moved it back and forth. "So, my love, we'll hide you in Angel's room until after the reverend's visit."

"He's coming here? To your home?" Llewellyn sounded affronted.

"We must be discreet with the clergy. Now, what should we do about this." She indicated the immobile women. "My love, your workshop's destroyed?"

"Completely." He sounded miserable.

"Well, then, they won't be back." She turned to Useless. "Get the wagon and take these two to the workshop. Kill them. But not a mark on Angel. Do you understand? Not one." Useless looked disappointed.

"However," she added in an off-hand way, "do whatever you want with Mrs. Stannert."

Useless' gaze melted on Inez. "Whatever I want." He licked his lips. Inez felt the sweat of terror slick the palms of her trapped hands.

Cat continued. "Remember, we want the map or the location of the claim. If she tells you, be a gentleman and kill her quick. Then get rid of the body. Toss it down a mine shaft, I don't care. Just be sure when you're done that no one—and I mean *no* one—will ever be able to identify her."

Llewellyn interjected, "Is this necessary?"

"Let me decide what's necessary and what isn't." Her fan tapped his chest. "A sensitive artist shouldn't worry about such ugly doings."

"If I'm not supposed to touch Angel, how do I kill her?" Useless sounded grumpy, as if ordered to clean out the livery stalls with his hands.

"Get the wagon. I'll tell you when you return."

Llewellyn addressed Cat after Useless left. "He's worse than useless, he's crazy! You can't let him do this. We've got to get rid of him."

She turned on him. "Who will stake and work the claim? Who will take care of these—" she nudged Inez with her shoe, "problems? You?"

Llewellyn shrank back in his chair.

"All men have weaknesses, my love. For a finely turned ankle perhaps, or red hair." Cat touched her hennaed locks. "Others, like Useless, have darker cravings. I keep him on a short leash with my girls, but with Mrs. Stannert, I'm going to let it slip. He'll lick my hand in gratitude. I know the men who come here in the evenings. During the day, they turn their eyes away, but I know each of them down to their boot soles. And their secrets. When I have the Lady Luck, they'll have no choice but to see me in the daylight at last."

With a determined rustle of silk, she rose and left the room.

Llewellyn looked mournfully at Inez. "My poor Catherine. Do you know her deepest sin? It's the same one that your poet assigns to his Prince of Darkness. You told me once." He leaned forward. "The sin of injured pride. She wants to be loved for herself. To be given proper due for the magnificent creature she is. My love and admiration apparently aren't enough."

He sat back, weary. "I'm sorry it's come to this, Mrs. Stannert. I enjoyed working on your painting. What a pity it'll never be finished."

Cat reappeared with a paper and a brown bottle. "Angel's room is on the second floor by the backstairs. Be careful crossing the alley."

She watched him depart, then glared at Inez, bitterness drawing hard lines around her mouth. "I want to leave you with one last thought about your husband. The oh-so handsome, oh-so charming Mark Stannert." She knelt by Inez, pulling her skirts aside from the blood-soaked carpet. "Last May, when he and I signed the contract to buy your saloon, he swore you and Jackson would go along. He took eight hundred dollars in partial payment and promised to return with your signatures by morning. I never thought he'd skip town, leaving a wife and child."

She smoothed the paper in her lap. "Llewellyn couldn't stand to see me so cruelly treated. He drew up new papers, Useless found receipts with your signatures, and…" She held up a forged contract for Inez to see.

"Your husband is gone, you'll be dead by morning, and Abe's as good as." She spoke as if ticking off a guest list. "When the hullabaloo dies down, all I'll need is a little help from our friendly bank manager and your saloon is mine. Your husband." She arched her eyebrows meaningfully. "He certainly knew how to distract a woman from all good sense, didn't he?"

Useless tramped in, arms full of canvas tarps. Cat handed him the brown bottle. "Laudanum. Hold Angel's nose and force it down her throat. She'll be just another girl who overdosed to ease the pain of a sporting life. No one will give her death a second thought. Bring her body back and we'll dump it in the alley. Maybe with the reverend's. Hmmm."

She spared Inez a last glance. "Think on what I said— and didn't say—about your loving husband as Useless speeds you on your way to Hell. When you get there, give my regards to Joe Rose."

Chapter Sixty-Two

Useless laid two tarps side by side, rolled each woman up separately, and tied the tops and bottoms shut like sausage casings. Inez's hope that Angel might gain the knife during the wagon trip evaporated.

On the dark, bumpy ride to Llewellyn's workshop, Inez's thoughts scuttled about like damaged mice trying to escape feline claws. She imagined Sands, sipping his last cup of coffee in Cat's boudoir. Remembered Mark, combing his mustache with extra care before leaving home that last time.

Mostly, she wondered how she and Angel would get out alive.

The sleigh runners squeaked to a stop. The wagon shuddered as Useless jumped off. After a long time, hands snared Inez's tarp prison and lifted her up. She was carried like a sack of potatoes, then lowered to another hard surface. The canvas parted.

Useless peered at her, dripping nose and worried eyes inches away. She screwed up her face, wishing she could spit at him. "Huh. Still alive. That's good." He ripped the saliva-soaked rag from her mouth. Inez coughed, trying to work out the nasty taste. "Holler all you want. No one's gonna hear you, except me and Angel." He went back outside.

Inez struggled to sit up and looked around. Llewellyn had not exaggerated the workshop's condition. Everything was ripped, smashed, or overturned, from the canvas stretcher to the small metal printing press.

Everything but the stove.

The stove gaped open, pouring a flickering red light into the room. It reminded Inez of some medievalist's vision of Hell. She broke out in a sweat and tried not to think why Useless wanted a fire.

Angel, who was lying some distance away, got laboriously to her knees, then feet, and stumbled toward Inez, hands still tied behind her.

"Right boot." Inez thumped her heel for emphasis. Angel lowered herself, sitting with her back to Inez. Gentle fingers fluttered into the boot. Inez sighed in relief as Angel slid the knife from the sheath.

A muffled thump and curse at the rear door alerted them. Angel threw herself down and rolled away from Inez.

The door squeaked open, and Useless reappeared with another tarp, a rope, and the laudanum. He opened the canvas square and arranged it close to the stove. Then, he approached Inez and lifted her as easily as if she were a case of whiskey. "So, gonna talk about that map?"

He lowered her with ominous care to the canvas surface. "Don't matter if you do or don't. 'Cause I have another plan. I'll just track Chet to the Lady Luck, then kill him when he's sleeping."

"You think you'll be able to sneak up on Chet in the middle of the mountains? You really are stupid." Inez injected scorn into her voice, hoping to keep his attention focused on her and her alone.

Angel—use that knife!

"I'm not stupid." Useless sounded wounded. "You always treated me like an idiot boy. All the time, you talked like I wasn't even there. Well, I was. And I heard. And I saw. I saw you agree to meet Nigel from the bank. Then I heard him asking questions about Joe Rose at the Crystal Belle. So I went to his office before you got there, told him you'd sent me. He didn't believe me." Useless sighed heavily. "Right after I killed him, you showed up. Sometimes my luck don't run real good. But it's changing. Right now."

He pulled out a knife and held the gleaming blade before Inez's eyes. "Recognize this?"

Inez fearfully examined Abe's old knife.

Useless switched it to his other hand, wiping a palm on his pants. "If I'd known I was going to get lucky, I'd've used this on Emma Rose and saved the one you gave Jackson for now. That would've been real sweet."

Angel stirred.

Useless whipped around. "Wanna watch, Angel? You can't get too close. Don't want that dress all blooded up. No marks. That's what Mrs. DuBois said." He walked over and grabbed her hair. Inez's hopes fell when she saw Angel's ropes intact.

Useless shoved Angel against the wall. "Sit tight, or I'll hurt you in ways that don't leave bruises. You know I can."

He straddled Inez on his knees and picked up the knife again.

She threw Angel a frantic look. *Use the goddamned knife!*

"We'll have some fun first," Useless mused. "Then, I'll skin you, throw you down an old mine shaft, and let the rats finish you off."

He drew the knife point gently down her throat to her shirt collar. She held still and tried not to swallow. The sharp point left a tingling in its wake. The tingling expanded to pain as blood welled and dripped to the tarp.

He let out a shuddering sigh and surveyed his work tenderly. "You look so pretty in red. Like that red dress you wore when you yelled at me for stompin' the rat in the saloon. I'm gonna cover you in red before I'm done. Now, lemme see what's under those duds. The way you strut around the saloon, it must be good."

Placing the knife at the top of her collar, he ripped down the fabric, scoring her skin. The knife snagged on the linen wrapped around her breasts. He tore the shirt open. "So that's how you fooled Flo."

He curled a hand over her trouser waistband and yanked. The first button popped off.

"You're a dead man." Inez poured certainty into her words, like acid into a wound. "Your life won't be worth two cents when you've outlived your usefulness to Cat."

He flinched. She saw a shadow of the Useless she knew. Then he snickered and tightened his grip. Material ripped and another button popped off. "Don't think so, Mrs. Stannert."

Inez talked fast. "Oh, not right away. I heard her discuss it with Llewellyn. They need you for the dirty work. But once you've sweated out a season of mosquitoes, mud, and rocks on the Lady Luck, all bets are off. Cat'll own the claim and she'll be hot to sell. One less partner means more money for her. So what's to stop you from becoming another corpse in Tiger Alley?" Doubt flickered in his eyes. She pressed on. "I just hope she cuts your balls off first. If she can find them."

Useless slammed her face with an open hand.

Near blind with pain, Inez kicked, catching him high on the inner thigh. He yelped, grabbed her boot, pulled it off, and flung it across the room.

He grabbed her other boot. Panicked, she curled her toes to keep it on.

Useless yanked it off.

"Shit!" He glared at the empty knife sheath on her ankle. Grabbing her by the neck, he shouted, "Where's the knife!"

He must have seen the answer in her eyes.

Useless dropped Inez and whirled to face Angel, standing behind him. Mark's knife was in her grip, the blade gleaming red in the stove's light.

Inez sat up, coughing, and scooted away. Useless tried to grab her foot. Angel darted forward.

Inez heard cloth rip. Useless whirled to face Angel, clutching his right side. Angel backed up. She twisted her wrist and the knife disappeared. Inez blinked, remembering Abe demonstrating that same maneuver: *Hold the handle so the blade points up along the inside of your arm. Your opponent can't see your blade, how long it is, or where it's pointin'.*

Inez looked around, saw nothing that would cut ropes. The closest object of any substance was the tipped-over printing press.

Gripping Abe's knife, Useless stepped toward Angel. She retreated, white skirts floating about her legs. He feinted, then slashed. Red bloomed on her sleeve. She transferred the knife to her other hand.

If there's a God in Heaven, help us now.

Inez climbed shakily to her feet. Useless, back to her, was intent on Angel. He stepped forward. The printing press, its black metal edges gleaming, now lay to his right. Inez calculated the distance, then charged on bare and silent feet. She hurtled herself at his legs, catching him behind the knees.

Knocked off-balance, Useless slashed wildly. Angel uttered a hoarse cry.

Useless fell, his boot hitting Inez's ear. His head hit the sharp corner of the press with a squashy thud.

In a heartbeat, Angel was on Useless. She ripped him open from abdomen to breastbone. He convulsed, hands rising to trap the entrails spilling out. She slashed him across the throat. Blood gushed like a cresting wave, splattering her face and the front of her dress. Useless' body jerked once, as if in protest, then stilled.

Chapter Sixty-Three

Angel spat at his body. *"Bâtard!"* She bent over in a fit of coughing.

Inez wheezed, "You talk!"

Angel wiped her face and the knife blade on her skirt, then cut Inez's ropes. "Only when I trust."

Freed at last, Inez rubbed her wrists. *I'll live to see my son, play the piano, ride in the mountains.* She felt deliriously happy. "Why didn't you yell for help? Tell someone about Cat, the counterfeit?"

"Scream?" Angel shrugged. "Ah. Women scream on State Street, day and night. No one cares. And tell who? *Policier? Monsieur* Harry? I trust only Abe. I don't tell him. *Pourquoi?* Until you tell me, I didn't know he was in trouble." She touched Inez's hand. "You and I, we share secrets. You know I talk. I know about your husband. We keep quiet between us, yes?" The speech sent her into another spasm of coughing. The red deepened on her dress.

Inez forced her to sit on the tarp. "You're hurt!"

Angel pointed at Inez: You too.

"It looks worse than it is." Inez touched a sleeve gingerly to her throat and examined the smear. "Not much blood. But you—" She looked with concern at the dark red patch. "We need to stop that."

Inez cut strips of canvas, binding Angel's arm and ribs. Angel began to shiver, despite the stove. Inez glanced around. "I don't see much we can use for fuel. We'll freeze if we stay. Besides, you need those wounds tended."

Inez ransacked Useless' body, taking gloves from his pocket and socks and shoes from his feet. Inez considered removing his jacket, but it stank, soaked with blood and body fluids. *Better for the dead.* His thick outer coat had escaped the bloodbath. Inez layered his footgear over Angel's dancing shoes.

Inez buttoned her own jacket and retrieved her boots, then pulled on Useless' gloves, hat, and heavy overcoat, saying, "When Useless doesn't return by daybreak, Cat and Llewellyn will vanish with the evidence."

Inez skirted the body and opened the back door. Snow poured in, wind whipping it in gusts.

"We've got to move fast. You'd best stay here, where it's warm. The less moving around you do, the better. The horse and wagon are probably in the outbuilding. I'll bring them around."

Angel gripped Inez's arm. "I'll not stay with *that*." She jerked her head toward Useless. "I come."

Inez drew a breath to say no, then looked at Angel's face. *Who am I to tell her what to do.*

Instead, she removed the overcoat and bundled Angel into it. "Keep your hands in the pockets," she told Angel. "I'll help you walk."

Inez turned up her jacket collar and opened the door.

Step by slow step, heads bent against the snow, they approached the outbuilding. Once there, Inez lifted the latch, and they fell into hay and animal warmth. Angel crumpled by the sleigh runners. Inez half lifted, half pushed Angel into the wagon bed, then fumbled to the door which had slammed shut in a sudden gust.

Pushing the door open, she faced a wall of blackness, heard only the wail of wind, felt the solid blast of snow in her face.

Whiteout. I can't drive in this.

Inez tugged the door shut. Taking the horse blanket, still warm from the animal's back, she crawled into the wagon, and covered herself and Angel. "We'll have to wait," she whispered. There was no response.

The roar of the storm receded as she collapsed into unconsciousness.

‹›‹›‹›

Inez awoke, stiff and sore, alarmed at the absence of sound. For a moment, she thought the building completely buried. She shook Angel gently and was reassured when the girl stirred.

Inez dragged herself out of the wagon and made her way to the horse's head. She stroked the beast's nose. He whuffed reassuringly.

Inez forced the door open against the drifts and faced a world turned from black to silver-white. Moonlight glimmered through shredded clouds onto the faraway peaks of Massive and Elbert. Llewellyn's workshop was a black shape with a silvered roof and light flickering through the window. She blinked. The light wavered and disappeared.

A door slammed.

"Inez! Angel!" Reverend Sands' voice lifted from the stillness.

Inez's shout erupted in a squeak, dissolving into a cough that tore at her throat. Desperate, she ripped the glove off her hand.

Joey's words to his mother on Christmas Day drifted back to her: "Three whistles means help."

She placed two fingers in her mouth.

The piercing notes echoed off surrounding hills and ascended the night air to the heavens.

Chapter Sixty-Four

Two figures came into view around opposite ends of the workshop, the moon throwing their shadows long across the open space. They converged and hastened toward Inez, pinpoints of lantern light growing into disks.

Reverend Sands arrived first, Bat Masterson close behind.

Inez fell into Sands' arms, giddy with relief and shaking with cold.

"Angel," she rasped to Bat. "In the wagon. Hurt. Needs a doctor."

Bat lifted the lantern high. "Jesus, Inez. You need a doctor yourself. That bastard do this to you? Deserved to have his guts ripped out. What happened to your hair?"

"Check the wagon, Bat." Sands held Inez tighter, as if she might disappear like a skein of smoke.

"Right. Angel in distress. My cue." He squeezed past them into the shack.

Ignoring the agony in her throat, Inez raced to say what she had to say before her voice gave out entirely. "The store-room in Cat's parlor house. Llewellyn's trunk, crate of counterfeit. Cat, Llewellyn, Cooke from the bank, they worked together. Cat killed Joe. Useless killed Nigel, hurt Emma. He was going to kill us both. Abe and I, we had nothing to do with any of this. I left my saddlebags with

Cooke. He fixed it so we were to blame. They'll leave if we don't get back by daybreak. Get Gus Brown in Denver."

Sands' voice in her ear was soothing, warm. "We know, we know. I saw your gun in Mrs. DuBois' house. We found Llewellyn; he told us where you were. He confessed to making counterfeit plates and implicated Cooke. Mrs. DuBois is in custody too. And mighty unhappy about it, as you can imagine."

There was a commotion from the wagon bed. Bat jumped down hastily. "Someone tell her I'm a friend. She tried to scratch my eyes out!"

Angel's face peered over the side, ferocious, her dark hair curling like snakes. She saw Inez and Sands, and relaxed.

"Cat had a signed bill of sale for the Silver Queen." Inez's voice was nearly gone. "A forgery. We never sold the saloon to her."

"Bill of sale for the Silver Queen?" Sands raised his eyebrows toward Bat, all innocence. Bat volleyed back the same bland expression. They looked like boys joined in a childhood conspiracy.

Bat scratched a corner of his mustache. "Hey, Justice, think that might've been the paper that sort of got caught in the breeze and ended up in the fireplace? The one Mrs. DuBois kicked up such a fuss about?"

"Ashes to ashes," murmured Sands, "dust to dust." He smoothed Inez's short hair. "The Lord giveth, the Lord taketh away. As Mrs. DuBois has discovered."

"In this case," Bat said, "the Lord had Justice on His side."

"I'll get these ladies to a doctor." Sands voice sharpened. "Bat, take the horses back to town, and tell Harry and Gus."

"Gus?" she whispered unbelieving. "Brown?"

Sands smiled. "He arrived before you did. With lots of questions."

"But I left him in Denver."

Sands' smile widened. "Gus is an old fox. He said he asked when you planned to return to Leadville. When you answered, he watched Joey. Said he knew from Joey's expression that you were lying through your teeth."

He held her out at arm's length. "We can talk more later. Right now, let me get a look at you. At least, you're walking, talking, thank God." He took in her face, her neck, and his expression tightened. "I'd've never picked Useless for being the type." His eyes traveled down her torn and bloody shirt, then stopped. "Jesus Christ. Did he—" His hands tightened, face stamped with sympathy and anguish.

Inez looked down, wondering what elicited such a strong response. Through the buttonless gap in Mark's pants, she saw Mark's gray woolen drawers, soaked with blood. Astonishment transformed into puzzlement. *Useless didn't even get close. What—?*

A familiar abdominal cramp provided the answer.

She closed her eyes and offered a silent prayer of thanks, then opened them and whispered, "It's not that. It's just…"

Comprehension dawned and Sands pulled her close again. "So your day-counting wasn't as far off as you thought."

Chapter Sixty-Five

During her convalescence, Inez gained an appreciation for the restorative powers of hot toddies, thanks to Doc, who believed in a high ratio of hot whiskey to sugar water. Doc also set her broken nose.

"I've done this hundreds of times, my dear. In a couple weeks, your nose will regain its normal size and shape and the bruising around the eyes will disappear. Your throat will heal as well. That laceration, however." He waggled a finger at the row of small neat stitches marching down her breastbone. "A little memento of your adventures. You may not want to wear low-cut dresses after this."

Reverend Sands called the day after Doc's surgery. She admitted him, with a purple nose, no voice, and many reservations. "I need time," she whispered from the refuge of her piano stool. Cat's musings and Harry's remarks roiled about, poisoning her thoughts.

Tapping his hat on the back of the loveseat, Sands didn't argue, although she saw a shadow cross his face, pulling a cloud over the sun. "When you're ready then." The silver fob on his watch chain glinted as he rose to go. "By-the-bye, Harry offered me a reward for breaking the coney ring. I told him you deserved it as much as I. Probably more."

"I don't want Harry's money!" she squeaked.

Reverend Sands played out the circumference of his hat between his hands. "The church's Widows and Orphans fund welcomes donations, if you're looking for a charitable cause." He settled his hat on his head. "I'll wait to hear from you, Inez. Maybe when Bat Masterson leaves town." Sands raised his eyebrows. Inez blushed through the purple and black bruises, wondering if he knew that Bat had called two hours earlier.

Abe was released within hours of Inez's return to town. To Inez's eyes, he seemed grayer, grimmer. He and Inez agreed to keep the saloon closed until they could hire more help. Angel and Abe rescued Angel's horsehair trunk from Cat's boarding house and transported it to Abe's home.

Emma recovered consciousness just as Inez's bruises faded from purple to green. Her memory, blessedly vague on most of the events leading to her condition, was clear where it counted. She told Marshal Hollis in no uncertain terms that it was Useless, not Abe, she'd surprised that gray dawn in her own home.

As soon as Doc related the news of Emma's recovery, Inez paid a visit to the hospital, Bible tucked under her arm. She found Susan Carothers visiting Emma as well. Susan's bright brown eyes lit up, and she rose from her chair to give Inez a hug, talking nonstop all the while. "I'm so glad you're up and around, Inez! I wanted to come see you, but Doc said I mustn't, that you needed complete rest. I'm dying to know what happened. Both he and Reverend Sands have been so close-mouthed, it must have been quite adventurous, whatever you did. All that the reverend would say is that you disguised yourself as a man and quite successfully fooled everybody. I wish you would've come to me when you were planning whatever you were planning. I could've helped. Although," Susan hesitated and eyed Inez's cropped locks, "I'm not sure I would have had the nerve to cut off my hair."

Emma exclaimed over Inez's hair and raccoon-like visage while Inez clucked over Emma's gaunt form. After assurances on both sides, Inez handed Emma her Bible. Emma clasped the book, looking up with a dread that Inez read as clearly as the goldleaf on the leather-bound spine. Inez glanced at Susan, who had settled into the chair and was beaming at them both. Inez abandoned her plan to tell Emma what she'd discovered in the Bible and in Denver. Instead, she sat on the corner of the bed and said, "I never opened the Bible. I couldn't stand to, after what happened."

Relief washed anxiety from Emma's face. "It's not important. What is, is that you saved Joey and ended all this business. You and Reverend Sands."

For the next two weeks, Inez focused her energies on Joey and Emma, helping them prepare for their delayed departure to Sacramento. She put off going to church, first one Sunday, then another, and another. When she thought of Sands, Inez remembered how it felt to lie close to him, her skin against his. His voice, warm and gentle as his hands. She shook the yearnings away. *I must think this through. No more jumping in with eyes shut.*

January was drawing to a close when Inez accompanied Emma and Joey to Denver. On the train platform, promises to write flowed between the two women. Inez hugged Joey and handed him a new leather volume of *Paradise Lost*. "When you read about the angel wars," she whispered, "remember your Auntie Inez." She stood on the platform a long time after the smoke had receded from the west-bound train.

Before leaving Denver, Inez paid a visit to the house on Holladay Street. Mattie Silks received her in the same rose and maroon parlor as before. Inez related an abbreviated version of the truth, deleting her scene with Harry and other judiciously chosen parts. Mattie listened, nodded, refilled their champagne glasses. The two women then exchanged views on horses, handguns, and the paucity of decent hired help.

"We need a barman and a dealer," Inez said. "If you know anyone reliable, send him with your recommendation. I've offered the position of lead dealer to Bat Masterson—"

Mattie raised her eyebrows.

"He's a *friend*," Inez emphasized.

Mattie rolled her eyes.

Mattie offered Inez the name of a Denver wigmaker. Inez declined, running a hand over her short-cropped hair. Privately, she reveled in the freedom from long tresses and the rituals of brushing, plaiting, and washing.

Missing husbands did not enter the conversation.

Returning to the hotel, Inez, on impulse, directed the driver to drive the length of Holladay. She leaned forward and gazed out the window, scrutinizing the men on the boardwalks, entering and exiting saloons, cribs, dancehalls, and parlor houses. She wondered what she would do if she spotted Mark at a door, adjusting his hat against the fading afternoon light. She shuddered and sat back against the cushioned seat.

<><><>

Inez returned to Leadville to find the Silver Queen open and operating and a new diamond-dust mirror along the backbar. The biggest surprise was Angel, working by Abe's side and wearing a wedding band.

Abe wiped his hands on a bar rag. "We got ourselves some first-class help. This bardog's a quick study and part of the family to boot. Mrs. Stannert, meet our new partner, Mrs. Jackson."

Angel, her hair pinned up and proper, twisted her hands in her apron. Her brown eyes were full of hope and hesitation. Inez rounded the bar and embraced her. "Congratulations. And welcome to the Silver Queen."

"As for the mirror," Abe said, "we needed something to hide that damn painting."

The final surprise arrived a day later: a thousand-dollar check signed by Harry Gallagher along with a sprig of mistletoe bound with an evening primrose. There was no note. However, the small bouquet spoke its own language, a language Inez still remembered from ancient deportment lessons: *I will surmount all obstacles, including your inconstancy.*

Abe squinted. "Mistletoe? Thought Christmas was over."

She crushed the glossy leaves and sulfur-colored blossom in her hand. "You're right, Abe. It's over."

The Independent reported Harry's departure on an extended business trip. The same article noted that an East Coast consortium headed by Isaac Eisemer had bought Silver Mountain stock valued at three million dollars.

A smaller item caught Inez's eye. Harry had paid Chet Donnelly fifteen thousand dollars for a claim west of the tiny gold camp of Independence. The transaction made hardly a ripple in the daily talk and discussion around Leadville. The town's attention was riveted on the Supreme Court decision giving the Denver & Rio Grande right-of-way to build a railroad line through the Arkansas Valley to Leadville. The D&RG promised to push the line through the long winter season and open the rails by summer.

‹›‹›‹›

In February, Inez's bruises paled to yellow and faded away. She resumed her place behind the bar and reopened the Saturday night poker games. Bat Masterson was a frequent visitor, walking her home after hours and filling Harry's chair on Saturday evenings.

One night, as she prepared to say goodnight to him on her porch, he leaned against the door, blocking her access. "Inez. I got a telegram this afternoon asking me to be a delegate to the Ford County Republican Convention. I'll be heading for Dodge tomorrow and probably on to Topeka."

"I see." She swung her key between her fingers. "Decided against making Leadville your home?"

"I'll be back. Late spring, early summer." He folded his arms and looked uncomfortable. "To tell the truth, I made a small fortune playing the tables, but it's still not enough to buy a place in Leadville. I want my own business, Inez. I don't want to work for anyone. Not even you." He sounded regretful.

"Well," she said, not certain if she felt disappointed or relieved. "I'd hoped to convince you otherwise."

After a moment, he took her hand. He played with her fingers, bending them one at a time as if testing their flexibility. Focusing on her fingers, he said, "Wondered how you felt about forming a partnership. We could mosey around Colorado or Arizona when I come back. See what's up."

She searched his face, still bent over her hand, and saw hope mingled with panic in a "What have I said?" expression. *He's so young.* Only a few years behind her, yet impatient, unsettled, hungry to see if the next town might prove better, hold more adventure, more silver.

I've already lived this. Ten years ago, when I said yes to Mark. The realization made it easier for her gently to withdraw her hand.

"I'm flattered you'd ask, Bat. But Abe and Angel are all the partners I need for now. And Leadville's as close to home as I have."

Disappointment darkened his expression, although Inez thought she also saw a glimmer of relief. "Well, think about it. Come spring, you might change your mind."

She smiled. "You might change yours, too."

Chapter Sixty-Six

Two nights later in the Silver Queen's office, Inez counted the evening's take while Abe and Angel closed up downstairs. After locking the safe, she paused by the window. Fat, slow snowflakes, more like spring than winter, drifted past. The moon hung below the clouds, so intense it shone like a beacon through the window.

Footsteps on the stairs recalled her to the present. She buttoned her gloves, addressing the door behind her. "I'm just about ready to go."

Her heart leaped to her throat when she heard Reverend Sands reply, "I was hoping we could talk first."

She turned and saw him, hands behind his back, the military man waiting to be recognized. The moon picked out the silver loop of his watch chain. She turned back to the window. "Abe let you in?"

"And left with his lovely wife. If you want an escort home, I'm it."

Silence.

"I've been waiting. Almost two months now. A long time."

Silence.

She heard him step forward. "Inez?"

"I understand Mrs. DuBois sold all her holdings to buy legal counsel for herself and Llewellyn." Inez touched the glass, so cold she could feel it through her calfskin glove. "Turns out, she'd bought Nils Hansen's claim using Joe Rose as go-between. And other claims as well." She shook her head. "Poor Nils. He was probably embarrassed beyond belief to discover his 'secret buyer' was a State Street madam."

He spoke from behind her. "Llewellyn escaped custody in Denver."

"So I heard. You don't sound upset."

"I don't work for the Secret Service anymore. If I did, and I'd been the operative making the collar, I'd be upset."

"But since you work for Harry, it's different."

Sands sighed. "My agreement with Harry was to break the ring in Leadville. I also told him I'd not take a single life in the process. That part of me was finished, I thought. Spiritual arrogance on my part. As a wise man once said, 'To thine own self be true.' We can't accept some parts of the self and toss out the rest."

"Shakespeare," Inez said half to herself. "That's from *Hamlet*, not scripture."

"Truth comes in many forms." Another step. "That night, when Llewellyn told us what Useless planned to do to you...I went to the workshop ready to kill him."

Inez traced a pattern of frost down the pane. "That night, Mrs. DuBois said you'd been a frequent visitor."

"Mrs. DuBois counterfeited truths to suit her needs. Yes, I visited. To listen, to observe. You and I, we unraveled the same mystery by different paths. You, through Joe Rose, me, through Harry."

"Harry. The Secret Service. There's a lot I don't know about you."

"And a lot I don't know about you. But we could change that. Inez," another step forward, "a delegation from the church has asked me to stay."

"Interim minister offered permanent post. Isn't that... irregular?"

"Opportunities presented are often not those one expects." He cleared his throat. "However, there's only one reason I would stay in Leadville."

She finally faced him. "Three months ago, I'd have sworn that my husband was dead. But now…Mark may be alive. In Denver. Somewhere."

Sands frowned, considering. "Have you heard from him?"

"No."

"Has someone said that, without a doubt, they've seen him?"

"No."

"What would you do if he walked through the door, right now?"

Inez thought. "Three months ago, I would have screamed, swore, thrown a few things. Then," she smiled ruefully, "forgiven him, I suppose. But now…I don't know. Too much has changed."

Reverend Sands was quiet a moment, then said, "I'm willing to take those odds."

"Odds." She shook her head. "In our first conversation, I accused you of being a professional gambler. Is that also part of your deep dark past?"

"I remember that meeting. I came to your house, angry that you hadn't notified me about Joe Rose's death. I was immediately charmed by your green-striped stockings. I thought, any woman who would answer the door wearing those stockings and no shoes was worth pursuing. So, Inez, shall we take a gamble? Start over, go slower this time?"

Inez turned and pressed her forehead against the window pane. The cold sank in, chilling her to the back of her bare neck. She closed her eyes and spoke slowly. "I can't promise anything, Justice."

"I'm not asking for promises. Just for a chance."

A loud crash out on State startled the street into silence. In the lull of drunken hoots and traffic noise, Inez heard a piano, backed by a brass band, swing into a waltz. The clamor returned, but the music rose above it.

"Inez." Sands voice was soft, pleading. "Dance with me."

She opened her eyes and turned around.

Shadows of large, flat snowflakes poured over the far wall, the loveseat, the reverend, and his outstretched hands.

He waited.

Inez moved at last. Placed one hand on his shoulder, the other hand in his. He held her by the waist. Close, but with room to breathe.

Inez and Reverend Sands danced slowly, without words, shadows of falling snow cascading over them and the bright and silent room.

Author's Note

First of all, there really is a Leadville, Colorado. You can drive there and experience it for yourself. Quick directions: go up I-70 from Denver into the Rockies, take a left at Copper Mountain, and follow the signs.

My intention was to use Leadville's history as a framework on which to hang my story. As such, I strove to portray the general feel and milieu of the times. As Stephen Voynick notes in his book *Leadville: A Miner's Epic*, "Leadville took her birth from the gold mines, her fame and fortune from the silver mines...." In April 1860, gold was discovered in California Gulch of the Arkansas Valley. By June, 4,000 men had arrived, staking 400 separate claims. By 1863, the gold rush was essentially over. Yet another, bigger one lay ahead.

In 1875, the heavy black sands that clogged the hydraulic equipment for extracting gold were discovered to be lead carbonate with silver. Enough silver to be interesting, even enriching. In 1877, the silver strikes began, and ordinary folks realized something extraordinary was going on in this Colorado mining camp up at ten thousand feet in the mountains. In 1878, the rush gained momentum and fortunes were being pulled from Fryer, Carbonate, and Iron Hills in the mining district.

A census in early 1879, about the time Leadville became incorporated as a city, shows a population of just over 5,000. By the end of the year, the city claimed a population of 20,000, a mine production of ten million dollars and an infrastructure that included a hospital, a water system, a police force, a fire department, a local telephone company, a gas company, and a post office. The railroad had yet to arrive in in this high mountain city, and all goods, from books to flour to diamond-dust mirrors, had to be freighted in by wagon at great expense. In addition, the law of "supply and demand" was in full operation as was speculation in real estate. Lots on Harrison Avenue that were twenty-five feet fronting the street and half a block in depth were selling for five to six thousand dollars, compared to two hundred dollars a mere year before. Saloons were plentiful (although only three women in the 1880 census laid claim to the occupation of saloon keeper or bartender, compared to 228 men).

I've alluded to certain real events, including the vigilante hanging of Edwin Frodsham, leader of a lot-jumping gang, and Patrick Stewart, a footpad, on November 20, 1879, the same day as the opening of the Tabor Opera House. As for the characters in *Silver Lies*, they are either fictitious or treated fictitiously. Among the true-to-life who saunter through the pages are Mattie Silks, who did indeed own parlor houses in Denver, Georgetown, and other Colorado venues, and Bat Masterson, who, although he probably didn't put in an appearance quite so early in 1880, by all accounts did come through this gambling mecca more than once. The Silver Queen is entirely fictional, although I set it up kitty-corner to a very real one, Wyman's Place, and appropriated Wyman's rules of the house.

Thousands of pages have been written about "Cloud City," as Leadville has been called, and its people. Those interested in learning more might try Edward Blair's *Leadville: Colorado's Magic City* or (for heavy hitters) Don and Jean Griswold's two-volume *History of Leadville and Lake County, Colorado*.

Regarding Leadville's miners and mining history, there's Stephen Voynick's *Leadville: A Miner's Epic*. For women's voices describing life in the mining camps and towns, I recommend Mary Hallock Foote's *A Victorian Gentlewoman in the Far West* and Harriet Fish Backus' *Tomboy Bride*. Malinda Jenkins' *Gambler's Wife* provides an interesting look at the life of an intrepid businesswoman and wife of a "sportin' man."

And yes, there really was a "Breakfast Bullets" column in the Leadville *Chronicle*.

Printed in the United States
81996LV00001B/1-39